The Brothers of the Virgin Gold

BY THE SAME AUTHOR

The Marvelous Story of Claire d'Amour
The Call of the Beast
Priscilla of Alexandria
The Angel of Lust
The Mystery of the Tiger
The Poison of Goa
Lucifer
The Blood of Toulouse
The Albigensian Treasure
Jean de Fodoas
Melusine

The Brothers of
the Virgin Gold

by
Maurice Magre

Translated, annotated and introduced by
Brian Stableford

A Black Coat Press Book

ISBN 978-1-61227-704-2. First Printing. January 2018. Published by Black Coat Press, an imprint of Hollywood Comics.com, LLC, P.O. Box 17270, Encino, CA 91416. All rights reserved. Except for review purposes, no part of this book may be reproduced or transmitted in any form or by any means, electronic or mechanical, including photocopying, recording, or by any information storage and retrieval system, without permission in writing from the publisher. The stories and characters depicted in this novel are entirely fictional. Printed in the United States of America.

Introduction

This is the last volume of a twelve-volume set of translations of Maurice Magre's prose fiction. It contains a translation of the novel *Les Frères de l'or vierge*, first published posthumously in 1949.

Volume One, *The Marvelous Story of Claire d'Amour and Other Stories*, contains translations of early short stories, including the collection *Histoire merveilleuse de Claire d'Amour suivie d'autres contes merveilleux* (1903) and six other stories from various sources, published between 1901 and 1913.

Volume Two, *The Call of the Beast and Other Stories*, contains translations of his first three works of prose fiction in volume form, *Les Colombes poignardées* (1917), as "Stabbed Doves," *La Tendre camarade* (1918), as "The Tender Comrade" and *L'Appel de la bête* (1920), as "The Call of the Beast."

Volume Three, *Priscilla of Alexandria and Other Stories* contains translations of the original version of the story collection *Vies des courtisanes*, first published in *Oeuvres Libres* 23 (1923), as "Courtesans' Lives" plus the additional story added to the version published in volume form in 1925, and the novel *Priscilla d'Alexandrie* (1925), as "Priscilla of Alexandria."

Volume Four, *The Angel of Lust*, contains translations of the novella, *La Vie amoureuse de Messaline* (1925), as "The Love Life of Messalina," the novel published as *La Luxure de Grenade* (1926), as "The Angel of Lust," and the chapter from *Magiciens et illuminés* (1930) entitled "Christian Rosenkreutz et les Rose-croix," as "Christian Rosenkreutz and the Rosicrucians."

Volume Five, *The Mystery of the Tiger*, contains translations of the novella *Le Roman de Confucius* (1927), as "The

Story of Confucius," and the novel *Le Mystère du tigre* (1927), as "The Mystery of the Tiger."

Volume Six, *The Poison of Goa*, contains translations of the novel *Le Poison de Goa* (1928), as "The Poison of Goa," and the prose poems contained in *Le Livre des lotus entr'ouverts* (1926), as "Lotus Blossoms."

Volume Seven, *Lucifer*, contains a translation of the novel originally published under the same title in 1929 and the novella *La Nuit de haschich et de l'opium* (1929), as "The Night of Hashish and Opium."

Volume Eight, *The Blood of Toulouse*, contains translations of the novel *Le Sang de Toulouse* (1931), as "The Blood of Toulouse," and the chapter from *Magiciens et illuminés* entitled "Le Maître inconnu des Albigeois," as "The Secret Master of the Albigensians."

Volume Nine, *The Albigensian Treasure*, contains translations of the novel *Le Trésor des Albigeois* (1938) as "The Albigensian Treasure," and the collection of vignettes "Communication avec la nature" from *La Beauté invisible* (1937), as "Communication with Nature."

Volume Ten, *Jean de Fodoas*, contains translations of the novel *Jean de Fodoas: aventures d'un Français à la cour de l'empereur Akbar* (1939) as "Jean de Fodoas" and the chapter from *Magiciens et illuminés* entitled "Le Mystère des Templiers," as "The Mystery of the Templars."

Volume Eleven, *Melusine*, contains translations of the novel *Mélusine, ou le secret de la solitude* (1941) and the collections of vignettes "Le Côté d'ombre des âmes" and "Révélation des mondes invisibles" from *La Beauté invisible*, as "The Dark Side of Souls" and "The Revelation of Invisible Worlds."

Although *Les Frères de l'or vierge* was the last work of fiction by Maurice Magre to be published, eight years after his death, it might not be the last one he wrote. Given that he dated the manuscript of the work that was published as *Mélusine, ou le Secret de la Solitude* June 1941, and died in December of that year, having been ill in the interim and resident in a nursing home in Nice, he surely would not have had time to produce the whole of what is by far the longest of his works in that interim, all the more so as he was probably still working on other projects, including his posthumously-published nonfiction book *Le Livre des visions divines* [The Book of Divine Visions] (1943).

Given that *Les Frères de l'or vierge* is a portmanteau work interleaving several related but distinct story-threads, some of which are complete short stories, it seems probable that its various parts were written over considerable time, perhaps beginning some six or seven years before, when he published two books of popular articles about adventurers in the Americas, *Pirates, Flibustiers, Négriers* [Pirates, Filibusters and Slave-Traders] (1934) and *Les Aventuriers d'Amérique du Sud* [The Adventurers of South America] (1935). The principal narrative thread is obviously incomplete, in spite of a brief concluding section that seems to be incompatible with the early chapters, and the second major thread also ends so abruptly as to suggest that more should have been added and might well have been projected, so the final preparation for publication was evidently an improvisation. Perhaps the author, realizing that he would not have time to finish the work properly, made what hasty provision he could hastily to adapt the material he had to hand in the autumn of 1941. It is possible that he might also have done something similar with *Mélusine*, which is also a patchwork; it too might include chapters that were not originally intended to be interleaved with its main narrative, and similarly abandons at least one significant plot-thread introduced in the early chapters and then abandoned.

The fact that *Les Frères de l'or vierge* is flawed in its conclusion, however, does not spoil it irredeemably as an ensemble. The very fact that it contains so many separate stories, many of which are properly concluded, means that there is a great deal of material in it that is admirable, and the main narrative thread, even though it peters out and leaves a badly

7

frayed end, is certainly not without interest. Nor can the published work consist entirely of work dating back to the mid-1930s, because the last of the completed subplots, the story of Hugues Borromée's triumph over doubt, as a result of celebrating mass in "the invisible cathedral," echoes very closely the convictions and sentiments of *Le Livre des visions divines*, which announces the belated discovery of a God far more orthodox than the pantheistic divinity featured with equal sincerity in *La Beauté invisible* and *Mélusine*: a discovery that Magre only made in the final months of his life.

Magre's interest in his native region, the city of Toulouse and the river valleys extending from the foothills of the Pyrenees, had previously been reflected in his fiction in images of the remote past—the early thirteenth century in *Le Sang de Toulouse* and the decades to either side of 1600 in *Le Trésor des Albigeois* and *Jean de Fodoas*. His previous novels set in the nineteenth century, *Le Mystère du tigre* and *Le Poison de Goa*, had been set in remote areas of the Far East. His attention had, however, been caught by a particular incident following the 1848 Revolution, when a considerable number of the inhabitants of the region between Toulouse and the Pyrenees, disturbed by the political upheaval, had emigrated *en masse* to America, seduced by the prospects supposedly offered by the colonization of Mexico and inspired with dreams of sudden enrichment by the California Gold Rush.

It seems probable, judging by the existing text, that what Magre originally planned to do in order to dramatize that occurrence was to produce a set of distinct short stories illustrating the fates of a series of exemplary emigrants one by one. The project must, however, have become unwieldy, partly because the introduction grew too massive and partly because some of the stories became too long and too complicated. The decision to pour them all into the same melting-pot to form a patchwork ensemble was probably belated, and the challenging task of designing a structure for that whole probably did not permit any elegant execution. Although the actual text, with the possible exception of a few of the final subsections, is very obviously Magre's work, it is conceivable that the assembly and organization of the chapters was the work of an editor. Whoever carried out the collation, however, it was not a problem capable of a wholly satisfactory solution.

In addition to the problem of its structure, *Les Frères de l'or vierge* also suffers slightly from the fact that Magre's occasionally casual manner of dealing with chronology and matters of geographical and historical fact stand out more obviously in this work than in his previous works set in the nineteenth century, and even more so in modern translation, because nineteenth-century America was far more familiar in common knowledge than India or Malaysia. Some of his inventions and improvisations must have seemed implausible in the 1940s, in France as well as in the USA, and one major error, in particular, must have stood out like a sore thumb; but that too is a peripheral issue that the reader is free to regard merely as an extra dimension of exoticism, which does not affect either the engagement or the argument of the text.

The supernatural trimmings characteristic of Magre's fiction are muted in many of the text's story-threads and completely absent from some, although not from its most important aspects. The principal story-line is emphatically supernatural, although the brutally hasty conclusion dismisses many of its earlier supernatural inclusions as irrelevant and inexplicable. Hugues Borromée's story is, however, flamboyantly fantastic, and although Noël Alga's communications with nature are limited, especially while he is away from his homeland, they might have come back into full flower had his story been continued following the moment of his return. The subplot featuring the ultimate descendants of the Bramevaque family and the Rosicrucian talisman they receive from a mysterious horseman before setting off is hardly developed at all, although it seems unlikely that they would have been given that device unless it had originally been intended to perform some quasi-miraculous function in the Mexican wilderness.

The disintegration of the principal supernatural plot-thread of *Les Frères de l'or vierge* is particularly regrettable because it cut off the development of a budding account of Amerindian sorcery that might well have been fascinating if carried through. The description of the naïve Dr. Fazeuille's visit to the remarkable brothel on the outskirts of Vera Cruz was probably designed as a distinct short story, but still contains promising seeds that would surely have benefited from further exploration and development. It might well be the case, however, that the author's sudden belated conversion to a more orthodox religiosity than the pantheism developed by the author in *La Beauté invisible*, Michel de Bramevaque in *Le Trésor des Albigeois* and the unnamed narrator of *Mélusine* would have cut off his interest in that development anyway, and might, in fact, have had something to do with his abandonment of the stories of Malvina de Noussoulens and Noël Alga before they reached the termini initially implied by their predicaments.

There is a sense in which Noël is effectively replaced as a sympathetic stand-in for the author by Hugues as the patchwork reaches its close, even though it is Noël who re-enacts a crucial scene that that reflected one of the author's enduring hauntings, providing a striking counterpart to the re-enactment of the same incident by Maurice, the protagonist of "Histoire merveilleuse de Claire d'Amour" (1903; translated in Volume One). Unfortunately, we cannot tell from the published version whether Noël was originally intended by his creator to go on to find a *consolamentum* for his loss in the resumption of his communication with Pyrenean nature, or whether he was to be left brutally bereft.

At any rate, Hugues Borromée's celebration of mass in the invisible cathedral became the author's last word on the *désespoir* that he declared, in the opening words of *La Beauté invisible*, to have been the central problem of his life, and which certainly provided the mainspring of all his artistic endeavors. It seems unlikely, however, that had Magre lived through the Second World War and still been alive in 1949 when *Les Frères de l'or vierge* was published, he would have been arrested at that point in his thinking. It was a symptom of his psychological and artistic predicament that none of the solutions he glimpsed satisfied him for long, even if they tantalized him with an appearance of light at the end of his tunnel. It would, therefore, be assuming too much to regard the author's ultimate divine vision as an authentic conclusion.

Lives inevitably end, but they always leave the work of living, as well as the work of writing, essentially incomplete, and its central threads awkwardly frayed. There is no need to regret that overmuch; not only is it better to travel hopefully than to arrive, as proverbial wisdom affirms, but it is surely also better—at least if one is a creative writer—to travel in despair than ever to reach the alluring but deceptive flame of enlightenment and true wisdom. Maurice Magre was a great creative artist, and was thus able continually to work the elusive alchemical trick of converting his ongoing *désespoir* into literary virgin gold. For that, his readers have cause to be grateful.

The following translation was made from a copy of the 1949 edition published in Paris under the Deux-Rives imprint.

Brian Stableford

11

THE BROTHERS OF
THE VIRGIN GOLD

Preface

How many vanished memories and how many beautiful stories lies dead on the stories of the hearths around which they were told! Histories blur and fade, the thread of stories wears away like an embroidery forgotten on a work-table. And yet the heroes ought not to disappear. For the chain of the living and the dead, they can extend their hands over the years. How many men of the land of Comminges raise their hairy heads eternally, in order to attest that they have loved and suffered and that even if they have done nothing better, at least they have lived.

In those days, the streams of the Pyrenees seemed to sing more loudly as they descended among the slate stones. The sawmills screeched and moaned with the life of wood cut in the corridors of all the valleys. Like a wind carrying seeds, the revolution of 1848 had brought promises of liberty and hopes of a better life to the smallest mountain villages. And then the wind had ceased to blow. One might have thought that the streams no longer caused their waters to fall back on the pebbles.

And another wind, more powerful, had passed over souls. For the passions never sleep, and from an inexhaustible source that is who knows where, a force escapes that reignites them. Along the interminable processions of poplars that extend in the valleys of Nebouzan, Barousse and Comminges, coming from Toulouse, the city of bell-towers, prodigious news had run: news that, along with the laughter of joy, would bring despair and death. It was the news of the discovery of gold in California.

Henceforth, there would be no more need to work hard to live. The evil law of nature was vanquished. Pleasure would finally be the portion of all. The disease of the century took on a more universal form. It was about to circulate over the entire earth.

But because of its purity, the race of the mountain men was to be more disturbed than any other by the poison. So, there was a land where gold was found in torrents: virgin gold, unalterable gold, such as it had been created by a younger and more beautiful sun at the beginning of time! And in order to go to search for it, all that was required was a little courage. Now, there was courage a-plenty among the sons of the Garonne.

In reality, that gold, discovered at that moment of the century, at a time of the wakening of souls, that Californian gold, was merely a signal. Who would ever know gold by what it had given? It announced the unleashing of the passions, the fury of enjoyment perceived by the men of the high lands, who had the habit every morning of going to wash their faces in the water of immaculate torrents into which a fern branch had been dipped.

This is the story of some of those men. Having believed, being ignorant of the vastness of the world, and of its different mores and climates, they got up and departed. There were good ones and bad ones. Some died of the difficulty, others harvested gold, but very few found happiness. Now, none subsists. The last old man has disappeared. But in the ancient dwellings of the Pyrenean valleys, their story is still told.

PART ONE: THE GOLD-SEEKERS OF COMMINGES

I. Malvina's Confession

Perhaps everything that happened subsequently, that folly of desire, the dancing flame that ran hither and yon, the force that parted the clouds in order to display an imaginary sun, all obtained its commencement on that winter evening.

The great winds that accumulate in the stone corridors and fir woods of the Pyrenees had never blown with such force.

Oh, it they could only carry me far away, to a place where there are no more men, thought Malvina, on the narrow path. And with the folds of her shawl she tightened her black tresses with golden glints, which the wind had undone, against her torso.

Was she not lost in a darkness that had never been seen as thick on earth? But no! She was still between the poplars, which, with their low courbettes and their strange signs, ought to take her all the way to the church of the Borromées. She had been walking for an hour. There, at least she would find a place sanctified by a great soul. She knew that in drawing closer to a veritable saint one draws closer to salvation.

Was the former bishop Nestor Borromée a veritable saint? Perhaps. First of all, was there even one veritable saint in the entire world? In casting a glance backwards at her life, she saw that she had only encountered wicked souls, creatures devoured by desire The desire for her, above all, the desire for her beauty. Only the ailing old man gave her the health of the soul when she approached him. She perceived his purity around him, like an atmosphere—and that so sensibly, for her, that she rediscovered that purity in the places where he lived, in his garden, around his house, and especially in the chapel that was part of his house and where he was the only one to say mass. And it was because of that influence that this evening, more tortured than usual, in spite of the rain and the tempest, she had slipped out of her house silently in order to go and pray before the altar that was Nestor Borromée's.

Pray! She would have liked to be able to do that with a sincere heart, but she was not sure that she believed. Too many misfortunes had struck her. There was too great a drama in her life. She had been born with incoherent forces in her, of which she understood neither the meaning nor the extent: a force of pleasure, a love of life, an appetite for immediate realization.

Suddenly, she stopped. The rain had just diminished. She listened. Had her father not followed her? Was there not a sound of footsteps behind her?

But no. Her father was too violent to follow her for an hour without running, shouting insults, attempting to bring her back by force. She looked in the direction of Mauléon, at the side of the mountain at the foot of which the Château de Noussoulens stood. In a clear interval in the sky she could only glimpse a somber mass. There was no sound of footsteps. She resumed waking under a further squall of rain.

And as distances are falsified in the darkness, it turned out that she had arrived when she thought that she was still far away, along the long row of poplars. She suddenly heard the noise that the Garonne made on its bed of cold stones, which she had not distinguished from that of the wind. To the left, she perceived the shadow that the abode of the Borromées made. The chapel was in front of her.

Malvina knew what it was necessary to do to get into it. On a nearby fence the key was hanging on a nail. In principle, it was there to serve a few local people susceptible of coming to pray, if the desire came to them, but no one made use of it except Nestor Borromée. Malvina took a few steps in order to pick up the key, but she stifled a cry of surprise.

The door was ajar, and she could even distinguish a vague light coming out of it. It was, however, impossible that anyone could be in the solitary chapel at this late hour of the night. The perpetually-suffering Nestor Borromée went up to his room as soon as the meal was over and did not come out before morning. It could not be old Catherine, his maidservant. To be sure, two of his nephews were there at the moment. Sulpice was pious, but not enough to pray in the middle of the night. As for Bernard, the strong mind, he did not even go to mass and was proud of being anticlerical and evolutionary.

Malvina suddenly remembered that on two occasions, old Catherine had bought a large candle with her savings and had lighted it when her master was ill. She even claimed that each time, a sensible improvement had coincided with the last flicker of the candle. Doubtless that light was coming from one of Catherine's ex-votos. She had lit the candle and forgotten to lock the door with the key. The wind had opened it...

Malvina advanced slowly as far as the threshold. No noise. *The chapel is deserted*, she thought. She had on her lips the first prayer that she counted on formulating in the place that she judged sacred; instinctively, she tied back her wet hair behind her head. She pushed the door and went in.

A light turned and illuminated her face. A large silhouette loomed up a few paces away. She did not have time to be surprised or frightened. It was only a man who was wearing a long shepherd's cloak, to which he had added a goatskin cape. It was bishop Nestor. Doubtless he had only come in a few moments before, because he still had his hood up.

Malvina did not attempt to see his features. She fell to her knees before him immediately, murmuring: "Since you're here, it's God who has guided me."

But who can tell where God guides them?

The lamp rose and fell twice. There was an absolute silence. Outside, the squall stopped, and one might have thought that the forces were attentive behind the walls of the church, as if they had been stopped by the redemptive power of the holy place. Two or three drops made a noise on the flagstones. They were not tears, but water dripping from the rain-soaked shawl.

Malvina started to speak very rapidly. She felt that a chance was being offered to her and that it was necessary not to let it escape. Everything that happened had been determined for her, somewhere in another world. The night and the storm were accomplices. A chance had arrived for her soul, perhaps the first in her life.

"Monseigneur," she said, raising her head slightly, "hear my confession."

She glimpsed a movement of recoil, a quiver of the lamp. She feared being put off until tomorrow. She knew that there was no confessional in the ancient chapel, devastated sixty years before. She extended her arms forward. "I beg you!" she cried, and immediately, she began to speak. She felt possessed by a strange facility of confession, a spirit of sincerity that abruptly illuminated her past with a light that surprised her. She saw herself in a perspective of misery and fatality and it seemed to her that all her sins were reduced to negligibility by the story that she was about to tell.

"I've always been very unfortunate," she said. "Monseigneur, you've known my father better than anyone. I ask you to judge what his daughter has been able to endure. I don't reproach him for anything, but you'll understand if I tell you that he has diverted to me the rancor that my mother had inspired in him. Perhaps the first cause of my misfortune was resembling my mother, having her face, her form, her soul—especially her soul. Oh, Monseigneur, I've never been able to understand that. The sons are punished for the sins of fathers, it says in the Bible. Why? Why? What is that heritage of beauty, sickness and sin? It was inscribed, engraved in my flesh, like an indelible seal.

"When you came to Noussoulens you must have seen, in the large drawing room, near the door, a medallion of a ten-year-old girl. All the visitors—there were still visitors then—

18

believed that it was a pastel representing me. 'What a good likeness!' they said. It was my mother. I can say it on this stone, on my knees before you. I resemble her. I've inherited her face, her character, and her vices. Yes, Monseigneur, may she pardon me for speaking thus. There is something in me that doesn't belong to me, an interior force that burns me, that makes me act, that is foreign to me...

"How can I tell you? I dare not speak, to tell all; I'm ashamed. And yet, since you're here, this evening, where I expected to be addressing God alone, it's you who ought to hear everything, to whom I ought to tell everything, even what other women hide with so much care when they're possessed, like me."

Malvina's voice had risen in order to compete with the sound of the wind outside. She raised her head to move away the trickle of her hair, which was running on to her bosom, and she saw that the lamp was no longer in the bishop's hand, but that he had placed it on the holy water stoup. She interpreted that gesture as a consent to hear her. She straightened up on her knees, and crossed her hands in front of her; her thin neck emerged from her shawl and she thought, without wanting to, that in that pose she resembled exactly a stone angel that an ancient artist had sculpted as a support for the stoup, which had resisted the effects of time.

It was in a low voice that she continued.

"Is it God who gives us these instincts, these evil forces, or is it us who draw them from our substance and delight in developing them? Sometimes I accuse myself, but at other times I feel that I'm not responsible. Since my childhood I've experienced the desire of men upon me, but I was also drawn toward them. What can one do when one is born thus? One begins by not knowing that it's a sin. And then it's too late. Certainly, my father guarded me well. But there was the example of my mother. I've never dared say that. But it's necessary that I explain...it's not to excuse myself...the true cause was in me. It's me who appealed, with a gaze, a movement of the shoulder. And then, I thought, I thought about men..."

Malvina no longer had to fear not being heard. The tall form with its hood, which made a shadow before her, was now leaning toward her. A keen attention enveloped her. "Go on," she heard.

"I'm sure that many women are like me, but they never say so, even at confession. Then again, perhaps you've heard worse...no, not worse than me. At fifteen, in summer, at night, I met a young man from Saint-Gaudens in the park. Then there was another one with whom I spent three entire days and three nights when my father went to Bordeaux for my mother's heritage. But that's nothing. There was a curse upon me. Yes, Monseigneur, something harassed those I went near, and me. I'm getting to the great drama of my existence. It was last year. There's a death in my story. Oh, not a crime, don't think that...but a misfortune..."

Malvina then had the sentiment that the bishop had taken a step backwards and raised his hand to pick up the lamp from the stoup. She raised her head, throwing back her hair. Her headscarf had slipped. She sensed that she had a face resplendent with temptation, a beauty that the evocation of the past must give her, and which was not appropriate to the moment. She fixed her gaze on the oval shadow framed by the hood. The arm extended toward the lamp fell back slowly.

"Go on," murmured a toneless voice, which gave the impression of coming from very far away.

"Perhaps you remember a man who arrived in Saint-Gaudens last year, and about whom there's talk at present. He'd reserved an entire floor in the Hôtel de France in Saint-Gaudens and hired a carriage with a coachman. He was a handsome fellow—too handsome. He said his family was Portuguese and he had a letter of recommendation for my father. In the vicinity they called him the magnetizer because he had given a public séance of magnetism, but his name was Maximo Avila. My father made his acquaintance and invited him to Noussoulens.

"I'll spare you the details. In brief, he became my lover, the first real one. You can't understand the distinction that a woman can make. And yet, there was something that distanced me from him. At night he climbed over the wall of the park, I opened my window and he came to join me in my room. I'd poisoned the guard dog Black, although he was a dog I adored. I've never been able to explain to myself how I was able to do that, but I did it, and this is what happened.

"No one ever heard mention of the Portuguese magnetizer again. He disappeared abruptly. But that was the moment of the revolution. People were only occupied with politics: the King, Napoléon, the Republic…what do I know? No one worried much about what had become of a foreigner. The hirer of the carriage took his rig back at the end of the month, and his trunk must still be on sufferance at the Hôtel de France. The Portuguese magnetizer is lying in our garden, at the foot of a beech. It was my father and me who buried him. He was dead in a second, in my room, in my arms. I didn't know that you could die so quickly."

Malvina stopped, for the time necessary to get her breath back. But the person who was listening must have been keenly interested by what she was saying, because he could not support that interruption. Malvina heard his voice, still stifled but becoming imperious: "Well, go on! Tell me everything. Yes, everything."

She was not thinking of hiding anything, for the breath of liberation was swelling her bosom. She was ridding herself of a heavy burden.

"He had come as usual, climbing up to my window. Nothing could lead me to think…I ought to say that he seemed to love me passionately."

"And you?"

Malvina would have been astonished by the tone of those two syllables if she had not feared herself putting too much realism into her story."

"Me? I don't know. Perhaps that's what people call love? I loved him, in a certain fashion…"

"How?"

"No, it wasn't loving. Don't oblige me, Monseigneur, to…he exercised a certain physical attraction on me. Perhaps it was magnetism. That evening, he didn't say two words to me. He was a brutal man. I'd put out the lamp and closed, or thought I'd closed, the window. He was very handsome and the room was illuminated by the moonlight.

"I've always wondered whether the death might have been caused by certain practices of occultism. He had told me that he held séances of evocation and that he obtained extraordinary, even terrible, results. I thought that he wanted to scare me, but it was true. He wanted to do experiments on me. I'd refused, but I would have ended up giving in eventually. He was lying beside me. I'd turned to the window and I said to him: 'Look. There's no wind, but he window is opening of its own accord.'

"It had just opened, as if someone had pushed it slowly. He didn't reply to me. I put my hand on his shoulder. I shook him. I called to him several times. At first I thought he'd fainted. But there's something mysterious about death that makes one aware of its presence. Suddenly, I understood, and was overwhelmed by fear. The window added to that fear. What could I do? I told myself that my father might kill me. I was running the risk of that. I put a mantle over my shoulders and went to wake him up. I had to shout, because he was sleeping very deeply. The servants sleep on the other side of the house, a long way off, and they couldn't hear.

"My father didn't throw himself upon me. He said: 'It's necessary to take care of him. Go fetch what's necessary.' I could only find his razor. But when we arrived in the room he understood that it was futile. Only then did he take my by the throat, and he took off everything I was wearing. He said that for my punishment he wanted me to go to fetch the gendarmes from Mauléon without any clothes, in the dark, and he dragged me as far as the garden. I stayed on the doorstep for I don't know long. I was weeping. I was scarcely conscious...

"Then I heard a low voice calling to me through the window. I found him sitting beside the dead man, his head in his hands. He let me get dressed. He said: 'I've reflected. They'll say that I killed him. I know the people around here. We're going to bury him here. No one will know anything. We're not responsible. His heart must have stopped. It happens.'

"We took the body downstairs together. It had gone stiff and cold. There was no longer a moon. I went to look for the tools. My father dug a ditch in a place where no one ever goes, under a beech where I used to play with my doll when I was little. He dug. It took a long time. I replaced him when he couldn't do any more. It was endless. He spent part of the night leveling the soil. I daren't go back up to my room. I waited until daylight in the drawing room.

"At about six o'clock I was dozing...I was woken up by my father's voice. I saw him outside with his rifle. He said to the gardener, very calmly: 'If Monsieur Maximo comes today, tell him that I've gone out hunting bears on the Cagire. I won't be back for four or five days."

"A man is very little, if he's alone, if he has no family, like Maximo Avila. I don't think there was even an enquiry into his disappearance. People were only occupied then with politics..."

At that moment the wind blew a little more forcefully. A bird flew in through a place where there had once been a stained glass window, traversed the chapel and alighted somewhere in the shadows. That prevented Malvina from hearing a halting respiration above her. The bishop had drawn closer to her, his arms extended.

"I haven't finished, Monseigneur. Listen to me, I beg you! I have something more to tell you."

She had thought that she noticed signs of impatience in the bishop. Perhaps she had taken too long. She pressed her arms against her breasts as if to concentrate the thoughts she had to express and which were the most difficult to translate into words. That prevented her from raising her head.

If she had done so she would have glimpsed a young and ardent face, distressed by evil, and the frightful form that desire takes when it is exasperated by jealousy. It was certainly not the noble and sad face of Nestor Borromée, a man of wisdom and meditation. It was that of a young man who was clicking his teeth with rage and who, in spite of the majesty that dresses any confession, in spite of the remorse of the usurped authority, was hesitating as to whether to throw himself upon that woman and possess her by force on the cold flagstones.

Long after, he repented bitterly of not having done so.

But the action required a decision of which he was perhaps not capable. He gazed intently at the woman, whom the evoked image of the dead man surrounded with a carnal corruption. He imagined the scenes that she had just recounted and those that she had not described. The unknown by which they were enveloped rendered them even more horrible.

The bird that had penetrated into the chapel flapped its wings three times, as if it were about to fly away, and three times it resumed its immobility.

"I have something more to tell you," Malvina repeated, in a low voice.

II. The Borromée Family

That evening, as soon as he was alone in his room, Bernard Borromée, the oldest of Bishop Nestor's three nephews, had heard an appeal analogous to the one that had driven Malvina out of her house at Noussoulens.

The voice of the mountain winds sometimes speaks about God and his consolations. The light of the nascent stars and the approach of a storm troubles certain souls in the same fashion. Bernard Borromée said very loudly that he did not believe in anything and yet, that evening, an inexplicable turnabout had taken place within him and he had said to himself: *Who knows?*

It was a strange family, that of the Borromées, in which a certain eccentricity had been transmitted like a tradition. Nestor Borromée, the bishop, had had two brothers. The younger had had three children and had died of languor, it was said, after his wife's death. But before then he had gambled and lost his fortune as well as almost everything his brothers possessed. The elder, Romuald Borromée, had astonished the region. There had been much talk about him, and then he had been forgotten. Ruined by his brother, he had cultivated a small field himself, let his hair and beard grow, saying that he was a philosopher, and exposing to peasants on Sunday a complicated theory of the world.

"That was the belief of the philosophers of antiquity," he added. "Personally, I'm not a partisan of the moderns."

The he began to have a horror of men and had made a vow of solitude.

"I'm quitting the region forever. I prefer to live with the wolves."

And he had gone to install himself in a shepherd's hut, high up in the mountains of Sacrous. His brother the bishop sometimes went to see him there, but there had come a time when illness and age prevented him from climbing the steep paths that led to his brother's hut.

"Come as far as the Hospice," said the solitary Romuald to his brother Nestor. "Bring the old hunting horn that we used as children, which is suspended in your house in a panoply. Blow it, as before, and the savage will descend from his solitude to see his brother who has remained in the world."

And several times, people had been surprised to see Bishop Borromée riding an old mule, which he borrowed from the churchwarden of Saint-Just, with an antique horn over his shoulder, plunging into the high valleys all the way to the Hospice of Venasque, where the mountain becomes a stone barrier.

But now, Bishop Nestor no longer had the strength to undertake that expedition. He loved his brother and he gazed with nostalgia in the direction of Sauvegarde, which dominates the Sacrous.

"Wisdom would be to join him," he often said.

With the years, the anxiety had grown in him of not having done enough good. He had, however, done as much as he could. It was at the moment when his health had prevented him from playing an active role in the church, at the moment when he had retired to his house near the Garonne, that the imperious desire was born in him for the immediate good deed. But at the same time, by a singular fatality, he had been obliged to give his brother's moneylenders what he counted on distributing to the poor. He saw that as an incomprehensible trick of Providence. His generosity had grown with the diminution of his means.

He had sold everything in his house that was superfluous—paintings; a few items of sculpted furniture; the objects in panoplies, with the exception of the hunting horn; and a part of his library—in order to distribute the money. However, he had kept portraits of his relatives who had occupied important ecclesiastical posts. There was a cardinal, a Franciscan superior and a missionary martyred long ago in America. Oh, if he had been able to sell the portrait of the Franciscan, which had

26

been painted by a master! But how could he resolve himself to that sacrilege? So, he had only been able to contrive a dust of alms.

A long time ago he had drawn up a list of families that he ought to help. The moneylenders of Toulouse had come and taken everything. He reproached himself for not selling his house, with the beds and the remaining chairs, his little garden and his dilapidated chapel, in order to enrich the families on his list. Would they have been enriched? Old buildings did not have much value. At least his conscience would have been satisfied. Had not all the great saints begged on the road and lived as ascetics?

He had told his brother: "A day will come when I will play three fanfares at the foot of the Sacrous. Then I will come up to you and never go down again."

But Bishop Nestor had a weakness that dated from his childhood. He was afraid of wolves.

"Are there many wolves on the Sacrous?" he asked his brother Romuald.

"Eh? There are some, as there are everywhere in the mountains, but they only come down in the autumn."

"What do you do then?"

Romuald laughed heartily. "I have my ax. I advance slowly, while looking at them, and I kill them with a single blow to the skull."

It was the thought of the wolves that forced the bishop to postpone the sale of his house. He was not made for wielding an ax. And he knew full well that Romuald was not lying, for he had in his cabin the whitened skulls of wolves, in which the wounds testified to the manner of their death.

And the bishop thought: *Who knows? Perhaps the solitude of winter nights makes a man revert to a certain savagery instead of bringing him closer to God?*

In any case, as the years went by, the bishop developed a singular tendency to live in the past. He remembered having seen Comminges and the entire regions between the Pyrenees and Toulouse covered in magnificent churches and abbeys.

With his great-uncle, the Franciscan superior, he had gone into cloisters that no longer existed. Churches and convents had been ravaged and destroyed during the revolution of '89. Nestor Borromée had not been able to resign himself to that. He knew all the archeologists of the Midi and had redrawn the plans of vanished monuments. He knew the location of several monastic cloisters around Saint-Bertrand de Comminges of which nothing remained but vestiges. He knew the names of the last priors.

"Today, I'll go to see the good Brother Henri and stroll in the cloister of Saint-Just."

And he spent his afternoon in a field where there was the phantom of a cloister.

"Today I'll go to see the venerable Anselme, the fried of Fénelon."

He ordered a carriage to go to the Abbaye de Sarrancolin. Not a stone of the Abbaye de Sarrancolin remained now.

That was a subject of mockery for Bernard Borromée, the one of his nephews who was the most distant from him, and for whom he had an unacknowledged predilection in spite of the atheism of which he was proud.

Hugues, the second, was concluding his studies at the seminary of the Missions.

"One never knows," Nestor had said. "Perhaps one day, much later, the atheist will become a saint and the missionary will only be a missionary."

As for Sulpice, the youngest, he worried about him because of his distressing timidity, his obstinate mutism and the impenetrable character of his nature.

But he did not think of retaining any of them when they came to stay with him for a few days.

"I don't understand the new generations," he said. "There are revolutions that trouble the brain. The year 1848 has lit a fire that won't be extinguished for a long time. It's time I went to join my brother on the Sacrous."

Once or twice he had even unhooked the hunting horn.

"What about your paupers? And me?" said his maidservant Catherine, who was eighty years old. "Are we also going to live with the wolves?"

And he put the horn back in its place.

The rain had started falling at dusk and Bernard Borromée had felt a bitterness that never quit him rising within him with more force.

So, destiny continued to hound him incessantly! Others were rich and loved by women. Others had a family in Paris. A family is the source of a thousand advantages. But he only had an uncle who was going senile and who gave the little money he had to strangers. Money was everything. It was necessary to have it at any price. His father had been criminal in not amassing it for his children. Not only had he not amassed any, but he had had mistresses, gambled and made imbecilic speculations. His father had despoiled him. He only had the little capital that had come to him from his mother, but his mother had never been very rich and it had been necessary to share the inheritance with his brothers. As if inheritances ought not to be divided in accordance with the value and intelligence of the children!

Bernard Borromée laughed bitterly as he cast a circular glance around his room, almost devoid of furniture. A bed, a table, a chair and books. Oh, books! There was no lack of them in what his uncle called "Bernard's room." Doubtless that was to convert him. What books, for him, the atheist! For he had, he did and always would sadden his uncle, an uncle who gave everything he had to the poor, without worrying about the needs of the only member of the family qualified to spend money—him, Bernard. For that was not given to everyone. It was necessary to belong to a certain aristocracy to spend money with the necessary style.

Bernard noticed that two candlesticks of no great value, which had still been on the mantelpiece during his last visit, had disappeared.

What was he able to get for them? he thought. *And for whom?*

Fate was set stubbornly against him. He distinguished an ill will in the sequence of the events of his life. He had arrived in Paris with letters of recommendation from the widow of General Compans. A fine protectress, in truth, whom his uncle had procured for him. She only recommended him to royalists, just at the moment when the monarchy was about to collapse. Oh, if he had been able to witness the days of February! But he had arrived in Paris too late. And he had written a letter of admiration to Barbès[1] on the eve of the day when he attempted to form a provisional government and was arrested. What folly it had been to believe himself compromised and to have returned to his homeland! No one cared about a twenty-three-year-old provincial. He ought to have proclaimed himself a Bonapartist loudly and denied his Republican opinions. After all, what was he, in sum? He wanted to belong to the party that succeeded. But his bad luck had always put him in the camp of the losers. If that continued, his brothers, those two incompetents, would end up surpassing him.

When he thought about his brothers, an ill-defined suffering awakened in him. He had always been jealous of them. As a child he had wished them dead. With the years he had acquired the measure of evil that takes the place of conscience, but he felt despoiled by his brothers. He had heard it said that Hugues was the most intelligent of the three and Sulpice the most seductive. What, then, remained to him? And yet he sensed a value in himself, a ubiquitous capability. A man of

---

[1] Armand Barbès (1809-1870), a fervent Republican, had been in prison since 1839 for trying to overthrow the monarchy when the 1848 Revolution broke out. After his release, he served in the new National Assembly for three weeks, but he was caught up in a demonstration that was perceived, probably mistakenly, as an attempted *coup d'état* and imprisoned again. Napoléon III pardoned him in 1854, but he lived in exile for the remainder of his life.

his intelligence could take up any métier and excel therein. But it was necessary not to be misunderstood, and he was. It was necessary for him to find his peers, men on his level—then they would see!

The rain was falling with regularity against the window panes. It was warm. He opened the window. He looked at the distant contour of the mountains, which the clouds buried, and found a certain comfort therein. He had the vague sentiment that nature did not misunderstand anyone and that she gave everyone the example of her immobility and her power.

Yes, but it was necessary not to fall into the stupidity of poetry, to be duped by things after having been duped by men.

A certain tender sentiment overtook him, though. Oh, if he were loved by a woman, a real woman—like Malvina, for example. Certainly, he had experience of women, and in that matter his brothers could not compete with him. Hugues, the hypocrite, was out of the contest, but Sulpice, even though he let nothing appear, had pretentions to please. That made him laugh. His poor brother! His timidity went as far as malady. But he was not timid, and if he succeeded in life, if he succeeded in obtaining money, then...perhaps he might aspire to the inaccessible Malvina.

His thoughts became more confused in evoking happy images. Now the tempest was unleashed and was sending great damp gusts into the room. He moved away from the window and took two or three steps in the shadows, where the wood of the furniture was creaking. Then he returned to offer his face to the rain.

And it seemed to him then that he was washed all the way to the soul by a supernatural water falling from the sky.

What if he had been mistaken from the very beginning? What if his brother Hugues was right? What if atheism was the greatest of human errors, and God existed? What if there were a witness incessantly poring over him, who read his thoughts and to whom he might appeal? That above all! To obtain justice. But how could one know?

Bernard Borromée had often heard it said by his uncle that the old chapel situated on the other side of his garden was a particularly holy place.

"I would swear," the bishop had said, "that if one dug under my old church, one would find the foundations of a much more ancient church, perhaps dating from the time of the first Christians. Prayer ought to find its path more easily here because of the great river of prayers that has obtained its source here."

Those words, which had once made him shrug his shoulders, suddenly imposed themselves on Bernard's mind.

If the manner in which I ought to live were to be dictated to me, it will be there and this evening. If my most ardent prayer is to be realized, I ought to formulate it there. I shall ask God to determine that I be loved by Malvina.

The young woman had never shown the slightest sympathy for him. Bernard had made his studies with the Jesuits of Toulouse. He had only come to Comminges during the vacations, and, in spite of his efforts, he had only had brief polite exchanges with Malvina. But if God existed, he could do anything.

The thought of Malvina gave birth in Bernard's soul to possibilities of ardent fervor. A bell, which had to be the bell of Saint-Bernard, chimed in the distance, and had the effect on him of a divine response. Who could tell whether his life might begin with that prayer?

His resolution was made. He closed the window again, and lit the lamp, after having carefully trimmed the wick so that it would resist the wind. He went out into the corridor and listened. His uncle's room was at the other extremity of the house and he knew that he was always profoundly asleep at this hour. In any case, when the bishop was reading in bed, a luminous radiance under his door revealed the fact.

He went downstairs quietly, traversed the antechamber and withdrew the heavy bolts that locked the door. The rain was so heavy that it seemed to be delivering blows upon the walls with large wet hands; it could be heard streaming over the three steps of the perron.

The distance to cover in reaching the chapel was not great, but it was sufficient for him to be soaked through by the rain. Then he spotted his uncle's large goatskin cape handing on a coat-stand. He threw it over his shoulders and pulled the hood over his head, smiling internally at the weight of the mantle and the resemblance it must give him to his uncle.

"I have something more to tell you."

Oh, yes, Malvina had something else to say, and it was the essential thing for her. Except that her words were now emerging with more difficulty. She was searching for her words as one searches for objects in a dark room. And that prevented her from being astonished at not having been interrupted, at not having heard any word, whether of benevolence or reproach.

"Nothing but a little hope, Monseigneur, I'm only asking you for a little hope. A creature can't be entirely doomed for one sin. It was a year ago and I wasn't yet twenty. You're the representative of God; everything that you say, I'll believe."

She must have misinterpreted a gesture of the man she believed to be the bishop, for she opened her arms wide as if to retain him.

"Yes, yes, you can do anything, everything depends on you, my entire life is in your hands. You'll understand. But I'm not asking you for anything, except a little hope for later, for a long time hence, when you judge yourself that the moment has come. I have a great love in my heart. I can even say that I've always had it, in spite of what has happened. For I've only been the victim of a stronger will. Yes, I've always loved, without telling anyone, even the man I loved. How could I have told him, anyway?"

She stopped for a moment, in the vague hope of an indulgent word. An invitation to continue would have been sufficient, even a gesture; the silence of her interlocutor appeared to her to be oppressive. She heard a halting respiration, almost panting. She spoke in a low voice.

"I love your nephew. Oh, not Bernard. On the contrary, Bernard repels me. To tell the truth, I don't believe he's good. There's something that separates me from him. I love Sulpice—Sulpice, from whom it's so difficult to extract a word. But it isn't those who speak who think the most. We've known one another for a long time. You remember. Once, he was always ill and he was kept here for the winter while his brother was in Toulouse. We never said anything that could have...no, never the slightest confession or the slightest plan... I understand that you think he's too young... Then, naturally, it's necessary to think of a situation beforehand.... But if I knew that one day...later...if I knew that you forgive me, that I'm not accursed..."

Malediction is the final word of hatred, and it seemed to Bernard that his soul was on fire. His hand fell abruptly on Malvina's shoulder and brought her to her feet.

"Yes! You're accursed, cursed forever by God!"

They were now face to face, but Bernard was careful to continue to play the role of the bishop to the end. He lowered his head in order that his features would still be hidden by his hood, and he spoke in a shrill voice that hatred rendered unrecognizable.

"Get out of here. You're soiling this church. Get out!"

He saw Malvina's face decompose, lose all beauty, express the greatest misery. But he had no pity for her. He marched toward her, arms extended, while she recoiled toward the door.

When she had arrived there her wide eyes gazed around the church as if to request the manifestation of a higher power than the human, from which she might obtain the forgiveness that would place in her heart the tiny glimmer of hope to which every creature has a right, in order to march along the road of life.

By virtue of one of the correspondences in which nature delights, there was then a response of sorts to her mute appeal.

The bird perched somewhere in the shadows suddenly opened its wings. It bumped into the pillar that sustained the vault, tumbled heavily, resumed its flight , and went to strike the wall, a symbol of all the blind beings imprisoned in the inexorable laws, which break against them the wings that they try to open.

Mechanically, Malvina folded her shawl over her breast. She was accursed, forever accursed. She knew full well that God was neither behind his representatives nor behind the figuration of his emblems. There was nothing to be expected from anyone.

The door was ajar. The rain had resumed. Malvina launched herself through the shadows.

III. The Return of Pierre Montanagol

For most people, 1848 had been the year of the Revolution. For others it had been the year of the discovery of gold in California and the commencement of great hopes. But for many, in the circle of the mountains of Comminges, 1848 was the year of the return of Pierre Montanagol.

How clever he must have been, that Pierre Montanagol, who had left the country barefoot, in rags, thrown out by his mother and his stepfather, big Malègre, and who had found a means of making a fortune in America well before the discovery of gold mines there!

The neighbors of the Montanagol farm had seen Pierre for the last time running along the road to Valentine to escape the fury of Malègre, who was pursuing him with a stick in his hand. Malègre was shouting that he wanted to kill Pierre, and he was perfectly capable of doing it.

Malègre was a bad man. For a start, he had no homeland. To anyone who asked, "What is Malègre?" the reply was given, "He's a former factory foreman who had the good luck to marry Françoise, the widow of Montanagol, who planted vines and grew rich selling the wine. Anyway, he comes from Paris, which says it all. And like all Parisians, he drinks. When he's drunk, he's capable of killing. And he's as strong as four men put together."

As soon as he had married the widow Montanagol, people had said: "He'll end up killing little Pierre." And when they heard screams from the big stone building, they said: "There it is; he's killing him."

And no one dared to go and see.

Little Pierre had done what it was best to do. He had left. He had not asked anyone for anything. He had gone along the road in the direction of Toulouse and had not been seen again. Fifteen years old and barefoot!

"What can have become of him?" people sometimes asked. But they preferred not to think about it anymore.

Malègre had brought his relatives—more Parisians. What people! A family ravaged by alcohol, like him. A brother who looked like a specter, and an uncle with a shaven head, like a former convict, with their wives and children. And that vermin had lived in the house and on the estate of the great Montaganol, the man of the vines.

Poor Françoise had not been able to live for long with that evil society around her. She had begun by no longer going out.

"How's Françoise?" people asked Malègre when he went by.

"What business is it of yours how she is?" he replied, without stopping.

People soon knew how she was. She was ill. And in the end she died.

Even on the last day, the Algas had seen her come out on the road. It was sunny and she had put her hand over her eyes in order to see further.

"The poor thing! She peers in that fashion in order to see whether her son might be coming back."

A short time after that, Malègre had started dressing like a monsieur and had tried to put on the manners of a castellan.

"He might well, damn it," people said, "with the Montanagols' money!"

And in front of the former farm he had taken it into his head to sow grass, with geraniums on the edge and a flower-bed in the middle, as in real châteaux. At the start there had been a lot of shouting and blows received, because the children, the donkey and the chickens did not want to give up the habit of playing on the former beaten earth that had become a lawn and flowers. But Malègre mounted guard on it with a big whip and he had ended up having what he called the front of the château respected. Every time he drank his absinthe—and that was several times a day—his little eyes, scarcely visible under his thick eyebrows, blinked in the same direction.

37

One morning, the first absinthe was scarcely concluded, and Malègre was picking up the bottle in order to pour a second when he remained open-mouthed with surprise. On the lawn, in the middle of his precious flower-bed, there was a rider on a horse, a rider who seemed to be of unusual proportions. He thought immediately of someone from a circus, because he had seen someone similar the previous year in a circus that had set up on Saint-Gaudens. He was a Mexican with a broad-brimmed hat such as had never been seen, a bizarre short jacket, and everything else in leather.

But he did not have the leisure to meditate on that costume, for the Mexican leapt down lightly in the middle of the geraniums, and called to Thomas, the farmhand, who was looking at him:

"Hey, you! Instead of looking at me like an idiot, come here and tether my horse to that tree."

He threw the bridle negligently to Thomas, paraded a circular glance over everything, shook his head two or three times and advanced at a leisurely pace toward the house.

Malègre's blood had only made one circuit. Surprise had nailed him to the spot at first. He got up with a bound and launched himself toward the whip.

On the threshold of the entrance he almost collided with the stranger, who was coming in.

"There you are, Malègre. Do you recognize me?"

Malègre had been obliged to take a step back. He shook his head.

"No, but you'll begin..." And he made a movement with his whip.

But the other shrugged his shoulders. "I'm Pierre Montanagol, and I've come back from the other end of the world, where I was very comfortable, moreover, for the sole purpose of breaking your head with a single punch. It's something I've done to others. But on seeing you, I've changed my mind. I only break solid heads. You've become a poor wreck. I imagined you as you were when you gave me beatings. Now you're almost an old man."

"You're Pierre Montanagol? You!" Malègre repeated, mechanically, seeking to realize the consequences of the eventuality, about which he had often thought with apprehension.

A door had opened to the right, where the entire Malègre family appeared.

"What do you want, then? Why have you come?"

"I've come to live in my house. I learned this morning that my mother is dead. I'm the sole proprietor. But we've said enough. I don't want to see you again. Get out. Right away."

"Me get out? Me!"

Malègre had cast a glance at his relatives, who had advanced into the room. He took a step backwards, with a gesture of defiance.

What followed was as rapid as the thought that animated the action. Malègre did not see his adversary coming. He was lifted up and thrown outside. The same force projected, in disorder, all the Malègres present.

Except that the one who resembled a specter fell near the fireplace, or perhaps let himself fall there deliberately. There was a heavy iron poker that served to move large logs. He seized it silently.

"Don't try to come back or you'll have to deal with me," said Montanagol, on the threshold. "I'll throw out everything that belongs to you; you have a quarter of an hour to clear off."

Doubtless a habitude born of the quotidian struggle permitted him to perceive the play of muscles behind him. Perhaps there was a shadow. He let himself fall almost to the ground at the moment when the poker would have struck his head obliquely. He launched his fist and the pale man, struck in the stomach, found himself sitting down, trying to recover his breath. A few seconds later he was brutally thrown outside.

"Don't try it again, because then it would get serious."

Then the shutters on the first floor windows clattered. Garments and various objects, including a few portraits with their frames, fell on to the lawn.

Pierre Montanagol was seen at the middle widow. Suddenly, a detonation rang out.

"Don't touch my horse, or you're dead."

Malègre's uncle had attempted to undo the tether that was retaining the horse. A bullet caused his hat to fly away, which he went to pick up and place on his head.

Montanagol was waving a pistol of an unfamiliar form.

"I still have five more bullets here, at your service," he said, in the tone of an item of information that one supplies, for he thought that the Colt revolver, recently discovered, might not be known yet on the banks of the Garonne. "You only have five minutes." And he leaned on his elbows, placing the weapon on the window sill.

But before the five minutes had elapsed, all the Malègres had disappeared.

Only then, from the gardeners' house on the other side of the lawn, did a little old lady emerge, with the smallness that only old age is able to compose with human matter. It was the grandmother of the farmhand Thomas, who had already been old in the time of the great Montanagol, the man of the vines. She gave the impression of a piece of barely-sculpted wood, and she did her best to run, with her arms extended.

Pierre Montanagol met her on the threshold and lifted her up in order to kiss her.

She had not lost her consciousness of things, and she immediately cried: "My poor Pierre! But they'll come back with the gendarmes."

Thomas had approached, as well as neighbors attracted by the event.

"Do you think I'm so stupid? I went to see the sub-prefect and the notary beforehand. There's a testament of the great Montanagol and another of my mother. Everything here is mine. They advised me to come accompanied by a bailiff. A bailiff! I've seen men much harder than the Malègres."

He raised his voice and spoke to everyone.

"Once, in a place that belonged to me, I found five men...but I'll tell you that story another time. We'll all going to have lunch together. There must be a good wine in the cellar. I invite everyone. And tomorrow, we'll start to rip up this lawn and beat the earth as it was before."

Pierre Montanagol, the son of the man of the vines, was seen all over the place, at the Saint-Gaudens fair, the markets at Aspet and Mauléon. He arrived on horseback with his big hat and his red poncho, and immediately sat down at a table in order to have a drink.

Certainly, no one took it into his head to say that he drank as much as Malègre, but he drank a lot. At first he had asked for a drink unknown in the region, of which no one had heard mention, which he called whisky. After having uttered all kinds of oaths because there was none, he did as everyone else did and drink wine—lots of wine.

And he told extraordinary stories, which were unforgettable.

He had come from a country, Mexico, where, in certain places, one only had to bend down to pick up gold nuggets.

"All the Mexicans are rich, then?"

The places where gold shone on the banks of rivers were inaccessible, in deserted mountains, and in order to reach them, it was necessary to brave dangers, to fight with bandits and redskins, and not to be afraid of anything. Sometimes it was necessary to dig in the ground to discover gold. But in sum, that was the true life, and when one had tasted it, one had a desire to go back.

Thus the rumor spread, confusedly, that it was sufficient for a courageous man to depart for Mexico to make a fortune and no longer to have anything to do than go into villages on Sundays and market days, drink and tell stories. The old law of labor had been abolished. A little courage and one would no longer have to push a plow, sulfurate vines and plant pickets to prevent the apples from being jostled by the wind. It was a marvelous promise, illustrated by the living image of a Mexican cavalier with a magnificent hat.

And a little later, when the newspapers were full of the discovery of gold in California, and societies of emigrants were formed all over the place, the naïve men of the Pyrenean valleys were ready for the most deceptive hopes. One of theirs had made a fortune before all the others! All those who had the youth and the health thought of departing, and especially of returning with a sleeveless mantle called a poncho and spurs larger than a man's hand.

IV. The Star Dancer

"I'm a star dancer," Margarita de Querigut had often said, in the time of her family's prosperity.

At twenty-five, she had never studied dancing, nor even sketched the slightest step as an amateur. But she was firmly convinced that she possessed a genius for dancing and had not been able to bring it to light because of the barbaric prejudice that prevents the descendants of an illustrious family from devoting themselves to any kind of art.

The Querigut family attributed a prodigious antiquity to itself. A Querigut had accompanied Charlemagne in Spain and had died in the Pyrenees, doubtless by Roland's side. Another had been the protector of Saint Bernard. But the last Queriguts had need, above all, of being protected. The old dwelling was crumbling and the mortgages taken out were going to carry it away even more surely than the wind and the rain.

The father and mother of Margarita de Querigut had just died at an interval of a few days, and it was perceived that the sale of the last small patch of land remained of the old estate would scarcely be sufficient to pay for the burials.

Relatives and friends were very anxious about Margarita's fate. But such anxieties only became manifest very slowly. General Compans' widow, who had devoted herself since her husband's death to the protection of the weak, had arranged a meeting at her old house in Salies,[2] the general's homeland, to see what could be done.

---

[2] Author's note: "In 1885, in Portet, near Toulouse, in a château belonging to Monsieur Biscons, at the confluence to the Ariège and the Garonne, there was a room reserved for General Compans' weapons. Why were they in Portet and not Salies?" Jean-Dominique Compans (1769-1845) had enjoyed a spectacular career under Napoléon, surviving numerous wounds sustained in battle, and continued to serve under Louis

"That girl doesn't have a very solid head," the general's wife had said. "If we don't get her out of difficulties, she's doomed."

The general's wife inspired a universal respect and had received many written responses to her invitation. There were invalids who could not come. Then again, times were hard. Everyone would ask round their relatives, ask about a possible situation. Only Adhémar de Bramevaque had come to the meeting. His poverty was proverbial.

"Of course!" said the general's wife. "He isn't risking anything. He has nothing to give."

But Margarita had not shown any affliction at the defection of her friends. When it had been firmly established, at about five o'clock in the afternoon, that only Bramevaque, known to be completely ruined and a trifle dotty, had come to the meeting, without really understanding its purpose, she had shown a shocking amusement at the efforts made by the general's wife.

"I'm poor, I'll earn my living. Aren't I by nature a star dancer?"

Now, Margarita de Querigut had received from nature a body endowed with abnormal thinness. Too tall and too slender, she had a cranium that, by an inexplicable phenomenon, allowed the design of its skeleton to be seen in an impressive manner. And on that death's-head, which bore the smile of an ingenuous young woman and an excessively shiny gaze, grew formidably long and curly red hair. Margarita de Querigut, especially when she laughed—a laughter always prolonged, with a disquieting tone—gave the impression of not belonging to ordinary humanity. The brightly-colored Spanish shawls that she liked and a large necklace that made a noise like rattling bones when she walked, added to the mortuary exoticism of her person.

XVIII before rejoining the deposed Emperor during the Hundred Days, after which he retired and was appointed a peer of France.

And a few days later, without anyone having been consulted, a poster in the square of Saint-Gaudens announced that on the opening day of the fair, in the theater hall adjacent to the Hôtel de France, the star dancer Margarita would appear in her repertoire of ballets.

General Compans' wife was only informed at the last moment, and she believed that it was her duty, given the irremediable character of the catastrophe, to try to save the situation by lending the patronage of her presence to the performance and asking a few friends to come with her.

"I've always thought that you were mad," she said to Margarita, "but I would never have believed that you would go so far. In memory of your parents, I demand that you wear a rigorously correct costume."

All the same, she sent a personal note to Commandant Bertrand de Chalabre asking him to come, with a circle of former officers of the Empire of which he had been a part.

"Try to save the situation," she said to him.

Margarita had obtained the collaboration of a group of local amateur musicians. There were two or three rehearsals. The leader of the orchestra, who had once been in the band of a regiment of zouaves, interrogated as to the quality of the dancer, had replied with a certain mystery: "I'll only say this..." and had clicked his tongue.

The owner of the Hôtel de France, who was to have half the receipts, had organized the room as for certain dramatic performances. At the hour when the market was in full swing he had the drum beaten.

The local bourgeoisie, fully costumed. piled into the front rows. In the middle there was a place of honor with a larger and higher seat, a sort of throne, reserved for General Compans' widow. She was surrounded by all that the region had of former officers of the Empire, to whom a word of order had been given.

"There's a situation to save."

There was Colonel Espondeillan, who had made the retreat from Moscow and had told the story a thousand times.

"Don't let young Espondeillan die," Napoléon had said to one of his aides-de-camp on seeing him sitting by the roadside near the Berezina. There was Zenon Fabregat, the philosopher, who had a wooden leg that he slapped hard in order to manifest his impatience; Colonel Bertrand de Chalabre, who occupied himself with astronomy after a military career; Julien de Miravel, the seducer, whose long moustache, which joined up with his side-whiskers, rendered him irresistible—he had never surpassed the rank of captain but everyone knew that there were stories of women that had retarded his advancement. There were others too, and they had all been electrified by the drum rolls.

The audience in the stalls had rendered a worldly manifestation, slightly bizarre in the fashion in which it was presented, but which was under the aegis of Madame Compans. They had come to see the descendant of a great family of the region showing off her artistic talents, for a charitable cause that had not been specified.

It was not the same, however, for a numerous popular public that occupied a sort of raised gallery above the stalls. There were cattle drovers there come for the fair, who had kept the long pointed sticks with which they pricked the animals, shepherds entirely dressed in sheepskin, and sawmill workers. A poster similar to the one that had announced Margarita's dances had advertised for the other days of the fair, either a dancing bear or a singer from Toulouse who was half-prostitute.

Margarita had only to appear for a rumor to burst forth in which there were sentiments of alarm and hilarity. Immediately, there was a treason on the part of the orchestra leader, who winked, in order to make it understood that he, a veritable artist, did not consider what they were about to see to be serious.

Margarita's inexpert make-up brought out the terrible character of her head strangely. She was wearing a fringed skirt that came down almost as far as the knees and rendered visible the design of legs of incredible thinness, covert in

46

stockings the color of whitened bones. The Spanish shawl was scarcely crossed over. The open-mouthed audience had the sensation of an animated skeleton agitating in amorous attitudes.

Madame Compans was like a stone statue. Her friends applauded politely. The so-called dances succeeded one another. But as soon as the effect of surprise had worn off, laughter and jeers began to burst forth in the crowd. They augmented progressively, mingled with the banging of staffs on the floor.

Bertrand de Chalabre stood up to his full height, turned to the audience and shouted in a resounding voice: "Come on, Messieurs, a little restraint."

He obtained a minute's silence. But the bursts of laughter, with which obscene remarks were mingled, resumed even more loudly.

Colonel Espondeillan attempted to intervene in his turn, but he was jeered. The officers rose to their feet. Julien de Miravel was heard asking several times who would like to step outside and measure sabers with him.

The officers were not popular. General Cavaignac's fusillades in Paris had echoed all the way to the Pyrenean villages. Insults were addressed to them.

Meanwhile, Margarita, with an ecstatic smile on her face, continued the same steps and the same attitudes of languor. Sometimes, the whim of the audience produced a thunder of joyous applause, which she interpreted as a manifestation of admiration.

"Stop! That's enough!" Malvina de Noussoulens whispered to her.

But she would not hear it. She went on to the end.

Outside, the square was jammed. There were carriages and flocks of sheep. A stray ox was bellowing and running back and forth.

"Has she measured the extent of the disaster?" someone asked.

Someone affirmed that they had seen her weeping at the moment when she bowed—but perhaps it was with joy.

Napoléon's officers were on the defensive. The battle was lost. They had seen many others! What was it, compared with Moscow in flames?

There was only the naïve Madame Toché, the notary's wife, to say to the general's wife, while shaking her hand: "Your young friend was charming, utterly charming."

They searched for Margarita in vain. Neither the unworthy orchestra leader nor the owner of the hotel had seen her. Scarcely had she left the stage, with her necklace making the noise of rattling bones, than she had disappeared.

And everyone imagined her, waking with a long stride along the road, where the mountain mist was now falling, overtaking moving flocks, sometimes receiving the light of a shepherd's lantern in her made-up face. And she would sit down alone, with her vanished dream, in the deserted Château de Querigut, whose furniture had recently been sold at auction, and all night long she would be whistled by the owls in the fir trees.

The following day, Margarita de Querigut went hither and yon, to the houses of her friends, to announce the good news.

She had been engaged by a passing impresario to give dance performances in Mexico. Providence had determined that the day before, Monsieur Alcide Pécouret had arrived in Saint-Gaudens and had chanced to see the performance she had put on. He was the representative of a large French emigration society. He had judged at a glance that, if her art was not understood by the vulgar Pyrenean peasants, it was exactly what was needed for the cultivated society of Mexico. There were fortunes to be made out there. He had only made one allusion to the rich owners of haciendas—that was what Mexican châteaux were called—for whom French women were ornamented with a great prestige and might become admirable suitors, but she knew that there were always saddled horses whinnying in the courtyards, and innumerable negro slaves running with sorbets because of the heat.

For the expenses of her voyage of course, it was necessary to have a few thousand francs for the society. The sale of her furniture, her last resource, represented exactly what was necessary.

Alcide Pécouret, who was a great lover of art, especially that of dance, had greatly admired her style of dancing. He had only formulated one reservation. He did not like the noise her necklace made—but that was nothing. Success was assured among the Hacienderos. That was the word she used. A marvelous future was opening in front of her.

Oh, no, there was no need to tell her that there was no Providence!

"You ask me what gold looks like when it's extracted from a seam, and obviously bears no resemblance of a *louis d'or* bearing an effigy of Napoléon," said Pierre Montanagol to a man who was sitting beside him and listening to him with admiration. "Well a piece of gold ore resembles the skin of that individual in a frock-coat coming out of the Hôtel de France, who has little russet patches under a sickly goatee."

The individual in question was Alcide Pécouret. A curious coincidence rendered his face, afflicted by a bizarre rash, similar to a block of gold ore. He was describing the gold of placers, a virgin gold, sparkling, he said: a chimerical gold, which did not exist anywhere; and one only had to look him in the lying eyes to see the color of veritable gold: the sad gold, the terrible gold of the earth.

V. Noël Alga

"Maman, I want to enjoy life," said Noël Alga to his mother, when a fit of sadness fell abruptly upon him.

"Aren't you enjoying it at every moment," simply by breathing in the sunlight," replied the aged Madame Alga, shrugging her shoulders.

Noël Alga made a gesture, signifying that he knew what his mother was about to say.

"I know. God knows what he's doing. He puts everyone in his place, and it's necessary to stay where one is put. Why, then, does he give us desires for change?"

"Can anyone know the intentions of God?"

And old Madame Alga went away, in order not to have to argue with her son.

She had had him late, after having lost her other children, and her sole dread was seeing him leave. Her husband had been the proprietor of a big sawmill in Saint-Béat. On his death it had been necessary to sell it, and the profit had permitted her, just about, to buy a little house in the valley at the foot of Saint-Bertrand-de-Comminges and to have a small income on which to live modestly with her son. She had never incited him to make money, to succeed, like all parents. At the first pretext of illness she had interrupted his studies, and had withdrawn him from the seminary of Saint-Gaudens.

At twenty, since he had to do something, she had obtained a position for him, in memory of her husband, as junior clerk to Maître Toché, the notary. But Noël was not made for stacks of paper and he had been unable to stay there. One morning, he had arrived at the office and sat down, as usual. Suddenly, he had got up, as if someone had summoned him, went out, and never came back.

He explained to his mother what had happened.

"There was a call. A slight breeze had risen and blew into the office. And at the same time as the signs creaked I heard a voice. It was very clear and it said: 'Come, Noël Alga.' The mountain had called me. How could I leave it without response, preferring the parchment face of Maître Toché to the mountain?"

When her son talked like that, Madame Alga did not know, exactly, whether he was serious or joking.

"In sum, perhaps you're right," she said, in the same tone, "since you were called."

And that day, Noël left for the mountain, and stayed there for three days.

In such cases, he took a small bag of provisions, a staff, a cape and a guitar. Sometimes, he put a book of poetry in his pocket.

Madame Alga was not anxious, even if the expedition was unusually prolonged. It was sufficient for her son to have indicated the name of the mountain that he was going to climb by showing her the contour from a distance, so that she could look in that direction in the evening and tell herself that he was out there.

"Tomorrow," he said, "I'll be in the meadows of Roumaingou. There's a forest partly knocked down by the wind, alongside the pond of storks. All the trees are my friends; they talk to me and I understand them as well as if it were you."

Once he had said: "There's an oak several hundred years old almost at the summit of the Cagire. It has sent me a message; I have to go and see it."

And the mother said: "Fine!" And she hastened to prepare ham, cheese, bread and wine in an old leather bag that dated from her grandfather's time.

"He's gone to see some trees that he likes, up there."

And, sitting on her doorstep, she did not lose sight of the skeletal design of the Cagire, the mountain on the side of which her son was sitting under a bald trunk, playing the guitar before going to sleep.

"You see, you can stay as long as you like. The essential thing is that I know the mountain."

"Tomorrow I'll be up there," said Noël, pointing to one of the peaks that formed the horizon.

There was another custom established between the mother and the son. At every return, scarcely had she said: "Oh, how black you are," or "How hot you are," than he seized her and lifted her up, in spite of a few protests.

"Noël! Are you mad! Let me go!"

He did that while dancing three times round the kitchen, if he surprised her in the house, or a large plane tree if it was in the courtyard.

"So? Have the trees told you beautiful things?" the mother said.

And Noël began a story, no matter what, while his mother busied herself laying the table or asking whether he preferred white or red to drink.

Noël was tall, thin and, for the sake of romanticism, wore his hair long. A slightly hooked nose gave him a certain austerity, was compensated by the joyous and sparkling gleam of his gaze. He was said to be savage because he did not run after he local girls. He thought them vulgar, dreaming of romantic amours, amazons in black toques, young women dreaming on the perrons of châteaux.

Those amours to come had given him a great preoccupation: he lacked knowledge of life. He did not know how to conduct himself at table in a grand dinner of important people. Men of the world must have a special manner of eating of which he was ignorant. Where could he learn it?

"What shall I do, Maman, if I'm invited to dinner by the prefect of Toulouse?"

"Wait for the invitation to arrive before tormenting yourself. You don't know the prefect. Anyway, I have the idea that the noblest people eat exactly like you."

But Noël had a graver concern. What conversation would he have with a young woman of high society to whom he was paying court?

"My son, I have the idea that young women of high society express themselves almost exactly like the others. Anyway, you don't know any."

Noël Alga's anxieties changed as rapidly as his joys. He loved animals, but he wanted to go further than any other man in their conquest. He dreamed of narrow communication, relationships of amity analogous to those between human friends. Evidently, he was separated from them by the impossibility of conversing, but who knew? Animals might well have a language. Why not arrive at understanding it, and even of speaking it? He understood the language of trees well enough. So?"

And when he was alone, walking on the mountain paths, Noël delivered himself to all sorts of trials, modulations of birdsong, whistles, grunts, croaking and braying. For a long time, in one solitary meadow, he had tried to penetrate the souls of donkeys, studying the different tones in which mothers called to foals or announced the discovery of a more succulent thistle. The results had been unsatisfactory. He thought he had had more success with a badger cub that he had found in the forest, picked up and tamed, for Noël claimed that domestic animals were perverted and that only wild animals had a virgin soul capable of love.

By whistling in a certain fashion he succeeded in making snakes emerge from their holes. He had been seen with a long grass snake wound round his arm. He had once been followed by a mole. He was proud of that, he said, because moles could not see him. It was therefore obeying an invisible force. And several hedgehogs, animals that, under their bristling carapace, one might think were strangers to any speculation, came to his door in the evening and showed no fear when he tried to speak to them by means of raucous cries. One of them would even have come into the kitchen if Madame Alga had not intervened, armed with a stick, saying that everyone ought to remain in their place, animals on one side and humans on the other.

To be sure, Noël, pushed by the enthusiasm of success, sometimes exaggerated his power over animals—notably when he claimed that the ants of a certain ant-hill, that one and no other, paused in their march and raised their antennae toward him as a sign of sympathy. He also affirmed that a crow that had a nest near his house, when he shouted "Five o'clock!" to it distinctly the day before, came to wake him up the next day at five o'clock by tapping his window pane with its beak five times.

It did seem that, in general, animals showed a particularly amicable conduct in his regard. His mother laughed at what he told her about that, and pretended to mock him, but sometimes she said: "Haven't I brought into the world a son who is something of a sorcerer?"

However, a goose compromised the confidence that Noël had in himself by pecking him rather seriously with her beak.

"I forgive her," said Noël. "It's the wickedness of humans that has rendered her wicked."

And he played his guitar in the mountains, very high, in the most inaccessible places, on the deserted peaks, in the hope of charming the truly savage beasts of the summits.

All legends have a foundation of verity, he thought. *Orpheus made tigers come to him. That's because music must act on the simple souls of the most ferocious creatures.*

And he did not despair of attracting the bears and the wolves. While he played, he watched the edge of the forest, and caves at the rim of precipices. He would have been content with the presence of a chamois with slender hooves and red-tinted horns. Perhaps he was not a great enough musician? Nothing is more difficult than charming—even beasts...

Noël Alga did not always go to play his guitar on the heights. On winter evenings, he practiced interminably, while his mother was asleep by the foreside.

Martin Bruno, a tall peasant of his own age, who lived in Barbazan and admired everything he did and everything he said, came to listen to him, and remained motionless nearby until the moment when Mother Alga, who had not heard anything, said: "I believe that music will drive me mad!" and gave the signal to go to bed.

On spring days he went to certain chosen places; he played for himself, falling into a sort of ecstasy that music alone can produce.

The place that he chosen in preference to any other was one where wild poppies grew under a mulberry at the extremity of the park of Noussoulens. The enclosing wall had collapsed a long time ago and the park was confounded with the common land of the mountain, planted with heather.

At the end of that day in May, when the guitar stopped, he had the surprise of hearing the sound of two hands applauding. In an abandoned pathway, which the lateral foliage obstructed by meting up, Malvina appeared.

"Thank you, Noël Alga," she said, coming forward "It's nice of you to have thought of giving me a concert this evening."

She smiled, feigning cheerfulness and ease, but the cheerfulness was artificial and the ease too great to be natural.

Noël did not notice something distracted that was in her eyes. He had stood up, and in his confusion he began to say that he had come there unintentionally, by chance.

Was it chance? There was a force that impelled him, unknown to himself, in the direction of the park of Noussoulens. He did not admit it to himself. He did not admit that it was the vague hope of encountering Malvina. In any case, he almost never crossed her path. What might she be doing all day in the park? And what point as there, anyway, in an encounter? Sometimes, on Sunday, coming out of mass at Saint Bertrand, he bowed to her and succeeded in meeting her gaze. But it was a haughty, hard gaze that scarcely posed on him. For scarcely a second he glimpsed a gilded gleam that immediately turned away. What pride there was in her! Did women become more inaccessible as they became more beautiful?

However, they had played together when they were little children. Martin Bruno's mother had been Malvina's nurse. When they were four years old, perhaps five, they had amused themselves together with Martin and, as he had been the oldest and most reasonable then, he had been the one in command! She was even under his protection, because Martin was endowed with an abnormal strength and did not yet know its proportions. But that time was doubtless forgotten. At least, for years, she had made a semblance of no longer knowing him.

And now, suddenly, he was in the presence of the most beautiful young woman he knew, the inaccessible and the proud, who was smiling at him in a familiar manner. Noël felt a surge of joy. But immediately, rising from the depths of his soul, came his old dread of not knowing certain customs and attitudes that aristocratic people must have when they encountered one another. He lacked knowledge of life.

"Do you often see Martin Bruno?" she asked, negligently. "Does he still live out there?"

She took two or three steps as she said that, and a slight movement of the head indicated to Noël that she wanted him to walk alongside her. He followed her across the park. She stopped frequently. She talked about a thousand things, volubly, about songs she liked, local people, and the long excursions that Noël made in the mountains.

Yes, she knew that. How could she have lost sight on an old comrade like Noël? She also knew that he had tamed a badger and snakes.

"So, you remember the times when we used to play in the Bruno barn?"

"Know that I don't forget anything, ever."

And she looked him straight in the face, as if that insignificant stroll were creating a secret between them, becoming an important moment in her life, which she could not forget.

At the end of the path in which they were walking, the château was outlined. Then she retraced her steps. Noël was walking as if in a dream. Knowledge of life no longer tormented him. He felt full of delight, He had the sentiment of eternal duration that certain sudden and intense joys produce.

He was talking to Malvina like a friend. He would have liked to tell her all his dreams, all his ambitions.

The light was beginning to die away. The bushes were buzzing with insects. The warmth of the spring rose up from the heated ground. They had arrived at a place in the park where the vegetation was so thick that it was necessary to part the branches with their hands.

"I'd like to reach that large beech over there," said Malvina.

She turned her face toward Noël and he saw an extraordinary gleam in her eyes.

"I don't know whether these bushes will permit that."

However, they arrived at the foot of the beech.

"It isn't such a long time since someone's been here," said Noël, pointing at the ground. "That part in the form of a rectangle must have been dug up only a year or two ago."

"Who knows? And what does it matter?"

Malvina had taken his arm and was squeezing it.

"No, I never forget. And yet there are memories that it's necessary to suppress at any price, that it's necessary to kill, in order that you don't die of them."

Noël did not understand her sudden vehemence.

She had quit him, she had taken a few steps under the beech, looking at the ground, as if measuring the place. Then she came back toward him, looking him full in the face, and Noël thought he saw a glint of gold dancing in the depths of her pupils. He had a desire to take her in his arms and he sensed that it would be an action as easy as that of drinking water from a mountain stream when it was very hot.

"But once, when I was four, perhaps five, and you were six or seven, didn't we cal one another *tu*?"

She was very close to him. Noël did not notice the distraction in her gaze. The guitar that he still had under his arm slid to the ground, and a string rendered a long, dolorous sound. Malvina had inclined her head and their lips met while the string was vibrating.

Then she pulled away, made the gesture of pushing her hair back from her forehead, as if she were also chasing away a sudden and unknown impulse, and she fled. Nevertheless, she made a gesture before plunging into the thick bushes at the end of the path: a gesture of adieu, the meaning of which Noël was to try to understand a thousand times, which might equally well have signified "Until tomorrow!" or "Never!"—a gesture that might as easily have meant: "What a folly we've committed" as "This is the beginning of a great amour"—or a gesture that might perhaps have no significance at all...

The next day, and the following days, Noël waited at the same time in the same place, in the midst of the poppies. He played the guitar and he took the same path that led to the beech, though the brushwood. Fearing an error, he even came well before the time when he had seen Malvina, only leaving when night had entirely fallen. He even came when it rained, with his boots and his guitar under his cape. *One never knows*, he said to himself.

He thought at first that Malvina was ill. He feared that, but above all he hoped for it. He did not see her at mass. Perhaps she had left on a journey. He remembered having heard it said that she had relatives in Bordeaux. He asked around. She was not ill, nor had she gone away. She had been seen in her carriage.

The beautiful Malvina, with her blue-tinted trees with flecks of gold! One only saw her at that moment. Ha ha! She certainly gave the impression of loving life, that one! Who was it who said that she had fire in her body? Oh, the girls of today! And have you noticed? The younger one locks them away, the more they do stupid things a little later. The beautiful Malvina runs after men...

If old Noussoulens held on to his daughter as he did, it was because he knew full well that she resembled her mother...

VI. The Rose of God

"Uncle, what is it necessary to do when one is invaded by doubt?"

Timidly, Hugues Borromée had asked that question of the former bishop, and he kept his eyes lowered, feeling a sort of shame at having asked it.

He had concluded his studies at the seminary of the Foreign Missions and he was only waiting for the order to depart. He had come to spend his last days in France at Saint-Bertrand-de-Comminges. And that May evening, not without difficulty, he had been able to force his uncle to listen to him. For Nestor Borromée was becoming more and more self-enclosed, fearing appeals to his theological science, or even advice to give.

Hugues went on: "Doubtless, in whatever country I'm in. I'll have long hours of solitude. It's then that, without any reason, doubt surges forth. Is there a means of keeping one's quotidian faith intact?"

They were both walking slowly alongside the poplars and yews of the cemetery of the church of Saint-Just. But Nestor Borromée did not have the start of surprise that his nephew feared. The word "doubt" caused him to sketch a gesture, as if to chase away a familiar phantom.

"Doubt! My poor child! But one is invaded by doubt until one's last day. Everyone! Even those whose faith is the most solid, even those who never ask themselves questions, even those who seem enclosed in their simplicity as in pure armor. I've listened to many confessions, seen into the depths of many souls. In all of them there's doubt, which lies awake in a corner, like a little malevolent lamp."

"The saints, however..."

"The saints more than the others! The serene faces, the hands clasped in long prayers are often only façades behind which there is the torment of not being sure. Evidently, in principle, one is sure. But everyone would like his personal proof. Everyone believes that he has a right to that. Everyone would like to see, and even to touch. But even if God manifests himself to a man, what can prove to that elect that he is not the victim of an illusion of his senses? Is there an authority who can say with certainty: this is a creation of the imagination; this is an authentic manifestation of God? There are saints who have doubted after having seen..."

He stopped. He considered his nephew's ingenuous face, which was filled with sadness, and he thought: *How wrong one is to speak! The truth is always dolorous and futile. I'm only discouraging him. I'd do better to shut up.*

In spite of that, he continued, driven by the mysterious need to express himself.

"I believe that everyone is born with his ration of doubt, which he cannot escape. The doubt is there. It surges forth, and then disappears. It's a companion from which one cannot separate oneself. When it starts to torment you, I don't know any other means than waiting patiently—waiting for faith to return."

Nestor Borromée stopped, and glimpsed a flash of desperation in the young missionary's gaze. They had arrived at the church of Saint-Just. With a vague gesture he designated the saints sculpted in the stone of the portal.

"There are aides, there are protectors. It's necessary to appeal to them. Sometimes, they respond. There are favored men who hear words coming from on high, but I'm not one of them. I believed that in advancing in life, there was a moment when serenity would come, when one was supported by an absolute certainty. Nothing of the sort. I'm more tormented than before as to what I ought to do. Ought I to give my property to the poor and go to live as an ascetic, like Uncle Romuald? I once believed that was my destiny, that I would find God in solitude. I'm no longer sure of it. It needs a solid brain o support the continual presence of a sky full of stars above the head. Here, one doesn't think about that terrible immensity, but out there...

"I went to see Romuald not long ago. The weather was fine. Catherine went with me. She carried the horn. I've always considered Romuald as a superior being. A man who has loved Greek philosophy to that extent, and knows Plato and Aristotle as if he knew them personally, isn't just anyone. He has eccentricities, evidently. I had deposited myself, in a corner of the cabin where he lives, a copy of the gospels hat had belonged to our father. I had said to him: 'Promise me to read the gospels from end to end.' I thought that he'd be touched by the light. Well, it was neither a believer nor a philosopher that I saw coming toward me but an almost savage being. His hair is falling over his shoulders, his beard is bushy. And he's proud of the hair that covers his body and which, by a phenomenon I can't explain, has become abnormally long.

"It was the end of April and it was cold. In spite of that, he was naked to the waist and his first words were to say to me: 'You see, I'm like a bear!' in a triumphant tone. And it was true! I wanted to talk to him about elevated subjects. I was well received! He always came back to the quality of the goat's cheese and ham that the wardens at the hospice brought him. Hs greatest joy is that of helping woodcutters to slide tree-trunks down the slopes.

"And then...I hardly dare tell you this...I heard it from Catherine, who's talkative and chats to everyone. He sometimes goes to meet an old peasant woman who lives ten kilometers away, and is slightly crack-brained. Solitude has debased him instead of elevating him. Yes, solitude is redoubtable. You fear that it will bring you crises of doubt. There are other dangers. Savagery. It can cause retrogression. And that is the greatest evil that threatens human beings."

They walked on in silence. They had retraced their steps back to the cemetery of the church of Saint-Just. They were walking slowly in the dusk.

"In sum, what would you do in my place?" Nestor Borromée asked his nephew.

The young man had hoped to obtain a line of conduct from his uncle, to benefit from the familial wisdom that he believed to be transmitted like a deposit by all the great ecclesiastics of the Borromée family, and now it was him, the young apprentice missionary, whose advice was being solicited!

"Yes, would you sell the old house to go and lead the life of a hermit in a cabin where there are the skulls of fifteen wolves? If do that, I abandon your brothers, old Catherine and all the people who count on me and come to ask for the support of my wisdom. My wisdom! I don't have any. I deceive them in giving them advice. Sometimes I fear that I'm talking nonsense. By selling everything I could do a great deal of good. The portrait of your great uncle, the superior of the Franciscans, has a considerable value, it seems. An art dealer in Toulouse knows a collector who would like it. And see how illusory everything is. In all good faith, that painting is no better than other paintings of the same epoch that I possess; the colors are even more tarnished. And yet that one has value, but not the others. My God, why is it sought after? Yes, that painting alone would yield a lot of money. But then another problem poses itself, an almost insoluble problem. Ought one to do good with money? What's your sincere advice?"

"I don't know, uncle. I've always thought..."

"That it's necessary to do the good. That's what everyone thinks, because they don't look at the enchainment of causes and effects. But experience has shown me that, in a very large number of cases, money received has been a cause of harm. I recently cast trouble into a family that was getting by, more or less, neither too fortunate nor too unfortunate, which had, at any rate, the equilibrium that permits one to get a little further in life. From the moment that I intervened the family was dislocated. I'll spare you the details. The son had difficulties in an affair; everything could be sorted out with a sum of money. With great difficulty, I procured it.'

"It was a matter of very worthy people, strongly united. I went to take them the sum and I gave it to the father, the head of the family. Well, without anyone knowing, the man had a mistress in Toulouse who needed the same sum of money. He yielded to a moment of folly and went to give her the money intended for his son. Chance played its role; I met the mother and the son the same day and I told him: 'I've just given the money to your father.'

"'When?'

"'An hour ago.'

"'But I've seen him, and he didn't say anything to me; he's gone to Toulouse.

"Everything came out. The happiness of that family has been destroyed. Who was the cause of that? The man who intervened in order to do good. Good engenders evil, and reciprocally. So, perhaps the best thing is to do nothing."

"But then, in my case, I ought to abstain from going to evangelize ignorant men, in order not to give birth to causes whose effects I don't know."

"Eh! Perhaps so...I don't say that. I don't want to give advice. I've arrived at fearing the slightest indication on my part. It's necessary to arrive at an advance age to comprehend the meaning of the word *responsible*. The weight of responsibility! It's a burden as heavy as that of the years and one receives it in as gradual a fashion."

Night had now fallen and they did not say any more until the moment when they felt the shadow of the dismantled belfry over them.

"Think that if I sold everything," the bishop exclaimed, "the new owner would have the right to have a modern villa constructed on the site of that chapel. There are Borromées buried there, although I don't know which. But they're there. Perhaps they were great saints. I'd make the happiness of a few living people, but the ashes of a few dead ones would be thrown to the wind. My God, what to do?"

In spite of the presence of the unknown Borromées, Hugues did not go willingly to pray in the chapel. He sensed something hostile there, whose origin he could not discern. It was not the placid and grave faces of courageous ecclesiastics that he discerned under the flagstones, but the passionate forms of beings tormented by desire who had not accepted the silence and shadow of death.

He had been born with an unusual clairvoyance that his life of meditation had only served to develop further in him. He feared that clairvoyance and strove not to believe in it, not being sure of the purity of its origin. His greatest dread was that of not being able to recognize that it came from God, and that it came from the great evil force of the world that he saw at work around him.

"My son, remember that when the moment comes, God always gives a sign to someone who has served him faithfully. The difficulty is in seeing the sign and understanding its meaning, for the divine language is always veiled."

He had recalled to mind that speech by his teacher at the seminary of the Missions, Père André, who had traveled the world for forty years before devoting himself to the instruction of new apostolic missionaries.

Why does God not speak clearly? Hugues often asked himself. Why did it require too much difficulty to find one's way? But where would the merit be otherwise? The law was universal. It was necessary to extract the truth with effort, in the same way that the peasant extracts his nourishment from the earth. Doubt itself as a necessary proof. It enabled the joy of belief to emerge more fully. And he sometimes rejoiced after an hour of dryness because he emerged from it with a greater love.

In any case, doubt was never anything but a temporary crisis for him. A sign quickly came that reminded him of the role that he had to play in the immense divine organization. And the sign was such that he sometimes thought that he was the object of a special attention on God's part. His gratitude was then infinite.

As long as pride isn't blinding me! he thought.

It seemed to him that his life would be too short to realize the good that he projected. How many men there were to save! How little time he had to teach the way to salvation to those who did not know it! The intoxication of action then took possession of him. He waited impatiently for the moment of departure.

Although he thought that the place of prayer was of little importance, he avoided long meditations in the chapel. He took the little path through the fields that led in the direction of Mauléon, toward the mountains. He reached the first foothills. There, abruptly, the route became a steep path through the midst of rocks, ferns and wild heather. He left to his right an apple orchard, near to which he paused to listen to the song of cuckoos. It was never the same, that song, depending on the hour and other reasons that escaped him. Who could tell? Could there not be warnings transmitted by the intermediary of cuckoos? Some of those birds came to flutter round him in a very familiar fashion. Might they not be messengers?

He continued his route through honeysuckle and continued to climb as far as a small platform where three old chestnut trees confronted a large flowering hawthorn. That place had a secret character. One might have thought that no one, neither lovers nor groups of children, had ever discovered it. Thus, when nature, with her earth, her plants and her woods, has realized a tiny perfect landscape, she defends it for a long time from human pollution, by some mysterious method.

Hugues sat down under one of the three chestnut trees, and sometimes let an entire afternoon go by in reverie and prayer, watching the wind agitate the branches of the hawthorn.

He had never encountered anyone on the path that led there and he had ended up considering that retreat as his property. He savored the harmony of the earth and the sky there, but he remained suspicious before the excessive seduction of the landscape. He knew that the beauty of living forms is the trap that the love of life and material enjoyment uses in order to awaken human desire. He had known throughout his adolescence the disturbance that comes from terrestrial aromas in spring, for trees swollen with sap and excessively captious flowers. He mistrusted reverie in the bosom of nature as much as the presence of an excessively beautiful woman.

One afternoon, as he arrived at the foot of the three chestnut trees he saw a freshly-cut rose on the stone where he was accustomed to sit down. It was not a wild rose but a flower that one sensed had been chosen from among the most beautiful on a rose-bush.

Someone has been here, he thought, *doubtless a woman, who has forgotten that rose.*

He considered it, placed it on the grass, but remained embarrassed by its presence.

The next day, when he came back, there was a new rose on the stone. It was perhaps more beautiful than the previous one, and must have been picked very recently. The other one had begun to wither slightly.

How much disturbance a flower could cause by its presence! His prayer was distracted. He could not help wondering who had brought the flower to this solitary place in the woods. Where were there such beautiful roses? Those in his uncle's garden did not have that splendor. Perhaps they came from the Château de Bramevaque, which was not far away, or that of Noussoulens. There were also roses in Saint-Bertrand. Yes, the most beautiful in the region were assuredly those in the cloister of Saint-Bernard-de-Comminges.

Suddenly, a dazzling idea sprang to mind. He remembered having seen roses as beautiful, similar to that one. He often went in the morning to the cloister of the cathedral of Saint Bertrand. That cloister, with its three Roman galleries, appeared to him to be one of the most beautiful places on earth, a marvel little celebrated, and all the more precious for that. The dream of beauty of great anonymous artists, sculptor monks of ancient times, was fixed in the stone, in the shafts of the colonnades, in the ecstatic faces of prophets, in the bas-reliefs of the sarcophagi. And the faith of the holy men who, for centuries, had walked under those arcades, had gradually taken on substance in the old marbles, the mortuary moss and the immemorial earth, with the result that the cloister, along-side the cathedral looking up like a fortress, was the symbol of the spiritual effort of the past, the divine stone impregnated by the sky, placed by God in the land of Comminges.

He remembered having admired astonishing roses around one of the pillars of the cloister, on which the four evangelists were represented, hugging a stone book. And other roses of an equal splendor covered a tomb, a tombs among tombs, the one that had contained the dust and the bones of a Borromée, the Bishop of Saint-Bertrand, in olden times...

He dared not conceive the hypothesis. He shivered thinking about it. A supernatural hand had cut a rose from the cloister and had transported it miraculously for him.

He let himself fall to his knees in a movement of gratitude.

He got up again immediately. He was the victim of his pride. He had not merited the sign of the rose. Or an unknown person, a passer-by had deposited that flower. Perhaps it was a manifestation of sympathy of a pious person who had surprised his daily prayer. The revolution had recently reawakened the old popular hatred of priests, but there was now a contrary reaction. He was saluted respectfully when he passed by, which had not happened the previous year. Yes, it was only that. And yet...

He found a new rose every day. The first time, he had not dared to take it. Now he carried it away and kept it amorously in his room.

Woe betide he man who does not understand the sign, especially if it is striking, he said to himself at times—and he felt surges of enthusiasm passing through him. *I have been chose for something very great and very fine.*

One afternoon, when he arrived a little earlier than usual on the platform of the hawthorn and the chestnut trees, he distinguished through the branches the silhouette of a woman under the trees. He arrived just in time to perceive her gesture. Visibly, it was her who came to deposit the rose. At the sound of his footsteps she moved away along a path that descended in zigzags to the right and was a short cut in the direction of the Château de Noussoulens.

Hugues recognized her immediately. It was Malvina. In any case, she did not try to hide. As she moved away she turned and smiled at him. His surprise was so great that he stood there motionless and made no response.

He had the sentiment of falling from a high tower where all was glory and beauty, and the summit of which he would not attain again. He had always been afraid of Malvina, afraid for others, because of a kind of power that was within her and that he assimilated to evil. But for the first time, he was afraid for himself. He had just distinguished, in the quality of her smile and her glance, intentionally too long, when she had turned round, a desire to please that had the effect on him of a burn. What he had believed to be a sign from God was only the maneuver of a perverse creature.

He looked around and the transformed landscape. Oh, how full of dangers nature was! In the buzzing of insects, the calling of birds, the movements of bushes, and the swelling of sap under the bark, he sensed the force of evil. And that evil was within him. He had communicated with its power via the intermediary of that daily flower that he had hugged so tenderly against him. A dormant force had awakened in his body. Would he be able to master it?

He cast a final glance at the shade of the chestnut trees, where he had found a deceitful exaltation. The hawthorn appeared to him to be malevolent. In the odor of the honeysuckle he thought he sensed an odor of flesh.

He drew away rapidly. He almost ran in order to reach his uncle's house. He went up to his room in haste. In a vase, on the table, next to a prayer-book, there were the roses of the last seven days, the freshest one radiant in the middle. Around the vase, faded petals made a circle. He swept all of them away in his hand, crushed the roses and went down into the garden, to the compost heap, on which he threw them.

He could crush the roses, but how could he annihilate the smile and the sidelong glance?

VII. Alcide Pécouret's Successes

One of Alcide Pécouret's greatest successes was the one that brought him into the circle of the former officers of the Empire on the day when he came to explain the advantages of the emigration society that he represented.

The circle had a room on the first floor of the Hôtel de France. Cards, liqueurs and military memories often prolonged the soirées until eleven o'clock. A pact bound the members, a pact based on a common resolution: the refusal to grow old. They had agreed two things. Firstly, they had to remain young, and secondly, they had to admire Napoléon.

The second was easier. Admiration of Napoléon was maintained by the story of past campaigns and received a powerful aliment every day, for the political prognostications announced the election of Prince Napoléon to the presidency of the Republic.[3] But eternal youth encountered unexpected obstacles from time to time. Once it was a rheumatism, another time it was an eyesight that admitted its deterioration.

It was only in the domain of seduction that there was no weakness—but Colonel de Chalabre declared that women were inferior beings, utterly despicable, because they were not military women, and he added, when the matter was discussed: "Even that wouldn't matter much, but have you ever heard mention of a female astronomer?" Because, in getting old, Colonel de Chalabre had discovered astronomy. The sky had revealed its mystery to him.

"I was sitting outside my door one evening, smoking my pipe and, by chance, I tipped backward in my chair. Suddenly, I saw the sky for the first time. I'd looked at it a thousand

---

[3] The election in question took place in December 1848, so the implication that it has not yet happened is not quite compatible with other datable references in the story, but the chronology is slightly askew throughout.

times before, but I hadn't seen it. Note that I might very well have died without making that discovery. The happiness of my life dates from that admirable evening."

Thanks to a small family inheritance he had built a tower above his house and had installed a telescope there. The sky could only be studied seriously from a tower. Above all, he was amazed by the distances of the planets, the figures of which he knew by heart and took pleasure in reciting.

"To remain young," he said, "it's necessary to have commerce with the stars and not occupy oneself with women."

But he was an exception in the circle of officers.

"I don't know what's happening to me," said Captain Montarache, who was suspected of not knowing how to write and was much the oldest. "There's a renaissance of my entire organism. I wonder if I'm not a phenomenal case. My hair and beard are growing three times as fast as when I was twenty. And there's an extraordinary growth of all the hairs on my body. My virile forces are five or ten times greater than before. Certain unsteady teeth have become solid and I wonder whether I might get new ones."

His poverty was extreme and he only had one miserable little room where he did his own cooking, but he simulated ease as best he could. Every year, General Compans' widow gave him a box of cigars for Christmas, and he only smoked one every Sunday, in order that the box would last all year. He said he had a horror of gambling and alcohol because of the expenses they might entail.

"I've always had a slightly sensitive throat," he repeated, to explain the eternal black scarf that he wore around his neck, which hid the absence of a collar, and often a shirt.

Zenon Fabregat, popular because of his wooden leg, never went out without a book by Descartes or Spinoza under his arm. He did not read them but if he encountered someone he touched the book with his finger. "Spinoza!" he murmured, in a pensive tome, even if he was addressing a mountain shepherd.

Since the departure of Romuald Borromée he affected solitude.

"He was the only man in the region with whom one could discuss the great problems of philosophy."

People laughed at him but he inspired respect because of the influence that that a thick book always has on anyone who would not understand any of it if they were to flick through it. And there was only General Compans' widow who, when he said "Spinoza!" to her, replied: "Zenon Fabregat, you're an ass!"

When Blaise Espondeillan, the president of the circle, announced that a representation of an emigration society had asked for an audience with the members of the circle in order to explain the advantages of his society, there was only one cry:

"What's the point? Do we look like emigrants!"

But curiosity prevailed. There was no talk of anything in the entire world except the discovery of gold in California. The newspapers invented extraordinary stories, accounts of millions gained in a matter of days. They could have details first hand. Alcide Pécouret was invited.

No man could be as far from them as that former notary's clerk with a face full of pimples and shifty little eyes. But a man who manipulates promises artfully triumphs over all antipathies. Alcide Pécouret was able to make certain words shine. It was the word "courage" of which he made use, and also the word "elite."

It was necessary not to hide that success was difficult out there—more difficult than was generally believed, more difficult than he had said himself, but that difficulty fell away when it was a matter of courageous men who knew how to fight. It was necessary to depart as if one were going to war. In California there were the dregs of the population of the world. There were the miners, and then there were the bandits who did not work and despoiled the miners. Everyone had to be led by the whip. One was obliged to risk one's life, but the result was certain, for what was most lacking was elite men. There was no elite in Mexico, and no elite in California. There was none even in the whole of America.

Alcide Pécouret lowered his voice. "I'm talking about a military elite. You obviously know the political situation of those regions?"

The officers exchanged glances and shook their heads. No one knew that situation—not even Alcide Pécouret. However, he knew the name of General Arista, the President of Mexico.[4]

"This is independent of the gold placers on the banks of the Sacramento or the San Joaquin. But in the end, there's not only fortune. When the fortune is made, one can think of glory. Now, General Arista only lacks one thing: elite men. If Mexico had elite men, it would be the foremost country in the world."

"It's ten years since I've sought to fight anyone with a sword," exclaimed Espondeillan. "I'd doubtless have the opportunity."

"Assuredly. You'd have that opportunity every day."

"Do you think that one would be able to find snuff?" asked Zenon Fabregat.

"For next to nothing."

"And cigars?" asked Captain Montarache.

"As many as you like. Think about it! Manila isn't far away. Ships full of cigars arrive in San Francisco. And what cigars! This big!"

And Alcide Pécouret measured in mid-air a chimerical cigar at least a foot long.

There was scarcely any mention of gold. For those men of action, whom years of immobility had caused to lose the

---

[4] Mariano Arista (1802-1855) was the President of Mexico from January 1851 to January 1853. The citation thus implies that this scene and the others contemporary with it are set in May 1851, but it is asserted twice later in the text that the departure for America takes place in 1850.

sense of reality, petty advantages acquired more importance than the promised fortune.

"And just think," Alcide Pécouret continued, "that for two thousand francs, the society, thanks to an arrangement with a great ship-owner, will transport you on a thousand-ton ship, nourish you for the duration of the voyage and furnish you with tents, collapsible wooden huts, tools and provisions for the first days. As for weapons..."

Everyone stood up. Weapons! They had weapons. The matter of weapons was their concern. Not only did they possess good weapons, but they knew how to use them.

Oh, Alcide Pécouret had no doubts about that. Champagne was brought. The officers consulted one another in low voices. The unpleasant little man with the goatee was definitely very intelligent. It was necessary to reflect. It was serious. Life would have to begin again. But a prodigious existence might be opening before them. They had all been in their twenties in 1815 and the flight of their heroism had had its wings clipped. Destiny was setting before them an opportunity that they would not find again.

They all raised their glasses to drink to the health of General Arista, whose name they had heard for the first time.

The Lyonnaise Emigration Society addressed itself, on the one hand, to the most chimerical of men, by promising them handfuls of gold with a minimum of labor, and on the other hand, tried to siphon off the most practical of men, those who only believed in the reality that emerges from the soil, in the form of wheat and vegetables, which dogged labor was ready to furnish. It flattered idleness with the lure of an immediate fortune, the appetite for labor with the promise of a piece of land to cultivate. It sent some to California to pick up gold on the banks of rivers, others to Guazalcoalco, where—so, at least, it affirmed—immense concessions of extraordinarily fertile land awaited arms to cultivate them.

It was, above all, on market days, in the large café of the Hôtel de France that Alcide Pécouret recruited his adherents.

"So, I'd become a landowner, just like that, on arrival? You're another of those Parisians who come to mock poor folk."

"It's as I tell you. Guazalcoalco is the part of Mexico that has the fewest inhabitants. The region, the soil of which is very fertile, is covered by enormous forests and fertile lands as yet uncultivated. The Mexican government is delighted to see foreigners come to cultivate its country. It gives them land. The Lyonnaise society has obtained large tracts on the edge of the sea. It has provided houses for the colonists, with plows and the necessary agricultural equipment. In any case, the question of property is envisaged in Mexico in a different fashion than in France. It's sufficient to plant pickets to delim-it the area of land that suits you."

"And one is a landowner?"

"Evidently. In the beginning it's necessary to work hard to till it. But because of the climate and the quality of the soil, the harvests come in with disconcerting rapidity. Just think that for two thousand francs, the society will transport you n a thousand-ton ship, nourish you for the duration of the voyage, and disembark you in Guazalcoalco on the very land that will belong to you. It will furnish you with everything necessary at the start, the agricultural implements and, notably, the axes to cur certain extremely hard woods, like mahogany."

"Mahogany?" exclaimed the woodcutters. "There are mahoganies?"

"Mahoganies of which some are fifty or a hundred me-ters high. There are forests of mahoganies, commerce in which has to be organized. Those who know their wood will be able to make fortunes there."

Those who knew their wood! They all knew their wood, those men of the mountains. The circle around Alcide Pécouret quickly became numerous.

"But all the same, one doesn't become the owner of land where there are mahoganies on arrival."

"Why not? It might well be that there are some on the lot that will come to you in the division. There might be a wood, a small forest of mahoganies there."

"And cedars?"

"There are cedars, palms and all kinds of trees unknown in the Pyrenees."

Discussions were held. All the same, it wasn't being given away. Two thousand francs: the society must be a famous operation. It was always the same; it required a little capital to make a fortune. Then again, was it all true? Imaginations worked hard. Above the Pyrenean forests, giant mahoganies were seen floating, saws of an unknown format were heard screeching, and trunks descended along glaucous streams to the song of parrots, on rafts that crocodiles came to bite...

"Naturally, Monsieur Pécouret, you must have a fine concession, and also a placer full of gold. Will you be departing on the voyage?"

Alcide Pécouret tugged his goatee and his eyes moistened, as if under the influence of some profound regret. No, he would not be departing. He had an old mother in delicate health in the vicinity of Lyon, and to abandon her to make such a long voyage would be to kill her. Life sometimes imposes hard sacrifices. Alcide Pécouret would prefer that people did not talk to him about it. It caused him too painful a regret. But duty is duty and the love of a mother is the best thing there is in the world.

There was in the region a man known as the Night-Owl, because he had no other métier than killing those nocturnal birds in order to nail them to doors of tree trunks. His Christian name was Auguste, of which people had made Augustou. He received a few sous for each owl he killed, for owls of the larger species came to steal chickens. At least, people thought so.

He had a head so big that people wondered how he was able to maintain it in equilibrium, because of the weight of the cranium. He laughed continually—or rather, the disposition of his teeth allowed the belief that he was laughing. He was deprived of certain faculties of mental coherency and memory. One could not give him more agreeable alms than an old top hat, with which he made great salutes to passers-by. Because of old stories, poorly elucidated, little girls were advised to avoid him on the roads. He sometimes had fits of intelligence, but they were brief.

One evening, Alcide Pécouret was coming back along the high road from Toulouse to Saint-Gaudens. He was satisfied. He had just signed two engagements for departure, one for California, the other for Guazalcoalco. Night had fallen completely and he was hurrying. He overtook a man who was also heading toward Saint-Gaudens and who immediately made him great salutes.

I'm beginning to be very well-known in the region, thought Alcide Pécouret, and immediately engaged him in conversation.

In the darkness he could only distinguish the gleaming teeth of his companion. The top hat made him think that he was dealing with some bourgeois of the town, of cheerful humor. What was there to do, while walking, except evoke the motives that had brought him to the region and the advantages of the Lyonnaise Emigration Society.

At first he made entirely general remarks. The French made the mistake of not leaving their native land. They were ignorant of the world's resources. They were too home-loving. Look at the English. The first advice that he, Pécouret, gave anyone was to learn a language, English or Spanish. Spanish permitted you to be at home in America, or at least a large part of it. Without a knowledge of the language, a traveler in a foreign country is like an owl exposed to the sunlight.

That comparison had a considerable effect on his interlocutor. The response was strange.

"A barn owl, five sous. A long-eared owl, ten sous."

Alcide Pécouret did not stop there. Carried away by his familiar subject, he gesticulated under the shadow of the plane trees. He talked about California, its wealth in gold, which was even greater than the newspapers said. The gold was in the placers, sometimes at ground level, but it was found above all in the steams. The silt of the streams was washed and gold was found therein, flecks of gold.

He heard a surprising response.

"It's the same here, but there's surely not as much."

Alcide Pécouret continued. "And note that for two thousand francs, the society will transport you on a thousand-ton ship, nourish you for the seventy days that it takes to arrive in California via Cape Horn..."

"Two thousand francs! But I can show you streams that are full of gold for five francs."

Alcide Pécouret laughed benevolently at that joke.

"Tomorrow, if you like. We can go on foot from Saint-Gaudens. All the torrents of the Pyrenees contain gold, heaps of gold in flecks."

They arrived at the first houses.

One might have thought that the gleam of the evoked gold awoke the dormant intelligence of Augustou, alias the Night-Owl.

"The Garonne, which flows near here, carries gold. That was known a long time ago. The proof is that in Toulouse, there was an entire street called the Rue des Orpailleurs, where the people were rich because their métier was extracting the gold of the Garonne. My grandfather had the idea of going to look for it in the sand of the torrents that flow from the Pyrenees. They're full of gold. He showed me those torrents before dying. I could be rich if I wanted. I prefer nailing barn owls to trees. The whole mountain is a gigantic block of gold with earth and forests on top of it. And you're asking for two thousand francs to go search in America for what one has within arm's reach here! Me, I'll only ask you for five francs and a few hours of walking, instead of seventy days."

They had just passed the last plane trees of the road. As they traversed the shaft of light escaping from a doorway, Alcide Pécouret saw that his interlocutor had a sandal on his right foot and that he left foot was bare. He was one of those mediocre minds who judge people by their costume. He made a vague gesture and drew away rapidly, while Augustou, to salute him, swept the road with his top hat.

VIII. Great Hopes
(Dr. Fazeuille's Journal)

Why is one driven to write one's journal, even when one has nothing extraordinary to report? I believe that a journal replaces the confessional. One recounts to oneself. Thus, one has all the leisure to explain one's bad actions and every facility to absolve oneself.

It's only worth the trouble if one says everything with an absolute sincerity. I'm beginning today, the morning after my arrival in Saint-Bertrand-de-Comminges.

I've just woken up in a little room in the Hôtel de l'Abbaye.

"You'll be very comfortable here," Sulpice Borromée told me yesterday on quitting me, "better than in my uncle's house."

I was originally going to sleep in his uncle's house, but it appears that it would make too much work for a certain Catherine. Then too, Sulpice's uncle has acquired a curious habit. He gives away his furniture. Suddenly, he's gripped by a desire for dispossession. He runs to his poor neighbors. "Do you need a bed or a table?" They always say yes. It's necessary, therefore, that his rooms are vacant. The occupant of one of them would risk finding it empty when he wants to go to bed.

Sulpice explained that to me without comment. But his brother Bernard lives in a constant indignation. If his uncle, a former bishop, were not surrounded by general respect he would have tried every legal means to prevent what he calls acts of insensate prodigality. According to the manner in which one sees things, the same action can appear to be insensate prodigality or noble charity.

I've decided to identify myself in this journal that no one will read, my faults and my vices, every time they present themselves and I'll be able to observe them. I have a horror of hard work: a profound, innate horror that I sense in every atom of my body. I felt perfectly happy this morning on waking up and contemplating the Place de Saint-Bernard-de-Comminges. The cause of that happiness was the absence of any obligatory work to be done.

Man is not made for labor. Man...I'm not, at least. I've gone into medicine without love, driven by a desire to soothe my fellows. But aren't there better ways of coming to their aid? Even admitting that I succeed in completing my studies, can I have a conscience at rest? Sulpice is right. He rarely speaks but he says sensible things. The spirit is superior to the body. The medicine of the spirit is superior to the medicine of the body. I have embarked upon an inferior career in which it is necessary to devote too much time to the work that I hate. Perhaps it's Providence that wanted me to enjoy the money of my inscriptions, which I'm losing. I would have been refused and the money would have been lost in any case. Is Providence occupied with our affairs? Sulpice thinks so. That's not my opinion. It's necessary that men sort things out between themselves.

It isn't only my desire to aid humanity that engaged me on the path of medicine. I was driven by my physical conformation. I have the physique of a doctor. That's indisputable. And I've had it for a long time. As a child, I was a herbal doctor. At eighteen, when I took my first inscription, I had nascent side-whiskers and a certain heaviness in the shoulders, and the enigmatic self-importance necessary to a man who is to pronounce on life or death. There are many professions— those of painter, poet and ecclesiastic—for which one bears the physique from birth. Is there a predestination? Perhaps everything is written in advance. How many insoluble problems life poses! Sulpice claims that his uncle can resolve them easily, because he's in communication with God. When I tell Sulpice that I don't believe in God he shrugs his shoulders and thinks, or pretends to think, that I'm joking. But even if God existed I wouldn't believe that his uncle communicated with him.

I have an innate, profound and even joyous liking for lying. I perceive it in the fashion in which I deform my character hypocritically and the pleasure I take from that. I lie in my good intention. But I ought to suffer from it. I don't suffer from it at all.

I'm in a royalist and military environment here. All the people I've met since I've arrived regret the monarchy. The Republic horrifies them and the election of Prince Napoléon to the presidency of the Republic is a catastrophe for them and the prelude to European wars. I think in an entirely different fashion; I think as my father thought, who fought during the days of 1830. Well, in spite of that, I enter into the views of the reactionaries, I flatter them, I even overbid them in their opinions. And I don't do that to please them, but in order to please myself, by means of a kind of suave satisfaction that lying gives me.

I've experienced an analogous pleasure in writing to my father. It's necessary that I explain the interruption in my studies in medicine, just at the moment when I was about to complete them and the title of doctor was about finally about to be achieved. I couldn't tell him that I'd gambled away the money for my inscriptions! Anyway, that's not the true reason. Strictly speaking, I could have found or borrowed that money. The true reason was an insurmountable state of apathy before the effort to be made for the final examinations. But all that can't be explained to a father who has been particularly laborious, and laborious for the establishment of his son. So I told him that that I was ill, ill because of having worked too hard at medicine, and that my masters had told me to take a few weeks' rest in the Pyrenees.

Thus, to all the worries that he has about money, I've added that of knowing that his son is ill. I've even added a further pain. I've given him reasons to think that I'd have had no pleasure in seeing him again. In coming to Saint-Bertrand it would have been easy for me to change diligences at Montauban and go to spend a day with him in Rabastens. But no, I didn't do it. Certainly, I feel remorse for that. But that remorse is only manifest when I think about it, and it's easy for me not to think about it. Well, although I analyze these things, in writing to my father and giving him details of my illness, I experience a bizarre pleasure, which is nothing other than the pleasure of lying.

Thus, the obligation to write one's journal has a certain character of justice. It puts us in the presence of the various facets of our soul, gives us a precise idea of ourselves, and incites us to reform.

Sulpice is a singular fellow. He speaks very rarely and only becomes eloquent when he depicts his desire to reform humankind. He would like it to become better and to devote himself to its happiness. I admire his noble sentiments and often share them. Sometimes, like him, I want to devote myself to some noble task. But horror! I'm obliged to observe that there is a secret desire in me to see all of humankind unhappy and me alone happy. It's necessary that I tear out the root of such perversity from my soul.

Sulpice has reached the conclusion that people are perhaps only happy in staying where they are born, cultivating the soil and living there on its produce.

This morning, as we came out of Saint-Bertrand by the Cabirole Gate, we were leaning on the balustrade that overlooks the plain, and Sulpice showed me, in the middle of the plantations, a field surrounded by poplars with the small rectangular house.

"The ideal," he said to me, "would be for us to buy that field and that small house. We could live there together, like peasants. Our existence would be in accord with God."

"I'd like nothing better," I replied, "than to live in accord with God—in whom I don't believe." I kept that reflection to myself, of course. But why, then, would I have done my medical studies, which have cost my father so much sacrifice?

"Well, you'd care for the plants and make them prosper. Isn't that a manner of practicing medicine?"

I kept quiet. Perhaps he's right.

Family ties don't bring about a veritable community of characters. All the members of the Borromée family are different. They give the impression of having come from far and wide and having encountered one another by chance in that old house full of portraits of bishops.

Today, the one Sulpice calls "my uncle the saint" said to us, during lunch: "I'm going to the Abbaye de Sarremezan this afternoon."

I note, with regard to lunch, that I make the sign of the cross like everyone else when the bishop says grace.

In the evening, he gave us a description of that abbey. Its cloister is on the same model as that of Saint Bertrand, except that it has a fountain with a water jet that rises very high and launches a very pure water skywards. Certain favored monks see in the spray of that fountain and the rainbows it forms all sorts of faces of saints and angels.

"It's truly extraordinary," he told us. "Once, those images were rather confused, but now, everybody can see them."

"You must take me to the Abbaye de Sarremezan," I said to Sulpice. "I want to see that marvelous fountain."

Sulpice replied in an evasive fashion. "I'll show you the admirable forests of the Cagire and the lake of Oc."

I had seen the bishop go off in a carriage. I asked Père Mauvezin, the proprietor of my hotel, whether I could go on foot to the Abbaye de Sarremezan.

"Sarremezan? You can easily get their on foot. But what abbey are you talking about?"

"Isn't there an abbey at Sarremezan?"

"Oh, I get it! It's the bishop who mentioned it to you. There are ruins beyond the village. A few stones here and there."

He sketched a gesture. I understood that he was about to touch his forehead with his finger. He stopped. I knew that he was putting on the face of a man who thinks well of others.

"Everyone has his ideas, don't they? The love of the past is respectable."

Sulpice and his brother Bernard make a surprising contrast, and they're both very different from Hugues the missionary,

But Bernard inspires unexpected thoughts. When I see
him I immediately ask myself the question: "Are there men
who are fundamentally evil, who have carried evil within them
since birth?"

Why does that question come to mind as soon as I am in
his presence? And as soon as the question is posed there is a
romantic desire in me to find myself in the presence of one of
those predestined to evil, and I would like it to be an entirely
exceptional predestined, satanic and terrible. Thus, when I was
a child, sometimes I wanted the moon to fall, the sea level to
rise, or some other great cosmic catastrophe, out of a simple
desire for novelty.

Bernard gives me a troubling sensation. It seems to me
that he hates his brother and also his venerable uncle. But these intuitive sensations are often deceptive. When I saw Monsieur Mauvezin for the first time, because of his accent, the
roundness of his face, his plumpness and a certain impulsive
frankness, I thought that he was a good and simple man with
no hidden agenda. Now I know that he's good, but not simple.
He's astonishingly cunning. Furthermore, he's part of the
council for the fabrication of the cathedral of Saint Bertrand.
Now my father has always said that a man who in a member
of any council of fabrication whatsoever is a Jesuitical individual whom it's necessary to mistrust. But ought I to believe
the letter of all my father's instructions? How many problems
to resolve!

I sensed clearly yesterday evening that Bernard desired
to make his brother suffer.

I ought to say first that I believe that Sulpice is in love,
and has been for a long time. He hasn't told me that because
he doesn't like talking about himself. But in Paris he talked to
me several times about a young woman named Malvina, and
every time he talked about her he lowered his voice. I've no-

ticed that when someone lowers their voice when talking about someone, it's a mark of veneration.

Once he told me that she had the face of a Madonna, and another time that she had the face of a siren. Once he said that she had blue hair, and another time that her hair was black.

"We were good friends during the time when I was ill in my uncle's house. She lent me books. She's very intelligent. Then there was a long period when she refused to see me and she only nodded to me when I encountered her."

"But why?" I said to him.

"I had my brother ask her the reason, and it appears that she replied—this is what Bernard said, exactly: 'I don't see him because he's a simpleton. Why would I waste my time with a simpleton? There's no other reason. I don't like simpletons.'"

I must confess that there is a touch of the simpleton about my friend Sulpice. I'm obliged to agree with that even though I like him a lot. I ought, however, to register that fault since I've promised myself to identify all my faults to myself, I have a certain satisfaction in observing my friend Sulpice's stupidity and that a very pretty young woman finds him so. Why? I don't know that young woman, so it isn't a matter of jealousy or rivalry. There are evil sentiments that are absolutely inexplicable. Unless it is jealousy and I'm obliged to inscribe to the deficit of my soul a natural tendency to jealousy.

So, yesterday evening, Uncle Borromée had gone to bed. He'd lit an oil lamp because night had fallen while we were finishing dinner. As he left us, he turned round on the threshold of the dining room and, raising his hand slightly, he said: "*Bonsoir*, my children!"—words that wouldn't require annotation if they hadn't been accompanied by an expression of benevolence so great that it was abruptly associated with the odor of oil, and that, on lighting my own lamp in my room and perceiving its odor, I saw the calm face of the bishop again, and heard, again: "*Bonsoir*, my children!"

Bernard lit a second lamp, complaining that Catherine hadn't trimmed the wick. He poured himself a small glass of quince liqueur without offering us any and immediately, as if he had been waiting for that moment to say it, he said: "I met Lucien Leduc this afternoon."

Sulpice didn't reply—me neither, naturally, judging the words devoid of importance. There was a silence, and it suddenly came to my mind what Sulpice had once said to me about a certain Lucien Leduc, the son of the president of the tribunal at Saint-Gaudens:

"A perverse individual who has no other occupation than pursuing women. Morally and physically corrupt. He joined the Algerian troops but he came back after three years because of maladies contracted with women. Our parents were linked. Although I've never done anything to him he's always detested me. As a child he never lost an opportunity to hit me, for no reason. He'd do the same now if he could."

He had told me all that with regard to natural sympathies and antipathies.

"Lucien Leduc is very intelligent," Bernard went on, as if he were following a road he had mapped out in advance. "And at least he knows how to conduct himself with women, He rules them with the rod. He told me that, and he's right. If you want to keep a woman it's necessary to give her a good kicking sometimes. He's absolutely right."

He laughed and waited. Sulpice stood up and poured me a small glass of quince liqueur, a family drink that's rather nasty. I believe he knew at that moment what his brother was about to say.

"And don't you know who Lucien Leduc has for a mistress at present?"

Sulpice shook his head with a resigned indifference.

I caught the glance that Bernard launched at his brother, which was like a sharp arrow.

"Malvina."

There was to reaction on Sulpice's part.

"Yes, yes, Malvina. Oh, women! One can imagine! It's sufficient to go there. Especially that one. And note what

Lucien Leduc told me: 'You know, whenever you want...it wouldn't bother me..."'

He added a few words of an extreme vulgarity, which I won't reproduce because the written form gives a value to things and such words don't merit being perpetuated, even for myself.

"Let's go for a walk in the garden," said Sulpice—and when we had gone down he took me by the arm and said: "It isn't true. I don't believe it. It isn't possible that it's true."

This morning Sulpice came to wake me up with eyes full of enthusiasm. He has an immediate task to which to devote himself. He's counting on me to work by his side.

"The fate of the land where I was born is at stake," he told me. "A poison is circulating that everyone is being made to drink: peasants, workers, townspeople. Souls are being poisoned gradually by a criminal propaganda. The newspapers are mixed up in it and approve the propaganda. It's a matter of making the people of the regions depart for the New World. The attraction of gold is being shone in their eyes. I'm sure that it's exaggerated. The promises are too marvelous to be true, but even if they correspond to a reality they'd be no less detestable. The richer men are, the unhappier they are. Gold, that so-called precious metal, which is a representation of wealth, is truly the means that evil uses to corrupt men and lead them to degradation. Don't you agree?"

"Oh, evidently. It's in accord..."

I had never heard Sulpice say so much. And I couldn't help thinking that if I had had a little of that gold, the miserable representation of wealth, a few weeks ago, I would have paid my inscriptions and I'd be much closer than I am to my title of doctor. But I immediately turned on myself. I was always thinking of myself. I was possessed by a profound egotism. I couldn't welcome a noble idea without looking first at what effect its realization would have on me.

It was early. Sulpice had come to find me while I was still in bed. I leapt out and began to get dressed. A reaction had occurred in my soul. I affirmed to Sulpice that he could count on me. I would help him to save the men of Comminges. I was ready. What was it necessary to do?

Sulpice didn't really know. He regretted not being able to speak eloquently. He thought that it was necessary to spread a propaganda contrary to that which a certain Alcide Pécouret was spreading, on behalf of a Lyonnais emigration society.

"If all the inhabitants of France were as sensitive to lies as those of this region, France would rapidly be depopulated and pass entirely into America."

"The mountains, the form of the trees and the air one breathes," I said, "create a mentality here different from elsewhere. Since I've arrived in Saint-Bertrand, I sense myself more given to illusion and great hopes. The water of the Garonne and the sun create mirages. I understand that the promises, as soon as they're enunciated, are magnified of their own accord."

We walked at a rapid stride though the matinal countryside.

"Let's begin," said Sulpice. And he indicated a charming little house with bindweed and nasturtiums framing its door and its two windows. "Perhaps we'll find an auxiliary in my friend Noël Alga.

As no one replied immediately when Sulpice knocked on the door, we made a circuit of the house, guided by the sounds of a guitar.

A young man, who appeared to me to be tall, handsome and likeable, was sitting on a stool in the middle of a little courtyard. He was surrounded by chickens and a cock, and I saw to my surprise that there was a sort of wild pig—it was a badger—and two hedgehogs running around. A bizarre bird was smoothing its plumage on the roof of the henhouse. Noël Alga was visibly playing the guitar for that gathering of animals.

He stood up and seemed charmed to see us. He immediately asked us not to frighten the hedgehogs—very intelligent animals, he told us, but rather timid and fearful of new faces.

"They all like music passionately," he told us. And leaning forward, he murmured: "Don't worry, I'll continue soon."

He was addressing the chickens and the hedgehogs. He also pronounced a few guttural sounds that might have been words in animal language.

The chickens continued pecking indifferently, but I ought to say that the bird took off and went to perch a little further away.

I liked Noël Alga a lot. He appeared to me to be intelligent and frank. He took us into a kitchen with a rustic hearth, where everything was shining with cleanliness. I noticed a portrait of Lamartine and another of Béranger.

"Can I offer you some milk? Or coffee? My mother has just made some."

Sulpice immediately asked him whether he knew a certain Alcide Pécouret, who had his headquarters at the Hôtel de France in Saint-Gaudens.

"I should think so. Who doesn't know him around here? I confess that what he's told me has enthused me." But he put a finger over his lips, nodding toward a door that led to a neighboring room. "My mother's in there and I'd rather..."

Sulpice explained his point of view. I did my best to support him. But Noël Alga remained thoughtful.

"I'll grant you," he replied, "that in principle, you're right. Yes, in absolute terms you're right."

"But in sum," Sulpice exclaimed, "I hope that you, who are known to be a lover of nature, who goes to spend entire nights in the forest in order to communicate with the trees, aren't thinking of quitting your homeland?"

Noël Alga remained silent at first.

"It appears that nature out there is unimaginable. Then, think about it, Sulpice. You know my situation. In our society, what's the destiny of a young man like me, who hasn't made studies and has no fortune? To be sure, I can live—or rather, subsist—modestly, but here's a force within me that wants more. I'd like to enjoy life."

"No one enjoys it more than you. You have animals, books. You're a musician. The Pyrenees belong to you."

"That's true. I often tell myself that. But I only have to play a tune on the guitar to see ravishing young women passing by in caleches, on a promenade by the sea, with mantillas, fans, and low-cut dresses of an unusual elegance. Where are those women? I don't know. In distant cities where they spend the evening nonchalantly... It's those women I desire, and to possess them, it's necessary to travel, to be rich."

"That's a poetic dream that doesn't correspond to any reality," I said. "Nothing is as deadly as poetic dreams. Lamartine and Hugo are very dangerous men, my father often says."

"I'd rather content myself with hedgehogs, crows and all the animals I tame. But even for animals, I'd have an infinitely richer field of experiences in Mexico. I know that there are strange animals in the New World that I've never seen: the tapir, the anteater...especially the anteater...."

"One doesn't make such a voyage to see an anteater!"

"But I'd make it to be in rapport with snakes! I borrowed Buffon from Madame Compans, who put her library at my disposal. Well, it appears that in the forests of the Americas there are thousands, millions of snakes."

"There are plenty here as well."

"Little snakes of no account. But out there is the true realm of snakes."

"That would be a reason for not going there. What do you want to do with those snakes?"

"It's difficult to say. I like them. I'd like to communicate with them. Except, it the same as for humans—it's necessary to see a great many in order to find one that's intelligent and sensible."

I nodded my head, while being privately astonished.

"You're really thinking of going, then?" cried Sulpice

"Quietly! Lower your voice. I don't want to torment my mother, even with an intention. I don't know. I'd like to go, it's true. But for a start, it requires two thousand francs. I might be able to borrow them—but there's my mother. Enough! I still have a few days to decide."

Sulpice was devastated. When we had quit the little house he marched for a long time in silence.

"Even Noël Alga! The government ought to intervene! It's a social disaster!"

And in the depths of my soul I felt a certain satisfaction rising, at the idea of a social disaster. The human heart is full of unsuspected mysteries. But have I the right to generalize, and am I not a particular case, perhaps unique? Am I not a monster of perversity?"

IX. Maximo's Treasure

In the Château de Noussoulens the father and the daughter had not had any conversation for a year. In the beginning the silence between them had been dramatic, but it had gradually been interrupted by a few words necessary to life.

"What do you want to eat tomorrow?" said Malvina, almost mechanically.

Then again, it had been tacitly agreed that the two aged domestics of the house, who also served as gardeners, should not suspect anything. They were used to petty family quarrels, to the father's fits of violence, to Malvina's bad moods. Long silences did not astonish them. But the meals, rapid as they were, had to be punctuated by a few remarks:

"It's nice out."

"Spring is early his year."

"The lilacs are beginning to flower."

"Are you going hunting tomorrow?"

Once, the big news of the region had been brought by the taciturn Mathieu while he was serving a leak lunch.

"Has Monsieur heard about it? It appears that in America one can find gold as one wishes in certain places. There's a society that takes charge of taking people out there. Many in the area have been inscribed to depart."

Malvina had listened distractedly. It seemed that old Noussoulens, almost uniquely occupied with bear-hunting, ought to have shrugged his shoulders and cared little for such a chimera as the pursuit of gold. Nothing of the sort. It appeared to interest him enormously. He asked Mathieu, who did not seem to know much more, for all sorts of details.

"It's said that there's someone representing the society at the Hôtel de France in Saint-Gaudens."

Noussoulens started pacing back and forth in the dining room. The news occupied him so much that he turned to his daughter and said to her—to her, personally: "Ten years ago, I read an article about that in a newspaper."

"Astonishing events happen in the world from time to time," said Malvina, in order not to leave that commencement of a conversation of sorts without a response.

Noussoulens went on: "Oh, if only I were younger! If I even had the strength I had four or five years ago!"

He made a sign to Mathieu that he was no longer hungry.

"And you! If only you were a man!"

One might have thought that his rancor was forgotten. Malvina took advantage of that. She started talking. Four or five years ago! Why that number of years? She had never noticed that her father's strength had diminished.

Noussoulens burst in to bitter laughter.

"First of all, I've shrunk. Yes, I've measured myself, and I'm smaller. Then, in my ears, my hairs have started growing in an extraordinary manner. I thought at first, naively, that it was a resurgence of youth. But old age doesn't forgive. It's more than six months since I've gone hunting. Why? I've never had as much desire to do it. It's because the last time, I thought I'd never come back. I was sitting on the ground and I stayed there for hours looking at the valleys, where some-where, there was my house. I had to come back slowly, be-cause my legs would hardly carry me. Oh, the bears can be quite tranquil now!"

From that day on the father and daughter recommenced talking. Noussoulens came back often to what seemed to be the essential theme of his ideas about life. Women were sluts, animals of a sort, who thought of nothing but lying down on their backs. His wife had been worse than the rest and his daughter was similar. But it was necessary to take them as they were. There was no point in trying to reform them.

But there was now another thought, equally capital, which filled his mind. There was a place on earth where gold was to be found, where one could make a rapid fortune. And when he talked about it to his daughter—it was always during meals—he came back to it. Happy with the semi-tranquility that enabled him to recover the habit of conversation, she asked questions, gave the impression of being interested in what the newspapers might be saying.

She noticed a certain reticence in him. He said things that needed explanation.

"To depart without information would be imprudent. But someone who could leave with a quasi-certainty..."

And one evening, in the garden, after a rainstorm, old Noussoulens bent down to kill a slug. He had tried to strike it with the secateurs that he was holding in his hand. From a distance, Malvina was surprised to see him remain bent over for a long time, then totter and sit down on the ground. He had lost consciousness. It was necessary for her to call Mathieu and his wife to help her carry him into the drawing room.

Ten minutes later, he came round, and immediately flew into a temper because everyone was gathered there and looking at him with astonishment.

"Well, what? What's the matter with you? It's nothing at all. It's you who are ill. Let's go to dinner. It's time, and I'm hungry."

Nevertheless, it was necessary for him to agree that his eye was jaundiced and that part of his face was paralyzed.

He had never been ill, and if he saw Dr. Tonniens from time to time it was as an old friend of his youth.

Dr. Tonniens was a thin and sickly man who was scornful of people who were too healthy. He strove to weaken them with bleedings. According to him, everyone was dying because they ate too much, especially too much meat. He had been arguing with Noussoulens about that for forty years.

"Those who want to live for a long time ought to have a weak body," he said. "Woe betide the colossus. Look at my case. I can hardly stand up, and I'll live to be a hundred."

"I don't want to see Tonniens," Noussoulens said, immediately.

He did not protest the next day, however, when he heard a carriage pull up in front of the perron and Malvina said to him: "I asked Tonniens to come anyway."

The doctor had looked modestly triumphant. Noussoulens would have preferred to hear him repeat: "What have I told you? Too much meat! Too much wine!"

He concluded that his case had become serious,

"Tell me the truth, old man. Am I finished?"

The doctor bled him and prescribed a diet. No excess, no emotions, water and tisanes.

"Might as well die right away, then."

"Why? You'll see that life is much more agreeable when you have a weak body."

The invalid asked whether there was any connection between the length of the hair in his ears and his attack of paralysis."

"No direct connection, obviously."

"And what do you think happens after death?"

"Nothing happens. One is a little weaker. One is better. It's necessary give up bear-hunting, of course."

"I already have,"

"Well then, you've done the most difficult thing."

The doctor was about to climb back into his carriage.

"If I'm finished, tell me."

"We'll see. I'll come back."

All through the evening, Noussoulens declared to his daughter with a somber expression and an elevated tone of voice that he was not afraid of death. He was finished. He knew it. Dr. Tonniens had had difficulty dissimulating his joy. But in sum, it was better to die. Life wasn't so funny! For all the satisfactions one got from it!

In reality, he was terribly afraid. Like many simple people he had never thought about that eventuality. It was a surprise for him. A new element had just surged forth: a threat of whose existence he had been vaguely aware, but which was presenting itself for the first time.

"And hear me well! Don't talk to me about confessions. Don't do for Monseigneur Borromée what you did for the doctor."

No, Malvina had not thought of doing that. She had even wondered, with anguish, what she would do to beg the bishop to come if her father asked for him. For not a day went by when she did not relive the confession scene, when she did not hear the words of the malediction resonate. As soon as she woke up, the shadow of the chapel, the silence, the tall silhouette with the goatskin hood, the lamp, the nocturnal bird and the stone angel supporting the stoup, whose pose she had copied for a few seconds, were in the depths of her soul. That malediction, she continued to attribute to the bishop, and she bore the weight of it. And that weight did not lighten. One can forget a pardon, but not the assurance of being accursed.

Perhaps Noussoulens would have liked to have his hand forced—but he did not want to go back on what he had said.

"No, no—no curé," he repeated.

He tried to convince himself of his strength of mind. It was necessary for that for someone to hear him. It was to his daughter that he repeated the same things. "Well, what? Death is annihilation. And afterwards? One sleeps, that's all."

But he was not absolutely sure of a solution so simple.

It seemed to him that he was having more difficulty moving his left leg. He thought that it was necessary to do exercises in order to stop it stiffening up completely. He now went for walks in the park, but it was necessary for him to learn on his daughter's arm. That was humiliating.

"I'd be perfectly able to walk on my own if I wanted to."

He multiplied hypotheses regarding death. He rejected as puerile the hypotheses of Paradise and Hell.

"That's absolutely impossible."

But without knowing why, he considered it as probable that he would encounter those he had known and who had died before him, and that prospect darkened his mood.

At the end of one afternoon he plunged further into the park than usual. It had been a long time since the pathways had been maintained and the bushes pruned. The box trees and the spindle trees rose freely. There was a region where the pink and white oleanders were in flower and falling in sheaves. The eglantines were clinging to the oaks, and after a meadow where the grass was very long, the honeysuckle and arborescent ferns were so dense that one could no longer make headway.

Suddenly, Noussoulens seized his daughter's arm violently. Malvina understood immediately on seeing her father's glazed eyes fixed on an ancient beech surrounded by poppies. He did not say anything, but Malvina felt his arm trembling with emotion on hers, while they drew away rapidly.

Her father emotional! *How things change*, she thought. Until now, his emotions had always been manifest in anger and violence.

They had never spoken again about Maximo Avila since the night when they had buried him at the foot of the beech. Twice, while they walked, Noussoulens looked over his shoulder, awkwardly—for he had difficulty moving his neck—and murmured: "Can't you hear them?"

"What?"

"Footsteps behind us."

"No. Who could be walking, anyway?"

"Evidently." The old man kept his head down. "It's an illusion I had, Can you imagine that I thought…I'm definitely getting old."

As they arrived back at the house he said: "It's not the first time that I've thought I heard footsteps in that direction." He pointed in the direction from which they had just come. "And it's not an effect of the attack that I had, which might have affected my brain. Before then, I'd already got up several times in the night because I heard footsteps in the same direction."

"Mathieu has told me that when he suffers too much from the rheumatism in his shoulder he goes out. He says that walking diminishes the pain."

"It's not Mathieu. He always wears clogs. What I hear is a light step: a step that doesn't resemble ordinary footsteps; a step that hardly touches the ground; a step…in sum, the step of a phantom…"

"You think that there can be phantoms here that come back?" said Malvina, trembling with terror but ready to simulate cold reason.

"No, I don't believe. Never, during my entire life...I don't know."

It was time for dinner. They could hear Mathieu setting the table in the dining room. The familiar noise was somewhat reassuring.

"It's because, you see, it's a matter of a particular man, who had communications with the afterlife. He made evocations. He even told me that he had been obliged to stop, because of certain hauntings. I shrugged my shoulders, then. But now I tell myself that if he was pursued by obsessions, why shouldn't we be in our turn?"

"That's not a reason," said Malvina, precipitately, who wanted to find objections, more for herself than for her father. "We didn't do anything to him. He has no reason to bear a grudge against us. We had nothing to do with his death."

She stopped. She had never evoked by words the terrible night of the death of Maximo Avila. She had had nothing to do with his death? Was she quite certain of that? She had often asked herself. Never before had she imagined a passion as savage as his. Might not the emotion of amour, pushed to its limit, precipitate death in someone who had that mysterious thing, a disease of the heart? For since then, she had made enquiries. One had a heart attack at the time one least expected it and without having suffered beforehand. The physicians knew nothing about it. But everyone knew that a great emotion can kill. Had not Dr. Tonniens said, with regard to her father: wear and tear of the heart...?"

They were both in front of the perron and, as nightfall progressed, they felt small and wretched, overwhelmed by the magnitude of the problem they were measuring.

"Our conscience is clear with regard to him," Malvina said, again, suddenly raising her voice, as if she wanted to be heard even in the depths of the park, by a being living in the midst of the ferns and poppies.

"Yes, yes, clear," murmured Noussoulens. "Not entirely clear. We should have...at least, I should have made an attempt to find his family."

"He had no family—or rather, he had broken with it."

"Yes, he had broken. That's what he told me. He had broken. But all the same..."

After dinner, both of them prolonged the evening for as long as possible, in the dread of finding themselves alone in confrontation with their thoughts.

Malvina had abandoned her room the previous year, but she had been obliged to take it back during the winter because almost all the flues in the house drew poorly except for hers. She had stayed there. Now, this evening, on going back up to her room, she perceived that her window was only pushed to. It was warm, the air was heavy. The flowers of a nearby magnolia were spreading a heavy perfume. There was no wind. She was getting ready to open the two battens of the window wide when they parted silently, as if a hand had pushed them from outside.

They opened suddenly like that on the night of Maximo's death, she thought.

At first she wanted to sleep elsewhere, but there were no sheets on the beds. It would have been necessary to wake Mathieu's wife, who must already be asleep. Her father would hear her. She would be obliged to give him explanations. Then, perhaps it had been a gust of wind. She was gripped by lassitude. She sat down on her bed and stayed there very late, listening to the sounds of the garden and the beating of her heart.

Noussoulens had another loss of consciousness. Dr. Tonniens came back. The same things were repeated.

"Tell me the truth, old man. I'm done for, aren't I?"

"No, you've only eaten too much meat, drunk too much wine. Look at me..."

"Why not tell me? It's the end. I understood that when my ears..."

"No, no, I'll come back..."

And one morning, when she went into her father's room, Malvina found him sitting on his bed, calm and lucid.

"I was waiting for you. I have something to tell you. And I have a document to give you. Sit down."

He made a sign for her to sit down beside his bed.

"I'll summarize, because I don't have enough breath to talk for long. Yes, I have something to give you. Perhaps it's your heritage. Providence has acted. I only understand now what Monseigneur Borromée once said to me about Providence. When I'm no longer here, you ought to see him, as often as possible. Everything he told me has come about. He told me that Providence never acts directly. It makes detours. But it's as if there were an intelligence full of attention that watches over every one of us and prepares their future, without seeming to. It has been thus for you. I ought to blame myself for not having thought enough about your interests, your fortune..."

Malvina made a gesture of protest.

"Don't interrupt me. I thought about hunting, and only preoccupying myself seriously with that. Once, your mother committed many follies. She threw money out of the window. She consumed her fortune and mine. I let it happen; I was wrong. You were the victim. Your mother threw money out of the window, but she occupied herself with it. She made investments, often bad, but in the end, she administered. Whereas I, since her death, haven't occupied myself with anything. I've lived—we've lived—on mortgages that Maître Toché has taken out on the house and the land. Now, there's nothing left. I've been very culpable. You have a small income from your grandmother, which you receive, with which you buy stockings and hats...almost nothing. There isn't the wherewithal even to live like a peasant. I wonder whether that isn't all you possess. Perhaps you have something else, given by Providence...you'll see..."

He stopped and breathed deeply several times. Then he pulled out from under his pillow a small wallet in black morocco leather, which did not seem to contain very much. His hand was trebling.

"Maximo Avila loved you—at least, I suppose so. I'm not asking you questions. That's the past. He didn't say anything to me. But in sum, I can't think that for him, you were just a temporary adventure. One can consider that what was his ought to revert to you. At any rate, it ought to revert to someone, and we don't know his family. He never said a word about them. There are many people on earth who are absolutely alone. Nothing is as fragile as a family. Even you, when I'm dead..."

He stopped the gesture that Malvina sketched.

"Do you remember, the night of his death, when you came to look for me? I stayed alone with him. I was able to think that he was carrying papers, the address of relatives, and indication about his identity. In sum, it was my duty to know who he was. He'd often talked about Lisbon, but to say that he'd left it as a child. I took his wallet and I kept it. I ought to tell you one of the reasons for his presence in our region. He had come to interest me in a business deal, or simply to ask me for a large sum of money. How did he know me? He had known your mother during one of his sojourns on Bordeaux, in the home of her aunt.

"Your mother, I don't know why, passed herself off in his eyes as rich. She had such weaknesses; it came from her immense vanity. He spoke of your mother as a friend. He must have been exaggerating. He simply said Lucie. The affair in which he proposed that I become a shareholder seemed to me at the time to be a chimera. He introduced it to me in a dramatic fashion.

"'Do you know that I'm much richer than you, Monsieur Noussoulens?'

"'I'm convinced of it,' I replied.

"'I might be the richest man in France and Portugal, and my fortune is here in my wallet.'

"With that, he took out his wallet and waved it like a flag. 'I possess an immense treasure,' he went on.

"I remember bursting into laughter and asking him whether he took me for an imbecile, for I didn't believe in hidden treasures. Laughing, he called me an old skinflint, like all rich Frenchmen, in fact. And as I showed signs of annoyance he told me that, being Portuguese, he didn't know the exact meaning of all expressions. 'For me, skinflint means having savings,' he told me.

"Oh, he was clever. He talked a great deal and he explained his affair as a matter of gold. There was a treasure in California. It was necessary to go and search for it. That treasure was a placer discovered by a gold prospector who knew its exact location. A placer, more than a placer, a veritable treasure, he repeated.

"I ought to tell you, and this I consider as certain, that he had been in America for a long time. But he was one of those men who don't like to explain their actions precisely, nor the motives for their changes of residence. It's a natural liking for mystery. Your mother was the same. When she went to her aunt's house in Bordeaux she'd write to me immediately to say that she was leaving for Bayonne and I'd learn later that she'd gone to Mont-de-Marsan. Your mother was strange, Ordinarily, one calls that lying. But it wasn't lying...

"Let's get back to the treasure. During his sojourn in America, Maximo had been put on the track of a gold placer by a Spanish adventurer named Esquiros. But that's where it gets complicated. The placer wasn't one. It was something else. He had employed that word to tempt me, because at that time, in France, people only talked about discovering placers. Anyway, he winked every time he pronounced the word, as if to say that it was a matter of an even more astonishing wealth. What he said let something filter through.

"Unfortunately, to begin with, I didn't believe him, and I scarcely listened. It bore too much resemblance to a feuilleton novel. There had been a great many crooks with tales of treasure. For one thing, I didn't have the money that he was asking of me, and was necessary, he said, because it was necessary to organize a little expedition, buy tools, tents and weapons. At the time he was talking to me I knew nothing about the matter. I told myself that he wanted to borrow money and was inventing a story.

"That wasn't unlikely. Maximo Avila bore too much resemblance to an adventurer. I've always distrusted men with side-whiskers. His stories of magnetism and his appearance—especially his side-whiskers—all contributed to devalue him in my eyes. But since then, I've reflected. An adventurer has more chance than anyone else of having adventures. The newspapers have since reported much more extraordinary stories that have happened in California and elsewhere.

"I regretted not having been more interested in what Maximo Avila told me. But it was too late. He was dead. Except that I still had his wallet. There were visiting cards and a piece of paper folded in four and enclosed in another sheet, doubtless to preserve it from wear and tear. That has to be the document, or a copy of it. It's in Spanish. It's nothing much, only the information necessary to arrive at a particular location in New Mexico, departing from a town called Paso del Norte, a town that I've found on a map, and arriving at another called Acoma, which isn't marked anywhere.

"With that document one can find it, although it gives the impression of being a summary of a more complete document. There are insufficient indications—follow a tributary of the Red River—and incomprehensible things that have nothing to do with an itinerary. One might think that they were the titles of chapters in an adventure novel: *the land where the Indians have blue eyes; the rock of El Moro; Antonio de Cochea, the magician bishop; the three hundred steps; the corridor of giant stones; the enchanted cathedral; find a saint for the mass.* There's a separate line that says: *In Acoma, find a man named Socrates and don't offer him money.* And at the bottom of the sheet: *Above all, don't pronounce the name of Esquiros.* He's the one who had discovered what Maximo still called a placer. 'An excellent man,' he said, 'with a heart of gold, whom I liked a lot. But like all men who are too good, he had a diabolically bad reputation.'

"I asked Maximo how he had met that Esquiros and how he had been chosen as the depositary of such a precious secret. Then he showed surprise. 'By virtue of personal sympathy!' he exclaimed. 'Everything fortunate that has happened to me in life has happened by virtue of the natural sympathy I inspire.' I remember that he even added, laughing: 'You too, you'll end up lending me the sum I'm asking of you, because, deep down, although you don't want to give the impression, I'm infinitely sympathetic to you.'

"He was exaggerating. Your mother liked feuilleton novels, and you've inherited her tastes, but I always held them in horror. Anyway, I was never able to read anything. People are divided two categories, those who read and those who don't. Someone who doesn't read ought never to marry a woman who does. Anyway, those who don't read are more intelligent than those who do. Maximo was a character from a novel. That's why you liked him. In what measure is it necessary to trust him? I don't know. However, I believe that his story was true.

"At first it seemed to me to be implausible. I wrote to Bordeaux to make enquiries. But your great-aunt, in whose house your mother met him, is dead, I could only address myself to one of her friends, an old lady who has gone completely senile and could only repeat to me: 'He's a gentleman, a veritable gentleman!'

"In any case, this is the story. For unknown reasons, Maximo found himself in Martinique, at Fort-de-France. There, one evening, he picked up a drunk and wounded man; that was Esquiros. According to Maximo's story, the person in question was a victim of destiny. He had escaped from a prison in Venezuela, where he had been unjustly imprisoned. Such an injustice is already a bad sign. He had gone to San Francisco and had resumed his former profession as a prospector. There were already a number before the gold rush. It was then that he made a discovery of extraordinary richness. I wondered why he didn't load himself with a large quantity of gold, sufficient to make him rich. The amount a man can carry constitutes a fortune. Then too, he must have had a horse or a mule.

"Undoubtedly, it mustn't have been as simple as that. It appears that it required implements and an expedition. That Esquiros had various adventures and ended up, wounded, in Martinique. The wound was a crocodile bite. As we've never seen a crocodile, such details give stories a romantic character. But in those distant countries it must be perfectly normal to be bitten by a crocodile. Maximo rendered various services to that Esquiros. Notably, he declared to the police that he had known him for a long time. He answered for him. The wound got worse. Gangrene set in. It appears that the odor it gives off drove everyone away, except for the courageous Maximo. And then, to thank him when he felt death approaching, Esquiros delivered his secret, or a part of his secret, to his benefactor.

"All that is possible. I even believe it. Habituated as certain people are to lying, there's a tone that isn't deceptive when they're telling the truth. I consider that the story of Esquiros is true. If I understood correctly, once Esquiros was dead, Maximo departed for New Mexico. He didn't succeeded, for want of money or courage, but he was able to assure himself that Esquiros' stories were true and he returned to Europe in search of money or companions. He thought I was very rich, according to what he was told by your mother, Lucie, as he said, without thinking that I might be astonished by that familiarity. It was of me he had thought in order to procure the necessary sum.

"And now he's dead; the chain of circumstances determined that I was in possession of the document, and I remember what Maximo said about that subject. I didn't ask him for it. Anyone else in my position would have taken the wallet. Anyway, it was my duty, to send it to his family. I would have had a struggle with my conscience if I had known that family. But Maximo never wanted to talk about them, and it's probable that they don't exist. This belongs to you. It's your heritage."

Noussoulens had made a great effort to say all that. He was now out of breath, but satisfied, and relieved of a great weight. His face had taken on a serenity with which Malvina was unfamiliar on his part.

Malvina was holding the wallet in her hand and, unwittingly, the power of chimeras took possession of her—for there is in stories of treasures a source of vertigo that few souls are capable of resisting.

"Keep it preciously," added her father. "I don't know how you'll be able to utilize what it contains, but so many people are going there at hazard, without the slightest indication. Perhaps you can obtain something from that document. I don't know when and I don't know how. That will be up to you to determine."

That evening, after a further lapse of consciousness, he replied once again "No, no curé!" to Mathieu's wife, who had brought him a glass of old brandy and said to him that it was always a good thing to see a priest, whether it be Bishop Borromée or the curé of Saint-Bertrand. The secret that he had kept must have weighed upon him heavily, for he was joyful and liberated.

"Above all, no, curé," he repeated again to Malvina. "Another glass of brandy instead."

"You can have both," said Malvina. And when the door opened and the curé of Saint-Bertrand came into his room, he uttered a sigh of relief, as if all his wishes had been granted.

That evening, he died without perceiving it.

During the afternoon, the entire neighborhood had filed through the old Noussoulens house.

Pale and exhausted by fatigue, in the drawing room with the faded furniture, the taciturn Malvina had listened to the same formulae of consolation on the subject of her solitude and the loss that she had suffered. She calculated that of all those she had seen at the cemetery, no one any longer remained to come. She went out on to the perron. Night was about to fall.

"You can go close the gate," she said to Mathieu.

A carriage came in at great speed, and circled round the lawn. With lightning rapidity, a rather stout woman emerged from it, wearing bright yellow boots and a riding costume.

Before Malvina had been able to collect herself, the unknown woman had taken her in her arms and hugged her.

"Malvina! You'll permit me to call you that? Such a beautiful girl! All alone! So unfortunate!"

Malvina sensed a heady odor of patchouli and perceived on the fat and mobile face that was against hers a ridiculously exaggerated grimace that was attempting to express dolor.

"It's sufficient for me to look at you. I love you already like a sister. But you don't know who I am? Yes, I see that you've guessed. I'm Teresa..." There was a silence. She went on: "Teresa Avila, Maximo's sister."

That sister, Maximo had never mentioned, Mute with surprise, Malvina continued looking straight ahead, without making any response. But her silence did not inhibit the visitor. In her hand, strangely gloved in red, she was holding a slender switch, with which she flicked her boots from time to time.

"Don't be astonished if I'm wearing riding costume. But in your little town up there, perched on a little mountain, it's impossible to hire a horse. And the owner of the hotel doesn't understand anything. Anyway, here you are! What fatality! I arrive on the very day of the death of Maximo's old friend."

Malvina said a few words and made a few gestures of greeting, but the face that she had before her was not the ambiguous face of the young man who had bewitched her, the face to which the thickness of the chin gave a hint of vulgarity. She fixed upon the black, velvet eyes of an immense depth, eyes almost devoid of true light, but with an irresistible attraction: the eyes of Maximo, to whom she had abandoned herself without really knowing why.

Truly, between the brother and the sister, the only resemblance was in the eyes. But these, which were fixed on Malvina intensely, with an ill-disguised gleam of interrogation, were hostile eyes, the eyes of an enemy. Malvina sensed that immediately. What did she know about her? What did she want?

Even if a woman is shrewd, she lets herself yield to a natural desire to talk. Perhaps Teresa Avila would have been able to obtain by surprise, thanks to the disarray that Malvina was in, the confession of which she had come in search. Malvina's silence was like a lake into which she cast the flood of her own words.

Oh, how delighted Maximo had been in the Noussoulens' home! Anyway, she experienced herself the extreme attraction exerted by these old French families. Tradition! Nothing was as fine as the tradition of ancient virtues conserved in these old French châteaux. And what pleased her, Teresa, most was the scorn for fortune that one sensed there. Oh, these old aristocrats who had great fortunes and continued to live in a dilapidated old château with one or two servants. One or two servants, solitude in the woods, not far from a town that resembled a fortress at a distance! And the bears…that was for the men—and yet she, Teresa, would have liked to hunt bears. Was that still practiced with a spear, or only by lying in wait? She was ready to wager that Malvina had often accompanied her father into the mountains and had helped him kill bears, spear in hand.

No, Malvina had never helped to kill bears, either with a spear or in any other fashion.

Oh, Maximo was a great hunter! He had had adventures! But Teresa would not talk about that. She wagered that he had told Malvina all that.

No, Maximo had not told her anything.

Him, so expansive! Was that imaginable? But he had great preoccupations during his voyage to France—the search for capital. Malvina must be up to date.

She was not up to date.

What! Was that possible? It was scarcely credible. Malvina for whom he had had such an admiration! For he admired her, not to say more. That, she knew for sure. Maximo had written to her about that. Him, who wrote so little. He had that weakness. But in sum, he had written once, a letter from Saint-Gaudens, where he was staying at the Hôtel de France.

Behind the defense that she had created with her silence, Malvina weakened. The emotions she had just traversed disposed her to the impulse to tell her story that is in all human beings. Confidence is a sort of enrichment. But confession was difficult. Her father had taken on a heavy responsibility, which she shared. If Teresa Avila had received many letters from her brother, there was every chance that he had told her about his liaison with her. That knowledge would have given her, without her being conscious of it in her mind, a kind of right to know more. But one single letter! Teresa Avila did not know anything. She was looking for her brother. She had come on the off chance. Did she merit a confidence, and what was the point?

And then, another problem posed itself in her mind. Had she the right to keep the document that her father had given her when he was dying? According to what she had always heard, property reverted after death to the relatives of the person to who it had belonged. That was the law. Maximo's morocco wallet was against her bosom, between her chemise and her bodice. She could feel its outline against her flesh. That was all that remained of a man who had been her lover. To be sure, he had only been that for a few brief nights, the memory of which was like a dream, but according to the rules of honesty that had been taught to her, her duty was to give it to the dead man's sister, saying: it was in these circumstances that my father took the wallet; your brother died in my arms; my father and I dug a grave for him out there in the park, and you can go to pray under the beech that shelters him.

Yes, she should have said that. She would have done, not long ago. But something had intervened: Bishop Borromée's malediction. One night, she had made an appeal to the one man whose goodness and disinterest she recognized, to Bishop Borromée, and he had rejected her in the name of God, cursing her. She was no longer within the circle of good souls. Their morality was no longer made for her. She no longer had to encumber herself with it. Maximo's sister could deploy her graces full of traps in her regard, but to no avail. She would keep what her father had given her. She would not run the risk of certain reproaches and unjust suspicions.

She had meditated a hundred times on all the suppositions that would have been made if the secret inhumation of that terrible night had ever been revealed. She knew the story that would immediately have been created by the malevolence of souls: her father had caught her in the night in her lover's arms, killed the lover with his hunting rifle and buried him in order to conceal his crime. She had imagined everything that would have happened: the magistrate, the interrogation, the gendarmes, the autopsy of the victim, the reconstitution of the so-called crime and the cries of the crowd surrounding the house. And she should put herself in the hands of this unknown sister? A force of hypocrisy rose within her. It was necessary to speak in order to have plausibility on her side. Eventually, she spoke.

Certainly, the sudden disappearance of a relative who had been welcomed amicably had been a great subject of surprise. Avila had come to dinner several times, invited by her father. Personally, she had liked him. Nothing more. No, nothing more. Had he and her father sketched out some common business affair? It was possible, but she did not believe it. Her father was a rather withdrawn man, not very accessible to new things.

In any case, everything reposed on an error relative to his fortunate situation. She did not know how such a legend could have been created. Perhaps the Noussoulens had had a little money once, one of those provincial fortunes that have an effect because of the château, because of the extent of the lands, but in these mountainous territories one can own a great deal of land and still be poor, because it is all rocks and ferns. Perhaps once...doubtless a very long time ago. But now? Her father did not say much, but all the same he had told her that she was ruined, that she did not even possess this old dwelling any more, encumbered by mortgages for more than its value.

Her father had probably explained that to Maximo Avila, and abruptly, he had disappeared. There was a connection between the disappearance and the disappointment he most have experienced. Evidently, one does not leave without saying goodbye unless one has not foreseen one's departure. But Mademoiselle Avila must know her brother. He was a strange man. And who could tell whether he had not wanted everyone to believe that he had disappeared, out of a desire for liberty or for some other reason? Does one ever know?

Teresa Avila experienced a great disappointment. She had expected something very different. She did not know what, however. But the loss of foolish chimeras is more sensible than that of a reality. She was certainly searching for her brother, but the Noussoulens fortune that did not exist had had the effect on her of a lamp toward which she had started walking, and by the light of which she had seen herself welcomed by a young woman in love as the sister of a beloved fiancé, in the luxury of a château of which her brother had described the imaginary splendors.

She continued tapping her garish boot with her switch, but the beat became gradually slower. It ended up expiring, along with her hope.

She listed all the enquiries she had made, for what she had found at the hotel in her brother's trunk had not been able to tell her anything.

"A dress suit, a hunting costume, toilet objects, his night-clothes and a large dagger, terribly sharp and terribly long. No books—he scarcely read. A few unimportant papers. But he almost never wrote, and poorly, I must say."

Oh, there was not a single letter! He had no need to confide in anyone, him! Nor was he a tender person, like his sister.

And then there were plaints, mingled with memories. He had cost his family so much money!—she did not say what family, and where all that had happened. It had been necessary

111

or his relatives to make sacrifices for him. And he found all that quite natural! Why? Why had she, Teresa, been deprived of all that should have reverted to her? For it was necessary to say that, although she never complained, she had been dispossessed. In any case, what did money matter? For her, the essential thing was to be able to mount a horse. Did Malvina not have a horse in her stables that she could lend her?

No, there were no stables any longer.

Well, she would go back to Saint-Gaudens in order to hire one. For she wanted to make a few ascensions in the Pyrenees. Who could tell whether her poor brother might not be lying at the bottom of a precipice, in consequence of an imprudence? For he was capable of the greatest follies. And all that since his encounter with a man who called himself Ascanio, and who claimed to be a reincarnation of Cagliostro. The world is full of crackpots, and dangerous crackpots.

Maximo talked to the dead as she, Teresa, was talking to Malvina de Noussoulens, for example, and much more familiarly. There were some he addressed as *tu*. It was incredible. There had come a time when the house in which they lived— she did not say where—had been full of phantoms. And what phantoms! Personally, she did not believe in anything—in God, of course, a God who judges us—but apart from that God and that judgment she did not believe in anything. But she had been obliged to believe in his phantoms, since she had seen them. One above all, which had the head of a mummy...

But that would take too long to tell. It was sufficient for Malvina to know that she, Teresa, had said to her brother: "Choose between us, between your family, who love you, and your Ascanio and the phantom with the head of a mummy." And what did Maximo do? He had chosen the phantom and the reincarnation of Cagliostro and he had left. For he had the folly of leaving, like that, abruptly, without even taking a toothbrush. It was for that reason that one could hope for anything. He could have gone and come back, and everything could have been sorted out. All his errors could have been repaired. For he really was on the trail of a fortune. He had such great qualities, such a gift for inspiring sympathies. He had a fortune in his hand. He kept it in his wallet. Certainly, Monsieur Noussoulens had known that. But he was dead. And Maximo, where was he?

From time to time Teresa Avila's gaze departed like an arrow in the direction of Malvina's eyes. The arrow fell. It collided with the indifference opposed by one creature to another when there is too great a difference of nature between the two of them.

And abruptly, Teresa Avila gave up. *I'm in the presence of a young imbecile,* she thought. *I've allowed myself to be deceived for the hundredth time by one of my brother's boasts. This provincial girl has a frozen heart and isn't capable of amour or of confidence. And I was told that French women were such sluts!*

She gave her boots two or three hearty slaps with the switch.

"Great God! But it's almost night. Bonsoir, my dear child!"

The coachman, imperiously stimulated, whipped his horses.

"I'll go close the gate," said Mathieu.

Malvina heard him draw away. But it was to something else that she was listening. Was that not the sound of light footsteps, in the other direction—in the direction of the old beech?

X. The Brother of Saint-Jean-de-Dieu

One day, Hugues Borromée had met a singular individual on the high road to Saint-Gaudens. He was a man with long hair, who must have been about sixty, clad in black, very poorly but with an affectation of austerity. He had looked at Hugues with a fixed and gleaming gaze, had stopped him and said to him: "I recognize you. You're a Brother of Saint-Jean-de-Dieu."

"Me? Not at all. I've just left the seminary of the Missions."

"I was right. A missionary! You're a Brother of Saint-Jean-de-Dieu at heart. I too am a brother of Saint-Jean-de-Dieu." And he laughed, bitterly.

Then, abruptly putting one knee on the ground, he kissed the hem of the young man's robe.

"My name is Jean-François the sinner," he murmured, getting up. "Brother, I have need of your pardon."

Then Hugues remembered having heard the story of the man who was before him. The Brothers of Saint-Jean-de-Dieu had once had several powerful communities in France, which had been destroyed in '92. The monasteries had been burned and the monks dispersed. They had only returned to France in 1815. But they lacked he money to rebuild their monasteries and churches. It had been decided that all the monks would go and beg along the roads and strive to accumulate the money necessary to reconstruct the old communities. They had set forth, and their renown had preceded them. The name of Brother of Saint-Jean-de-Dieu was an entitlement of welcome. Some received large sums of money. Those accumulated sums permitted the reconstruction of fine edifices and new chapels.

Brother Jean-François was passionate and eloquent. He was not much over twenty when he took up the staff of a mendicant pilgrim. He excelled at assembling people at the crossroads of villages and describing the delights of the monastic life, and the necessity of communion with God in solitary meditation. He had great success wherever he went. People in châteaux summoned him. Those who heard him attributed to the Brothers of Saint-Jean-de-Dieu a direct communication with Heaven.

He received considerable sums and transmitted them faithfully. In his regard, a highly-placed ecclesiastic was reported to have said: "Brother Jean-François will be a luminary of Christianity." But pride entered into his heart. Was everything not permitted to a man who rendered such great material and spiritual services? And an appetite for pleasure also took possession of him, but pleasure in a vulgar form. He liked drinking and conversing at night with people of a base existence.

"I am like Our Lord; I shall covet prostitutes and murderers."

Several times he was robbed of everything he had on him. What did those paltry sums matter? Did he not have the faculty of having a thousand times more? And he set about drinking and gambling.

He knew that in the outlying districts of towns, no matter of what size, there were select taverns where all that humanity has of the most degraded gathered. It was there that he went every evening, always with the objective of conversion.

At first the community had turned a blind eye. But the scandal burst. A rich chatelaine of Pau entrusted a large sum of money to him. It was never passed on. Several times, attempts were made to bring him back to one of the now-prosperous monasteries and keep him there. He went with the brothers who came to fetch him, but abandoned them on the way. He was threatened. He was obliged to quit the robe from which he drew all his authority. He fell, and became a beggar who spoke to God.

Years passed. He continued his task as an apostle of the monastic life, but it was no longer anything but a caricature of an apostolate. After having occupied the opinion of the Midi—for he never quit the shadow of the Pyrenees—people ceased to talk about him.

Now he was walking beside Hugues along the dusty road, and there was admiration in his wild eyes.

"I've been like you," he said. Then, after a pause, he went on: "I've ceased to believe in it. But redemption exists. There is redemption for everyone." He looked to the right and the left and added, forcefully: "Even me."

He rummaged in one of his pockets, from which a crust of bead fell that he did not attempt to pick up. He took out a frightfully dirty playing card.

"Look. I've drawn it at random. Do you know that figure? Who knows? Perhaps you've never had it before your eyes. It's the queen of hearts. Oh, how many queens of hearts I've seen, in the abject places where I pleased myself, and where I went to sit down, clad in the sacred robe of the Brothers of Saint-Jean-de-Dieu. Look, another: the jack of clubs. I've known them too, jacks of clubs. The world is full of them. We'll go past some of them on the road.

"It's an extraordinary thing, you see. Once, an artist—or, rather, a magician—of genius painted the figures of a deck of cards. He painted the human passions—or, rather, evil. For evil acts by means of passions. But that's a great mystery. The person who possesses the figures, who handles them, who plays with them, is playing the game of his own death, the death of his eternal soul. How is that transmission possible? How can such human powers be contained in images painted on pieces of cardboard? Who will ever know? In a minuscule seed there is the reduction of an immense tree.

"There are other mysteries as astonishing. But I've experienced that one. I've seen many men fall who owe their fall to the mysterious manipulation of the accursed figures. As you see, I still carry them on me. They're all there. There's lust, with its beauty, the fatal pride of the king of spades, the bloody fury of the jack of diamonds, and then the inferior sins, whose significance is given by the numbers of the cards, in accord with their emblems. But I've vanquished them. Redemption has come."

He fell silent and walked alongside Hugues. The young missionary had understood that any response would be vain and that, in any case, his interlocutor did not care.

"After having been Jean-François the apostle, I've become Jean-François the sinner. In order for a sin to be pardoned, it's necessary that the person who has committed it repair his fault. How can a man do that who has stolen a great deal of money and has dispersed it? How can he return it to its legitimate owner? I've calculated that, even by working with my hands for a century, I couldn't earn what I owe—by working with my hands according to the order established here. But great news has reached me. There's a distant land beyond the sea where one can find in one day the gold that would be earned by a lifetime of labor. Today, I've learned that it's possible to redeem myself. If I can reach that country, I'll find the necessary gold and pay my debt to the prior of the Brothers of Saint-Jean-de-Dieu. He knows the figure and so do I, for nothing is forgotten. There's no sponge that effaces sins; it's necessary to repair them."

His eyes were shining and his face was invaded by the expression that only a vivid hope procures.

"I'm marching along the road of reparation. I'm still strong and courageous. I'll repair."

They had arrived at a crossroads. Hugues was about to take a minor road to the right.

"Pardon me, Brother of Saint-Jean-de-Dieu. You're a Brother of Saint-Jean-de-Dieu even if you don't know it. You're working on the construction of a community that will embrace the earth. I have need of the pardon of pure men. Extend your hand. Simply say: 'I pardon you.'"

"I pardon you with a glad heart," said Hugues.

"Thank you."

They drew away, each in his own direction. Hugues looked back and he saw that, while walking, Jean-François the sinner was dropping behind him, one by one, the cards of his deck, which made a trail of images in the dust.

XI. The Brothers of the Virgin Gold
(Dr. Fazeuille's Journal)

I am advancing in the discovery of my soul like a traveler in a forest full of monsters. I have just discovered in myself a cupidity, an avidity to possess riches that I had never counted among my faults. The light of introspection permits me to know that that disinterest was only an illusion. That skillfully-projected light permits me to see the origin of my cupidity.

The cupidity in question is recent. It was born in the last few days—a terrible thing—it is growing and developing in force. How has that been able to happen? I can see its origin in the moment when I began to speak in Sulpice's company against the appetite for riches, the thirst for gold. Then temptation was born within me.

I even know the exact moment when its first nucleus developed. It was the morning when I received the petty sum that my father sends me every month. That sum, when it arrives, usually brings me delight. It is sufficient to fulfill my petty desires. I also know the difficulty my father has in sending it to me and I have a pious thought of gratitude for him every time.

Now, that morning, I did not have that thought. I experienced a great dryness of soul and, shrugging my shoulders, I was invaded by the bitter sentiment of my poverty and the poverty that has always been my portion.

Then too, I sense that certain words, magical in character, are acting on me as they are acting on the other people of the region. Virgin gold! What an evocative force there is in those syllables! I didn't know that there was gold that was virginal and gold that wasn't. The virginity of gold! We only handle impure gold. But under the waters, the pure and singing waters, in inaccessible places, the virgin metal reposes, such as it was formed in the first days of the world's creation.

Everyone in the region is talking about virgin gold, and a group has even been formed, which calls itself, I believe, the Companions, or the Brothers, of the Virgin Gold, and which brings together almost all of those who have given their adherence to Monsieur Alcide Pécouret.

Sulpice is indignant. He is preparing a speech in which he is gathering all his ideas. He has resolved to deliver it at the imminent meeting of that association, which we are due to attend.

We have attended the meeting that took place on Saint-Gaudens, in the main room of the Hôtel de France. I ought to have obtained a great profit from that evening, for the sight of men assembled always entails a lesson. I did not. I was anxious, troubled. The lamp of introspection laid bare the evil aspects of myself. I thought that I was modest. I have been obliged to observe that I am nothing of the sort. I would have liked to play a role in the debates that I was witnessing, and a role in the foreground.

I no longer know at what moment in the discussion and for what reason, an individual that I did not know and who did not know me, pointed at me and shouted: "You, Monsieur, who must be a doctor, you must know..."

Indisputably, I have the physique of a doctor. That man had recognized it and was asking me for some unimportant testimony. It was very little. My head started buzzing. So an appeal was being made to my competence! In the milieu of that meeting, I was a doctor. A frisson ran through me. I was flattered. I regretted not having been in the hot seat for a long time. I had a desire to shout: "If you need any more information, you can ask me. I'm here. I'm a doctor."

A few minutes later, I heard an interior voice that said to me: *You're just a wretched braggart. Remember that you haven't yet passed your final examination in medicine.*

That assembly was curious. There were people of every sort. All the Bonapartist officers were there. I wonder why those men of a certain age want to try their luck in America, instead of living peacefully in their retirement. There were even a few rich people. And they want to depart in order to be richer! There are some who have ludicrous motives. Old Captain Montarache went from group to group, saying: "It appears that there are cigars as big as this..." And with his hands he designated the length of his arm. "It appears that even the poor smoke them in the port."

What port? He would have had difficulty saying. Me too, in fact.

Alcide Pécouret was always surrounded. Someone had brought him a little table and I noticed that the receipts he was handing out bore a ship in the corner with its sails deployed, which seemed to be sailing toward a palm tree.

That meeting did not concern the agriculturalists, the ones who have been promised land and who are to embark for Guazalcoalco. Their voyage will be shorter. Those who were gathered were the gold seekers who will be departing on a ship called the *Avenir*, a ship that, in order to reach California, has to go round South America, passing Cape Horn—where there are, it appears, unusual tempests—and sail northwards again along the coast of Chile. Everyone has consulted his school atlas. About eighty days of navigation, it's said.

There were even women! Do they intend to dig in the ground and filter streams to find virgin gold?

"Look," said Sulpice, gripping my arm, "That's her."

I understood that it was a matter of the famous Malvina. I recognized her by her mourning-dress, for she has just lost her father. For several days I had no talk of anything but that death from Sulpice. He felt sorry for her. She was going to be all alone. What would become of her? Ought he to buy black gloves in order to pay her a visit if condolence after the burial? Such was the custom, and it was an absolute custom, but the color of the gloves wasn't prescribed. Sulpice had some dark gray gloves. Would they suffice? I assured him that they would. He agreed with my opinion, which was the wisest, for it took account of the viewpoint of economy. He thought that I was right, but at the last minute—which is to say, in the morning before the burial—he changed his mind and took advantage of the milkman's cart to go and buy black gloves.

"My instinct always informs me of what it's necessary to do," he told me. "An interior force drove me to go and buy black gloves."

It's one of his errors to believe that his instinct is never mistaken.

He came back from his visit very emotional and told me immediately what had happened.

"I don't understand it at all. We went to the château together, my uncle, Hugues and me, for Bernard preferred to make his visit on his own. When we arrived, the Miramonts were coming out of the drawing room and old Madame Miramont embraced Malvina. My uncle went in first. Malvina looked at him with a fixed stare, as if she were struck with terror, and she fell down in a faint. In the meantime, Madame Compans arrived. She had smelling salts in her carriage 'I'll stay with her,' she said. 'The poor child has been too hot, but in a quarter of an hour there'll be no trace of it.'

"We left, and we heard Madame Compans saying: 'A mourning is like a battle. It's necessary to stand firm until...' She was about to say 'the last man' but she changed her mind and said: 'until the end.'

Sulpice was sad not to have met Malvina's gaze.

"Personally, I'm sad for the needless expense of your gloves," I told him.

This Malvina is a young woman such as there are in the novels of George Sand. She's a fatal beauty. She scares me a little. I prefer more vulgar women, with whom one is more at ease. She stood as motionless as a statue and her green eyes were sparkling though her mourning veil.

I took account, in her considering her, of the fact that my utmost depths were common, lacking in refinement. Immediately, I invoked the image of a café prostitute called Maria, a creature very much of flesh, with forceful breasts, whom one finds sitting outside her door in a back street in Saint-Gaudens. A band of the local lads who were having a good time on Saturday night took Sulpice and me to her café. Sulpice gives evidence of a profound disgust in such places and he's right. I sincerely wish that I felt a similar disgust, but I don't. I put my elbows on the table, I raise my voice, and I feel at ease. Then, I drink gladly and I feel a beneficent warmth.

Maria is a sort of inferior queen who dominates those who approach her. Her hair is cut short at the front and she has gleaming teeth, ornament of a constant laughter. Her neck is so short that her head seems to be born directly from her shoulders. She gazes fixedly and for a long time. I experienced the fixity of that gaze several times. Why? For sure I've pleased Maria. Certainly, it's not flattering. And yet I remember that internally, I felt a certain vanity in that.

"Let's go," Sulpice said to me, severely, when he noticed that ploy.

And I'm obliged to note that for a few seconds, I said to myself: *Sulpice is jealous*, and it required the nocturnal freshness to dissipate that insensate idea.

But let's get back to the meeting of the Brothers of the Virgin Gold.

The admirable Malvina had taken her place in her mourning veil in a dimly-lit corner of the room. Imagine my stupor when I saw Maria come to take her place in the opposite corner! She was affecting a modest appearance and, in order to seem respectable, she'd put on a caricaturish hat. She stared at her feet, and, after staring at them for a long time, she only raised her eyes once on the assembly—and that single glance settled on me, by virtue of a mysterious communication that I can't explain, and which filled me with confusion.

The two poles of amour! I thought, trying to orient my thought toward philosophical considerations, while discussions of every sort filled the room.

There were a lot of speeches. Improvised orators gave enthusiastic descriptions of California, about which they doubtless knew no more than me. The name of a town called Monterey was revealed to me.

I nudged Sulpice's elbow two or three times. "I believe the moment has come," I said to him. "You can reduce these stupidities to nothing."

"I'd like to know," he replied, "why Malvina is here this evening"—which had no connection with what I'd said.

Then the members of the group voted to elect a president. There was talk of appointing the oldest of the former officers of Napoléon. That was Captain Montarache, the man of the big cigars.

Doubtless he was solicited to accept by telling him that reason, for I heard his strident burst of laughter, and he exclaimed: "Me! Get away! I have teeth in the process of growing."

And I saw his jaw open, showing his teeth by the light of a match.

Then the names of the two colonels were pronounced, Bertrand de Chalabre and Blaise Espondeillan. It was agreed that they ought to nominate the second, the better known. But the first was interested in astronomy and had a telescope on him.

"He knows the stars! If we're lost in a desert, he'll be able to direct us by the stars! And even during the voyage, he'll be able to save us from a shipwreck."

The two colonels are fast friends and they declared that electing either one of them would be the same thing, in view of the amity that united them. It was Bertrand de Chalabre who was elected, and in spite of his declarations I saw Blaise Espondeillan dart a glance charged with bitterness at his friend.

"Well," I said to Sulpice, "this is the moment."

"I'm wondering why Malvina is interested in this whole affair," he replied.

And he did not make any speech. He maintained the silence that he always has the habit of observing.

I saw a shepherd with his hooded cape, who had listened attentively, approach Alcide Pécouret and I heard him ask:

"How much does it cost, everything included, to get as far as the place where the…gold is?"

He hesitated. He dared not say "the virgin gold" because he didn't understand that expression very well. He must have been thinking that in the rivers of California he would find gold coins with the effigy of Louis-Philippe. And he paid with louis that he took from a leather pouch that was wrapped in a big blue handkerchief.

"Speak before he's paid," I said again to Sulpice, pointing at the ingenuous victim.

But he could not take his eyes off the corner of the room where Malvina was sitting.

Then I didn't pay any more attention to the speeches. Was I the victim of an illusion? But it seemed to me that I had attracted the attention of the young woman and that her green eyes were fixed on me. But how was that possible? Perhaps she was saying to herself: "Why, there's that young doctor, who's a friend of the Borromées..." In the provinces, anything can happen. But no, that was my wretched vanity coming into play again.

I turned away and I saw Maria, who was looking at me, showing her teeth. She had stood up and, with her head in her shoulders, she looked like a thickset worker going to accomplish a task. Summoned by the duties of the little café, she went away, trying to remain as inconspicuous as possible, and directing one last glance in my direction from the doorway.

Everyone was on the move. We went on foot with Noël Alga. Sulpice Borromée and he were arm in arm. Malvina had left the room as discreetly as Maria, but I was sure that her image preceded the two young men. Both of them were burning to speak to her, to seek the motives that had bought her to that meeting. Either of them could have gone to sit near her and exchanged amicable words, but the mourning veil had stopped them. Now their fear of showing too keen an interest in her held them back.

"I don't understand," said Noël Alga, "why Buffon doesn't say anything about the intelligence of ant-hills. He doesn't even say with certainty what can be found in California."

"Buffon is very incomplete," said Sulpice.

And not far away from us, in a group marching alongside us, we heard Colonel de Chalabre explaining that the stars of the American sky were not the same as those of France.

"Go on—you're making fun of us now," replied a voice in the shadows. "God hasn't amused himself creating two different skies, one for us and another for California."

I didn't hear the response, but the grumbling voice of the one who had replied said: "I'll end up thinking that the ignorant know more than those who know something!"

I feel sorry for those who don't possess an interior lamp with which to see their soul. I've resolved to submit all my thoughts to a minute examination in order to purify them; I've burned the inexorable lamp of introspection and in spite of that, I haven't arrived at seeing much of myself. I see faults and I try to expel them, but new ones appear incessantly, and what was a firm conviction the day before is no longer one the next day.

I thought that I had a great firmness, but I don't have any. I didn't think that I was susceptible of being influenced, but I'm weak and subject to influence.

Dinner, at Uncle Borromée's, took place yesterday in the most extreme agitation. Hugues had just received the letter he was expecting from the Superior of the Missions. He showed us that letter, signed by the Prefect of the Propaganda and the Superior of the Missions of Paris. He was proud of it.

"It's the commencement of my apostolic life," he said, his eyes shining, and he looked into the distance, above our heads.

His uncle hugged him.

"Aha! The sin of pride!" murmured Bernard, with a perfidious smile.

That pride was increased because he wasn't being sent, like the majority of missionaries, into a remote region of China. He was being sent to America. The Society of Missions had renounced evangelizing America since Canada had been lost to France. There were only isolated missionaries in Louisiana. But a few years before, the Bishop of Cincinnati had made a request for missionaries. And now Pope Pius IX had created an apostolic vicariat in New Mexico and had decided that missionaries would set forth for all the savage regions of the country. Hugues would be the first. The letter he had just received enclosed flattering words about him. Not only was he to convert people, as all missionaries do, and organize local clergy, but they were counting on his intelligence to judge whether the immense regions of Arkansas, Texas and Colorado necessitated the sending of further missionaries.

"You're going to depart with all those imbeciles who are going to look for gold," said Bernard, as everyone got up from the table, for he never ceased mocking those who were proposing to depart. However, he had not adopted the same point of view as Sulpice, for he also mocked his brother for what he called an equally great stupidity: wanting to aid humankind.

"Someone has just brought a letter for you," said Catherine. And she held out a big blue letter.

Letters have a physique, like humans. A letter can have the physique of a coquettish young woman, just as I have the physique of a doctor. Even without opening it, one can recognize an anonymous letter. A letter from someone one loves always has a radiance. That letter disengaged a mystery. Everyone sensed it.

Bernard said: "Good!" like someone who cannot be troubled by any letter, and went to the window in order to read it by the last of the daylight.

Sulpice had seized me by the arm and he dragged me into the garden.

"I recognized Malvina's handwriting!" He told me.

"What can she have to do with your brother?"

"I'm wondering that."

The next day, to our great surprise, Bernard had changed his attitude completely.

"According to certain conversations I've had this morning with competent persons, it appears that the presence of gold in California is entirely real. The whole thing, in life, is not to act like an imbecile. As for saying that gold is evil and useless, as Sulpice does, that's pure childishness, and that childishness resembles stupidity."

Sulpice made no reply. Shortly afterwards, Martin Bruno arrived. He's a young man of gigantic proportions whose strength is renowned throughout the region. He speaks less than Sulpice and is extremely timid. He gives the impression of being very benevolent, albeit a trifle puerile. He told us that he was going to pay Alcide Pécouret. He lowered his eyes as he admitted it to us, after darting a fearful glance at Sulpice. He knew his ideas and was expecting a speech. Sulpice did not say a word.

I thought that he must have a particular reason to keep silent, but that the cause we had embraced ought to be defended. Perhaps, with a little eloquence, Martin Bruno might be saved?

I started speaking, telling myself that I was the champion of a good cause. The art of oratory in not foreign to me, since I'm a doctor—or rather, I will be when I've passed my final examination. I don't stammer and I know how to expose what I think. But my words rang false and I even stammered two or three times.

"Go on, then," said Bernard, ironically, when I paused.

I darted glances in vain in the direction of Sulpice. He looked at his feet, obstinately. Martin Bruno was like a schoolboy caught at fault, but I had the sensation that he wasn't listening to me.

I was annoyed, and I ended up getting to my feet and saying: "And after all, wealth and poverty, nature and artificial life, I don't care about that."

But I knew that I wouldn't be at peace with myself, And now I'm writing these lines, and I'm holding the lamp of introspection over my soul, I'm less at peace than ever. I wonder what's happening in me, and I can only see darkness.

XII. The Intoxication of the Departure

An intoxication of departure and adventure took possession of the land of Comminges. Only the courageous and the
audacious were going. But those who were not going regretted
being retained in France. The illusion was communicated from
the former to the latter, extending over all souls.

On market days, one heard a man leading an ox by a hal-
ter asking a merchant of chickens: "Are you leaving for California or..."

And instead of Guazacoalco it was always a strange so-
nority that was emitted.

"Oh, that devil of a country! They've given you its
name!"

"Of course. It's not everyone that can go there! It's not
everyone that can even talk about it!"

"Are you departing on the *Avenir* or the *Invincible*?"

At an interval of a few days, those two ships were setting
sail in the last days of June, one from Nantes and the other
from Cherbourg.

"It appears that the *Invincible* is a ship of eight hundred
tons. It must be very big."

"They're now beginning to build veritable floating cities!"

And one glimpsed, under the trembling whiteness of
those tall sailing ships panted in the illustrations in books of
voyages, a floating city, with its provisions and its streets, the
cabins of which were houses, its meeting rooms, its turrets,
even its churches. And the city was gliding over phosphores-
cent waters, followed by thousands of sharks, in the midst of a
spray of flying fish, toward fantastic continents rich in mystery and beauty.

A merchant ordered from Toulouse a job lot of military
equipment, belts and cartridge-cases dating from the Revolution. He sold them outside the Hôtel de France in Saint-
Gaudens in a single day. A peasant bought a large metal can of

considerable weight that he strove to keep on his shoulder all day. That was in anticipation of a certain fearful desert that it might be necessary to traverse, which was between the Sierra Nevada and a big lake called the Salt Lake. Thus he would accustom himself to carrying the can and everything else necessary to a gold prospector...

The Salt Lake! The Mormons! There was a strange sect not far from the Salt Lake called the Mormons. The Mormons had several wives; that was all that anyone knew about them. As in antiquity! Like the Muslims! And the jokes never dried up. "I'm going to be a Mormon," said the most austere shepherds of the mountains. Some nudged one another, others laughed. Some even made serious plans.

"Why not, after all?" they said. "Out there, one returns to nature."

The Maire of the village of Valentine was obliged to remind the elder Ducouret that, except at carnival time, one could not go out in disguise. He had bought a broad-brimmed that from a Spanish colporteur and had his wife make a sort of red velvet bolero, as he imagined the Mexicans must wear.

"If one goes to another country it's necessary to have the national costume," he said. "No one will notice me."

As for the younger Ducouret, he was tranquil. The rocks of the Sierra Nevada were no more difficult to scale than those of the Pyrenees. A hunter of chamois and bears, he never missed his shot. He was not afraid of the redskins or the trappers, whose celebrity to newspapers spread. In order to follow a trail they could put his sense of smell to the proof!

Tins of food were piled up, rope hammocks were woven, people learned Spanish feverishly and practiced firing a revolver. They days went by. The floating cities were out here, in the ports, and would soon be ready to depart...

Of the great family of the Bramevaques, apart from a son who was completing his studies at a college in Versailles, only two descendants still remained, one of the elder branch, which had supplied important functionaries and members of the parlement, the other of the cadet branch, which had perpetuated a tradition of crankiness. Such traditions never perish in families; they are more enduring than courage or honor.

The family of Bramevaque had not recovered after the French Revolution. For several centuries, one of the two châteaux, the one in the Pyrenees, had been nothing but ruins; but there subsisted, on a hill near Mauléon, a great fortress where the two cousins, Adhémar and Antoine de Bramevaque, had taken refuge.

They were both in their forties and had a great simplicity of mind. They lived like peasants, on the vegetables that they had ended up persuading to grow in a kitchen garden situated in the former ditches of the château. The absence of linen and costumes had virtually caused them to cease all social relationships, but they did not complain. Their eccentricities of character were inoffensive.

Adhémar claimed to be able to see the future—that of individuals and that of peoples—by tracing figures in the sand. Tracing those figures occupied him during the day.

As for Antoine, he went around all the houses in the vicinity and collected kittens from excessively numerous litters, which people were about to throw into the nearest river. That was because he claimed that the woods were full of cats that had gone wild, which one never saw, but which were redoubtable, especially for chickens. He had found a means of warding off the danger. In the evening, he exposed the kittens that he had been given on the edge of the woods. He never found them again the following day. That was because they had been carried away by the terrible wild animals. What happened then? The beasts adopted the newborns and became familial creatures occupied in the care and education of the young, of which there was no longer anything to be feared.

"That doesn't do any harm to anyone," people said, when they talked about him.

No one ever knew how those simple men got the idea of expatriating themselves. No one ever knew how they were each able to find the two thousand francs necessary for their departure. There was mention of a hiding place situated in the cellars of the fortress. After their departure there were people who went to search for it, but the cellars had the reputation of not being very solid and the searches did not go on for long. It was remembered that Adhémar de Bramevaque's father was said to have been received at the court of Louis XVIII and that a protector of the family in decline was paying for the youngest's studies. It was known with certainty that Adhémar repeated the following story several times:

It was the day of his departure. He was to catch the diligence in Saint-Gaudens that was to take him to Toulouse. His baggage was packed, and there was little of it. His cousin had departed the day before and they were to meet up in Barbazan. The somber Château de Bramevaque was outlined against a sky illuminated with pink.

"I had gone down the zigzag path that leads to the château. Everything I was carrying was in a cloth attacked to the end of a stick placed over my shoulder. When I got to the foot of the slope, where the zigzags end at the Mauléon road, I saw a horseman coming toward me. He was an ageless man with a beard, a man of my sort, but with long hair. He seemed very intelligent and cheerful by nature."

"'I nearly arrived too late.' He said to me. 'How early you're leaving! The sun has scarcely risen.'

"I was very surprised. I asked him who he was.

"'I used to know your grandfather, who was a very distinguished man. I've known members of your family who are now all dead. And in memory of them, before you leave, I wanted to give you this.'

"He removed a ring from his finger and held it out to me.

"'It's a ring with a stone devoid of value—commercial value, at least. Keep it. Put it on your finger. I don't know when, but that ring might be useful to you one day. Look, there's a design on the stone. Destiny is a singular thing. Men are various. If your life were in danger, perhaps, by showing what is engraved there, things would turn around. I say *perhaps*. One never knows.'

"It's an extraordinary thing that a man arrives on horse-back from who knows where at six o'clock in the morning, a man one doesn't know from Adam, to give you a ring, and has nothing else to say to you. I looked at him in bewilderment. Perhaps I was a little too bewildered. He started laughing, as if he were mocking me.

"'Call it a talisman, or a good luck charm, if you wish. That's it—I'm giving you a good luck charm.'

"He turned his horse around. He made an amicable gesture with his hand. He said, again: 'Good luck!' And he drew away at a trot. He had come just for that! I was never able to explain what it meant. Here, look—I don't know what this stone is. It was a clearly-designed cross, but a bizarre cross. There's a rose blooming in the middle."

General Compans' widow had put on the dress that she wore for ceremonies of mourning. Her coachman, known as Brisquet, a former sergeant in the Imperial Guard, had a jacket for such occasions on which the buttons of his old uniform were sewn, which glittered in the sunlight. General Compans' window said that the actions of everyday life ought to be considered as military actions: transpositions of encampments, battles and forced marches. When people saw her coachman's buttons gleaming, they knew that she was setting forth on an expedition.

The carriage went into Saint-Gaudens at a gallop. It traversed the town, reached a side-street of gardeners and stopped in front of a minuscule house preceded by a small garden planted with salad vegetables. Its noise caused a bizarre human form leaning over the ground to disappear. The general's widow did not care about that. She emerged from the vehicle as if she were charging, traversed the garden and opened the door of the house.

"Zenon Fabrégat, you're an ass," she said to Commandant Fabrégat, who was dozing on a rickety chair, and who immediately stood to attention.

She explained her thinking with vehemence. "Have you got a wooden leg, yes or no?"

He was obliged to admit that he had.

"When one has a wooden leg one doesn't go running off adventuring in California. There's no point in citing Spinoza, of whom you understand no more than I do. Spinoza and all the rest have nothing to do with it. Zenon, you're not going."

Zenon struggled as best he could. He had covered great distances on foot with his wooden leg. He was still vigorous.

"And don't tell me that you've handed over two thousand francs to that thief. You'll give me your receipt and I'll take charge of getting them back. Anyway have you thought about La Souillon, whom you'd be abandoning?"

La Souillon was a miserable creature who was only known by that name. She was old, it was said, when Commandant Fabrégat as twenty, and had met her. She was only seen from a distance, with unkempt hair, cultivating the vegetables while Zenon smoked his pipe.

"But it's for her that I'm going, in order to ensure the ease of her old age."

"Zenon Fabrégat, you're a liar. Give me your receipt."

The general's widow took the receipt and departed in a fashion as abrupt as her arrival.

"To Colonel Espondeillan's house!" she shouted to her coachman

General Compans' widow did not have a preconceived theory about the discovery of gold in America and the departure of a few Frenchmen for that distant land. She was obeying the last instructions of her husband, who had told her to watch over his old comrades from Comminges. And watching over them entailed making them respect a particular conception of honor.

"Blaise Espondeillan, you're going to leave!" she said, when she was in the little apartment facing the church that the colonel occupied.

"Me! Depart with that band of ingrates! Never in this life!"

"You have to go. There are men who are engaging in a sort of battle. It's appropriate that they be commanded by the man at whom Napoléon pointed his finger during the return from Moscow, saying: 'It's necessary to save young Espondeillan.'"

"They knew that, and they didn't even appoint me president of their association!"

"They're counting on you. You told them all that you were going. Some of them probably wouldn't have decided without you. They thought about Napoléon's finger, which designated you. You have to go."

Blaise Espondeillan remained silent for a long time.

"It's Compans who is speaking to you through my voice," the general's widow added.

"Very well, I'll obey Compans," said the colonel.

And he made a military salute to the invisible shade of his general.

"No, Maman, I have no intention of going," Noël Alga said every day to his mother. "Anyway, you can be tranquil. Where would I find the two thousand francs that Alcide Pécouret is asking?"

"Oh, if it were a matter of your happiness, of your future, it's not the two thousand francs that would stop me. But I know full well that it's not necessary to go so far to be happy. And then, it appears that those lands are filled with bad men. There are still savages with arrows. If you said to me that you wanted to buy a little farm, even if it were a long way from here, as long as it was in France, I'd say: 'That's all right.' If you were to tell me that you wanted to but a very expensive Spanish guitar for two thousand francs, I'd say: 'That's all right.' But to go beyond the sea! I'm sure that I'd never see you again."

Noël repeated for the hundredth time that he had no intention of leaving, even though it was a unique opportunity that wouldn't present itself again in his lifetime.

His intention to go was irrevocably settled. Maître Toché, the notary of Saint-Gaudens, had advanced a few people in whom he had confidence the two thousand francs necessary, reimbursable by contract the following year. Noël Alga, whose family he had known for a long time, was one of those privileged few. But Noël, although he did not lack natural courage, had none with regard to his mother. He refused to see any sign of chagrin on her face. And the existence of that chagrin was infinitely less serious in his eyes than the reaction that he might feel. The essential thing was that he did not see it. He had the fortunate faculty of not thinking about what was painful to him—a faculty that is the prerogative of youth.

Madame Alga lived in a rather solitary fashion, and the echoes of the world only reached her via the mouth of her son or those of a few neighbors. It was very easy for Noël to deceive her.

"You can see very well that I'm not going," he simply said to his mother. "The deadline has passed. I could throw myself into the Toulouse diligence and it would be too late. I wouldn't be able to catch the ship in Nantes. You can sleep tranquilly."

That morning, he was careful not to embrace his mother any more than usual. Maître Toché had lent him a supplementary thousand francs for equipment expenses. He intended to buy everything he needed in Nantes. He only took his guitar, as usual.

"The wind has finally dropped," he said, when he had drunk the cup of coffee that his mother had just given him. "There'll never be a more beautiful day. I'll finally be able to reach the lake that is, it appears, at the foot of the Foumero peak. You can see Sauvegarde from here. To the left there's Picade. The Foumero peak is beyond that. You can tell yourself this evening that I'm there. Shortly before the lake there's a cabin with thick straw, where I'll sleep."

"The straw is very thick?"

"So I'm told. The muleteers that go to Viedallet have the habit of sleeping there."

Madame Alga put the bag containing provisions around her son's neck herself. She did not ask him how many days he would be away. He had said twenty times that he did not want to fix a time, because that would oblige him to remain away longer, in order to demonstrate his liberty.

"From tomorrow on, I'll light the lamp as usual."

Noël had once come back from the mountains on a very dark night and, after having passed through Barbazan, had difficulty determining the direction of his house. Since then, she placed a little lamp behind the pane of one of the windows, which was to indicate the right path to her son.

"Yes, from tomorrow on." He hesitated momentarily. "From the day after—that will be sufficient."

One only recognizes presentiments when the events have occurred and they are no longer of any use. Madame Alga always affirmed subsequently that she had had a presentiment. Oh yes, she knew when he hugged her and said: "Take good care of the hedgehogs."

She knew, but she only knew later that she had known then.

"Don't drink cold if you're hot," she said to him again, as she habitually did. And to show that she was not alarmed by that brief absence, she smiled. "You'll tell me everything the trees have said that grow near the lake?"

And he drew away, making a habitual broad gesture of farewell.

"My son is at Lake Foumero," said Madame Alga the next day to an old woman known as La Ménine, who brought her vegetables every week. La Ménine had been in the main square of Saint-Gaudens when the diligence left for Toulouse. The diligence was full, and the Hôtel de France had rigged up an old rattletrap, and antique diligence dating from the previous century in order to take the excess of passengers. She had seen Noël take his place in the second vehicle.

The desire to talk is powerful, but there is sometimes a little pity in certain old souls desiccated by an unfortunate life.

136

La Ménine had pity. She remained silent. And then she said: "And where is this Lake Foumero?"

"You see Sauvegarde. You have only to follow it to the left. There's the Picade and then the Foumero peak. Oh, my son knows the mountains!"

La Ménine looked at Sauvegarde, than the Picade to the left, and shook her head.

"Oh yes, the mountains! He loves them. They retain," she murmured, and she pushed her little cart along the road more rapidly than usual.

It was only at the end of the fifth day that doubt entered Madame Alga's soul. Her son could not have lied. But an accident might have occurred on the mountain. Some people broke arms and legs in precipices.

She put on her big black hooded cape so that no one could distinguish her features if she happened to weep, and she went to Saint-Bertrand.

"An accident! Oh, my poor lady!"

She was immediately informed.

"And how long does that voyage last?"

"Two or three months."

"My God! And how long does one stay digging the ground and deflecting watercourses?"

"A year, two years, perhaps more..."

"My God! Is that possible?"

"And there are women who entice you, who prevent the men from leaving again but everything finishes...four years, perhaps five years."

She was very old. Oh well, she would live, she would wait, and she would be at a mother's post, in the house...

She went back at a resolute pace. She stopped at the last grocery in Saint-Bertrand and bought a large can of oil. It was necessary that the lamp burned behind the window. One never knows, when sons depart. One never knows when they will return. Noël might come back at night.

PART TWO: IN MEXICO AND CALIFORNIA

Prelude

When will you surge from the sea like an oceanic gift, O land of America, toward which the arms of thousands of Christopher Columbuses are incessantly extended? The ship of the finder of worlds is forever *en route* and his hope flies before him like the albatross with great wings. Between the gilded foam and the roseate algae it holds its course eternally on the road that parts the moving waters, leaving the past to the right and memory to the left.

I see a wreck drawing away, like an insensate whale, and a tree traveling straight ahead, torn from some shore, which seems as solid as if its roots were plunging into the clay of the planet. It passes majestically alongside our ship. Tree of America where are you going?

Now the clouds are dispersing and the mountains appear. They become increasingly compact on the horizon. They stand out from the waves like gods laying themselves bare and letting verdant robes fall. Far away, in the inaccessible heights of the skies, there is a huge flock of birds deployed like a bow.

The water has changed color. It is mixed with mud, terrestrial debris and animate things. The wind trails an odor of sap, seeds and rotten wood. Long live the earth where there are vegetables with magnanimous hearts, houses of humans whose roofs smoke like a great respiration, brushwood that shelters jackals and tapirs, subterranean tunnels where populations of ants live.

I can hear the parrots chattering among themselves and telling stories of the forest; I can see rhododendrons whose thorns are as long as Francisco Pizarro's sword, and opening magnolias dripping a viscous juice, each drop of which could scarcely be held in a Spanish alcarazas. I can hear the slithering of snakes along branches, the footfalls of tortoises running over the sand of broad rivers, and the explosion of aloe flowers in the silence of clearings.

It is in the heart of the distant mountains that the great streams of subterranean gold are fixed. Of what primitive emanation were they born? Was there a time, when the world was in birth, when gold was a pure virgin liquid? Under the empire of what secret force was it mutated into metal? We are going to snatch it from the place where the creative powers have placed it, and it will become for us the joy of living, the materialization of our dreams.

Be welcoming for us, land of America! Let us travel up your rivers, between the walls of forests, traverse your deserts without their sand burning our lungs. Perhaps there is a time marked for the continents when they must give their substance to humans. Your century has come, land of America, and now, on the seas that encircle you, traveling toward you, are those that have received that promise and have come to realize it.

I. The Lie
(Dr. Fazeuille's Journal)

It's a mild night. I can hear the noise that the *Reine Marie* makes as she cleaves the waves and I'm writing by the light of a miserable candle while my cabin companion is asleep above my head.

How did I get here? I'd have trouble explaining that to myself. When I get back I shall have to have a long conversation with Monseigneur Borromée about the march of events and the power that he calls Providence. I ought to have had that conversation when I was seeing him every day. When will I see him again now? I renounce casting light within me.

But I've just made a discovery relative to the subtle domain of life...

There are periods, places and groups of men who are suddenly enveloped in mystery, without the reason for it being absolutely determined. The mystery comes down like a cloud. It troubles souls, gives birth to unjustified terrors, accomplishes unexpected actions. Some men march thereafter as if surrounded by a halo, and the things they look at are invested with a particular color. The sound of their voice is no longer the same, they're perpetually in a state of expectation, and fear takes up residence in the background of their consciousness. They don't know that the mystery has enveloped them, and they go on unaware of its presence. The mystery is sometimes within them and it grows by virtue of the work of their imagination. But sometimes it's exterior to them, dependent on distant events, decisions that have remained in suspense, sometimes unpunished crimes, unknown tragedies that can no longer continue in events, following their course in an invisible fashion and causing to float over those who approach them an imprecise and obsessive menace.

And now I, who did not seem at all designated for that, have been thrown by an unexpected series of events into the middle of a cloud of mystery.

We had only quit Le Havre a few hours before and the vessel was cleaving quietly through the waves. I note in passing how marvelous it is, for someone unversed in marine matters, that a mass as enormous as the *Reine Marie* can move so swiftly when there is only an insignificant wind, which seems to change direction every five minutes. At any rate, the captain found that wind quite sufficient—or rather, he paid no heed to it—and he lavished smiles on the notable passengers who were on the deck. I was one of them. It is an advantage to appear older than one's true age. He must also have known that I was a doctor.

The captain, whose name is Courtin, was walking with an individual that he must have known for a long time and to whom he showed a certain consideration. He was a man of about fifty, with bright eyes. He was abnormally supple for someone of his age. His body undulated slightly when he walked, and that undulation immediately made me think of a panther, although I've only seen that animal once. But I had the sentiment that there was a slight affectation of suppleness in his case. Assuredly, he knew how to resemble a panther and took pride in it. His black moustache formed two points raised upwards and extraordinarily well waxed. His carefully-trimmed beard bore traces of a greasy substance, as if each hair had been subject to an individual treatment, and the bottom of his lower lip was clean-shaven and pink, which gave his face an expression of sensuality. He gave the impression of being intelligent, cunning and dangerous. Such, at least, was my first impression.

"It's a matter of blood...," he was saying to Captain Courtin when he passed close to me.

At that precise moment Malvina appeared at the top of the stairway and leaned on an iron balustrade for a few seconds. Then she perceived a group formed by Bernard

Borromée, Noël Alga and Martin Bruno; she headed toward them.

I looked at the face of the man who was talking to Captain Courtin. The points of his moustache rose toward his eyes by means of a movement that I tried in vain to imitate subsequently. His head oscillated, and I heard him say, in an indifferent tone: "But...isn't that a young woman named Malvina de Noussoulens"

"Why, yes," the captain replied.

And they drew away.

Those simple words had sufficed. I had perceived at that moment the mystery in which we were going to live. And in the depths of my being, the sentiment awoke in a painful fashion that I had imprudently embarked on a dangerous adventure.

However, that reflection had nothing extraordinary about it. I've forgotten to note that the man in question was wearing trousers of a singular form, tight at the knee and very broad at the bottom, that his waistcoat was very short and made of red velvet and that it allowed the sight of a broad leather belt doubtless adapted to carry weapons. How could a person dressed like that know Malvina, a young woman of an old Comminges family who, according to Sulpice, had never left home? Never, in the Midi, nether in Saint-Bertrand nor Villefranche-de-Lauragais, had a man wearing trousers of that form been seen. I confess that those trousers, and also the red waistcoat, had much to do with the enigmatic appearance of the individual in question Then too, "It's an affair of blood." What blood? What did he mean by that?

At any rate, it was at that moment that the mystery began to extend over us.

But in order to clarify my own ideas, and although I'm desperate to clarify them completely, the lamp that I project internally producing too feeble a light. I'm going to summarize, as if on a chart, the events that motivated my presence on the *Reine Marie*. It will be the chart of causes. As with all the causes that drive men to act, there are lies, perfidies and insanities. I'm obliged to observe that I didn't see anything and didn't understand anything—or rather, understood too late— by virtue of a natural blindness that impels me to mistake for truth any affirmation made in speech.

Early one morning, I was woken up in my hotel room by Bernard Borromée.

"I have to talk to you," he said. He addressed me as *tu* for the first time. "Henceforth, we'll address one another as *tu*. We're comrades, and it's absurd not to use *tu*, all the more so as you already use *tu* with my brother."

I understood that he was trying to flatter me with that familiarity. And what's more, I was flattered, without quite admitting it to myself at the time. *Aha!* I said to myself, internally. *He's trying to tighten his intimacy with a doctor.*

"I have an important affair to propose to you. You know what I've always thought of people who depart blindly for California, believing that they'll make a fortune there. They're imbeciles. They leave without any information and think they'll pick up gold as one picks up pebbles here. But it's an entirely different matter if one goes to America with a precisely defined goal, with a plan, to search for a treasure already discovered. Do you understand?"

I replied that I understood such a simple thing, but that the difficulty was in possessing such a precious indication.

"Well, I have it—or rather, a person in whom I have every confidence has a document indicating the place where a considerable treasure is to be found. In any case, you'll know who it is. It's Malvina de Noussoulens. She's chosen me to direct an expedition that she will join. She's chosen both of us, Sulpice and me, because she's known us since childhood and has confidence in us. It's a matter of reaching a distant and rather dangerous place. There ought to be several of us, and as we don't have any capital, we'll take advantage of the facilities offered by Alcide Pécouret's society and recruit our companions from among those who are departing, only counting on their lucky star. They'll be only too glad to have a certainty, or something approaching it.

"We need people who are both energetic and honest. I thought of Martin Bruno and Noël Alga. One is a slightly awkward colossus, the other something of a crackpot. With Sulpice and me you'll make the fifth. I'm convinced that your father will provide the necessary two thousand francs from his savings. I've seen Alcide Pécouret. I've arranged everything with him. We've consulted the maps. We won't take the same ship as those who are going to San Francisco. We'll make a much shorter voyage on a ship departing from Bordeaux, going to New Orleans, which will deposit us in a city of which you might have heard mention, called Vera Cruz. You have just enough time to leave, persuade your father, and join us at Bordeaux, where we'll embark. I believe that your father lives in Villefranche-de-Lauragais. That's almost on the road to Bordeaux. If you talk about it to my uncle, he'll tell you that it's a manifest sign of Providence."

I remember that it was on that word that a vertigo took hold of me. I had no liking for Bernard; I knew all his faults and I had a particular horror for the jealousy he nourished for his brother Sulpice. In spite of that, everything I had just heard seemed to me to be marked with the seal of verity and good sense. The treasure was a certainty, whether it was a placer discovered by an audacious pioneer or gold accumulated by some Mexican king or some international pirate. I had an extraordinary chance to be in the number of the privileged few who were about to depart on its conquest. It was necessary to profit from that chance!

It was excellent to be on familiar terms with Bernard Borromée. Fundamentally, he had a much better nature than I had thought. One can be so mistaken in the judgments one makes! All the theories that Sulpice had made me share vanished in an instant. In any case, Sulpice was leaving with us— at least, that was what Bernard affirmed to me, and I attributed that decision, in opposition to his ideas, to the joy of setting forth with Malvina.

It was there that I sinned, by virtue of a lack of reflection and a credulity that I cannot explain. When Bernard told me all that, Sulpice had gone to Saint-Gaudens, sent by his uncle for some reason I don't know. He would not be back until the evening. Now, according to Bernard, the hours were counted. If I wanted to join them in Bordeaux and devote two days to my father—even those two days were a minimum—I had to take the diligence that was about to pass through Barbazan heading for Toulouse. I only just had time to pack my modest valise and set off. Bernard would accompany me. There was no bill to settle with Monsieur Mauvezin, since I had been Uncle Borromée's guest. I would take a few minutes to bid farewell to that uncle; Bernard would explain my departure to Sulpice in the evening. In any case, we would all meet up in Bordeaux.

When I said that my presence was still dependent on the hypothetical acceptance of my father, Bernard told me that his refusal was not a sufficient reason. Malvina de Noussoulens would see Maître Toché during the day and would doubtless obtain an advance from him. She would advance the sum in question to me. It was a matter of an affair whose return would be enormous. I need have no scruple.

Uncle Borromée made no objection to my abrupt departure. I knew that his belief in a certain fashion of the action of Providence forbade him from worrying about the decisions what people made in order not to contradict Providence.

What determines events? I nearly missed the diligence at Barbazan. If I had not left until the following day I would have seen Sulpice in the evening and I would have known exactly what he thought. The diligence stopped for a few minutes in Saint-Gaudens. I looked around outside the Hôtel de France, where it was picking up passengers. Sulpice might have chance to pass by. He didn't. The chain of causes and effects is the great directive force. When will I know, now, the measure in which Bernard deceived me, and deceived his brother in order to leave without him? A lie is very difficult to discover when it is cleverly mingled with the truth.

I would also like to know Malvina's intimate thoughts and her true nature. What motives are governing her actions?

Is she uniquely driven by the desire to make a fortune with the aid of a document whose exact value no one knows? Does she see this voyage more as a means of satisfying her appetite for adventures? If, as Bernard, always avid to debase and depreciate, has let it be understood, she found herself after her father's death in a critical situation that would be aggravated by her solitude in an isolated old château, there might not have been a better reaction for her than this expedition among young men more or less in love with her. But why did she write to Bernard rather than Sulpice, and leave it to him to persuade his brother to depart? I know that a misunderstanding exists between them, caused by Sulpice's incapacity to express his sentiments. Silence is not golden. In any case, speech is a very pure silver. But I'm convinced that if the problem had been explained clearly to Sulpice—to depart or not to depart with Malvina—he would have departed without hesitation. I have no proof, but I'm sure that there was some complicated machination on Bernard's part.

"Voyages are instructive," said my father, sadly, when I left him. "Perhaps you'll travel by railway."

That is an experiment that I have to desire to make. It surpasses my sense of the order of things. Man is not made for traveling on a machine at a speed of thirty-five kilometers an hour.

We were due to meet at the Hôtel des Navigateurs, on the harbor, the address of which Bernard had obtained from Alcide Pécouret. Bernard, who had arrived the day before, was waiting for me when the diligence arrived.

He told me that we would be departing the day after next and that, in consequence, I would have time to make a few indispensable purchases. He did not ask, however, whether I had the money necessary to make them, nor did he ask how I had arranged things with my father.

"Sulpice will only join us tomorrow," he added, incidentally.

"What!" I exclaimed. "Sulpice isn't here?"

"No. I'm sure he'll arrive tomorrow." And he asked me not to tell Malvina that I hadn't seen Sulpice on the day of my departure from Saint-Bertrand. I had the weakness to accept.

I've already noted the intimate pleasure that lying gives me, but the discovery of a fault is not sufficient to annihilate it. Who can even tell whether its root, because it is exposed to the light, might not plunge more joyfully into the soul? I experienced a confused satisfaction in being mingled in a sort of conspiracy relative to Malvina. An interior voice immediately said to me: "You're wrong," but what credit does one give to interior voices, which are often contradictory?

I met Malvina in a little drawing room in the Hôtel des Navigateurs, the walls of which were entirely covered in pictures representing ships of every form. Noël Alga and Martin Bruno were sitting with her. In spite of her mourning she was wearing a Scottish cape with a hood and a black felt hat. Her face was full of the animation that adventure gives and she appeared to me to be even prettier than in the landscapes of Comminges. I remembered the particular fashion in which her eyes had fixed on me on the day of the meeting at the Hôtel de France, I recognized immediately that special gleam in her eyes.

She explained to me that she was staying in that little hotel in order that none of her mother's relatives would know about her plans and her departure.

"My mother's family was from Bordeaux. I still have an old aunt and an old uncle here, who are both in their eighties. Imagine what they'd think if they knew that I was leaving with a group of young men! Captain of gold seekers! They'd die of it."

She laughed, and her laughter had something so engaging that I felt that I was ready to follow her to the ends of the earth.

"But you, who are Sulpice's intimate friend, must know whether he'll arrive tomorrow."

"Undoubtedly. I believe he'll be here, He can't do otherwise."

Noël Alga and Martin Bruno had the same opinion. I thought privately that there was no reason for Sulpice not to have left with them, if he had resolved to depart, and I could not imagine what machination of his brother's had held him back.

The day I spent in Bordeaux was not marked by any event. I scarcely saw Malvina, who spent part of the day with her family's notary. My other traveling companions were running round the shops making all sorts of purchases.

"You ought at least to have a revolver," Bernard told me.

I replied that it was quite sufficient for me to have a medical bag. I had one, of which my father had made me a gift a few months before, and I was proud of it.

Noël Alga is an agreeable person, but singular. We shared the same room at the Hôtel des Navigateurs. He is only occupied with his guitar. He considers it as a small living creature. He gets up at night claiming that he had heard it moan. "It doesn't have the appropriate orientation," he told me. "Then it can't sleep." He moved it, and assured me that it would rest peacefully like that.

Sulpice did not arrive, of course, and when we went to take our places aboard the *Reine Marie* I saw that Malvina had the taut expression on her face that discontentment produces when one doesn't want to let it show.

And now we're sailing toward America. What conclusion ought I to draw about myself? For the knowledge that one has of oneself is the only important thing. I can observe that I'm brainless. I've allowed myself to be persuaded of the existence of a treasure whose reality reposes on a document that I haven't even seen, for I've stupidly put my pride in showing that that I was trusting. I've set forth in pursuit of riches, having as a principle that wealth is evil and an element of corruption. I'm profoundly illogical. And by the light of the interior lamp that outlines the contours of the soul, I can see that in all this, Malvina's gaze has played an occult role. If I welcomed the idea of departure with such rapidity, it's because I'm departing with her. I even wonder whether I don't have a certain satisfaction because Sulpice isn't with us, whatever the deception was on his brother's part of which he might have been the victim.

I daren't go any further in my self-examination. I've looked out of the porthole and the expanse of the moonlit sea. The waves fade away in the distance, infinitely, and a thousand glints play over them. I think about Monsieur de Lamartine. I ought to have a moving sensation of beauty. Nothing of the sort. The spectacle of nature doesn't procure me the stirrings of the soul of which poets speak. Nature bores me. I've already observed the uniformity of all sunsets. They resemble one another like the faces of pretty young women devoid of intelligence. Ought I to criticize myself for not savoring the magnificence of those colors spread with profusion and comparing them to pictures too hastily painted by hurried artists? I don't know. That must be a fault of my nature. But alas, I'm incessantly discovering graver ones.

II. *Aboard the* Reine Marie

"It's absolutely evident," said Noël Alga, "that those thin white birds that pass back and forth between the masts and give the impression of melting into the darkness, are the souls of dead mariners."

Dr. Fazeuille did not yield to the evidence in question.

"There is a subtle life that unfurls around us and in which it is sometimes permitted to us to participate. It only lasts a few seconds. I'm sure that it has happened to you, as it has to me, to hear those voices, to perceive things that have their existence in another world."

Dr. Fazeuille shook his head. It had never happened to him.

"Once, in the mountains, I went to sleep in a clearing. I was woken up by the sounds of a flute. It sometimes resonated to my right, sometimes to my left, always close by. The sun was about to rise. I went this way and that to discover what that early morning musician was. But the woods, especially above a certain height, are full of little creatures, which are almost all musicians and love to make fun of humans."

"Perhaps I've never gone up high enough in the mountains."

"Well, I can see that a ship transports in creatures with it, but of a different nature. It's only natural that the spirits of mariners who have been shipwrecked, which are wandering over the waves, would attach themselves to a passing ship. But I wonder..."

Dr. Fazeuille was not sure whether Noël Alga was serious, but as a matter of principle, he did not contradict anyone. He did not smile.

"Yes, was I the victim of an illusion? Last night I got up and I went up on deck. I went to the rear, where the emigrants are accumulated. Some of them were singing. I listened to them for a long time, and then I came back. I was going along the passageway where the cabins are. There ought not to be more than twenty people in those cabins and for two days I've known the silhouettes of all the passengers. Well, I went past a woman that I'd never seen: a young woman, in fact, and singularly seductive. I went past her just at a place illuminated by a tremulous lantern. Her head was wrapped in a fire-colored mantilla and I think I remarked that she was wearing red sandals. She wasn't hurrying, and there was something provocative in her gaze.

"She looked me full in the face and for a moment I thought that it was Mademoiselle de Noussoulens; I'd swear that they resemble one another. In any case, they have eyes of the same color. If I'd said something to her she would have replied. It was surprise that prevented me. When I wanted to do it, it was too late. She'd disappeared. But what is strange is that I didn't hear any door closing. And it seemed to me that she wasn't making any noise as she walked. Her red sandals, in the silence of the passageway, ought to have had a certain resonance. I saw, but I didn't hear. I wonder..."

"It could well be that there's a passenger we haven't yet seen. She was walking a quietly as possible. Her coquetry ensured that, even to traverse an obscure passageway, she knotted a flame-colored mantilla round her head. All that's normal. Tomorrow, perhaps that nocturnal apparition will take her meal with us."

"I'm not sure about that."

"I believe, Mademoiselle de Noussoulens, that I knew your mother in Bordeaux. My name is Anastasio Alaman, and perhaps you've heard my name pronounced."

Anastasio Alaman had swept the deck with his immense white felt hat.

"Oh, that happened many years ago—a long time, even a very long time—and when I saw her for the first time you had only just been born. I saw her again when you were a little girl and I can even tell you that you made a journey to Bordeaux when you must have been about five years old. I saw you then, only for a few minutes, but I haven't forgotten it, for my memory is reliable. You must certainly have known Madame Alfortas."

That name projected something akin to a beam of light into the mist of Malvina's memories. Oh yes, she had heard the name of Madame Alfortas. "She's a fine procuress, your Alice Alfortas!" That remark of her father's was engraved in her memory because she did not know what a procuress was and, in spite of long research, she had not been able to divine the meaning of the word. And that Anastasio Alaman had often been mentioned in the Château de Noussoulens! Malvina had only listened distractedly then.

"He's very respectable," her mother had said. "A man like any other, I assure you."

Her father had laughed bitterly. "A bandit is a man like any other. He can be well-dressed, as polite, and pay court to women in the same fashion."

"But Madame Alfortas wouldn't permit herself..."

"Aha! Let's talk about her. I knew her husband. Alfortas was a pirate. The English put a price on his head in Jamaica and Cuba. And he was invited to dinner in good society in Bordeaux!"

With regard to the good society of Bordeaux, Malvina remembered, her father never ran out of insults. "You'll never go to Bordeaux," he had often said to her. She had, however, gone there. Her father, in a moment of weakness, had let her mother take her for a few days. And now a rapid scene returned to her memory. There was a park enclosed by walls along an extent of water that must have been the Gironde. Night had fallen. It was at Madame Alfortas' house. Malvina was playing in a drawing room with other little girls. Her mother came to fetch her. It was raining, but in spite of that her mother had dragged her into the park. Near a carriage, someone dressed in a big overcoat was walking back and forth. Malvina remembered that her mother had said something like: "I promised to show her to you. Here she is."

The man in the overcoat had looked at her curiously, and said: "She's really quite lovely."

She had heard other words spoken that she could not remember and had not understood. She had had the sentiment of an atmosphere of sadness, perhaps of adieu.

"You can go back in now," her mother had said, and she had departed at a run.

All that was very confused, blurred in the past. Perhaps it was an imaginary scene. She was astonished, however, that her mother only returned a few minutes after her, in spite of the rain. And now she was wondering whether the individual who had once leaned over in the sad park had not borne a resemblance to the man who was now in front of her. Both had those moustaches with turned-up points, which had to be the object of constant care. Perhaps it had gone gray over time— but it was the same face, curious, mobile and passionate.

So, Anastasio Alaman was before her. What an incomparable seduction a bad reputation can provide! How much he knew about the unknown lands toward which she was going! How eloquently he talked! How he loved his country, that Mexican.

In the evening, the passengers formed a group on deck, of which he was the center. There was Malvina and her four companions. There was a shoemaker from Saint-Béat who had not been able to embark on the *Invincible*. There was Blaise Espondeillan, who had allowed his companions to embark at the last moment, promising to meet up with them out there— "out there," meaning Mexico as well as California, the distance between the two countries not being very clear to anyone. There was a fencing-master; an Alsatian who thought he would make a fortune selling dark glasses to the Mexicans, who said "It's a country where the sun is ardent and dark glasses are only known to a few merchants; and a Mexican general who affected a mysterious air and only consented to speak to Colonel Espondeillan.

"We, at least, are soldiers." And he had added, confidentially: "Don't trust that individual in the white hat who's holding forth in the midst of your compatriots."

"Ah," said Anastasio Alaman, "a new world is going to appear to us—or, rather, worlds, which are infinite in their variety. You might reach the land of Culiacan, full of guavas, orange trees, palm trees and trees such as you've never seen; the Guasteca, where ponds alternate with forests, Guadalajara, filled with silver mines and where it's sufficient, in order to make a fortune, to exploit the abandoned seams: Mechoacan, where the Tarasque Indians live; Tlascala, which is an ancient Indian republic—a republic older than yours, you understand; the province of Oxaca, flourishing with nopals, where the julep root is found; Tabasco, where there are woods of giant cedars; and Verapaz, where the sugar canes are more than fifteen feet high."

"Do you know a town called Acoma?" Malvina asked.

No sooner had she spoken those words than she regretted it. Anastasio's face did not show any surprise, but he remained silent for a few minutes. He reflected.

"How do you know that town?" he asked, in the most natural fashion. But his voice had a different tone, involuntarily, and his keen gaze was studying Malvina's face.

"I don't know. I've hear it mentioned. Oh, vaguely...people talk so much about America."

"Acoma is a long way from Vera Cruz, a long way even for Mexico. It's dangerous country. Do you have the intention of going there?"

She started to laugh to attenuate the curiosity that her question had awakened.

"No, I don't think so. We don't know yet. We'll see, we'll reflect."

"It's just that, for some people the name evokes tragedies, and for others hopes."

They talked about something else. Some of Anastasio's listeners got up and walked along the deck. He continued talking and the conversation returned of its own accord to everyone's preoccupation, the goal that had impelled them to change their destiny: the search for gold.

"Mexico is the classic land of hidden treasures. Although, when one has a certain experience of life like me, one perceives that the pursuit of treasures is more impassioning than their discovery. There are a great many men in Mexico, perhaps the most intelligent, who, instead of enjoying life, march bent over toward the shadows of the earth, with the hope of discerning riches there that they would not know how to use if they fell into their power. There are patriots, scholars and artists, as elsewhere, but the best of their activity is secretly turned toward the mirage of hidden treasure. Thus, for example, I have a son whom you might perhaps know..."

"You have a son?"

Anastasio was doubtless about to talk about his son; but the Mexican general, who was pacing the deck with Colonel Espondeillan, went past the group at that moment. He slowed down, pretending to be occupied in launching the smoke of his cigar toward the sky in successive spirals. Anastasio perceived that movement and fell silent. The general drew away, but those few seconds must have served to orient the Mexican's thoughts in a different direction. He made a gesture that might have signified: *We'll talk about that another time.*

"Why are there more hidden treasures in Mexico than elsewhere? Mexico is the land of gold. Great civilizations succeeded one another there, civilizations in which the most ordinary objects were made of gold. Every time there were conquerors and vanquished, the vanquished hid their riches at the moment of flight. And that was still happening not long ago. Oh, all that there might be in Vera Cruz, forgotten, lost, dead!

"Might there not be the treasures of the Jesuits, the six or seven hundred monks who came to Vera Cruz at the time of the expulsion of the Order, with long files of mules laden with all the treasures of their convents. They were embarked for Europe having only the right to take with them the robes on their backs. What became of their riches? They're within the limits of Vera Cruz, but where?

"Somewhere there is a life-sized statue of the Virgin of Guadeloupe, sculpted in solid gold. A Tlascalan chief from Jalisco, having roused the Indians to revolt, formed the project of taking possession of it and founding, with the same block of gold, a stature of the god Huitzilopochtli. He was also going to blow up the Viceroy's palace. That was discovered, and the statue of the Virgin was moved in order to protect it. But it never returned. Where is it?

"And Mexico City? Mexico City is constructed on the ruins of Tenochtitlan, which Cortès knew to be the richest city in the world, where enormous quantities of gold were contained. When Cortès penetrated into it, after a three-month siege, he found almost nothing. The gold had disappeared into wells with invisible rims, into tunnels whose entrances were buried under water. The channels and lakes hide treasures beneath their silent mud. Mexico is still even richer than California. It is, however, toward California that all the pilgrims of fortune come from the four corners of the world.

"Oh, the folly of hidden treasures! I've had it, like everyone else. But now I say to myself: What's the point? I wonder whether it isn't after their misfortune that people are running. Perhaps there's more joy in the puff of smoke that I blow than in the great mass of virgin gold of which the sacred pyramid of Tenochtitlan was made..."

Anastasio Alaman had a singularly mobile gaze, and he was watching, without appearing to do so, the impression that his speech had on his listeners. Malvina was particularly subject to his charm. One thing, however, astonished her. When Anastasio told stories about his youth, the name of Alfortas often recurred. That name was well known to Malvina. Madame Alfortas had been her mother's friend. It was in her house that she stayed in Bordeaux. One of her father's principal grievances, with regard to her visits to Bordeaux, was the amity of Madame Alfortas.

"Perhaps I wouldn't have anything to say on her subject, except that she's a procuress by inclination," he said. "But him! He's well known. He's been able to marry a d'Andignac.

157

He's nevertheless made a fortune as a sea-rover in the Antilles Sea. I'm not taking about trade in blacks. That's nothing—but he's a pirate, a veritable pirate, now mingling with the flower of Bordeaux society."

And Malvina remembered her father striding back and forth in the dining room, amid the large sideboards of black oak, gesticulating and menacing, and her mother remaining silent, with a scarcely visible smile, because she knew that the rude bear-hunter was too weak to exert his authority other than in violent words.

"My friend Alfortas," Anastasio Alaman said, putting into the syllables of that name the particular intonation of the evocation of memories. "You have the same eyes as him."

And Malvina saw again the picture once created by her childish imagination: the deck of a ship where women and children were on their knees in the middle of dead mariners and men with atrocious faces, their heads surrounded by red kerchiefs, a knife between their teeth, scaling the rails; a naïve image that the word "pirate" caused to surge forth in her mind's eye.

"It was after Moscow, in complete disarray. Wounded, unable to do any more, I was sitting in the snow. What would have become of me? God alone knows. It was at that moment that the Emperor's coach went by. I can still hear him saying to Duroc, who was beside him: 'We mustn't let young Espondeillan die.' Those were his own words."

And Colonel Espondeillan recounted how he had passed over the Berezina..

General Ozorno's principal concern was being superior to any event, and not being impressed by anything.[5]

"The great Napoléon knew men," he contented himself with replying, disguising his admiration.

---

[5] The General's name is rendered as Orsono here in the original text, but changed to Ozorno when he reappears again in Mexico City.

While Blaise Espondeillan told other stories, though, he meditated, and he finally spoke.

"You see, Colonel, it's a considerable title, in Mexico, to have known Napoléon. The great Iturbide had beside him as an intimate counselor a veteran of the Emperor of the French, and a milliner who had sold hats to the Empress Josephine, by virtue of that fact alone, dictated fashion in Mexico for years. Alas, our current President, General Arista, is unable to distinguish men of value. He keeps them away, even systematically, from power. He has the scruple of honesty. How can one occupy oneself with honesty when one governs? Don't talk to me about honesty! It's a pettiness that shackles all great ideas. Honesty immediately engenders economy, and if a person in power wants to make economies, he does nothing. Furthermore, he's been abandoned by all men of value, who need lucrative appointments, for it isn't just that talent should be limited by mediocrity. Integrity! General Arista says that he has integrity! I hope, Colonel, that you're not a victim of the weakness that is integrity?"

The colonel had that weakness. At any other time he would have responded with severe words. But he had entered into a new life. He was going to frequent new men. Ought he not to make a few concessions?

"The functionaries are being diminished, the troops reduced, to make economies! Arista will lead Mexico to ruin if he's allowed to continue. But we won't let him do it. There are men who are working n silence for his removal. You've certainly heard mention of Santa Anna?"

Espondeillan knew nothing about Santa Anna.[6] He thought it politic to lie.

---

[6] This seems unlikely; Antonio Lopez de Santa Anna (1794-1876), sometimes called "the Napoléon of the West" in spite of being one of history's greatest agents of military catastrophe, was world-famous long before 1851, having already served as President of the Mexican Republic and lost two wars against America, in the course of which he even made heavy

"He's a great man, the victor of Tampico, our former president. Oh, he didn't economize! His carriage was drawn by eight white mules, the most beautiful in Mexico, and in all his displacements he was accompanied by his cocks, whose nourishment he supervised personally. A great president ought to organize cock fights everywhere he goes, for the joy of the people. Think that, at official dinners, he always had six colonels in dress uniforms standing behind him, and protocol demanded that there were a dozen generals in his box at the theater.

"And what is even more extraordinary about him is that he loved the French! I say that it's extraordinary because it was a cannonball fired from a French ship that had cost him a leg at Vera Cruz. Well, in spite of that he's seeking Frenchmen and gathering them around him. He's counting on them to inform him. For he's awaiting his hour, which is imminent. I'm telling you this because I'm authorized by my master to make certain promises, to certain Frenchmen of quality. But I can't tell you any more for the moment. I must ask you for absolute secrecy regarding what I'm about to say.

"At this moment Santa Anna is in Venezuela, where he has bought a hacienda. He's taking advantage of his leisure to construct a tomb of immense proportions, his own future tomb. He needs a reliable man near him who will receive the title of Director of Santa Anna's Tomb—with a high salary, of course. I thought that you might be that man. We'll talk about it again later, in Vera Cruz or Mexico. Note that there's no need, in order to occupy that post, of architectural or mortuary knowledge."

Colonel Espondeillan thought that the singularity of that title—Director of Santa Anna's Tomb—was part of the new

---

weather of taking the Alamo. He was, however, invited back from exile in 1853 after a weak liberal government was overthrown and became President again. His right-hand man during that resurgence was the ultra-conservative Lucas Alamán (1792-1853).

order toward which he had started marching. He was at a loose end, and, above all, solitary. He had no one in whom to confide. All his compatriots embarked on the *Reine Marie* were too young for him, or of a social rank inferior to his own. He considered Malvina to be brainless, perhaps wanton, and he was scornful of the four young men who were accompanying her.

He wondered why he had left. His pension and the income from a small property in Boussens had been sufficient for him to live on. He had been carried away by the prospect of command. He had seen himself at the head of a small troop of gold-seekers who would be disciplined and militarized. And then that troop had appointed another leader! That was the wound from which he was suffering. Should not Colonel de Chalabre have refused to be elected in his stead?

They were two intimate friends and equals in amity, at least in appearance. But the superiority of Espondeillan over his friend was obvious from all points of view. At least, he thought so. In their interminable conversations, in which they revised the strategy of all the Imperial wars together, his opinion was always the correct one. When, face to face across a table, they displaced armies represented by little pebbles, when they recommenced Austerlitz and Waterloo, he was always the one who had the upper hand.

The thing was never clearly expressed because Chalabre was the silent type, poorly endowed from the point of view of speech. But Espondeillan had always considered himself to be infinitely superior to his comrade. It was only in dueling with a saber that they appeared to be almost equal, and even then, Espondeillan judged himself superior in that too. Often, though, he had deliberately allowed his friend to seem to be the victor in order not to humiliate him by surpassing him in everything.

Now, he suspected Chalabre of having had joy in being proclaimed the President of the Companions of the Virgin Gold in his stead. Yes, he had seen that joy in his gaze. Chalabre must have been jealous of him for a long time. Now he was enjoying his triumph. He had become a leader. He was in command, while he was alone and did not know exactly toward what destiny he was going. He remembered their last conversation. Chalabre had begged him not to quit him.

"You're my brother," he had said to him. "If we don't depart together, we'll never see one another again. I can't admit that idea." And he had proposed abandoning the gold-seekers and departing with him.

But that was a hypocritical offer! And anyway, in saying "You're my brother," should he not have added "and my master"?

The last word had not been said. They would see of what Colonel Espondeillan was capable. Who could tell? Perhaps he had been judged too old. Chalabre was two years younger than him, and he suspected him of dyeing his hair. By means of artifice, he made people judge him younger than he was. And then, there were the stars. The famous stars, of which he made so much. Was that not ridiculous? He had ordered a telescope from Toulouse in order to see them better, and had built himself a tower, which he called an observatory, in which to put the telescope. As if it were not sufficient to raise one's head, quite simply, to contemplate the extent of the sky.

Oh, he only realized now, while pacing the deck of the *Reine Marie*, that his old friend Colonel Bertrand de Chalabre was nothing but a joke.

Well, he would accept the post of Director of the Tomb of Santa Anna, strange as that title might appear at first glance. It was a question of mentality. In the New World, one could be a director of a tomb, just as, in France, one could be the director of a school. He would get to know Santa Anna, he would conspire, he would arrive at an important position, and it would be known throughout Comminges!

But there was something that he would never know. That was the peace of mind, the amicable mildness that he had experienced almost every evening when, on the road to Saint-Béat, he had accompanied his friend to the house of the telescope and the tower, and, as he drew away in the distance, he shouted from a distance: "Adieu, Chalabre!" and heard the voice of Chalabre reply: "Adieu, Espondeillan! Until tomorrow!"

"I believe I'm in love," said Noël Alga to his friend Fazeuille, one evening when they were exchanging confidences in the little cabin that they shared.

"You aren't telling me anything new."

Noël Alga shook his head.

"It's not what you think. Anyway, I don't understand very well myself what's happening within me. I'm in love with the young woman I passed the other night, who has eyes almost the same color as those of Malvina de Noussoulens."

"I've already noticed that one is attached to the same model of human beauty, and that one only loves creatures who have a certain resemblance to one another. But didn't you tell me that the young woman with the red sandals belonged to an immaterial world?"

"I thought so. I've been undeceived. I've talked to her."

"In a terrestrial language?"

"Yes. When you're asleep, you know that I sometimes go up on deck. In this calm weather the nights are delightful. That's the moment when she walks with her father."

"Her father?"

"She's Anastasio Alaman's daughter."

"Why doesn't she take her meals with the other passengers?"

"That's a whole story, which she told me, because she sometimes walks on the deck on her own. She told it to me without disguising anything. At first, she thought about masking the truth, and then she laughed and I understood that she had decided to tell me everything. She even did it with a certain cynicism. Perhaps too much. Mexican women don't resemble those of our homeland."

"There are cynical women everywhere. I even knew one in Rabastens.

"The one you told me about as the great love of your life?"

"Yes, Gisèle. She was cynical—also too much."

"This one is called Carlotta. She stays enclosed in her cabin, where her meals are brought to her, because her father fears her liking for liberty—that's the expression of which she makes use, but it means the excess of her temperament. She had herself abducted by the son of a businessman in Bordeaux. Her father was able to take a ship that left from Vera Cruz the next day but nevertheless arrived in Bordeaux two days before the one his daughter was on. That Anastasio Alaman gives the impression of being a man who knows life. He had warned the father of the young man, with the result that Carlotta and her lover were greeted on the quay at Bordeaux by their respective fathers, after a few weeks' honeymoon in an uncomfortable cabin. Carlotta is a minor and it was easy for Anastasio Alaman to reembark her immediately. And this is where the young woman's cynicism bursts forth. She said to me: 'Fundamentally, I'm not sorry that happened. The experience was sufficient for me. The young man from Bordeaux was a simpleton, much too jealous for my taste.'"

"I'm struck by the resemblance of character between that young woman and Gisèle. She also found me too simple and too jealous."

"I'm wondering whether there's a very clear difference between confidence and stupidity. That young woman doesn't wear a fire-colored mantilla and kerchief in vain. She was born under the sign of fire. Those who get close to her will be burned."

"Beware, then I too have been burned, a few years ago."

"Mexican fire is terribly ardent. Every night, Carlotta comes to join me on deck, when her father is asleep. I believe that that Anastasio Alaman in a very shrewd man, but the shrewdest of men has a weak point. That one is a heavy sleeper. I believe he drinks. According to what his daughter has told me, he's accustomed to a sort of alcohol the Indians drink, called mescal, and he can't do without it. Carlotta and I go to sit down between heaps of rope at the front of the ship. I even play her tunes of the guitar softly. And we make plans for when we disembark."

"What plans?"

"You'll see."

"And I thought you were in love with Malvina."

"Perhaps I am. I don't know. I wonder if one isn't in love with a single young woman who presents herself in life under different aspects. For, after all, almost all young women say very nearly the same things. They have very nearly the same thoughts. Some resemble one another physically. So I tell myself that one is wrong to experience excessive suffering when one passes from one to another. Fundamentally, it would be wise to consider that it's always the same one who accompanies you in existence, with only a few slight changes."

"You see," said Dr. Fazeuille, in a melancholy tone, "I would have like Gisèle to accompany me through existence. But she didn't want to. I would even be content with an imitation of Gisèle—her double, even one worse than her. I've never encountered one and perhaps I never will encounter one. In amour, it's primarily a question of physique. It's necessary to have a physique that pleases women."

"Without being complimentary, you look fine—apart from the beard...I don't know why you wear the beard."

"The beard gives the face gravity, and one has a tendency to conform to what one represents."

"Without your beard, I'm sure that you'd please many women."

Dr. Fazeuille made a vague gesture and changed the subject.

As she went up on deck, shortly before sunset, Malvina was struck by a spectacle that seemed to her to be singular.

Since the previous day, a large shark had been following the ship. It was following it very closely. The passengers went to see it, measured its size and exclaimed. Now, leaning over the water, Anastasio Alaman, his arms extended, was intoning a bizarre chant, in a language with harsh sonorities. A number of attentive mariners were grouped around him.

Malvina approached Captain Courtin.

"What is he doing?"

"He's supposed to be driving away the shark."

"But how?"

"Anastasio Alaman flatters himself on possessing many secrets," Captain Courtin said, "and perhaps, in fact, he has a few. His mother was an Indian sorceress from the island of Cerralvo in the Gulf of California.[7] It's an island where all the inhabitants are pearl-fishers. A few women there know—or are supposed by tradition to know—certain magical chants that have the power of driving away sharks when her men are diving. The Gulf of California is, with the Gulf of Mexico, one of the locations in the ocean most tormented by sharks. Anastasio Alaman has inherited his mother's secrets. As you see, he's in the process of making use of one."

"I'd like to know whether it's true, and whether he's succeeded."

As she arrived at the rear, Anastasio had just stopped. Night had fallen and the waves became abruptly agitated. It was difficult to see whether the shark had obeyed the incantations.

"It ought to have gone," said Anastasio, in a tone that was only half-serious, "but night had fallen in time to prevent us from making sure of it. Nature always arranges to hide the proof of everything out of the ordinary."

"I'll take advantage of it to give you some advice," said Captain Courtin, drawing Malvina to one side. "I'm Bordelais and I met your mother once, a long time ago. There was a slight amicable bond between us. I often see you conversing with Anastasio Alaman. I would like, not to put you on your guard—that would be to say too much—but, in sum, to observe some reserve with him in regard to your personal affairs.

---

[7] The former Isla Cerralvo is now called Jacques Cousteau Island.

166

Oh, he's a fine man. He has important affairs, although no one knows exactly what they are—he has a large fortune, the origin of which no one knows. But in Vera Cruz he is greatly feared.

"A strange story is whispered in his regard. When people talk about him they say: 'That's the man who possesses Santa Anna's leg.' I'll explain to you. When a French fleet laid siege of Vera Cruz, a cannonball fired from the sea off San Juan de Ulloa broke one of the legs of Santa Anna, who had taken command of the resistance. It was necessary to amputate it. Shortly thereafter, Santa Anna was elected President of Mexico. The city of Mexico did not know what to do to render him honors. His admirers thought of this: they brought Santa Anna's leg from Manga de Clavo, where it was buried and it was placed solemnly in the cathedral.

"But Santa Anna lost his popularity. Paredes beat him, and one day, the rabble of Mexico found nothing better to do than steal the leg from the cathedral and pull it through the streets at the end of a rope. It's here that Anastasio Alaman enters the scene. It appears—for it's not a certainty, but a story that is told—that Anastasio and his elder son were seen that day following the band of leperos that were dragging the leg. In the evening, they brought the leperos drinks, distributed a few piastres, and took away the leg—not without killing one of the leperos, it appears, who, more cunning than the rest, wanted to keep it.

"What can one do with a mummified leg, you ask me? Apparently, nothing. But it's necessary to know that Anastasio and his son are occupied in magic—what is generally called black magic. It's also necessary to know that if one wants to cast a spell on a man successfully, it's essential to have a fragment of him. One normally makes use of hair or nail-clippings. Personally, I don't believe in any of that, and I think that magic only exists in order to make the fortune of charlatans; but the Mexicans are extremely credulous in that order of ideas, infinitely more than our compatriots. I'm sure that you've never heard talk of spell-casting or anything similar?"

"Almost never, in fact. However, I knew a Portuguese who believed in it firmly."

"But this is the important part of the story. Santa Anna is a man who believes in magic, and Alaman must have known that. When Santa Anna learned that his leg had been disinterred and that it was in Alaman's hands, he was terrified. First he tried to buy it. Then he tried to get it back by force. Alaman disappeared for some time. Has he indulged in blackmail since? No one knows. But when he's been drinking he boasts of being able to send Santa Anna either headaches or stomach aches—any pains that he pleases—and he affirms that he can dispose of his life. I'm telling you this story in order to depict the man. He's perfectly courteous, intelligent, and brilliant, but no one knows what there is behind that appearance. So I'm telling you: be wary of him."

It was too late. Malvina had already told him everything about her projects. That had happened the same morning. Anastasio had encountered Malvina alone on the deck.

"Look me in the face," he had said to her, giving a character of levity to his gestures and the tone of his speech. "That's right, straight in the eyes. I'll show you my qualities of extra-lucid sight. You have a slender gold chain around your neck. Something very precious is suspended from that chain. When a woman has something she wants to conserve, she wears it on her person, suspended on a chain like that, of which everyone can glimpse a part, beneath your hair. Well, I'll tell you what there is on the end of that chain. It's a document. And in that document there's mention of the town of Acoma, a certain Socrates, and a Spanish cathedral."

Struck with astonishment, Malvina had not had sufficient strength of mind to disguise the fact that it was true. She had stammered: "But how can you know that…? It's impossible that you know that…! I haven't said anything to you…"

"I've seen accurately, haven't I?" exclaimed Anastasio, delighted at having achieved his objective. "But I don't want you to believe in my powers of sorcery. I can't see through a young woman's garments the secrets that she carries at the end of a gold chan. I simply made a series of small deductions. For you to enquire about the town of Acoma, lost in the middle of deserts, there had to be a reason. Now, you've named someone who, to my knowledge, has passed through that town, stayed there, and had reasons for returning there. And I knew, moreover, that the person in question was to go to Bordeaux, where he had friends.

"In the minuscule sachet that is at the end of that chain, I glimpsed a piece of paper through the mesh. What could that piece of paper contain, if not some indications related to the goal of your voyage? For it needs a powerful motive for a young woman who lives in the Pyrenees to set forth across the seas, and for her to group around her a few resolute young men. I have reasons for believing that the motive in question includes as essential givens: the town of Acoma, a region where the Indians have blue eyes, and, above all, a cathedral. And I can add that the possession of those details still leaves you far from the total."

Having said that, as if he were the victim of a kind of spell, which he had cast on himself without meaning to do so, Anastasio Alaman fell silent. Although he had sought to know Malvina's secret thoughts and the goal of her journey, and although he had employed a ruse for that, he suddenly appeared disinterested in what had previously impassioned him. His features expressed various sentiments, but fear was not absent therefrom. There had to be an evocation that was perhaps redoubtable in the name of the town of Acoma and in a cathedral standing somewhere in the middle of a savage country where the Indians have blue eyes. He was looking at the distant horizon of the sea, and perhaps the silhouette of that cathedral was designed there for him.

He turned toward the stupefied Malvina.

"I dare not give you advice, for one never supposes that advice is disinterested, but if you are wise, if you value your life and those of your companions, you should destroy the document that you believe to be precious and never think about it again. Above all, avoid pronouncing before any living person the names that it contains and the name of the man who gave it to you."

He drew away. Abruptly, he retraced his steps.

"I don't know exactly what the document you posses contains. Perhaps there is mention of someone named Socrates. Never do that. Anything is preferable. Remember what I'm telling you at this moment. Never try to see a man named Socrates."

The *Reine Marie* stopped over for two days in New Orleans before departing again for Vera Cruz. Anastasio Alaman had promised his new friends to take them to visit the city.

"You'll see that there are shops and restaurants unlike any in Bordeaux, or even Paris. I know a place on the shore of Lake Pontchartrain where one can eat crayfish cooked in the creole style and steamed fish from the Mississippi, that one doesn't find anywhere else in America."

Anastasio, Malvina and her companions were slightly astonished that Noël Alga did not accompany them. He only gave confused reasons.

"I haven't come to America to see negroes."

But they were aware of his whimsical nature. No one was unduly astonished.

"What a pity," said Malvina, on the second evening. "He plays the guitar so well and knows so many Pyrenean songs. He would have loved these banjos and these songs that we French have never heard anywhere."

"Who knows?" said Bernard Borromée. "He might be listening to other banjos and other negro songs. We haven't arrived yet, and already he's separated himself. In my opinion, one should never put one's confidence in someone who plays the guitar."

The *Reine Marie* was due to depart early the next morning. Dr. Fazeuille was on deck before sunrise. The previous evening, late into the night, he had waited for his cabin-mate. When first light showed through the porthole he had woken up and observed that Noël was not there. He had dressed in haste and had gone up to warn Captain Courtin.

The latter, a man full of benevolence, was like many weak men. When it is necessary for them to defend a resolution, they become more severe that the situation requires, in order to disguise their weakness.

Captain Courtin had taken on the forbidding aspect of a pitiless ship's captain, a slave of decisions and discipline.

"Two passengers are absent. So much the worse for them. The *Reine Marie* needs the morning breeze to tack. She'll depart at the appointed time."

Two passengers! Dr. Fazeuille divined who the other was when he saw Anastasio Alaman leaning on the rail. He strove to snigger on seeing the doctor, in order not to let his anger show.

"I suppose your friend is busy amusing himself in New Orleans, eh? You, who are a doctor, must know that it's physiological in our old European races. There are many men whose blood is degenerate, who think of nothing but pleasure, women, good food—and a guitar to give oneself the illusion that one is an artist. It's all a matter of blood."

He was speaking with rage, in the direction of the quay, with the hope of seeing the silhouette of a young woman in a red mantilla appear. Dr. Fazeuille attempted to explain, softly, that Noël Alga did not belong to the category of degenerate men that he had just mentioned, but Anastasio was not listening. He spoke as if the doctor were informed of the existence of his daughter.

"And to think that I foresaw everything! It's necessary to believe presentiments and not reject them as follies. I thought about throwing your friend overboard by seizing him by the feet one evening when he was looking at the sea back there at the rear. There was a shark following us. Everything would have been settled."

The doctor interrupted him to remind him that he had driven the shark away himself by magical practices.

For scarcely a second, Anastasio measured the sum of irony contained in that remark; then he continued:

"I'll give you some good advice. It's the wisdom of my entire life. When one is facing an adversary—in a brawl or a business deal, it's the same thing—it's always necessary to strike the first blow. In the brawl, one looks, one hesitates, one feels one's knife. The victor is the more audacious, the one who strikes first. In business, it's necessary to steal before one is robbed. I should have attached my daughter with a chain, like an animal, and thrown the guitar-player to the shark. The first blow—that's everything. Remember that, Doctor. In Mexico, it's always necessary to strike the first blow."

Anastasio Alaman reflected, and then, suddenly, seemed to make a decision. He ran down to his cabin, and when he reappeared on deck he had a striped blanked over his arm and his big white hat on his head. He had also put on his leather belt, garnished with weapons. He searched with his eyes for Captain Courtin. He did not see him, and changed his mind again. He threw the blanket on to a banquette at the foot of the mainmast, and sat down. He leaned back, affecting nonchalance, and lit a cigar.

The *Reine Marie* began to move.

"Doctor! Doctor!" he shouted.

The latter approached.

"A doctor knows better than anyone. Men, women, we're pigs, nothing but pigs. We like enjoyment, eating, putting ourselves on our backs. We only live for that. Miserable humanity!"

III. The Adventure of the Shoemaker
from Saint-Béat

Here is inserted the adventure of Barthélémy Dalbiès, native of the village of Encausse and shoemaker of Saint-Béat.

"You're a man of simple tastes, Barthélémy; you have everything you need here. What the devil's got into you, going to look for gold in America?"

Barthélémy Dalbiès earned his living in Saint-Béat. His shop was minuscule, but he had more work than he could handle. He was laborious and, above all, a man of his word. He was proud of delivering what he had promised on the dated fixed.

"If I've said Wednesday, you can count on having your clogs on Wednesday, That's Barthélémy's law. I always keep my word."

Clogs were his specialty. He also excelled in all solid footwear, country footwear, and in the restitching of old boots, to which he rendered life until the ultimate limits of old age, but he took to extreme perfection the rustic clog, with which one confronts mud in labor and sunken roads, which one stuffs with straw and keeps the foot warm in winter.

The previous year, Barthélémy had lost his wife, the severe Marinette, a good housekeeper, but tight-fisted. Since then, Barthélémy, always so punctual, had become more taciturn. He was a man who scarcely went out, who had no curiosity, and, with so many sabots, he was assumed to be well off.

"But after all, what would you do with money, if you found any?" his neighbor, the baker, had asked him when he learned that, without consulting anyone, Barthélémy had gone to see Alcide Pécouret and had given him two thousand francs in order to be inscribed among those that the Lyonnais society took charge of taking to America.

Barthélémy had replied: "First of all, one never has enough money. There are farmers who have a pair of clogs that could hold their feet for the rest of their lives. Neverthe-

173

less, they order another pair from me, and then another. They never have enough clogs. Money is similar. Then, perhaps you don't know what Marinette was like. She lived modestly, but she had a taste for houses such as the rich have. Then when she was about to die, I promised to build her a tomb that would be the most beautiful in Saint-Béat cemetery—a tomb with marble, such as one only sees in Toulouse. I'm a man of my word. I promised Marinette and she must be impatient. I have to find the means to build that tomb."

"But if you don't find anything, if you don't make a fortune, not only will you have spent all that you have, but you'll die of hunger yourself in the midst of negroes and redskins."

"A man who has a trade and is laborious can always exercise that trade," Barthélémy replied, with a great deal of common sense.

And he left—but not with his compatriots. In accordance with a misconception that was commonplace among chimerical souls on the banks of the Garonne, it did not matter to him whether he disembarked in one place or another in America, because there was gold everywhere and a resourceful man had his fortune assured no matter where he was. He had asked to be disembarked in New Orleans.

"It appears that they speak French there, as in Saint-Béat," his wife had said to him one day on reading a letter. "It's exactly like here with regard to society, except that there are a lot more negroes."

That letter had been received three years before. It came from Eugène Peytava, Marinette's brother, who was out there, placed as a domestic in a big house—not an ordinary domestic but a kind of steward in a very large house of very important people, said Marinette, when she talked about her brother. And her husband never failed to add: "Eugène is one of a kind!"

The letter, with his brother-in-law's address, had been lost. But Barthélémy had no doubt that he would be able to find Eugène Peytava easily as soon as he arrived in New Orleans. Eugène Peytava the steward could not pass unperceived! He was one of a kind!

Aboard the *Reine Marie*, Barthélémy Dalbiès had passed almost unperceived. He was intimidated by Malvina, by Bernard and by Colonel Espondeillan. The daughter of Noussoulens, the nephew of Bishop Borromée and the man who had known Napoléon were individuals from another world, to whom he was content to address a respectful salute in the morning and evening. He had asked the passengers who were designated to him as residents of New Orleans whether they knew a steward by the name of Eugène Peytava. The response had been negative, but that had not discouraged him. He was not at all troubled, either, by the idea that he had had no news of his brother-in-law in three years, in spite of the intimacy that had once bound them together. He was certain of being welcomed with open arms—for the more imprecise a hope is, the more power it has in the soul.

They had passed the bar with its great line of foam. The *Reine Marie* had gone up the yellow waters of the Mississippi. Amazed, the inhabitants of the banks of the Garonne gazed at an infinity of low-lying ground, the desolate realm of floating mud, partly-dried clay and stagnant waters, a world never seen and never imagined, the haunt of crocodiles, turtles and water-snakes. Sometimes, however, carriages ran along a dyke, and negroes passed by with baskets, their heads enveloped in brightly-colored scarves.

In the midst of the pools there were houses that evoked insecurity, between cypresses with uncovered roots. One wondered how they could be reached in the midst of that sodden terrain, those semi-liquid fields where a heron occasionally alighted only to fly away immediately. Everything was immense, surpassing known proportions: the trees wrenched from the banks that brushed the hull of the *Reine Marie*; the paddle-steamers they passed with their huge wheels and intermittent flame; and the river itself, as vast as a sea. The New World, with its sky, its waters and its low lands, gave the travelers the impression of their own smallness before a previously-unimagined infinity.

Leaning over the rails, they saw great forests appear, and lakes shining among fissured trains. Finally, after two days traveling up the Mississippi, the houses began to multiply, and they saw fields of sugar cane and cotton. Little boats began to follow the *Reine Marie*. Merchants with coffee-colored faces sold curious things: heron plumes, fans, muskrat pelts. Then there were the suburbs, the bend in the river, an immense dyke, and red tiles alternating with wooden roofs.

The emigrants who were to disembark in New Orleans had emerged from the depths of the ship, and baggage, sacks and crates were piled up on the deck. The preliminaries of the arrival, before the *Reine Marie* touched a quay in a basin covered with flat boats, were interminable. The capital scene of Barthélémy's life was about to unfold in a matter of minutes.

Captain Courtin in person, and all the people from whom Barthélémy had received advice, had made him the same recommendation:

Don't lose sight of your baggage. When you arrive in New Orleans, the deck will be invaded by a crowd of negroes. One of them will throw himself on to your trunk in order to transport it to a hotel. Fix a price with him beforehand. Designate a hotel of your choice.

And a small boarding house in the French quarter had been indicated to him, which was simply called the Hôtel des Français. There, Barthélémy would pay a modest price, would find a compatriot speaking his language and would have every chance of obtaining news of Eugène Peytava.

He was an optimist by nature. *Who knows?* he said to himself. *When things begin to succeeded, they succeed completely. Perhaps Eugène has had changes in his life. Why should he not be managing the Hôtel des Français now? Perhaps it's him who will greet me on my arrival.*

He held what was most precious to him in his hand: his shoemaker's tools, the leather of soles and a large selection of nails.

"With this, I'm very strong," he said, familiarly, striking with his hand the package that permitted him to accomplish the finest actions of life.

He shook hands, he received good advice and sympathy from the travelers who were continuing their voyage aboard the *Reine Marie* in order to disembark in other cities as mysterious as the New Orleans, the vastness of which filled him with surprise.

Suddenly, there was a great clamor. A gangway had been extended from the quay to the deck. The emigrants were on their feet. Cries resounded, appeals formulated in English, Spanish, French and absolutely incomprehensible creole dialects.

Barthélémy only knew French, and he had heard it said that everybody in New Orleans spoke French. He perceived that it was in languages unknown to him that almost everyone was expressing themselves.

"*Au revoir*," Martin Bruno said to him, shaking his hand. "Perhaps..."

He was suddenly interrupted.

Barthélémy had a large trunk in front of him and, in accordance with the numerous recommendations of experienced people, he was not losing sight of it. But his gaze quit it for the space of a second because, when one shakes hands with someone who is expressing an amicable wish, it is necessary to meet his gaze.

Only one second, and the trunk had been moved! Instead of being on the deck of the *Reine Marie* it was on the back of a gigantic negro, a joyful negro who was laughing at the weight of the trunk and uttering a few strange cries.

No, it was not a phrase susceptible of having a meaning; they were interjections that could not correspond either to the address of a hotel or a price, or anything sensate.

In any case, Barthélémy did not have time to reflect. Still laughing, the negro had launched himself lightly through the crowd toward the gangway that connected the ship to the quay. Barthélémy hurled himself after him. But while the negro had traversed the crowd of men laden with their baggage easily, Barthélémy was stopped several times. He lost ground.

He saw the negro stop for a moment as if to wait for him, and turn a laughing face in his direction. Then he shouted an imperious order to stop and to fix a price for the transport of the trunk so audaciously seized. That was, however, an imprudent waste of time. The negro, who was only clad in light white twill trousers propitious for running, had just launched himself forward with a surprising agility and a horrible insouciance for the owner of the trunk.

The heat was oppressive. Barthélémy was hampered by his packet of tools and a Pyrenean cape that he was caring over his arm. Nevertheless, he launched himself in pursuit of his trunk, without overmuch fear at first. Surely the porter, the unloader of boats, had received the mission from some hotel to attract travelers by that method who allowed it to happen. But he was not one of them! He would not stay in that hotel, he swore to that! And the negro, in spite of his stature and a sort of childish ingenuousness in his laughter, would see with whom he was dealing.

What streets! What a strange city! He could have believed that he was in Spain, in the towns in the Pyrenees that he had visited in his youth with muleteers from Luchon. There were wooden balconies and perforated moucharabies, as in Spain. Sometimes he tried to shout, to stop the bearer of his baggage in his course, but he arrived at a street corner and no longer saw him in front of him. He must have turned right or left. But which? There was a man standing in front of a cigar shop, a motionless man leaning in an arrogant attitude, smoking a big cigar.

He interrogated him. Which street had a negro carrying a big trunk—his trunk—taken? The man must not have understood. He launched a puff of smoke at the sky and did not reply.

Barthélémy took one of the streets at random. He was covered in sweat. Despair had taken possession of his soul. In the meantime, with an abruptness in which there was malignity, night fell. He knew that it was a phenomenon habitual in that part of the world, but he saw it as a ploy of destiny, which was decidedly against him.

He struggled, however, he went along streets at random, retraced his steps, made further enquiries. The people did not seem to understand and replied in English. The quarter he had reached was no longer Spanish. The houses were tall and sordid in appearance.

Exhausted by fatigue, he was about to lay his shepherd's cape on the ingrate and dirty ground of a street in New Orleans when he thought he perceived, as if in a dream, a little further on, by the vague light cast by a lantern, a negro laden with a burden. And that silhouette seemed to disappear into a wall with the rapidity that certain images put into disappearing in dreams.

He gathered his strength and ran. There was a sinister intersection with a lackluster shop that had several barrels of rum stacked up in its window. A confused music of banjos and low, drawling singing was escaping from it. Opposite was a porch. It was there that the silhouette had been absorbed. There were shutters clicking here and there, laughter and appeals in an incomprehensible language.

Barthélémy almost collided with a thickset negro elegantly clad in black, who was holding a cane with a gold pommel, and then an old woman who appeared to him to be a barley-sugar seller. Under the porch there was a stairway. He took it.

The hum of life made the house quiver. On the first floor there was a balcony illuminated vaguely by a bowl of oil placed on the floor, in which a wick was dipped. That balcony connected the part of the house where he was with another building, which appeared to be vast. It surrounded a rectangular courtyard and it seemed to him that he could see clusters of children hanging over balustrades of exceedingly thick wood.

He had thought that he heard a heavy tread going upstairs. A man carrying a trunk has a heavy tread. He made haste. There were whispers, and stifled laughter. Doors opened and closed. Through the gap in one of them he perceived, for a second, an interior with a multicolored Chinese lantern, like a lantern whose form had once caught his attention at a fair. A black woman of enormous proportions, who was only wearing a skirt, with the illumination of teeth appropriate to the black race, stepped out on to the landing, then closed the door again, leaving an odor of patchouli, sweat and rum.

He arrived on the second floor. There was another corridor and a balcony, on to which he ventured with the sensation that the heavy tread had steered in that direction. Suddenly, a door opened wide in front of him and he saw a mulatta dressed in a pink calico dress with a low neck, who appeared to him to be delectably beautiful. The room behind her was barely illuminated, but the presence of a large mattress made it a paradise for a weary man.

"Mon chéri!" she said, tenderly, and added, in French: "Me waiting for you. See charming bird."

She pointed at a parrot that was perched gravely on a stool.

"Good rum! Good rum!"

And, while pulling him gently by the sleeve, she showed him an earthenware jug set beside the mattress.

Those few words spoken in French, even in a French whose accent was different from that spoken in the Pyrenees, were like a mild balm upon Barthélémy's anxiety.

He had arrived. He would go no further. It was only for form's sake that he asked her whether a negro in twill trousers carrying a large trunk was somewhere in the house.

"All full of negroes. Good negroes. And here good rum. You like rum?"

Barthélémy had never seen such a beautiful creature. She leapt up and down, laughing; she had taken his cook and his package, and she filled two glasses with rum.

"Him Tomlinson," she said, pointing at the parrot, which immediately started flapping its wings. That lasted long enough for him to lie down on the mattress.

"Me, Rose."

The laughter resumed, and she took off his shoes.

Barthélémy drank a rum that seemed to him to be better than any rum he had drunk before. He saw that the lantern on the ceiling was also a Chinese lantern. That must be the local custom, he thought. The room, although untidy, was agreeable, the hostess even prettier than he had thought on first seeing her, and her gaiety, which seemed to be shared by the parrot, was so continuous, content with motives so minimal, that he told himself that life must be an eternal joy next to such a cheerful woman.

Assuredly, there must be police in New Orleans to recover trunks from negro thieves. But he had time. The important thing was to savor the joyful sweetness of such a new experience, which did not resemble anything that a shoemaker from Saint-Béat could imagine.

He drank another rum and fell asleep.

And he lived there for twenty years, almost without going out, in the most perfect happiness.

He did not find his brother-in-law Eugène Peytava, and did not even search for him. Nor did he go to the police in order to have his stolen trunk recovered. He had the intention to do so, the day after his arrival, on waking up in the room of the freed former slave, Rose, but something happened.

He had opened his package to show his shoemaker's tools, for every man likes to glorify his profession and ornament with beauty the ordinary objects of which he makes use, if he makes use of them lovingly. Those objects provoked an unexpected joy and admiration on the part of the mulatta. She wanted to share that joy with another mulatta who lived next door.

That one did not speak French. She was of mature age and grave humor. She did not perceive the beauty that the tools displayed, but she understood their utility. And she brought him a pair of shoes whose soles needed to be changed, without delay. The price was settled with Rose—at a discount, of course. By way of service, Barthélémy set to work

181

immediately, and gave his word that the shoes would be ready the following day. He installed himself on the balcony and started working joyfully, while Rose went to buy what was needed for a meal.

Naturally, Barthélémy's presence did not pass unperceived, and all the inhabitants of the populous house, all the tenants of all the balconies, of every race and every color, came to contemplate him while he worked. They all had shoes to sort out, and there was soon a large pile next to Barthélémy. If he respected his word given in Saint-Béat, he also respected it in New Orleans. The promises he made, and the mysterious urgency that people experience in all latitudes to have their footwear sorted out with the shortest possible delay, retained Barthélémy at his work and drove away the thought of the stolen trunk. The enchantment caused by Rose's perpetual laughter, and the leisure time spent with the parrot Tomlinson enabled him to find the hours prodigiously rapid.

An old Frenchman with white hair came to sit down beside him every day. He did not give details of his past. Once he had nearly taken part in the Empire's wars and he had passed through Toulouse. Wine, rum and a beverage unknown to Barthélémy, whisky, had played a large role in his life. They still held the first place therein.

His words were in conformity with Barthélémy's ideas: a laborer who works hard at his trade can live comfortably anywhere.

"The whole thing is to do it with an appetite," the old man invariably added, watching admiringly, but without envy, as the shoemaker chose his nails or polished his leather. He had never exercised any profession himself.

"Not everyone is made for work," he said, "but those who work are the first among men."

He also said that he had once heard mention of Saint-Béat, and he was sure that he had seen the Pyrenees from a distance. "What a beautiful country!" he repeated.

A man's happiness is never complete unless he has someone to admire him in his profession. The old Frenchman contributed to the happy life of labor and amour that the shoemaker of Saint-Béat led.

The negroes had kept the habit of barter. They sometimes brought him objects, poultry and vegetables in exchange for footwear. Once, a Jewish second-hand dealer came to offer him a trunk that he had in his shop. It was unusual in form, he said, and must be of foreign origin, but it was very solid. Barthélémy only had to come and look at it.

Moved by a presentiment, he went. It was his own. Certainly, he could have had a search made. The dealer gave the impression of a receiver of stolen gods. Happiness and ease inclined him to forbearance. All the same, he felt a certain emotion. He had the trunk brought and he gave the Jew a superb pair of lined boots.

Many years later—it was after the war of 1870—the Maire of Saint-Béat received a letter from New Orleans. It was signed with an unknown name, but the old men of the town that he questioned recognized it. It was a matter of the sale of a little house that was falling into ruins and dishonored a street by its sordid aspect. It was also a matter of transforming a tomb in the cemetery and erecting in its place a marble tomb for which an American architect had drawn up a plan. But the grave had not had a perpetual concession, and it had been dug up to make way for new tombs. In any case, the nature of the ground was such that it possessed an unusual power of assimilation and consumption, with the result that no vestige was found of the dead that it had once received.

The Maire wrote to Barthélémy Dalbiès to that effect, but never received any reply.

IV. A Social Soirée in Vera Cruz

"You'll come to take the evening meal tomorrow in the old dwelling of the Alamans," Anastasio Alaman had said to Malvina and her companions with some solemnity. "Great Mexican families have a decorum and a liking for protocol and ancient customs that it will be necessary for you to excuse. In the house we have changed nothing of my ancestor's way of life—the one who was called, with reason, the great Alaman. He proclaimed the constitution with Apodaca,[8] and he, at least, was not afraid of shedding blood. Furthermore, as you'll see, he's still there. His portrait presides over all our meals. I'll tell you the history of that portrait, which is rather curious."

Almost all the French passengers of the *Reine Marie* had had a pleasant surprise on disembarking in Vera Cruz. They were staying at the Hôtel de la Merced, near the Alameda, and had been welcomed by French proprietors, who were even Bordelais, the Garisse brothers. All the hotel staff were French too, and had thus been able to initiate them very rapidly in petty Mexican habits, the value of the once and the real, to inform them that it was necessary not to throw stones at hideous vultures because of the services they rendered, and how to recognize certain ragged individuals as soldiers or senior policemen.

Bernard Borromée, Dr. Fazeuille, Martin Bruno and Malvina had felt a deep impression during their first stroll through the city. What churches! What convents! What crumbling but magnificent ostentation in the openings of portals,

---

[8] The naval officer Juan Ruiz de Apodaca (1754-1835) was the Viceroy of New Spain but was overthrown by a coup following the defection of most of his troops—including those led by Agustin de Iturbide and Santa Anna—when he refused to join the independence movement.

184

the proud sculpted façades and the square turrets marked almost everywhere by the hole of an open window. Sometimes they had the surprise of seeing a majestic church loom up with its saints and its stone angels, which was, when they got closer, no longer anything but a skeleton without a roof. Or behind a great paved courtyard where grass was growing, they perceived a big house whose crumbling floors were suspended one atop another. The result of wars and revolutions!

Everything attested to a lapsed Spanish splendor, a forceful religious life whose sap had dried up. But in the evening the air as full of hymns, sung canticles, somewhere in distant convents—no one knew where—and those songs were bizarrely mingled with the music of guitars and dance tunes coming from invisible courtyards in narrow streets over which balconies, in joining up, extended and eternal night.

But the Alameda, the great portals with triple arches overlooking the sea, the tall churches, the distant silhouette of San Juan d'Ulloa and the avenue bordered by old trees and ruined palaces that extended all the way to the pool of Malibran, all evoked for the young people from Comminges the vision of an arrogant aristocracy, proud of its privileges, set in its habits, its costumes and its disdainful pride.

The evening before, they deliberated with a certain anxiety. Above all, there was the important question of what to wear. Martin Bruno excused himself. He would write to apologize for not coming. He only had a traveling costume. He also considered himself to be a peasant, who did not dine in society. Bernard and the doctor had the formal clothes that young men buy at the beginning of their career. They had thought that they would not have to use them, but had brought them just in case. And behold—they were going to wear it on the second night after their arrival! That made them proud, but also apprehensive.

They consulted the elder Garisse. He was a thin man with a long goatee, which he tugged when his prudence had to be exercised. At first he remained silent on hearing the name Anastasio Alaman, and tugged his beard forcefully.

"The Alamans! You know the Alamans! Damn!"

"So what?"

"Great family! Very great family! The grandfather married an Indian, the daughter of a pearl-fisherman. The great Alaman! Do you know what Anastasio's nickname is? El Demonio!"

"Doesn't that mean demon?"

"Exactly. That's the translation. But the nickname doesn't signify anything. Decorum is of great importance in that house, especially because of Anastasio's uncle and aunts. It's very closed milieu, where strangers are never received. Dress as if for a marriage."

Malvina spent part of the day unfolding her dresses and ironing them with the aid of Madame Garisse the younger. The doctor and Bernard ran to the city, one for a white cravat and the other for a black hat.

"I hope you have a good time," said Martin Bruno, laughing.

Monsieur Garisse took the doctor to one side.

"Doubtless the son won't be there. Yes, the son Ezéquiel...it's better if he's absent."

"Why?"

Monsieur Garisse tugged his beard. "He's a...how shall I put it...he's a charming man, but strange, very strange...and also, perhaps, violent...that's it, violent,"

"That happens to a lot of people—me, for example. I'm a calm man, and I want to be calm, but it sometimes happens that I'm possessed by surges of anger."

"That's the case. He has surges of anger, and then he lets himself go...but he's a tender, a tender soul. And he has faith in his mission."

"What mission?"

Monsieur Garisse, who had let go of his beard, took it in hand again, perplexed.

"I don't know exactly. But under the seal of the greatest secrecy, I can tell you one curious thing about Ezéquiel Alaman. Will you swear to keep the secret, Doctor?"

"I swear."

"A year ago, at about this time, I was coming back from Tlascala, where my occupation as a hotelier had taken me. Beyond the Ottumba farm, the Tlascala road goes past a temple where, it's said, the worship of the ancient gods of Mexico is still celebrated. It appears—I can't guarantee anything—that the temple, which has been secretly repaired, was once consecrated to two divinities. I've retained the name of one of them: Cochiquetzal, a somewhat erotic goddess, I believe.[9] The second has a barbaric name that means 'the goddess in the jade skirt.' And it's said—these are rumors that I can't guarantee that prostitutes, and even hermaphrodites, come in procession to celebrate ceremonies that must have a character of obscenity."

At this point, the elder Monsieur Garisse's face reflected the base gaiety that possesses men of fifty at the evocation of a pleasure of which they are beginning to be deprived.

"Prostitutes and hermaphrodites—it's unimaginable! So, I urged my horse forward, for you'll learn that the Mexican roads are never safe. At Ottumba, the doors and windows were closed. Nothing is as disagreeable as spending the night near the temple. I saw silhouettes on the road. I thought they were thieves. I only ever travel with a trivial sum of money, just sufficient not to annoy anyone who might stop me too much. There was a bright moon and I distinguished clearly a man who was turning on to the little path that goes from the road to the temple. It was Ezéquiel Alaman. Well, Doctor, he had bulging eyes, and his entire body was as stiff as the body of someone who is magnetized. His face was smeared with blood

---

[9] I have retained Magre's spelling of the name of Aztec fertility goddess and personification of sexual desire Xochiquetzal, also known as Ichpochtli." The goddess with the jade skirt" is Chalchiuhtlicue, that being the meaning of her name; she was a water divinity—and thus associated with fertility—also associated with serpents, often represented as a beautiful young woman.

or another red liquid, and he was clutching in his hands, as one holds a Holy Sacrament, a white cock! I have no advice to give you, but I engage you not to link yourself with a man who goes by night to offer white cocks to immodest goddesses."

Dr. Fazeuille made a gesture indicating that there was no possibility of any such liaison.

"Anyway, you won't see him. He's at sea. Yes, at sea, which is another story. And what's more, you're sure, if you don't see the son, of not seeing the daughter either."

Monsieur Garisse's face took on a saucy expression again. But a carriage came into the courtyard of the hotel. Although the Alamans' house was not far way, Monsieur Garisse had assured his guests that they ought to take a carriage.

Malvina had never been as beautiful as in the black taffeta dress that a couturier in Toulouse had made for her. The arrangement of her hair, and the wearing of a unique ring, testified that she had understood how much sobriety and measure add to charm. She held herself very straight, and a timidity that she did not want to allow to disappear hardened the gleam of her eyes. Bernard affected to combine within him all the authority of the group, and he deliberately spoke loudly. Dr. Fazeuille measured that false importance with a little sadness, and only thought of not falling foul of it. He was embarrassed by his suit, which was several years old, but which he had only worn two or three times. As he had lost weight, the garment hung slightly loosely, and he was aware of it.

As soon as they arrived they were seized by fright at the excess of pomp. Night had just fallen and the lackeys lifting large bronze chandeliers ran forward to welcome them. A half-caste dwarf who must have been very old was playing the role of steward and giving orders. The candlelight, as it was displaced, caused panoplies of weapons to gleam, and illuminated great somber dressers and a crucifix that rose up to the ceiling, opposite a marble staircase.

Anastasio appeared on that staircase, clad in black velvet, in the fashion of the ancient Spanish caballeros. And as he had a mirror behind him, and that mirror was face to face with others, the three guests saw, in accordance with the whim of the candles, a host of Anastasio Alamans solemnly descending staircases reflected to infinity.

Their first impression only increased when, having arrived on the first floor, they suddenly saw looming up before them, in the reception room where the meal had been prepared, the members of the Alaman family. They all advanced together, like a familial group on parade, presenting the appearance of old people allowing themselves to be passed in review.

There was Anastasio's uncle, very old but upright to the extent that one might have thought that some sort of paralysis was the cause of that extraordinary rectitude. He extended his hand like an automaton, and pronounced a few words of polite welcome; and when the three young people drew nearer to him they were surprised by the complete atonality of his gaze. There was a person that they could not identify, and who was introduced as "the Colonel." He gave the impression of being a carbon copy of the old uncle, but appeared to be even older. Both had magnificent but faded uniforms.

In the same line, the two aunts and another woman, who might have been a friend or a lady companion, advanced simultaneously. Large tortoiseshell combs maintained their white hair, which descended in bands over their ears. Their thin necks emerged from identical black silk shawls. They were the same height and equally wrinkled. Apart from the length of their noses, the only thing to distinguish them, they were so similar that they could have been mistaken for one another. They made the same gestures, pronounced the same words in Spanish, and, letting their arms fall in parallel, they remained motionless, as if they were a long way away, in a universe where all was shadow, mourning and majesty.

Malvina and her friends had had the leisure to remark the characteristic of all Mexican houses: destruction alongside splendor. The marble staircase had a broken step and a domestic was posted there to illuminate it especially. The damasked velvet of the furniture was torn in places. A candelabrum that should have had seven branches only had six. A life-sized portrait had several round holes in the breast that must have been made by bullets.

Anastasio Alaman spoke abundantly and did not seem to take account of the great distance that separated his family from their guests. The great distance that separates beings so different had something garish about it. Perhaps he was amused by it.

One place remained empty at the table. He pointed his finger at it and then designated the portrait.

"We leave the place that the great Alaman occupied empty. His image is here, his spirit is here. The portrait we see is an extraordinary likeness. That's a mystery. I accommodated for some time an Italian painter, the descendant of a princely family almost reduced to mendicity. He wanted to repay me for my hospitality and proposed to make a portrait of my ancestor, who had just died. There was no document. He painted the picture in accordance with the character traits that I described to him. The painter had talent, for the portrait is marvelously accurate, even though its author had never seen the model."

The meal went by slowly. The dishes lost their importance by virtue of the solemnity with which they were resented. Every spoken word was weighed down by its own emptiness. Malvina struggled heroically against the potency of Mexican peppers, to which she was not accustomed. Dr. Fazeuille had a strong desire to ask who had been audacious enough to fire revolver shots at the image of the great Alaman, but he dared not.

Suddenly, there was a noise that must have come from the ground floor. That noise must have been interpreted as a threat. Malvina saw one of the lackeys on the threshold freeze, and his face suddenly took on an expression of fearful expectation. The aunts sat up straight in their seats and the mummification of their features as accentuated. The uncle made a sign to the colonel, as if he had to hold himself in readiness for a battle Only Anastasio Alaman remained smiling, but the calm was that of someone on the alert.

"I seem to recognize Ezéquiel's voice!" And he added, looking at Malvina: "He's my son."

The noise became a racket. One might have thought it an altercation. A thick and drunken voice was perceptible, uttering insults in a joyful fashion, and a fragment of a sentence reached them, which no one wanted to understand.

"If the old swine aren't there..."

The lackeys at the door were shoved aside and a pale young man of tall stature appeared on the threshold. His face, with regular features, was very handsome, but, in spite of an affectation of gaiety, there was something naturally tragic, and even desperate, in his features. His black hair was escaping from a fine silk kerchief and falling over his shoulders. He only had a light shirt, tapering at the neck, and his belt was stuffed with weapons. His gaze scanned the circle of guests but, in posing on Malvina, it stopped for a few seconds—long enough to cause an atmosphere of embarrassment. He kissed his father on both cheeks and took him in his arms as a supplementary expression of tenderness. Then he bowed ceremoniously to everyone present, with the exception of the old uncle, who, when he went past him, remained in the immobility of a stone statue, his eyes fixed.

"You can come up, no one will eat you," shouted the young man to someone who must have been on the staircase.

"I hope that isn't the captain!" said Anastasio, swiftly.

"Oh, as long as it isn't that man who...," murmured an aunt, without finishing, and she veiled her face with a hand—a gesture that the other two old women immediately reproduced.

"If it's the captain...," said the colonel, in a tone that permitted the belief that he was ready for an extreme resolution.

"But yes, it's the worthy Montaria, the most courageous man in Mexico," said Ezéquiel, pretending not to perceive the

191

general movement of reprobation. At the same time there was the expression of indulgence and gaiety inspired in a joker who has just caused laughter. "Come on, Montaria, you're welcome. Don't wait to be begged—your place is set."

Ezéquiel had cast an imperious glance at a lackey, who ran forward to set another place.

"I hope that he isn't going...," Anastasio said to his son, making the gesture of firing a pistol shot.

"No, once is enough. Don't worry..."

There was a trailing step, and Captain Montaria came in

"Good God! My cigar is out" he cried, tapping off the ash with his fingertip. He approached one of the candelabra on the wall and was obliged pick it up several times. Everyone was able to observe, with consternation, that he was staggering.

"I salute everyone," he said.

Captain Montaria was short and stout. His face was crimson. His eyes had the fixity that alcohol gives, but joviality as the dominant note of his expression.

Ezéquiel had pushed him on to a seat—that of the great Alaman.

"He's an extraordinary man, with whom one's never bored," he said, addressing Malvina directly, as if to excuse himself for having such a companion. A place had been set for him beside her. She hastened to smile at him, and the banal words she pronounced had a tone of sympathy. Was it not necessary to do her best to struggle against the heavy atmosphere of embarrassment that was already hanging over the gathering and had just been further aggravated by the arrival of the newcomers?

Only Captain Montaria was entirely at ease. He had put his cigar on his plate and having met the gaze of Dr. Fazeuille, he addressed him personally.

"We used every possible means to beat them, Oh, the swine wanted to get us. Did you hear the cannon about an hour ago? That was my forward gun. I think, in fact that the *Aquilon* has been sent to the bottom."

Dr. Fazeuille had not heard the cannon. But could one hear it from the Hôtel de France? He did not know what the *Aquilon* was.

That unleashed the captain's laughter.

"Hey, Señor Anastasio! He doesn't know what the *Aquilon* is. We know, don't we?"

"It's the customs schooner," said the uncle, with a tone that expressed horror.

"Well, it's on the bottom. You hear that? It's my forward gun that pierced its hull and it was that damned Espandrillo who pointed it! Oh, he's a sharpshooter! You should have brought him, Ezéquiel."

There was a general shudder caused either by the loss of the *Aquilon* and the threat of its consequences or the idea that the cannoneer Espandrillo might have been added to the number of the guests. Ezéquiel got up swiftly and went to whisper a few words in the captain's ear. But the latter had reached the point of drunkenness where reason ceases to have the slightest value.

"The courageous Ezéquiel is ashamed of his actions! Me, I'm not afraid of anyone and I'll say to Arista himself that I sunk the *Aquilon*. I'll say it to Santa Anna if he becomes our tyrant again."

That name awoke joyous memories in the captain's soul. He repeated "Santa Anna" several times. He leaned toward Dr. Fazeuille. "Don't forget that we're in the home of El Demonio, in the house of the leg."

And he emitted a loud burst of laughter. But that burst of laughter was without echo. He did not care. Mexican custom dictates the drinks are only served after the meal. The captain gave an imperative order to a servant to bring him an aguardiente and specified the one that Ezéquiel kept in reserve for him.

Ezéquiel was no longer thinking about the captain. His eyes were lost in Malvina's. He said no matter what to her, about her, about her voyage and about Mexico, and she replied in the same tone, possessed by a similar intoxication, but of which she took no account. A first encounter between two individuals who experience a mutual attraction gives to the gaze a language that they never find again, which is perhaps the most eloquent of all those they have to exchange. The gaze renders a first appeal that no word can express thereafter, and they will have forever the sentiment of profound things once said and never to be rediscovered.

From time to time, Ezéquiel interrupted his conversation with regret in order to make a gesture of indulgence regarding the captain. He said in a low voice: "He's a worthy man—the only mariner who knows the Gulf of Mexico."

And twice he turned toward his father at the moment when the latter's face was about to express a violent determination.

"Remember that he's saved my life, and several times."

The captain heard and replied: "The life is nothing. Old friend, I've saved you from prison. But that damned Rosario is fighting the sharks this evening."

The uncle had got up several times. Every time, he had coughed, and struck the pose of someone who is about to say something. Doubtless he was going to say that the dignity and that of his family could not support the presence of a person so completely deprived of elementary usages as Captain Montaria. He had begun: "It's intolerable that in the house of the great Alaman..."

Each time, Anastasio, losing the familial respect that he had shown until then had shouted to him: "Shut up!" while making an imperious sign to him to sit down. And he had murmured to Ezéquiel: "The essential thing is that he doesn't recommence as on the day when..." Raising his hand, he made the gesture of shooting with an imaginary pistol.

Now, at that same moment, under the influence of the aguardiente, the idea came to Captain Montaria to recommence. Already, he had pointed at the portrait of the great Alaman several times, and then turned his head.

"But why is he staring at me? Is it because of Rosario and his boat?"

194

In the end, he shouted: "I've had enough of being looked at like that." and he took a large pistol from his belt, which he cocked.

"Ezéquiel, I bet you that I can put a bullet in the right eye."

The guests had pushed back their chairs, but no one dared to stand up first, in order not to designate himself to the terrible captain as a target.

Only Ezéquiel had launched himself forward and attempted to extract the weapon from his friend's hand.

"Here, drink this glass," he said, serving him.

But the captain did not want to be dispossessed of the revolver. While he was struggling, he even had another idea, which enthused him.

"I'm going to break your aunts' tortoiseshell combs. I'm sure of my shots. Tell them not to move."

A shot departed and the bullet lodged in the ceiling.

There were piercing screams, and everyone got up in tumult.

Ezéquiel had shouted: "Octavio!" That was the name of the half-caste dwarf who served as a steward. He must have had he habit of such scenes, for he seized he captain by one arm while Ezéquiel took the other, Both of them drew him away without difficulty, for the sight of the old half-caste had the effect of rejoicing Captain Montaria, who started to shout: "Hurrah for Octavio!"

Anastasio Alaman offered his guests profuse apologies.

"What can you expect? He's my son's companion. All mariners are a little like that."

Malvina and her friends were secretly surprised, believing that they understood that, although Anastasio was criticizing the captain's conduct severely, he did not appear to be overly shocked.

"Anyway," he added, "there was nothing to fear, even for my aunts' combs. The captain is a very bad shot."

195

The carriage was in the courtyard. The young people climbed into it, and, as soon as they were alone, Bernard Borromée gave free rein to his indignation.

"We were in the home of bandits, veritable bandits. In a lair: it's a gang."

Malvina said, timidly, that the old ladies in the black shawls, whom one could reproach for not being very welcoming, were not, in any case, susceptible of belonging to a band of brigands."

"Personally," said the doctor, "I don't understand why we were invited."

Bernard contented himself with laughing at such ingenuousness.

But Malvina was no longer listening. The carriage had entered the courtyard of the now-silent hotel, She got out and looked at the sky. She seemed lost in a profound ecstasy. Bernard touched her arm lightly to bring her back to reality.

"One would think that they aren't the same stars as if France," she said, in a low voice.

"Eh? All stars resemble one another..."

"These seem to me to be more beautiful."

Somewhere, a bird made a few discordant sounds heard.

"Listen—that song is delightful," said Malvina.

Bernard shrugged his shoulders. The door of the hotel was open. Malvina waited for a few more moments. What she had called a song was not renewed. But she carried an interior music away with her.

"I'm wondering whether all soirées in Mexican high society resemble that one," said the doctor, as he crossed the threshold.

VI. The Convent of the Dead
(Dr. Fazeuille's Journal)

Monsieur Garisse the younger is much smarter than his brother, although I thought the opposite at first. He's an observer. But as I'm not writing this record to clarify the psychology of Monsieur Garisse, hotelier of Vera Cruz, but for my own interior instruction, I won't go on at length about his qualities. I'll only note my lack of perspicacity, which caused me to mistake the elder Garisse's prudence for sagacity and the younger Garisse's reserve for mediocrity.

"Are you occupied with the occult sciences, Doctor?" the latter asked me, as I was walking on my own in the paved pathways of the hotel garden while waiting for lunch.

"I consider that all things are occult," I replied. "Occult science is that of the world."

He paid no attention to the attempt at profundity that I had put into that reflection.

"I'd like to know whether you've noticed that Mademoiselle de Noussoulens is prey to certain hauntings."

"My God! I haven't remarked that precisely, but in fact, perhaps sometimes..."

"According to what I've understood, she believes that she hears footsteps—footsteps that don't exist."

"Has she told you that?"

"Yesterday I was going along the corridor on to which her room opens. She opened the door abruptly and exclaimed, on seeing me: 'Oh, it's you, Monsieur Garisse!' She seemed anxious. She was about to go back into her room when she changed her mind and asked me: 'Was it you that was walking back and forth outside my door ten minutes ago?'

"I replied that I had been in the stables ten minutes ago, that I had just that moment come up to the first floor, and that I hadn't had any idea of walking back and forth in the corridor. She was troubled, and she said to me: 'I thought I heard...it seemed to me...about ten minutes ago...' And she went back into her room. Note that I'm not a skeptic, and I believe that anything is possible."

We talked about this and that, and I told him that I wasn't a skeptic either, but that I had not seen anything personally that escaped the natural order of things.

"I could perhaps show you something extraordinary. Extraordinary, at least, for an observer. For there are people who go into that house—it's a matter of a house, and even of a public house—who don't notice anything. I won't tell you anymore. We'll make an experiment. You're a bachelor, I understand, and French. You won't be shocked by going into a house where there are women taking a glass of aguardiente. It doesn't commit you to anything. We'll spend an hour there and we'll come back."

We arranged to meet that evening at six o'clock. As Bernard never quits Malvina for a moment, I judged it futile to invite him to come, and, at six o'clock I took my place with Garisse in a bizarre hotel caleche driven by a negro, which must have dated from the last century.

The city was full of a racket of fandangos and guitars. We went down the Almeida and found ourselves, on the other side of the Porte de la Merced, on a new avenue bordered by sumptuous abandoned dwellings. I perceived a herd of swine between the paneled walls of a drawing room.

"Spanish luxury is dead," said the younger Garisse, with a sigh. Like all hotel proprietors, he has a veneration for great families and wealth.

Abruptly, however, we emerged on to a sandy expanse bordered to the left by the sea, and after a few minutes we took a path between trees. Very special trees, in truth! Giant cacti with redoubtable claws, aloes, deformed magueys, spiny yuccas, Barbary figs sweating thorny: all that demonic vegetation was bristling with spikes, and distilling poisons in the ooze of its gums.

"Look over there, a short distance away—that white wall is the old cemetery of the Franciscans. Take note of the distance. Note the distance carefully."

I noted it, distractedly.

"For the house where we're going and whose great portal is over there, is a former Franciscan convent purchased by Anastasio Alaman, only a part of which has been redeveloped. Singular as it might seem, it was Anastasio Alaman's grandmother, the Indian woman, the sorceress of Isla Cerralvo, the former wife of the man they call the great Alaman, who keeps that house. Oh, it isn't because of the profit. She's very old, and does it by inclination, or for reasons that escape everyone, except for her son. Incredible reasons, of which one scarcely dares emit the hypothesis, and which are to do with the most terrible magic. But I'm not telling you anything. Anyway, it's impossible to understand anything without some knowledge of things of the occult world. Have you read Gaffarel's *Book of Unusual Curiosities*?"[10]

I replied no, after a moment's hesitation, for I was ashamed to be less learned than the younger Garisse, hotelier of Vera Cruz, and ignorant of Gaffarel.

"It's an unusual curiosity. In Vera Cruz it's said that Anastasio wanted to get his grandmother out of the city and that he's very glad of the money that the former convent brings in. Pure absurdity! It's also said that it's in the former Franciscan convent that he hides Santa Anna's leg."

We were about to arrive. Garisse spoke more rapidly in order to have time to finish.

"You're going to ask me how the former sorceress could have at her disposal a large number of young and pretty women, not one of whom has been recognized as being from Vera Cruz?"

---

[10] *Curiositez inouyes sur la sculpture talismanique des Persans* (1637), by the astrologer Jacques Gaffarel (1601-1681), known in English as *Unheard of Curiosities*, was a surprise best-seller in its day.

I had not thought of asking that question, but I nodded my head.

"Yes, not one from Vera Cruz! It's truly astonishing. A few years ago, families of pearl fishers from Isla Cerralvo emigrated and came to settle in this little village, behind that sand dune and not far from the cemetery. It's said that the sea was then full of pearls from Vera Cruz to Goazalcoalco. Yellow fever annihilated almost all the fishers. A few still remain, but very few—not enough to aliment old Alaman's house. So?"

The carriage had just turned in front of a massive wooden door. At first a loophole opened. We went in behind a tall negro who wore a sort of livery and carried a sharp metal rod under his arm, as one might carry a cane.

He marched in front of us and, after having taken an obscure passage and gone passed an old holy water stoup and a pedestal with no statue we found ourselves in a little cloister with walls of blue faience, where orange trees and palm trees grew and astonishingly green water sparkled in a worn stone basin. A very tall tree with a white trunk, known here as a zebaa, loomed over everything and covered the cloister and the surrounding buildings with its shadow.

On a bench, like statues, four or five women were sitting, who seemed young to me but heavily made up. Their faces were entirely painted. They wore large colored rebozos that enveloped them from head to toe. Not far from them, in a large armchair, a little old lady, covered in wrinkles, was rolling a cigarette. Her feet were negligently placed on a small table in front of her.

She did not get up, but made an amicable gesture to Garisse. I noticed, on the table, a prod similar to the one the negro carried under his arm. I heard Garisse introduce me as one of his French friends. The little old lady ordered punch to be served

The women had got up and they started to laugh and babble. They seemed to me to be Indians. There was one mulatta, however. Without my inviting her to do it, she came to sit on my knee.

"I believe she's the only one who speaks Spanish," Garisse told me.

She did indeed speak Spanish, but she only seemed to know one sentence of it, who she repeated: "Yes m'sieur, good weather for picking grapefruit..." And she laughed, showing her gleaming teeth. I tried in vain to obtain other words.

I have a fundamental austerity in me and there are memories on which I don't like to dwell. My conclusions regarding life make me think that one should not seek pleasure for pleasure's sake. But can we not make an experiment? Then too, I was stimulated by Garisse and—who knows?—by the successive glasses of punch we were served.

I followed the mulatta into a small cool room that, in olden times, must have been a monk's cell. There, a Franciscan full of faith had once elevated his soul toward God. It required an effort for me not to think about that pious man and make an abstraction of the disorder of the room—a disorder that might be called dirtiness.

"Yes m'sieur, good weather for picking grapefruit..."

In truth, I wondered why Garisse had brought me there, and what there could be to remark there. Perhaps I was devoid of all subtlety. That vexed me. When the mulatta and I returned to the cloister, the women were sitting down again—a little too stiffly, to be sure. The old Indian woman was nonchalantly blowing puffs of smoke toward the branches of the zebaa, and Garisse was smiling, with a glass of punch in his hand. He seemed to be saying to me: *Well, what do you think? Isn't it unusual?*

He got up and said in a low voice: "You owe two piastres."

I hesitated. I turned toward the mulatta.

"Yes m'sieur, good weather for picking grapefruit..."

Oh, no, no, enough…! The extended hand of the old Indian made me understand that it was to her that I had to give the two piastres.

Darkness fell with its habitual abruptness, almost without transition with the daylight. As we went into the law corridor that led to the cloister, I looked back, and it seemed to me—but I cannot affirm it with certainty—that the women seated in their attitude of parade had become transparent, as if they had drifted in the motionless evening air. I could even distinguish the trunks of the palm trees in the garden through their bodies. It was a momentary impression, which might have been produced by my desire to find something astonishing in the very ordinary aspect of everything that I had seen.

"Well?" said Garisse, as soon as we were in the carriage. "I assume that nothing escaped you?"

Still animated by the same sentiment, I replied haphazardly. "It's truly extraordinary."

"I've heard it said that that's frequently practiced among the necromancers of the Antilles. It's very curious to see the combination of negro magic and Indian magic."

"Very curious."

"And did you notice that bizarre repetition of the same phrase?"

"Oh! I should think so!

"Bizarre in appearance only."

"Yes."

"For is sum, one cannot expect of…how shall I put it?…those creatures, an ordinary memory. Perhaps they repeat in a mechanical fashion the last phrase they pronounced when they were alive."

"Perhaps."

"And do you know what put me on the track? For, naturally, I'm the only one to know it. A few months ago, a few cases of yellow fever were still being identified. Someone claimed, rightly or wrongly, that it came from the fact that the pearl-fishers from Cerralvo had been buried at ground level in the Franciscan cemetery. The governor of Vera Cruz sent a gang of workers to bury them again. That was considered a profanation by the inhabitants of the village, who stopped the workers completing their task. The governor would have had to send soldiers. He didn't do that, and it appears that that was a consequence of an intervention by Anastasio Alaman.

"What could it matter to him whether the dead were five feet underground instead of one? But I have the following fact from one of the workmen who had begun work on the graves on the first day. He's a man worthy of faith, who came to work at the hotel. Having dug a ditch he set about uncovering a mound where a young woman had been buried about three years before. Three years, you hear—and she had died of yellow fever. Well, according to what he claimed, the body was intact. And that simple man added: 'If she had had make-up on, she would have appeared to be alive.' As one doesn't trifle with yellow fever, he put her in the ditch anyway."

But what has that to do with it? I was about to ask—but the carriage had just arrived at the hotel, and I kept quiet.

"How many incredible things there are in the world," said Garisse, as he quit me.

I went for a walk in the hotel garden, reproaching myself for being ignorant and slow-witted—and suddenly, I was gripped by an unspeakable horror.

VI. Sentenced to Death
(Dr. Fazeuille's Journal)

Tragedy sometimes slips into life secretly, unknown to everyone. One chats, one strolls, one meets up very day and one does not know that a new element has been introduced into life to turn it upside down. That was what happened to us in Vera Cruz. When I remember that period, I criticize myself for not having divined anything, for having been almost totally blind, and the only consolation I have is thinking that I could not have changed anything in the course of events.

I will not go into any detail, since the purpose of this journal is not to tell the story of other people's adventures. Then too, it gives me no pleasure to remember what happened to us in Vera Cruz.

Our existence was dominated by the folly of Malvina and the ill humor of Bernard Borromée. Once, she declared to us that she was handing over the direction of our expedition to Anastasio Alaman. For what reason? Experience, and above all the great honesty of that man. Another time, she made us party to her decision to settle permanently in Vera Cruz. She seemed to be living in a joyful ecstasy and in the expectation of some unknown, unexpected and fortunate event.

The event occurred, but it was of an atrocious nature.

Now, I ought to confess in all sincerity that I have not understood anything either of the causes of that event, nor of the role that Bernard played in it. I have not even been able to measure the dolor that Malvina experienced and the art she put into disguising it. How I envy the intuitive, who see the motives behind actions easily!

On scrutinizing the secret intentions of destiny, as it is appropriate to do in order to understand the meaning of life, I see that everything was triggered by the cannon-shot fired by a certain Espandrillo, which had sunk the brig of the Vera Cruz customs. Scarcely had that cannon-shot resounded out to sea in the Gulf of Mexico than events prepared in advance were set in progress, one leading to another, to end in the scene that I am going to describe.

No, I cannot believe that Bernard played an important role in what happened. I prefer to believe that he was only a passive witness, like me. And yet...

What was inexplicable was the rapidity of events. Perhaps there had been a delay in the order of things and that delay had to be made up? When Providence is in a hurry, it has no fear of riding roughshod over usages, and it causes to collapse into a short duration time that it might have spread out into a number of days if it had not been in such a hurry.

The entire city was talking about nothing but the loss of the *Aquilon*, and everyone was whispering in confidence: "It's the work of Ezéquiel Alaman. But who can prove it? And even if there were proof, no one dares touch the Alamans..."

Only the younger Garisse said to me: "Governor Ambrosio detests the Alamans, and if he had formal proof, Ezéquiel would be doomed."

And there were people who said: "That Ezéquiel is a murderer." Others: "He's a madman." And others: "He's a sorcerer sold to the Devil, like his father."

Scarcely three days had passed.

"Let's go fetch Malvina," Bernard said to me. "She's asked me to go and pick her up in the old church of the cloister of Saint Augustine."

I started. "But I thought Malvina had sworn an oath never to enter church again!"

Bernard uttered a bizarre laugh. "Oh, women's oaths!"

Night was about to fall. The street where the church of Saint Augustine stood was silent and empty. For unknown reasons, it had once been closed by chains, the stumps of which were still visible. The church seemed forgotten, lost, and dead. We went in through a low door. There was a candle at the feet of a Madonna that could not be seen. I nearly bumped into several black forms that were prostrate human creatures. The contours of Malvina's face were outlined by the little aureole of the candlelight. She had not heard us coming. Bernard was about to touch her shoulder with his finger, but he stopped, and I understood that he was listening to the inconsequential words that she was pronouncing.

Inconsequential! Perhaps they did have a consequence. A name was repeated frequently, and it was that of Ezéquiel.

It is impossible to say that a movement of anger is heard or seen. And yet I had the perception of a breath, a painful element, made more of rage than dolor, that was emitted by Bernard.

"Let's go," he said to me in a low voice, and when we were under the porch of the church he added: "Let's leave her to her prayers. Let her pray as much as she likes!"

And he drew way. He only came back to the hotel late.

Assuredly, I cannot affirm it, but I have the sentiment that a great part of the events that followed had their cause in that minute of silence when Malvina was praying on her knees and Bernard was standing behind her.

I shall not tell the story of the events. We learned the next day that the President of Mexico had sent a special judge from Mexico City, known as the great judge, to search for the authors of the sinking of the *Aquilon*, and the same day, the rumor went around of Ezéquiel's arrest.

Everything is different in France. One does not send a special judge, and when someone is arrested, even for a crime, there are advocates, a long trial, numerous witnesses and a public debate. Nothing like that took place. A wind of terror passed over the city. Everyone was afraid of being implicated in the affair. The brothers Garisse instantly recommended that we not even pronounce the name of Alaman, and, although of a rather courageous nature, I believe that they would have preferred not to have people in their hotel who had dined with the Alamans.

"It's over. You've had a narrow escape, but it's over," the younger Garisse said to me one morning. "Ezéquiel has been sentenced to death."

Destiny continued to make haste to finish it. Perhaps the special judge sent from Mexico was also in a hurry to get back home and was even more pressed for time than destiny. The execution was to take place in three days.

An execution is a little like a bullfight: it is a spectacle, but of a graver order. It takes place in the main square, where the condemned man perishes by the garrote, and all the high society of the city who can take their places at the windows of houses witness it, dressed up for the occasion.

Now, the Garisse brothers had a balcony at their disposal, and they made the error of asking Malvina whether she wanted to watch the execution, without consulting me beforehand. She accepted, and begged me to accompany her, Bernard having refused absolutely to do so. He would even absent himself that day, he told us, in order to go in a coach to visit the region in the direction of the Orizaba mountains.

The moment of sunrise can sometimes be a terrible time. I imagine that Judgment Day will be announced by trumpets that will resonate at sunrise. The color of the light can be very beautiful, but it also contains an icy horror, depending on the state of mind one is in. Ezéquiel was to be executed at sunrise. It fell on a Sunday.

I found Malvina strangely calm and her eyes shining. I could not help thinking that there is in young women a mysterious liking for bloodshed, an attraction that impels them to contemplates images of dolor and death.

It was still dark. We were at the bottom of the hotel staircase and we waited there, standing up, for a few minutes. A step creaked lugubriously several times.

"That's a warning to go back upstairs," I said to Malvina, "and go back to our rooms."

She did not reply.

The young Garisse emerged from the gloom. I don't know why, but he had put on dark glasses and a large cape that made him resemble a policeman of the Empire. We followed him into the dark streets, through which a silent crowd as moving.

The main square was not far away. Garisse knocked on a large portal, which opened with precaution. The terrible face of a man of about fifty, with tousled hair and a large moustache, appeared in the gap of the door and shouted: "It's young Garisse—damn, he's in disguise!"

I knew that our host was a French painter who had married a Mexican woman and tyrannized his wife's family by means of his whims and the jovial authority of idle men.

We traversed a patio where a pale and slightly plump young man was sprawled, clad in an embroidered robe that might have been a nightshirt, and who was trying to play the guitar while singing.

"Hey, Antonio!" cried the painter, severely. "That's my brother-in-law. He only knows how to sing and play music. He even gets up at night to do it. But this isn't the right time, damn it!"

Antonio continued, without even glancing at us.

We went up a broad staircase and into a room whose balcony overlooked the square.

"You'll have the best seats in the house," our host said, addressing Malvina. "Excuse the señora—she's such a sensitive soul that she can't bear this kind of spectacle. Then again, it's a bit early for her."

We saw a shadow emerge from a corner of the room. It was a very old priest, all wrinkled, who bowed very deeply to us. He seemed very sympathetic, and I would have liked to talk to him, but he went back into the shadows from which he had emerged. His face was very pale. The appearance of his luminous face gave me the sensation that a kind of sun was somewhere behind me.

In this country there must be a spectacular liking for romantic representation, which every man must bear within him, and which is realized in festivals, religious ceremonies, and even the executions of men sentenced to death. When I advanced on to the balcony, everything seemed to me, in the slight paling of the morning, so out of the ordinary that I recoiled, having the sentiment of being an actor ill-prepared for his role.

We were opposite the cathedral, the great portal of which was closed. One sensed that it was about to open. Monks clad in white robes with black hoods stood in two rows, and their silent file extended as far as the scaffold, which was situated in the middle of the square. A mute crowd surrounded it. Almost all of the spectators were wearing black headscarves, perhaps as a sign of mourning, because of the presence of death. One side of the square was occupied by the governor's palace. All the windows were garnished with functionaries and military men, with their families. There was a profusion of extraordinary uniforms, jewels, brocade dresses, and pointed swords. In the center, on a large balcony, straight and thin, in a black robe from which a face the color of wax emerged, stood the man called the great judge, surrounded by people whose attitude one sensed to be determinedly solemn and composed. On every side the houses were animated. A few lamps went out, one by one. Down below, the crowd of headscarves undulated.

"Look at the Marquise," said the painter to Garisse, pointing at a balcony.

I did not ask "What Marquise?" What was the point? A prodigious fat woman clad in lace, with a low-cut dress, covered in necklaces, was agitating above a crimson curtain thrown over the wrought iron of the balcony for the occasion. In spite of the morning chill she was fanning herself with a fan made of feathers. She must have been uttering little cries and pronouncing ridiculous words, for I could distinguish smiles on the faces of the people surrounding her.

I felt my arm gripped very forcefully. It was Malvina. She wasn't addressing me in particular.

"Oh my God! A miracle is still possible, isn't it?"

I looked at her, and she moved me to pity. I thought it appropriate to shake my head negatively.

"A miracle is always possible, my child," said a soft voice beside us. It was the old priest, who had overheard. "But it's necessary not to ask for it," he added. And, lowering his voice, with humility, he said again: "It's necessary never to ask for anything."

Malvina was about to say something else, but she couldn't. Abruptly, as if it were participating in a performance, the light was transformed. There was a stream of blood that came from the sky, which flowed over the houses, caused the red stones of the governor's palace to catch fire, and lit up the stained glass windows of the cathedral. And at the same time, as if a stage-manager had regulated the sun, the earth and the movements of men, the bells started to ring, the door of the cathedral opened slowly, and all the monks intoned the *De profundis*.

Red and black everywhere! Red and black cut by the lines of white monks: that was how that funereal square appeared to me in the light of the rising sun, in a theatrical symphony whose arrangement was so well regulated that it became horrible.

The condemned man had spent the night with his confessor before the main altar of the cathedral. That was the custom. Behind the soldiers carrying halberds and bizarre head-dresses that gave them the appearance of creatures emerge from Medieval Spain, behind an order of monks who were devoting themselves to prayers for the dead, Ezéquiel finally appeared, alongside a very small priest who stood up on tiptoe at times in order to reduce the difference in height between himself and the man he was supposed to sustain. The ivory crucifix that he was lifting up was illuminated by a red reflection on the threshold of the church, and one might have believed momentarily that it was painted with blood.

Ezéquiel had a facial pallor that seemed curiously related to the one that had struck me in the face of the great judge. He ought to have been covered by a black hood, but, doubtless by tolerance, he had been allowed to throw it backwards. He darted a circular glance around the square, as if he were looking for someone.

Malvina uttered a stifled cry. She addressed herself again to me: "Go, go tell them that it's not him! Run, quickly! He hasn't done anything. There's still time. They'll believe you. We'll testify."

They were insensate words. I had drawn her back into the obscurity of the room. I perceived the silhouette of the priest. He took Malvina by the arm, gently, pronouncing words in a low voice, which I did not hear. I saw his eyes fill with tears. I thought that everything was decidedly well ordered in the world, since a holy man emerged, at the moment and in the place where a holy man was necessary, to replace a doctor with a slightly dry heart.

"There are the members of the Acordada!" Garisse said to me.

Men in a red costume were shoving the crowd around the scaffold brutally. I don't know where they had come from. Garisse explained to me that they were a special police force created at the end of the eighteenth century, who had been given the power to crucify brigands caught with weapons in hand. They formed a fallen and obsolete fraternity, but reappeared on certain occasions, thus procuring the pleasure of those who liked to dress up in uniforms.

"Look at the Marquise laughing," murmured the painter.

Garisse, leaning toward me, said: "Old lady Alaman must be somewhere, at a window. You, who know magic, ought to know..." He interrupted himself suddenly. "Hold on, in that small window on the third floor, look."

It was a little too far for me to distinguish clearly, but I did indeed see, immobile, like a statue, the silhouette of an Indian woman, the face half-hidden by a black mantilla. It seemed to me that she was holding something in her hand that was burning.

"I'll wager that she's making an appeal to Metzli, the god of Light, for him to intervene and save her son."

Rumors and cries were now running through the crowd:

"To death!"

"*El saltádor!*"

211

And also: "Courage, Alaman!"—but those cries were less numerous.

Suddenly, there was a muffled clamor. On the scaffold, which was composed of a platform surmount by a large stake, a silhouette had just been outlined: that of the executioner.

I saw, with amazement, a negro of tall stature, naked to the waist, with an abundant curly white hair that overflowed a red bonnet. He had a black mask, doubtless because of an ancient tradition that wanted the executioner's face to be unknown, but he was a popular individual. He had folded his arms and, leaning on the stake, one sensed that he was enjoying that sinister momentary glory profoundly.

The condemned man, whom his confessor was holding with one hand, while brandishing his crucifix, ivory once again, in the other, climbed the steps of the scaffold. They had been nailed hastily, and one of them almost tilted. The crowd shouted. Ezéquiel Alaman took advantage of it to parade an anxious glance from house to house. He was searching for someone.

Suddenly, his gaze remained fixed on the balcony where we were. I felt my heart beating forcefully. I turned slightly and saw Malvina, her head leaning forward, in the attitude of a creature that has been magnetized. Ezéquiel climbed the last few steps slowly, inattentive to everything, his face appeased, his eyes still turned toward Malvina.

A functionary wearing a metal necklace made an imperious sign that urged the proud executioner to hurry. In a matter of seconds, the negro, whose teeth were gleaming, shoved Ezéquiel brutally on to a stool, jammed his head against the stake and enclosed his neck in an iron collar that made a horrible metallic sound. But Ezéquiel's eyes, in his now-twisted face, never quit Malvina's.

A great silence suddenly covered the square. The executioner had put his hand on the lever of the garrote. He only had to press it and the collar would break the condemned man's spine. But the confessor had to read the prayer for the dead. His shrill voice, whose tone he strove to raise, going as rapidly as possible, gave the impression of the song of an insect, the hymn of a solitary cricket.

"Lord, have mercy, receive his soul into thy arms," the old priest beside me said, in a tone whose sincerity wrung the heart.

The insect song stopped. At the same time, all the monks, of all the orders, all those who filled the cathedral, the greater part of the crowd, and those hanging out of the windows, intoned the prayer for the dead, which unfurled toward the heavens like a tempest of pity and desolation. Sobs were heard and, here and there, the cries of hysterical women. The executioner had pressed the lever. Ezéquiel's eyes, while his body was dislocated with a jerk, did not quit Malvina's.

Full of horror, I left the balcony, almost dragging her away by force. The nature of women is incomprehensible. She found an appearance of calm very rapidly.

"You'll excuse the señora," said the painter, shaking her hand. "She can't get up so early."

In the patio, the indifferent brother-in-law continued to extract notes from his guitar.

"It's very curious," said the painter, "that my brother-in-law is blond." And he repeated several times: "He's a blond Mexican. There are some."

VII. The Adventure of the Stagecoach

Colonel Espondeillan had resolved to reach Mexico City. Three days in a stagecoach! What was that? Had he not made the retreat from Russia? It was only in Mexico City that he could make his fortune. And he wanted it to be a political fortune. He wanted his value to be recognized, for people to talk about him. Oh, his compatriots had preferred his friend Chalabre, the star man, to him as president! It was necessary that they admit one day that they were wrong, for them to say: "If only Colonel Espondeillan had been our president, we wouldn't be in this mess!"

For they would not succeed. They were poorly led, Poor Chalabre! He loved him, all the same. But he had always considered him as a sort of disciple. From the viewpoint of strategy, Chalabre was an infant. And similarly in life. Once, he had almost lost his head because he was about to start a lawsuit, and if he, Espondeillan, hadn't taken the matter in hand... It was only in battle, with a saber in his hand, that he was almost equal in strength, and even then...

They had cut long laths of supple wood, with which they had measured themselves during the long afternoons in Saint-Gaudens. Evidently, the number of victories and defeats was equilibrated. Commandant Zenon Fabrégat, who judged the blows and struck the ground with his wooden leg when a head would have been split, affirmed that they were equal in strength. But he was an artilleryman. Poor Chalabre occupied himself too much with the stars. And to think that it was because of that that he had been chosen. They would see!

"We'll meet again in Mexico City," General Ozorno had said, who knew men.

The colonel's baggage consisted of an officer's trunk that was placed on the diligence. But there was also a pair of sabers wrapped in leather, which he wanted to have under his eyes. An argument ensued.

214

"A man without weapons doesn't exist!" he shouted, loudly.

But the nine places in the stagecoach were filled; it was necessary to place the sabers far from their master's eye, beside the trunk.

"You're a French officer?" asked a man with a big moustache and a terrible face.

"I'm Colonel Espondeillan."

"I'm Colonel Nacome."

The two men shook hands.

"We're men of war," said the Mexican colonel, darting a scornful glance at the other passengers who were installed in the stagecoach. And, lowering his voice, almost in confidence, he added: "Believe me, it's better that the weapons are on top. You'll see in due course why."

"Jesusita! Jesusita!" cried a fat woman with a piercing voice. "I commend Jesusita to all of you!"

Jesusita was a beautiful young woman of sixteen or eighteen, who had a sort of angelic disguise. Pale blue and faded white were combined in her costume with sufficient artistry to give a celestial impression. Nevertheless, she did not have wings. A light pink gauze floating in the wind attempted to substitute for them.

"Your Jesusita is all alone?" asked a fat man of well-to-do appearance.

"Lord God, yes, she's traveling all alone."

"That's very imprudent. When I take the stagecoach for Mexico City I only carry twenty-five piastres. They know me. I'm good for twenty-five piastres. But a young woman like that, one might well estimate her at five hundred piastres."

"Lord God! Jesusita isn't for sale!"

"It's not a matter of that. But one doesn't allow five hundred piastres to travel alone on a stagecoach from Vera Cruz to Mexico City."

"What! You think so? It's possible that..."

"Eh? Damn it, I don't think anything! I don't have anything to say. Don't make me say what I haven't said."

Espondeillan had heard that conversation. He removed his hat gallantly. "If it's a matter of the protection of a young woman, you can count on me."

"Lord God! I thank you."

Colonel Nacome tugged Espondeillan's sleeve urgently,

"Don't stick your neck out. You don't know where that might lead you. Jesusita's departure might have been signaled..."

"Signaled to whom?"

"Lower your voice. One can see that you're a foreigner." Drawing him a few paces aside, he added: "Look at that man with the tall hat. He's the one going to climb up beside the coachman and take care of the horses at each relay. He seems to be listening to everything. I don't like his sly air."

Espondeillan could not ask for an explanation, because the stagecoach was about to set off. *It's true*, he thought, *that the fellow's hat is an unusual shape, but that's no reason to mistrust him. Anyway, on what subject?*

There was a subject of dread about which all the passengers were thinking, but it was a familiar subject, not overly frightening, because they were accustomed to it.

"Hold yourself in reserve," said the man who resembled a well-to-do merchant, in a low voice, leaning toward Espondeillan's ear. "That young woman sitting opposite Jesusita has just declared that she's from Huamantla."

"Beware! The young woman with the big nose is from the village of Huamantla," whispered an old lady in black lace to her neighbor.

Espondeillan perceived that name on her lips. "What is Huamantla?" he asked.

A shiver ran around. The pure Jesusita was the only one not to manifest any disturbance.

"Huamantla? But that's my village," said a lively young woman with dark eyes, who would have been judged quite pretty if she had not been marred by a big nose, casting a fiery glance around the audience.

Colonel Nacome, who was sitting beside Espondeillan, leaned toward him again.

"Huamantla is the village where the robbers of stage-coaches are recruited."

He had thought to impress his neighbor, but the latter only started laughing.

"I don't fear thieves. If they present themselves, they'll have to deal with me."

But that did not reassure the audience. There was a sudden silence. People looked at one another. The young woman from Huamantla fixed Espondeillan with and inquisitive gaze. Then she looked at the woman in black lace, who shivered and exclaimed: "I don't know him. I don't know who he is."

"Then permit me to introduce myself," said Espondeillan. "I'm a French colonel, who has no hesitation in declaring to you that you have nothing to fear from thieves."

The young woman with the big nose burst out laughing. "But there are no thieves. At any rate, I can guarantee that here are none in Huamantla. It's my homeland, and I only know worthy people there."

Everyone joined in chorus, while the stagecoach rolled on, inviting the passengers to sleep.

The first stage went as far as Perote. Espondeillan took advantage of the evening to recount all his campaigns to his new friend, Colonel Nacome.

"A man like you isn't cut out for this country," said the Mexican, sententiously. "Here, men don't fear death, but they have an extreme fear of the incidents that provoke it. Explain that however you like. It's necessary not to be too brave. Life isn't organized for that. Look at Santa Anna. He's a hero, everyone recognizes that. In spite of that heroism, he's always run away at every opportunity. In your place, I wouldn't keep that big revolver on me. It's imprudent."

Before departing, Colonel Espondeillan had bought a superb six-shot revolver of an American model. That weapon no longer quit him and he had invited Colonel Nacome to admire it. The idea of separating himself from it caused him to shrug his shoulders.

"Take note," said Colonel Nacome, "that there will be danger this evening, when passing through the Pinal."

"What danger?"

"Thieves."

"Two resolute men are worth a whole troop."

"Evidently, two men…two…"

The sky was leaden. The travelers dozed, and then ate. The conversation resumed. They arrived in Huamantla. The young woman with the hooked nose was not going any further. She bid everyone farewell amicably.

"How cheerful and charming she is!!" said all the travelers.

"Too cheerful! Perhaps ironic," murmured Nacome.

Huamantla was a village like all villages. Espondeillan saw villagers such as there are everywhere, and on a street that sloped downwards he saw a red-faced priest with a paternal expression who was walking slowly leaning on a staff. A low and very ancient bell-tower seemed to be gazing over the houses.

This is a very peaceful place, Espondeillan thought.

They set off again.

"It's a fatality," said the well-to-do merchant, "But one always passes through the Pinal at the end of the day."

"Will we soon be in the Pinal?" asked a thin and stiff woman whose husband never ceased coughing, clutching a large red handkerchief to his lips.

"I sell chaplets," said the merchant, "and it would be a good idea to carry some with me, if only for that accursed Pinal. Twenty-five piastres! I only have twenty-five piastres on me."

"Oh, the Pinal!" said the man who had stopped coughing as soon as he word *Pinal* had been pronounced.

"Fundamentally," said the chaplet merchant, stimulated by what he had drunk in Huamantla, "Everything can be evaluated by a sum of money. Each of us has a value. Well, I think it insensate to put into a stagecoach that traverses the Pinal, without a defender, a young woman like this one, whose name is Jesusita—a young woman who represents, in my opinion, a value of at least five hundred piastres."

"She has a defender," Espondeillan put in modestly.

But at that moment there was a noise of hoof-beats on the road. The stagecoach was enveloped by a group of riders. At first there was a murmur of fear among the passengers, which changed into delight. The horsemen were carabiniers, known as "regulars," by contrast with the numerous "irregulars" with whom Mexico had been filled for forty years.

The stagecoach had stopped. Colonel Nacome knew the lieutenant who was at the head of eight soldiers. He stood up and got out in order to go and shake his hand. The lieutenant was a young man of pretentious appearance, but amiable. He uttered reassuring words. The road and, in particular, the Pinal, were tranquil. As Nacome climbed back up, Espondeillan, to his surprise, saw that the groom in the tall square hat had approached the officer and was chatting to him in a familiar fashion. He even thought that he saw the officer receive something, which he put into his pocket precipitately. He made the observation to Nacome, who had also seen it.

"I don't much like that," he said. "The officer is from a good Mexican family, but everything degenerates, especially good families."

The stagecoach and the horsemen set off in opposite directions, with equal speed. Night was approaching.

"We're in the Pinal, said a slightly hoarse voice.

Rugged rocks loomed up to the right and left, bristling with stunted pines. The road, carved into the stone, rose and then descended, and seemed to shrink. What followed unfurled with great rapidity.

"Halt!" cried a resounding voice on the road, and at the same time, a man was seen, running and making signs.

But the stagecoach was on a slope and horses were galloping.

"Halt!" cried another voice, while a second silhouette became visible.

"I beg you, pass me your revolver!" said Nacome, squeezing Espondeillan's arm. The latter saw that he was very pale.

"I'm an excellent shot," he replied.

"But it's to disarm it and throw it on the road. You're risking everyone's lives. I beg you, for the honor of Jesusita, whom you're putting in danger, throw away your revolver quickly."

The coachman struggled in vain with the horses; the slope was too steep. The carriage hurtled downhill. A detonation resounded. The coachman fell forwards and tumbled from the vehicle. The groom seized the reins and succeeded in stopping the horses.

The stagecoach filled with cries.

"Above all, don't move!" cried the chaplet merchant. "This has happened to me before. Stay in your seats or you're dead."

Nacome had thrown himself on Espondeillan and attempted to snatch his evolver.

"I beg you. You have to throw it away. There's still time."

The door of the diligence opened. A form stood there, under a large sombrero.

"Women, to the right, first. Get down, colonel."

Nacome hastened to get down, raising his empty hands. In the shadows the voice of another man resounded, who was wearing a red headscarf. "Pass me Jesusita."

Before the young woman, chilled by horror, had moved, Espondeillan extended his arm and fired. The man collapsed. Suddenly rejuvenated by the atmosphere of combat, the colonel leapt lightly outside, where the women were crying out, and sent a second shot at the man with the sombrero, who recoiled, uttering imprecations. He fell too. The intuition of a combatant made Espondeillan turn around at the precise moment when the groom, crawling toward him with a knife in his hand, was about to leap upon his back. He fired a third shot, to which a howl responded. With both hands over his bloody face, the man started running. There was a noise among the pines of men fleeing and calling to one another.

"Nacome, pass me my sabers. You go take the horses—and you women, shut up!" shouted Espondeillan, in a tone of command that brooked no reply.

Nacome got the sabers down, murmuring that it was insensate, and that they would never reach Puebla alive. The chaplet merchant took the horses. Espondeillan, his revolver in his hand, went back up the road, which was becoming ever darker, until he reached the coachman. He made sure that he was dead. He called Nacome to help him, and they both took the body, which they hoisted up, not without difficulty, on to the top of the stagecoach.

"We'll never arrive in Puebla," murmured Nacome. "First of all, who's going to drive?"

"I'll take charge of that."

Espondeillan ordered everyone to take their places again. He took that of the coachman, and put his saber and his revolver beside him. He cracked the whip in a resounding manner, while the women repeated prayers inside the diligence.

The diligence arrived without encumbrance in Puebla, where they were to spend the night.

The event did not arouse any great emotion.

"Poor Pablo," someone said, talking about the coachman.

"If everyone acted thus, there'd be no more thieves!"

But the unanimous opinion was that the presence of such a courageous man represented too great a danger for those who accompanied him.

"What imprudence!" everyone said. "And what's going to happen to him?"

The road from Puebla to Mexico City was known to be the only one where security was absolute. Troops circulated along it almost every day. In spite of that, when the diligence set off again the next day, with a new coachman, Colonel Espondeillan found that he was the only passenger, except for

221

Jesusita The colonel could not tell whether the young woman had taken account of the danger she had run.

"Lord Jesus! There you are!" said a fat woman very similar to the one who had accompanied Jesusita in Vera Cruz, when they arrived in Mexico City. After a slight nod of the head to her traveling companion, Jesusita drew away with her.

With his trunk and his sabers, Colonel Espondeillan booked a room at the Hôtel des Arcades. No one noticed his arrival. Three days later, he was celebrated throughout Mexico. Colonel Nacome, whose affairs had retained him for a day in Puebla—so he said, at least—had taken it upon himself to tell the story of the evening in the Pinal, with a few slight modifications regarding the role that he had played. He had remained sincerely wonderstruck by the precision of Espondeillan's revolver shots.

"First of all," he said, "those six-shot revolvers are extraordinary. But that Frenchman fires without taking aim. I've seen him drop his man at three hundred paces, and in the dark."

Colonel Espondeillan became the best marksman in Mexico. That reputation was to be useful to him.

"You've killed two of them and wounded a third," Nacome said to him. "Here, blood always calls for blood. The highway thieves form a very powerful association. Beware."

Espondeillan was fearless. In spite of everyone's advice, he went to gambling houses and places of pleasure and came back late at night.

While lingering once following a game of monte in a small basement, to which an officer of his acquaintance had taken him because it was picturesque, he noticed a man with a bandage over his face and a square hat of a form that was not unknown to him. The man disappeared as soon as Espondeillan's gaze settled on him.

Much later, the colonel quit the game of monte, in which his resources had not permitted him to take part, and headed toward the Hôtel des Arcades. On the way, whistle-blasts were heard in front and behind him. He had arrived at an intersection, and in all directions, by the light of blinking lanterns, he saw human silhouettes.

With the strange lightness that he discovered at the moment of combat, he departed at a gymnastic pace straight ahead, his revolver raised in his right hand. Then, stopping suddenly, he gave his voice its full amplitude and he shouted, loudly enough to be heard by the entire group that was running toward him: "Look out! I'm firing!"

A single knife was hurled in his direction, but it must have been with an ill-assured hand, for it missed him by a long way. In all directions at once, he heard the sounds of hectic flight, a precipitate stampede.

They knew that the foremost marksman in Mexico never missed his man, even in the dark.

VIII. The Bandits' Camp

The men of Comminges who disembarked at San Francisco after a seventy-one day crossing, had a different state of mind, fashioned by storm and sadness.

When the cry of "Land ho!" resounded aboard the *Invincible*, they did not see a city with steeples and houses. The absence of houses, in particular, struck them. At the foot of a severe line of fir trees, which dominated the amphitheater of a bay, they only perceived wooden huts and tents. Fortunately, when the ship had penetrated into the bay and had drawn closer to land, the silhouette of a deer that was gamboling on a ridge was outlined against the sky. That gave them the sensation of a friendly wilderness in which hunting would be easy and nature welcoming.

But the majority, if they could, would have departed again toward the mildness of the villages of France.

When the emigrants disembarked with their tents and a few collapsible wooden huts that turned out to be impossible to assemble, they did not know at first where to go. Everyone had told them that it was necessary to mistrust a population of adventurers who did not speak their language. They asked where there were Frenchmen. A promontory covered with forests was indicated to them, where a French camp was located about a mile from a place called Contra-Costa.

They set forth, carrying on their backs the collapsible houses, tents, tools and weapons. In the middle of a vast clearing they found bearded and hairy men who had constructed a vast dwelling out of tree-trunks and palm leaves, into which the rain must stream, but where they were able to spend the first night.

"Where is the gold?" they asked, immediately. "Where are the placers?" They were greeted with bitter laughter. The gold was a long way away, at least ten days' march in the direction of the mountains. To be sure, one could get there. But the majority of those who set out never came back. It was necessary to reflect, to make preparations. In the meantime, if you were a good shot, you could kill game and go and sell it. And there were many other métiers that you could exercise, if you were clever, without risking your life in unknown mountains full of Indians, lovers of scalps.

Not all the men of Comminges were clever. Being clever, for the Frenchmen of Contra-Costa, meant, in sum, being a thief, or very nearly. It was a matter of having an aptitude for exploiting and despoiling the gold-seekers who came back with their dust and nuggets, the famous virgin gold of which there had been so much talk and the evocation of which had sent so many men to adventures.

The men of Comminges split up. Their fraternal association was dissolved. There were the courageous, who set forth, and the hesitant, who remained. And among those there were the honest, who tried to work at their trade, and the others, who were tempted by the gambling dens, improvised theaters and bars aligned along the harbor, prostitution and its thousand resources. The mere radiation of virgin gold exhausted energies and decomposed souls.

By virtue of the mysterious law of sympathies, Vincent Malbosque, a good and simple man from the valley of Barousse, was immediately selected as a companion and friend by the man who was known as "the lord"[11] in the camp of Contra-Costa. He had received that nickname because of the aristocracy of his manners, a certain attitude of scorn that he never abandoned and the red side-whiskers that he maintained along his cheeks with care. He resembled the idea that the Californian adventurers had of a lord.

---

[11] This nickname is given in English in the original. Although I have equipped most of the nicknames employed in the text with a capital letter, as Magre usually does, it would be inappropriate to do so in this case, for obvious reasons.

That morning, the lord had killed a roe deer and he was carrying it on his back. He called to Malbosque.

"I'll teach you something that you need to know in order to be a man."

He spoke in the tone that a master adopts in speaking to a disciple. Malbosque listened respectfully. The lord threw the roe deer at his feet and took a large sharp knife from his belt, which he carried in a sheath.

"It's the first thing that it's necessary to learn. You're a child at the teat as long as you don't know it. It's just a trick, but it's still necessary to know how it's done."

Malbosque looked on with his full attention.

"I'm going to show you on the deer's hide the place on the back where the hairs are longest. The important thing is to cut it with the knife. You dig it in, holding it flat, and you trace a circle, a little as if you were opening a can of food. It's necessary to do it quickly; the art is in the speed. Then you take the hair firmly in your hand and you pull. But in order that it's done in a single thrust, you put the foot on the man's chin."

So saying, the lord had had torn away the circular patch of skin from the back of the roe deer, causing blood to drip.

"You see, it's a fake scalp. There are some jokers who hang several like that from their belt."

Malbosque widened his eyes, not understanding yet.

"But it's necessary not to forget the foot on the chin. That's quite hard. And it can happen that the man experiences a sharp sensation, and if he's stunned or mortally wounded, he starts to howl. Now, silence is always necessary. Personally, I always finish the man beforehand."

Malbosque had understood. His peasant wisdom had taught him to listen to everything without protest. It was necessary to learn the mores of the land. He felt himself blushing.

"But I've no intention of...doing that," he said, simply.

The lord began to laugh. "If you don't do it, someone will do it to you. Not scalping one's enemy is a sign of weakness. In France, there are decorated men. They're respected.

Here in California, if you want to be respected, it's necessary to have scalps on your belt. Patience, though. If you go to the Rocky Mountains you'll have some too, and you can't know the pleasure there is in adding one to your collection."

On his parents' farm Malbosque had a young cousin of sixteen called Laurence, of a delicate temperament, whom everyone loved. But it was necessary not to kill a chicken in front of her because the sight of blood made her faint.

The fake scalp was swinging in the lord's hand, and a drop of blood sometimes made a slight sound as it fell on his boots. Malbosque could find nothing to say. He thought he could see his cousin's face, her eyes fixed on his belt.

As he got out of the launch that had transported him to land, Colonel Bertrand de Chalabre twisted his foot. He was taken to a nearby house, where a Spaniard consented to keep him until he was healed. The old Spaniard, respectable in appearance, knew a physician who lived not far away and who achieved extraordinary cures.

"A Spanish physician! You know that the Spaniards are the foremost physicians in the world."

Everyone was unaware of that, but the colonel had confidence and his friends left him in the Spaniard's house.

Julien de Miravel came back immediately from the Frenchmen's camp. "All the women there are horrible to behold," he declared.

It seemed to him that there were more resources in San Francisco. He discovered a gaming house adjacent to a single-story wooden hotel. Wooden huts formed dependencies of the hotel all around it. Fifteen women of all races were installed there. In order to strike the eyes, each wore the national costume of her homeland, but with a theatrical exaggeration. The Spaniard never quit a Basque drum found who knows where, and had sewn little metal roundels to the hem of her scarlet skirt. A Syrian had arranged rags and gauze veils that made her resemble a fairground Scheherazade. A Frenchwoman caused a sensation with the exaggeration of her crinoline.

Julien de Miravel installed himself in their midst. He was dazzled.

"I've spent twenty years of exile in the honest little town of Saint-Gaudens. I've rediscovered the veritable life."

And it was agreed that his companions would come to look for him there when the moment came to depart for the distant region of the placers.

Captain Montarache became the leader of the expedition. Initially, he had the pretention of militarizing the members of the association of the Brothers of the Virgin Gold. In the morning, in the middle of the camp at Contra-Costa, they had to respond to the appeal, do exercises and run at a gymnastic pace. That took place on the first day, before the bewildered and ironic inhabitants of the camp. There were still a few faithful on the second day, but on the third the captain was alone with the excellent Malbosque. For the sake of principle he continued his lessons in fencing with a bayonet, while the lord and his comrades, not far away, amid laugher, devoted themselves to caricatures of exercise. It was necessary to stop.

In any case, Captain Montarache had been experiencing since his arrival a disappointment far more serious than that of not being able to exercise any military authority. He had not found the cigars of his dreams, the cigars "as long as this" that the humblest stevedore on the harbor was supposed to smoke. Not only had he not found those gigantic cigars, but he had not been able to procure any, even of the most reduced format.

"Oh well! When we get back from the placers I'll go to Manila."

He did not know where Manila was, and imagined that he would reach the city of cigars one evening on horseback, in the depths of a valley, in the midst of the enchanting vapors of tobacco. Accustomed to an extreme poverty, he did not suffer any privation. He only suffered from not having the cigars that he had never known and the deceptive delights of which he had created himself.

But he had marvelous compensations. The activity, the illusory authority with which he was vested, and the aspects of the nature that surrounded him, contributed to a return to juvenility.

"My hairs are growing more quickly since my departure from France, and they're more numerous," he said. "It's the same for all the hairs on my body. I have singular phenomena in the jaw. I wouldn't be astonished if new teeth were growing." And he clicked his jaw, laughing.

In the evening, around a wood fire, he listened avidly to the stories that the Frenchmen of Contra-Costa told. There were many stories of violence and rapine, calculated to frighten an honest French pensioner, especially one of particularly austere mores such as him. But he thought: *Every country has its mores. It's necessary that I accustom myself to the existence of these men, harsh in appearance but fundamentally excellent.*

The camp did not only bring together Frenchmen. There were other foreigners, all remarkable for a strong personality, almost always expressed in a criminal appearance.

There was a Methodist preacher who went to the gaming houses to harangue the gamblers and then went begging. As soon as he had enough money he would depart for Rome, where he was certain of converting the Pope. He gladly recited the conversation that he would have with him.

"In matters of dogma I fear no one, and the Pope will yield to my arguments."

But his companions knew his old habit of picking pockets and sometimes recovered their property from him by violence.

A man they called Robinson Crusoe possessed a large umbrella, to which he had fitted a very long shaft, which he could stick in the ground in order to sleep in its shade. He had sharpened the other end, and sharpened it incessantly. He claimed that with that umbrella he was not afraid of any wild animal.

"There's no tiger, or even a snake, that can resist the terrifying effect of an abruptly-opened umbrella. And if, in addition, its muzzle is traversed by a sharp dart, it never fails to run away." Once, he had stopped a charging bison dead. He only feared wolves. For mysterious reasons, wolves, when they were numerous, took no account of the umbrella.

The Kentuckian Joe, known as the Chinaman, excelled with carbine and revolver. He spent his time furbishing his weapons while explaining his means of making a fortune. He had a particular love for China and the Chinese, although he was not acquainted with them. He had only frequented the wretched specimens of the Chinese that were seen in San Francisco. He had a plan to make a fortune, thanks to China.

"That country is very vast. We only see poor coolies here, but China is full of mandarins and princes. As soon as I have a considerable sum, I'll buy rifles of the latest model and those marvelous six-shot Colts. I'll go to China, and those mandarins and princes, who still make use of bows and arrows, will undoubtedly buy my weapons for enormous prices, ten or twenty times what I'll have paid"

A man known as the Emperor had such a majestic physique that one was tempted to attribute a kind of sovereignty to him. His hair fell over his broad shoulders and a gray beard descended over his chest. He was tall and his gestures were slow and noble. He claimed that after a shipwreck he had been cast up on a Pacific island where the indigenes had prostrated themselves at the sight of him, and where he had exercised an absolute royalty. He gave descriptions of an island of forests and marshes, which might be situated in Malaysia. He talked about lacustrian villages where it was necessary to defend oneself incessantly against huge water-snakes. He had had ministers, wives and children.

One day, however, a ship, half-merchant and half-pirate, had dropped anchor in the island's only bay. The captain had spent a few days with him, and had shown him the greatest regard. He had offered to take him aboard and bring him back to civilized lands. He had accepted, and had taken with him a treasure of admirable pearls fished up by his subjects. But scarcely was the ship at sea than the captain, careless of the services he had rendered, had obliged him to replace a member of his crew who had recently died and had had him given twenty lashes right away to teach him the rigors of discipline.

The Emperor only recounted the continuation of his story when he got drunk, which he did every time he could.

"I had been a cook in the first phase of my life. I make it a principle only to act by cunning, and I had always found that it paid off. In order to maintain myself as a king on an island I needed a great deal of cunning, especially in the early days, when I didn't speak the language. I made the captain believe that I accepted my fate. Then I talked to him about my talents as a cook. It was agreed that I would replace the man who worked in the galley, who was ignorant of the first elements of his métier. I happened to have brought with me a vegetable poison of great violence, prepared by one of my wives, which was an instrument of my reign on the island. I didn't waste time. I surpassed myself once with a dish of fish and rice of which I was a master, and in the evening, they demanded the same dish with the same preparation. I put my poison in it, of which I knew the infallible effect."

In the camp of Contra-Costa stories were told in the evening before great fire lit in the open air, where the products of hunting were roasted. When the Emperor reached that point in his story—for he told it quite frequently—there was laughter and great enthusiasm. When the Frenchmen from the banks of the Garonne heard it for the first time, a few of them remained thoughtful.

"Of how many men did crew consist?" asked Captain Montarache.

"It was a ship of three hundred tons, and there were only eleven men in total."

"And they all died at the same time?"

"Almost. I knew the poison. In case of incomplete success I had taken an ax and barricaded myself in the galley. I knew that it was necessary to wait for twenty minutes.

"But among those eleven men there must have been a few worthy ones?"

"I couldn't choose the good and the bad. They were pirates. Except one, perhaps—the only one who had treated me well, a Dutch colossus. He didn't want to die. The poison had only dazed him. I was obliged to finish him off, because it was necessary to think about the future, and what he might have said. Mine was a terrible situation. Alone with eleven cadavers and a ship adrift. My first concern was to throw the bodies in the sea, for the poison rendered the faces terrible, and it wasn't comfortable. I acted under the spur of emotion—too quickly. See the fatality. I couldn't find the pearls, of which the captain has taken possession. He must have had them on his person. I'd thrown my fortune into the sea. That troubled my brain. When a Spanish ship picked me up, my explanations must have seemed awkward, for they kept me in prison for six months in the Philippines. Judge my fate: to have been an emperor, and then receiving strokes of the lash, and spending six months in prison."

Captain Montarache contented himself with twisting his moustache.

A little later, Dardignac, a worthy man from Toulouse, said to him in a low voice, seeing him anxious: "Well, Captain, other lands, other mores. I believe that fundamentally, the heart is here all the same."

However, the newcomers formed a human bloc that had difficulty mingling with the former Frenchmen of Contra-Costa. Natural antipathies were manifest with more force than sympathies. An unreasonable hatred put the lord at odds with Jean-Marie Dutasta, who had immediately been nicknamed the Braggart.

Jean-Marie Dutasta, a former sub-officer in the cavalry, was a small town dandy. He was a fine talker and knew how to dance. Tall and blond, he gave the impression of a redoubtable sheep; he was cowardly in the extreme but boasted about his heroic exploits. When Robinson Crusoe told stories of wild animals, he immediately overbid hem by talking about hunting lions and panthers in Africa.

"I've been the companion of Bombonnel,[12] and he said to me: "Dutasta, you're better made than me.' You've heard mention of Bombonnel? Well, several times, before French officers in Algeria declared that he considered me to be his master for killing panthers."

Such speeches exasperated the lord. Silent by nature, he accumulated within him the sort of rage that has explosive force when it has been compressed too long.

They were talking one night about knife fights, and someone said that the Italians excelled at them. The lord was known to be very redoubtable when he had that weapon in his hand. Pushed by his evil genius, Jean-Marie Dutasta declared that he feared no one in a combat. Once, in Genoa...

He was unable to recount the false story in question. The explosion took place in the soul of the lord. After insults in a language that no one knew, he summoned Dutasta to fight with him with a knife, unless he was the miserable coward he thought.

Dutasta was that coward. He contented himself with sniggering, without taking any account of the proposition. The lord approached him and covered his face with a great jet of saliva, of which he knew the secret.

It was late. All the energetic and sensate men who might have been able to intervene had gone to sleep, either in the large common cabin or in huts of branches that they had constructed in the vicinity. The fire was dying, and threw out occasional burst of vivid light. Scarcely anyone remained but the lord's companions, who considered a knife fight as a choice spectacle as well as a legitimate way of settling a difference.

A cry of joy rang out. It had been uttered by the Feverish. She was a woman of about thirty with red hair that was always unkempt. Tall and thin, she was incessantly in a state of extravagant agitation. A tic caused her head to move up and

---

[12] The big game hunter Charles Bombonnel (1816-1890) published his autobiography. *Bombonnel, le tueur de panthères* [Bombonnel the Panther-Killer] in 1896.

233

down. She had vestiges of beauty, screeched at everyone, was always in a state of fury or joy, and received and gave blows. The lord claimed to have rights over her, but she was to some extent everyone's. She started running around the fire proclaiming that the two men were about to fight.

Still sniggering, Dutasta was content to wipe his face. The lord was two paces away from him, his hand on his belt, more redoubtable than Bombonnel's panthers, of which the former sub-officer evoked the memory so frequently.

"What are you going to do, Dutasta?" said a voice beside him, trembling with emotion. That was Jean-François the former brother of Saint-Jean-de-Dieu. Possessed by his obsession, he had hardly pronounced a word since leaving France, not confiding in anyone, living within himself. That scorn was experienced by Dutasta more than any other, for he remembered having seen him begging on the roads of the Pyrenees.

"Nothing," he said. He got up and headed for the cabin.

The lord went to catch up with him, but someone shouted: "He's gone to get his knife."

The Feverish ran back and forth, stamping her feet joyously. Sleepers appeared in doorways. A moon the color of gold gave a somber mystery to the edges of the forest.

Suddenly, the sound of a trumpet resounded. On great occasions a man known as the Thin Fat Man made a tour of the camp in a grotesquely solemn manner playing a fanfare. He was a former obese man whom illness had stripped of all fat, and whose cheeks sagged. It was only when playing the trumpet, he claimed, that he recovered his full face of old. He stopped playing occasionally to shout:

"Ladies and gentlemen, wake up to watch a duel to the death with knives between the lord and Jean-Marie Dutasta, the celebrated killer of panthers."

"Set up the table!" someone shouted.

It often happened in the gambling dens of San Francisco that adversaries fought on a table in order that the audience could enjoy the combat more. The duel of the French adventurer, in particular, was famous.[13]

Jean-François had followed Dutasta. "It's necessary to fight, you have to fight. The honor of your countrymen is at stake."

But the wretched Dutasta sat down on the ground, holding his head in his hands. "It's sending me to the abattoir. The lord is a murderer who has never missed his man with the knife."

Jean-François was as tremulous as him. "You can't do otherwise," he insisted.

Meanwhile, the table had been set up. It was long and low, and only permitted the combatants a few steps of retreat. The lord had bounded on to it and, with his jacket wrapped around his left wrist, he was keeping his right hand hidden. His raptorial profile was outlined by the firelight. Beside him, the Feverish was uttering cries of delight.

All doors had opened. People were calling to one another. The majority did not understand. "A duel!" some shouted. Those who were informed were looking at the cabin, from which they expected to see Dutasta emerge. The lord was becoming impatient, and stamped his foot on the table.

In the doorway of Dutasta's cabin it was the former brother of Saint-Jean-de-Dieu who appeared. His eyes were lowered and he seemed to be in a somnambulistic state. Sud-

---

[13] Author's note: "De Pindray, a French gentleman, was celebrated for some years in California, where he was the leader of a band of adventurers. He was found murdered in their midst." Charles de Pindray (1816-1852) fled the French police, who were pursuing him for forgery, after the Revolution of 1848. He joined a westward-bound wagon train, distinguished himself by his hunting skills, and continued making his living by that means, based in San Francisco, where his custom of dressing as a seventeenth-century musketeer made him stand out. In December 1851 he set out to found a colony in Mexico, but was murdered not long after arriving there.

denly, he fell to his knees, his hands clasped in front of his breast. All the inhabitants of the Contra-Costa camp were expectant. A few minutes went by. Even the Feverish had fallen silent. Only an owl, somewhere in the woods, uttered a cry.

Jean-François suddenly stood up. He ran forward, with a surprising lightness, as far as the lord.

"I take you all as witnesses," he said. "It's me who is taking Dutasta's place. This man wanted to fight a Frenchman. He'll fight with me."

And with a bound, he was on the table, a knife in his hand.

All sorts of cries resounded. Some wanted to intervene. Others said that Jean-François was known to be mad. But those who were the first inhabitants of the camp, the lord's friends, sure of his victory, did not want to be deprived of a combat and the pleasure of seeing blood flow.

Someone threw Jean-François a piece of cloth to ward off thrusts, but he did not understand the usage and rejected it

"Accept," someone shouted to the lord. "He needs a lesson."

Perhaps because he had seen Jean-François on his knees and had a confused fear of that appeal to an unknown power, the lord hesitated. He said something that no one heard.

"You're afraid of that runt! He's afraid!" said the voice of the Methodist preacher, who was the most avid of all for the promised spectacle.

Then the lord started to laugh. He seemed to be saying: *You'll see, you'll be amused!* And he put himself on guard.

The combat only lasted a second. The brother of Saint-Jean-de-Dieu, doubtless animated by the mysterious strength that is like a grace of another order, the grace of the body, pounced like a tiger, reached the lord, knocked him down, rolled off the table with him, and his arm was seen to strike a mighty blow. Then he stood up and stood motionless, his arms stuck to his sides, his eyes lowered.

There was a clamor. The Thin Fat Man sounded the trumpet. The combat was over.

Colonel Bertrand de Chalabre's sprain did not heal, in spite of the cares of the Spanish physician. He came three times a week, kneaded the colonel's foot, said: "It's getting better," and went away again, after winking at the owner of the house. The colonel consoled himself by drawing up a map of the sky, such as he was able to see it from the beach of San Francisco.

Sometimes he received a visit from Julien de Miravel. The later wore a broad-brimmed round hat, trousers split down the side, a jacket with rounded edges, a rolled a multicolored poncho around his body. He only told stories about women or boasted about his gambling prowess.

"Be careful," said Chalabre. "You're almost as old as me. You're past the age of womanizing."

Captain Montarache also came and told the story of what was happening in the camp.

The affair of the lord and Dutasta had caused great disturbances. The lord had not died of his wound. He had been watched over devotedly by Jean-François and had recovered very quickly. He had remained taciturn, and one sensed that his hatred was not appeased.

But another event occurred, which caused upheaval in the camp.

In a place called Tamascal, not far away, there was another camp, occupied by Yankees. They were men of brutal mores, universally hated by the Californians, the Texians and foreigners in general, but they became more numerous and more arrogant every day. The Yankees of Tamascal had had several quarrels with the Frenchmen of Contra-Costa.

One evening, however, one of the Yankees had asked the French for hospitality. He had arrived by night and begged them to give him a bed. He said that he had gone astray while hunting. He was a man of honeyed speech, with long blond hair and hands that were always damp and entirely covered in tawny hairs, so that when one shook his hand one had the sensation of squeezing a moldy vegetable. He was nicknamed the

Oily, because he had conquered a certain sympathy, especially among the women. He admired the disposition of the camp and the convenience of the different access routes to the forest. He stayed for several days, eating and drinking abundantly, telling stories about the splendors of American cities. It was quickly perceived that he spent his time chasing the women.

"We Yankees don't have any women at Tamascal."

He invited the only virtuous woman in the camp to leave with him. She was an Englishwoman of abundant forms named Mary, who had married a few months before, with as much solemnity as possible, a former mariner from Saint Malo named Leblanc, about whom nothing was known except that he had been a convict in Peru. The Oily offered her a gold ingot, which she took without granting anything. He considered it stolen and, having followed her into a solitary place where she was hanging laundry, he attempted to take her by force.

She struggled energetically, and as she was strong, she got away from the Oily and shouted for help. Men from the camp came running, but the Yankee, who had his revolver, held them at bay, did not manifest any regret for the violation of hospitality, went to the cabin where his bag and weapons were, took them and went away, shouting that all the French were miserable dogs. He added, in spite of the manifest contradiction of facts, that their women were all bitches that everyone could have at his whim without even needing a gold ingot.

That evening, of course, everyone swore that he would chastise the Oily personally as soon as the opportunity presented itself. But it did not present itself. It was something else that happened.

On a moonless night the camp was woken up by screams, the sound of struggles and gunshots. Everyone was shouting in the darkness without knowing what danger they were facing.

Finally, a voice shouted: "The Yankees!"

It was, indeed, them. Everyone threw himself on his weapons, but it was impossible to make use of them. There were a few gunshots. A torch striped the night; it was carried by a Yankee known for his tall stature and his facility in imitating the howl of a wolf. Whinnying was heard, then the noise of a cavalcade in the direction where the horses were. Then silence fell again.

Lamps were lit, they gathered, and took stock. Captain Montarache issued vibrant commands, assigning everyone a defense post. But it was all over. The purpose of the attack was understood. Its goal had been the abduction of several women, firstly Mary Leblanc and then the two daughters of a former trapper, Malpart, known as the Beaver. They were fourteen and still seemed children. The Feverish had also disappeared, but, according to various items of evidence, she had gone voluntarily.

One young man had received a blow from a rifle butt so violent that he had been killed instantly. The Beaver, while defending his daughter, had been slashed in the face by several knife-thrusts. He was an old man whose faculties had been weakened. He loved his daughters passionately. Without paying any heed to his wounds, he shouted their names desperately in the night. It was necessary to bandage him by force.

Indignation was at its peak. Everyone wanted to depart immediately, in the dark. It was Montarache who demonstrated the insanity of that project, in view of the intense obscurity. They would never be able to recover the women. The Oily's departure, holding everyone at bay with his revolver, and the absence of punishment for that insult, had made the Yankees think that the French were cowards. They had not even hidden during their attack, sure of their impunity. They were also more numerous than the French. Certainly, their surveillance would relax very quickly. It was necessary to wait for the moon to extract a resounding vengeance.

"The suffocating heat of the nights must have the same effects in their camp as ours. They must sleep outside their cabins in the open air, next to fires of green branches whose smoke drives away the mosquitoes. An hour before sunrise, nature dictates that those men will be slumbering most profoundly. If we're wise enough and patient enough to leave at sunset in small groups, we can meet up in the middle of the night and crawl until we have the camp under our rifles. The moon will permit us to ire accurately. We'll see them as they get up, and our first fusillade will fell a considerable number of them."

Everyone rallied to that opinion, and Captain Montarache received supreme command. Only the Beaver protested in a desperate manner. Those few days of delay would deliver his daughters to the Yankees irremediably. The objection was raised in vain that what he feared could be accomplished in a few minutes and that the essential thing was to recover the children alive. He spent the night cursing his companions' lack of courage.

It was noticed that Leblanc of Saint Malo only showed a mediocre chagrin, and no haste to recover his stolen wife.

The expedition was realized as it had been conceived, for the greater glory of its leader; for the unexpected element of life does not always manifest itself.

The moon was full, the heat was overwhelming. The French numbered about fifty. The day before, the former brother of Saint-Jean-de-Dieu had disappeared; it was thought that he found bloodshed repugnant. The six groups formed came together at the appointed place, thanks to guides who knew the forest. Then they deployed in a fan, with orders to be within half rifle-shot of the camp an hour later.

Everything went as desired. The hours elapsed, everyone waited, a short distance from the camp. The French were surprised to see that it was composed of log cabins, infinitely better constructed than their own, each of which gave the impression of being a small fortress. The moonlight was almost blinding, but they could only make out the mass of those redoubtable houses, with their shadows beside them.

Discouragement took possession of souls. If the Yankees did not come out of their houses, they would shoot down the attackers to the last man without risk to themselves. According to the hypothesis formed by Captain Montarache, the Yankees were already outside, sleeping under the stars—except that they could not be seen, and the mosquito-repelling fires were extinct.

Kentuckian Joe, a man full of experience in the matter of ambushes, murmured in the captain's ear that the wise thing to do was to beat a retreat. He had made war in Mexico with General Taylor and was one of those who had mounted a night attack on the ramparts of Monterey.[14] Montarache was impressed. In spite of that he made a sign to young Adolphe, who was known without any reason as Adolfo, to launch the attack. The courageous young man was supposed to run into the camp, a torch in his hand, firing revolver shots, and try to set fire to a cabin. Then he was to fall flat at the moment when the French fusillade began. The delicate point was not dropping too late.

There was an element of risk in that attack, but the ploy worked. Adolfo acquitted his task marvelously—except that he dropped a little too late and received a bullet in the back. The Yankees, who, in accordance with Montarache's hypothesis, were sleeping outside their houses, got up in the greatest disorder. A large number were hit, because almost all the Frenchmen were admirable shots. The rest did not resist the impetuous assault that followed, and dispersed through the surrounding woods.

Captain Montarache, who had rediscovered the joy produced by being a leader, saw that joy disappear rapidly. He did not know the kind of men he was commanding. He witnessed a scene of pillage and a massacre; and his amazement was great when he saw the lord and the former trappers scalping

---

[14] Zachary Taylor's forces attacked Monterey on 21 September 1846, beginning a four-day battle that became one of the most famous of the Mexican-American War. The nocturnal attack in question, by the Texas Rangers and two infantry corps, took place before dawn on 23 September.

the dead and proudly suspending the scalps from their belts. He had a great deal of difficulty convincing them to retreat.

Another incident completed his disturbance. As the French were returning, laden with booty, with all the Yankees' horses, one of the Yankees wandering in the woods allowed himself to be captured by them. Montarache wanted to release him, but there were protests. A prisoner might be a useful hostage; they might as well keep him for a while. He was taken away, carefully bound.

Misfortune dictated that one of the Beaver's daughters recognized him and indentified him to her father was one of those who had subjected her to violence. It is only in novels that captive young women are found, when they are liberated, as pure as before. Reality is very different. The Beaver threw himself on the man and it was with great difficulty that he was prevented from killing him.

Captain Montarache therefore charged Malbosque with protecting the Yankee until the next day, firmly determined to set him free when the fever of combat had calmed down. Once in camp, the prisoner was tied to a tree and, as the Beaver continued to cry vengeance, it was agreed that Malbosque would finish the night beside him. But Malbosque sat down and fell asleep. He was woken up by a terrible scream. The prisoner had also fallen asleep. The Beaver had crawled up to him and pierced his eye with a needle. He wanted to do the same to the other, and it was very difficult to prevent him.

There were still no police or authorities, but the Yankees in San Francisco became agitated. Everyone was agreed in thinking that the punishment had far exceeded the crime.

Leaning on a cane, Colonel de Chalabre came to the French camp. He had finally understood that his injury was being maintained by the Spanish physician and he had started walking again since letting nature take its course.

He gave his visit a certain solemnity. He asked to talk to the captain in private.

"Captain Montarache," he said, "You've become a captain of brigands."

It was three days after the expedition against the Yankees.

"I know," said Montarache, sadly. "I've meditated for three days on what happened, and I believe that I've led the worthy men from our homeland into the midst of a gang of murderers."

"Leave today! Leave before nightfall," said Bertrand de Chalabre, as an order. "I'll join you a little later, when I'm fully healed."

During the day, the Thin Fat Man made a tour of the camp several times, playing the trumpet. The tents, the sieves for sifting gold from sand and the implements for prospecting, were piled haphazardly on to a few mules, and those who had decided to follow Captain Montarache mounted the stolen horse. The captain strove not to think about the fact that his mount as the fruit of pillage, but he quickly perceived that it was only docile when one spoke to it in English.

The former brother of Saint-Jean-de-Dieu had not reappeared. Malbosque and three others decided that they would wait for Colonel de Chalabre to be healed. It was understood that with him, they would not get lost in unknown deserts, because of his knowledge of the stars.

The expedition was guided by a man who claimed to know of placers in the direction of the sources of the river Merced. He seemed very excited, and said contradictory things, but it was necessary to leave, to quit the men the captain called murderers. None of the first occupants of the camp went with the expedition. They had lost faith in the placers.

Colonel de Chalabre, leaning on his cane, followed the caravan as far as the last houses of San Francisco.

"Rendezvous at the sources of the river Merced," he said as he might have said: *We'll meet up outside the Church of Saint-Bertrand-de-Comminges*. And all the riders waved their hats simultaneously.

Nothing more was ever to be heard of them. They disappeared in the light of the mountains whose torrents carried gold, as if that gold had the power to destroy those who aspired to its possession.

Three years later, an expedition of American troops charged with chastising pillaging Indians brought back from the Indians' camp a saber of the Napoleonic era, the blade of which was engraved with the words: *Dupin frères, armuriers, Toulouse.* As Colonel de Chalabre, who was at that time attached to the general staff of the President of Mexico, had requested officially that a search be mounted for a French caravan in California, he was shown the saber, which he recognized as that of Captain Montarache.

He sent it to Saint-Gaudens, where he thought that there were still heirs of the captain.[15] Many gold-seekers were unable even to send back a saber to those who had hoped for a fortune from them.

---

[15] Author's note: "In 1897 this saber was still in the possession of a certain Dabut, a rentier in Saint-Gaudens."

IX. The Duel of the Two Colonels

Mexico had always been the most agitated country in the world. It was at that time more so than in any other epoch. The treaty that had given Texas and California to America had rendered patriots desperate. They formed groups, leagues and associations, and demanded from President Mariano Arista a powerful army modeled on the armies of Europe. That army would have the mission of repressing the banditry that had robbed the roads of all security and rid the frontiers of Anglo-Saxon filibusters who attacked the towns and pillaged caravans.

Mariano Arista had learned that among the immense quantity of men whom the promise of gold had attracted to California there were French officers in quest of adventures. There were even former officers of Napoléon. He sent emissaries to California to make them offers.

Colonel Bertrand de Chalabre's foot had finally healed. He had promised his compatriots to meet up with them at the sources of the river Merced. He did not want to wait any longer. He was residing then in a long cabin rented from a Californian half-breed, for he no longer wanted to hear any mention of Spaniards, especially Spanish physicians. That house was situated at the northern end of the beach and had a little garden, where the colonel had set up his telescope, which never quit him. In that garden he also indulged in fencing bouts with the cavalry saber, with an Italian master-of-arms whose acquaintance he had made and who was waiting in San Francisco, like so many others, for the right moment to depart for the placers. Amateurs came to admire those contests of arms and sometimes took part in them, but the victory was always the colonel's.

With a great deal of difficulty, they had procured sabers with blunted edges deprived of points.

"With the saber, you're the strongest man in the world," Enrico Ferri, the Italian fencing master, said every day—who, being notoriously vanquished, had an interest in only being beaten by a unique prodigy. He learned with an ill humor that there was someone in the world who was the equal, or very nearly the equal, of Bertrand de Chalabre.

"Victory always remained uncertain," said Chalabre modestly, "when I measured myself against my friend Colonel Espondeillan. How many afternoons we disputed that victory, which we were never able to obtain!"

The amateurs quivered with admiration at the idea of such a duel.

"Oh, what wouldn't I give to find myself face to face with my friend again, saber in hand," said the colonel, in a melancholy tone, thinking about the rivalry that had darkened their friendship—for he loved his companion of the long days in Saint-Gaudens sincerely.

Jean-François, the former brother of Saint-Jean-de-Dieu, had come to see Bertrand de Chalabre. He only had confidence in him. It was him alone that he wanted to follow in order to reach the placers.

"A few more days! I'll soon be completely recovered. We'll depart for the sources of the river Merced. But it's necessary that my foot is completely solid."

He had admirers. The nights were clear and, through the lenses of his telescope, the stars appeared more beautiful to him than in France. He refused two guides who appeared worthy of confidence, one after the other. He was in no hurry.

Jean-François went here and there, living on alms. Sometimes he recovered his old flame of speech and preached to a small audience. He could only do so in French because his knowledge of Spanish was limited to a few words and he considered English to be a barbaric language reserved for heretics. In consequence, he could only address himself to his compatriots, who were not numerous. His desire to make a fortune in order to render to the fraternity of Saint-Jean-de-Dieu what he had once taken from it, remained ardent within him, but a miserable life destroys noble aspirations. The goal of his voyage was gradually effaced. He began to drink when he had the opportunity.

One evening, near an open air tavern, he talked about God to an old Italian woman who did not understand him. For long months she had been waiting for her son, departed for the placers. She was comforted by the ardor of Jean-François' gaze and the tone of his voice. Not knowing how to thank him, when he drew away, she ran after him and put a deck of cards in his hand. Jean-François stuffed it in his pocket without looking to see what it was.

In the course of the night, however, he felt that his head was on fire, with an unaccustomed desire to drink, to sing and to forget himself among human creatures. He went to roam around the taverns and the gambling dens.

What's the matter with me? he said to himself. He finally thought of looking at what the old Italian woman had given him. He saw with horror the figures symbolic of the passions. His first impulse was to throw them far away, but he did not yield to it. He folded up the pieces of cardboard marked with fingerprints in the page of a newspaper in which they had been wrapped. And he thought: *I'll keep them, but I won't touch them.*

He walked for the rest of the night, too troubled to lie down on the sand of the beach, which was his bed every night. He was carrying temptation.

It was a few days later that a visitor presented himself at Colonel Bertrand de Chalabre's house. How did he convince him so rapidly? Perhaps the man known as the star man had realized secretly that the life of a gold prospector was not for him. Perhaps he had seen reason, thinking that digging the ground, diverting streams and passing sand through sieves, or attacking rocks with pick-axes, was not work for a man in his sixties. Perhaps he said to himself that, in order to practice that métier, it was necessary to be a sort of ascetic of poverty, like Captain Montarache, whose hair and teeth were growing again with the advent of mature age.

Perhaps he was flattered by the celebrity of the messenger who had come in search of him: Melchor Ocampo in person, the greatest intellectual in Mexico, the governor of Michoacoam.[16] Out of patriotism, in his desire to see the Mexican army reorganized, he had agreed to come to California to search the human flood that had washed up there for the few remarkable men who might be useful to his country.

It was agreed that Colonel de Chalabre would recover the rank he had had in France and would command a garrison in the capital temporarily. Melchor Ocampo had received from the President the powers necessary to make that promise. But it was necessary to travel to Mexico City without delay, and in order to do that, to embark with him at dawn the next day on a brig that would deposit them at Masatlan.

Colonel de Chalabre felt an immense pleasure at the idea that he could wield his saber in earnest again. He dared not express the desire that Mexico recommence the war against America. He obtained permission to take Malbosque with him.

As he was devoid of jealousy and generous of soul he hastened to speak to Melchor Ocampo about another colonel, a man of great military merit, Blaise Espondeillan, the man whom Napoléon had pointed out to his aide-de-camp, saying "We can't let young Espondeillan die."

To his great surprise, he perceived that his friend Espondeillan was not unknown to Melchor Ocampo.

"Yes, yes, a remarkable marksman, a master of the saber, a man of great courage; he's already famous in Mexico." But he collided with a dismissive conclusion: "A dangerous man,

---

[16] The liberal Melchor Ocampo (1814-1861) was governor of his home state of Michocoan during and after the Mexican-American War but was forced to flee the country when Santa Anna returned to power. He continued his political activities in exile and drafted new civil laws that survived his assassination, the eventual partial adoption of which ensured his posthumous celebrity.

who immediately entered into the opposition and has made a pact with our enemies. I assume that he's now in prison."

A few hours after the colonel's departure, Jean-François headed for the little house in the garden of which the telescope was set up, and where the voices of duelists and exclamations flowing clashes of arms could be heard in the afternoons. It was necessary for him to know the date of departure, in order to master temptation.

But everything was mute and silent. The telescope had disappeared. The door was locked.

He interrogated a neighbor.

"The man who looked at the stars left with his weapons this morning. He embarked on a brig that could still be seen, not long ago, on the horizon, but must be far away by now,"

Jean-François had no more hope. He was all alone, and his old enemies, the passions, were in him.

In Mexico, Colonel Blaise Espondeillan had fully enjoyed his reputation as the best marksman in Mexico to begin with. When people talked to him about his merits, he never failed to say: "I'm a very moderate marksman, but it's well known in Europe that I'm the strongest man with the saber in the French army."

That reputation was added to that of marksman of its own accord.

"The government will make you propositions," people said to him.

He awaited them with impatience, for he estimated that it was necessary to show himself, and his funds were rapidly running out.

General Ozorno got in ahead of the government.

Colonel Espondeillan received a mysterious message at his hotel, which enjoined him to be outside the main door of the cathedral at seven o'clock. He went, not without having the marvelous revolver to which he owed his celebrity ready to hand.

A man with the cloak and hat that might be considered as the uniform of the conspirator asked him to follow him, in the name of General Ozorno. It was, indeed, his former traveling companion that he found, in a rich dwelling into which he only penetrated after passing through three solidly bolted doors, which only opened in response to three different passwords. He found the most notable men in Mexico gathered there, who welcomed him with the most flattering words. They all wanted to hear exactly what the great Napoléon had said to him on seeing the young Espondeillan wounded by the roadside.

Now aging, Espondeillan told the same story for the ten thousandth time. "It was not far from the Berezina..."

But there was one man more avid than all the rest to hear hat story and make use of the colonel's military qualities. That was Santa Anna, the future dictator, for whose return the notables present were preparing, while drinking punch every night in a hermetically sealed house.

Not only was the title of Director of the Tomb of Santa Anna promised to the colonel, but Santa Anna was waiting impatiently to have first-hand information from an authentic officer of the Grande Armée regarding Napoléon's court, the emperor's habits, his way of life, and his everyday decorum. Several times Santa Anna had been duped by adventurers claiming to be former acquaintances of Napoléon. There had even been a Greek who had flattered himself with the title of the Empress Joséphine's lover, who was not only ignorant of the French language but had never set foot in France.

But it was necessary to join Santa Anna right away. The future dictator would soon regain control of Mexico, but before then, he wanted to have a few days of solitude in order to question the French officer at his leisure.

"I'm ready," said Espondeillan.

"It's necessary to leave for Cartagena right away."

Having returned to the hotel, the colonel asked for a map of America in order to search for the situation of that town, the name of which he had seen in old stories of filibusters. He was alarmed by the distance. For thirty years he had been habituated to not making longer journeys than the one to Toulouse, only separated from Saint-Gaudens by a few hours in a diligence. But he reflected, and said to himself: *Did I not once go all the way to Moscow?*

When the moment came to depart, in order to go and embark in Vera Cruz, Genera Ozorno gave him some friendly advice:

"Remember that in Mexico, it's not situations that are difficult to obtain but the salaries attached to them. It's in order to get hold of those salaries that it's necessary to employ all one's art. Santa Anna will only ask realizable things of you. It will be easy for you to become enough of an architect to occupy yourself with the tomb. Santa Anna has a particular conception of death. He insists that his tomb should contain a large room with thick mats. He thinks that his shade will need to pace back and forth as when he was alive and he doesn't want it to be walking on bare paving stones because, he says, shades are sensitive to the cold and their feet shouldn't touch cold ground.

"Make, with no argument, a big walking-room with thick mats. But there's another thing that you ought not to accept if he proposes it to you: that's to be the leader of the search relative to what might remain of his leg. If he doesn't find those vestiges he fears being obliged, after his death, only to walk on one leg. All great men have had eccentricities and the greater they are, the more irrational those eccentricities are. In any case, no one knows who is wrong and who is right. But never agree to get mixed up in the story of the leg. You'll lose your life in that."

During the voyage to reach Cartagena, which was very long, Colonel Espondeillan rehearsed the phrases that he might employ when he was questioned about the mores and habits of Napoléon's court. In view of his ignorance, he was very anxious—but there was no need.

When he finally arrived at Santa Anna's hacienda near Cartagena, after he had seen the enormous silhouette of the monumental tomb outlined behind a wood of centenarian mimosas, Santa Anna, after a few brief courtesies, commenced thus:

"I'm a child of the Tierra Caliente. I need tropical vegetation in order to blossom. The juice of magueys and convolvulus flows in my veins. I was rocked to sleep the sound of parrots, and mockingbirds came to laugh over my cradle. You know that there are always certain prodigies at the birth of men who are to have a great destiny. My mother told me in great secrecy that on the evening that she believed to be that of my conception, a white eagle circled the house three times. I have one hero and one model. That is the great Emperor Napoléon, and I believe that I'm his brother—not materially, which is impossible, but in a spiritual order that escapes human reason."

And for days he continued talking to him, recounting his adventurous life, which was the most prodigious romance that a man had ever lived, from his infancy in the hacienda of Manga de Clavo, though his early days in the Spanish army, his first proclamations of the Republic, his victories, the time when he was the hero of Tampico, to his numerous defeats, which he was always able to transform into victories, the epoch when he had supreme power, when he played with congresses, when eight plumed white mules pulled is carriage, when he received thousands of love letters every morning sent by the most beautiful women in Mexico, to the epoch of Texas and the evening in San Jacinto when he was obliged to flee in slippers and was taken prisoner in an oak wood, all the way to the days when the region between Vera Cruz and Mexico City resounded with American artillery and the days of exile when it was necessary to go overseas and take advantage of his leisure to lay the foundations of a comfortable tomb.

In truth, Santa Anna was like all men who are growing old. He only asked for advice in order to give it. If he made a semblance of wanting to be instructed on some point, it was in order to demonstrate that he had a perfect knowledge of it. He aspired, above all, to recount, untiringly to tell the story of his

252

eventful, varied and dramatic life, such as few men had known.[17]

It was known in Mexico that Santa Anna as going to return and take possession of power by a forceful coup. He was on the way, it was said, and had sent emissaries ahead who had worked on the Mexican proletariat. All sensate men deemed that it would be deplorable to lose the honest Arista, who had attempted to introduce an organization of the country based on law, economy and honesty. But those things were too new, How could they resist a man who followed his proclamations with the announcement of cock-fights and who was invariably accompanied in his travels by a carriage full of elite cocks.

A day had come when Arista was told: "It's set for tomorrow. The city will be attacked by a troop of bandits on horseback, who will try to imitate regular troops. The mob will be commanded by a French adventurer."

Arista had summoned Bertrand de Chalabre, the commandant of the garrison. "Are you sure of your troops?" he had asked him.

"No, General."

Arista had meditated. "Troops are never sure, here at least. They fight anyway. Because of the heat, revolutions only ever take place at sunset. Try to hold on until midnight."

Colonel de Chalabre did not ask the reason for that deadline. He was filled with joy at the idea of fighting, and only feared one thing, which was that the revolution might not happen.

---

[17] Author's note: "A life of Santa Anna would be a prodigious adventure story in which one would see how destiny takes pleasure in alternating highs and lows in the same life and brings you near to death without precipitating you into it. It is worth noting that biographers are more tempted by mediocre lives than those that are varied and picturesque."

Poring over a map of the city, he spent the day distributing the troops at his disposal as best he could. He was aided by Captain Estevanillo. He was a courageous man, with a slight paunch, intelligent, astute and rather jovial.

"But colonel," he said, "if anything happens, all the men will raise the butts of their rifles in the air and shout: 'Long live Santa Anna!'"

"I don't think so," replied Chalabre, with a severe expression.

The foot soldiers were dispersed in the gardens of the Alameda, where the colonel would be stationed, ready to run to any position under threat. The elite of his troops, some two hundred well-armed cavalrymen, the only ones wearing uniforms in good condition, would remain in the courtyard of the barracks behind the cathedral, not far from the Plaza.

In the afternoon, they learned that the presidarios, convicts employed in road-works, had been liberated from their chains and even weapons, and were now outside the city. Then it was announced that horsemen were arriving via the road to Puebla, who seemed to form a kind of general staff around a uniformed leader.

"It's them that it's necessary to counter," said Chalabre. "I'll take charge of the leader."

The streets were full of people. Bands of young men were circulating to the cry of "Long live Santa Anna!"

Colonel de Chalabre asked for new orders from the President. No one could see him. The response was: "Hold on until midnight."

The heat eased. A cool breeze rose, ran through the streets and lifted hearts. The Plaza filled with a hostile crowd. Stones began to rain down on the National Palace, as closed and mute as a tomb. At that moment, the bells of the Convent of the Incarnation rang out, to which those of the Convent of Santa Domingo replied. They did not stop.

Someone came to inform the colonel that armed groups were marching toward the Plaza from several places. He sent an order to Captain Estevanillo to come and join him with the cavalry. The captain came on horseback himself, but alone. He was pale, but remained jovial.

"Colonel, as I foresaw, the men are refusing to march. They're in the courtyard of the barracks. The officers have left. I gave the order to mount up, but they were content to snigger."

"Follow me," said the colonel.

He leapt into the saddle and traversed the distance that separated the Alameda from the barracks at a gallop. Once in the courtyard he stopped his horse, facing the men. He drew his sword, and in a placid but loud voice, he said: "Is there one of you who refuses to obey? In that case, let him come forward."

Because of the accent of his poor Spanish, he had never given an order without an ironic grimace appearing of a few faces. This time, parading his glittering gaze from right to left, he watched out for the slightest grimace. He saw nothing but frozen faces.

He held himself as motionless as a statue, facing his men. He shouted: "Mount up!"

With a single movement, all the cavaliers leapt into the saddle.

"Forward march!"

And he emerged on to the Plaza with Estevanillo at his side and his troop behind him.

The crowd was swept away. Men who were carrying a wooden beam to use as a battering ram against the door of the National Palace dropped it and fled. On all sides, the windows lit up. Torches were seen waving on terraces. The sound of seats being dragged on to balconies as heard. The inhabitants of Mexico were coming to see the revolution, as a spectacle.

Stones had wounded a few soldiers. A woman, having seized the foot of one of them, had tipped him off his horse. They wanted to take their revenge. Chalabre was now sure of his men, at least temporarily.

He ran to all the quarters where movements had been signaled. Everywhere he dispersed the mob. Sometimes, a gunshot wounded a man, but the darkness and the sped of the horses protected them. Chalabre sensed the intoxication of victory.

"It seems to me that our troop is diminishing," said Estevanillo, two or three times.

He's brave but sees everything in black, Chalabre thought.

Sometimes, they heard appeals:

"Hey, Pepe!"

"Hey, José!"

They were the relatives or friends of soldiers, who recognized them in passing, and ran after them, exhorting them to dismount and join them.

Pepe or José slowed down, dropped back and then disappeared.

Estevanillo is loyal but he doesn't have the faith, Chalabre told himself, and he took no account of his captain's advice. In any case, he only had one idea: to find himself face to face with the leaders of the revolt, whose entry into Mexico City had been signaled to him. He did not succeed in finding them. He only encountered groups of presidarios, which his cavaliers, becoming less and less numerous, dispersed easily.

Time passed. The horses and the men were exhausted. But it seemed that the crowd was multiplying with the night. The bells of the two convents continued to respond to one another.

At the moment when he emerged again into the Plaza, all the windows of which, save those of the National Palace, were illuminated, the colonel turned to Estevanillo.

"Take a few men, break down the doors if necessary, but go to the Incarnation and Santa Domingo and make those damned bells shut up."

The captain bowed, smiling. "A few men? Good!"

He made a sign and drew away, followed by a few men.

At that moment, on the other side of the square, which his arrival had emptied, Chalabre perceived a group of horsemen emerging near the Casa de Cabildo. A tall cavalier was advancing at their head.

Finally! It was them! It was him!

The colonel darted a glance at him men. O stupor! There were only two of them left, two loyal old soldiers. No matter. He launched himself forward. The horseman facing him did the same. His troop, fearing a trap, remained prudently outside the square.

Colonel Espondeillan could not be recognized by his friend. In order to command the miscellaneous troop that was under his orders, he had thought it good to dress in a costume intermediate between that of a brigand chief and a military uniform. He had a striped sarape, trousers open at the side and an immense sombrero covering his face. For his part, he did not recognize Colonel de Chalabre, imagining that the chief of the garrison was giving his orders, alongside the President, from inside the National Palace. He thought he was about to make short work of some cavalry officer that hazard was putting in his path for the single combat he had desired for so long.

And between the two men animated by the same desire, between their armed partisans and the crowd, there was a tacit accord. Each party understood that a duel was about to take place—which is to say, a spectacle as attractive as a bullfight or a cockfight.

A circle formed. Spectators crammed the windows. On the terraces, raised arms held up lamps.

Chalabre felt his fatigue disappear. He stood up in his stirrups. He too was sure of victory. The horses' heads met. Blades were seen tracing circles.

Each of the combatants thought he was playing with the other, and delighted in his mastery of the thrusts delivered. It was necessary not to end the pleasure too soon. Then too, there was a certain responsibility with regard to the spectators. As always in similar cases, the horses took part in the combat, biting one another, rearing up and wheeling.

Almost at the same moment, the two colonels recognized that they had a serious adversary before them and, in the certainty of their strength, they experienced the same joy. The game was serious. So much the better.

Why the devil aren't those bells stopping! thought Chalabre.

He was to learn subsequently that the few men who had gone with Estevanillo had immediately dispersed and that he, left alone, was unable to catch up with them because of the crowd.

Is it possible that a Mexican officer possesses a mastery of the saber to that extent? thought Espondeillan.

And the circles, the vertiginous thrusts, and the suns made by the blades multiplied around the two men.

Suddenly, an immense cry sprang from the lungs of all the spectators.

An audacious lepero, doubtless unaware of the usages of the chivalry of brave men, had crawled as far as the combatants, with a long knife in his hand. He succeeded in planting it is the belly of Chalabre's horse.

The animal reared up and fell, but in the same second, the colonel launched a blow of the cutting edge at the lepero, disengaged himself nimbly from his stirrups and found himself upright, sword in hand.

It was that prowess that drew a clamor from the crowd and caused the torches on the terraces to dance. It was recounted the next day that the lepero had been cut in two.

The fight had become unequal. But Espondeillan did not hesitate. He leapt from his horse, affecting the same ease as his adversary and the combat recommenced.

But when they found themselves on foot, the thrusts delivered and parried, the attacks and feints, succeeded one another with the same rhythm as in the past, when the two colonels had disputed victory with fencing weapons in Saint-Gaudens. Both of them estimated that no one in the world was capable of praying certain irresistible bows—with one single exception.

Enlightenment dawned on them almost at the same time, as if the sparks of their blades suddenly permitted them to make out their faces. And at the same time, they thought they heard Captain Zenon Fabregat's wooden leg striking the ground firmly when he thought that a head had been split.

Thus, the victory so sought-after during the afternoons in Saint-Gaudens, hazard had enabled to be sought-after again, but for real, and before thousands of spectators. The intoxication of fighting one another was such that their thrusts redoubled in intensity, their blades were bound together, and they almost arrived at embracing one another.

And embrace one another, in fact, they did. Their chipped sabers fell at the same time.

"But it's you, my old friend!" they both said, hugging one another breast to breast.

No one on Mexico City understood exactly what had happened. All the lamps were agitated. The two combatants were enveloped by a group of notable men of the city, partisans of Santa Anna who were going to the National Palace to proclaim the fall of Arista. They went with them, arm in arm, too emotional to speak.

Colonel Chalabre looked at his watch. It was midnight.

I hung on, he said to himself.

And that was a great comfort to him.

In a carriage with four fast horses, President Arista had quit Mexico City several hours before, soon enough not to be overtaken. He was the only President who did not carry off any of the riches of the State. He left Mexico no richer than when he had arrived, but it was his integrity that had rendered him unpopular. By the same token, Santa Anna was adored because he represented a superior banditry.

X. The Story of the Unlucky Pharmacist

Here is placed the story of Thomas Bordes, pharmacist of Saint-Gaudens, of whom everyone said from his childhood on that he was unlucky.

There could be no argument with that. There was a determination of fate that followed him step by step and which caused him to say: "I was born under an unlucky star." He was so sure of a particular persecution that he often scrutinized the sky by night, saying: "I'd like to know which one is my unlucky star."

He did not discover it, but he saw in every event a malign intention against him. Perhaps there was an aspect of things that escaped him. He said for example: "See what bad luck I have. My father is a man so sad that he discourages all his clients. He doesn't give advice when people ask him for it. Everyone prefers to go to Marvejol, who is installed opposite us, who is amiable, and has a pleasantry for everyone. When I replace my father, the pharmacy will no longer have any clients."

He did not see that his father, in spite of his sadness, was profoundly good, and that he was lucky to have him, for the most favored of men are those who see the early years of their lives go by in an atmosphere of benevolence.

"I've had the bad luck to lose my father," he said, at twenty-five, when his father died.

In fact, a host of petty misfortunes struck him whose origin was natural, but in which he saw the stamp of an invisible enemy.

He had a cyst in the neck that obliged him for a long time to tilt his head slightly to the right. He greeted people with a bitter smile and, pointing to his neck with his finger he said. "You see, always my bad luck. I have a cyst."

It happened that, when he took the diligence one Saturday in order to go and spend two days in Luchon, it tipped over. He was unharmed.

"That was bound to happen. If I take the diligence, it tips over."

His hair fell out precociously. A pharmacist has numerous treatments at his disposal. He did not make use of any of them.

"It's my bad luck. There's nothing to be done."

Twice he frequented families with the desire to be married; but he did not have any faith.

"It's necessary to have luck to marry well. My baldness is beginning to be visible. Then too, people know that my pharmacy is going downhill."

It was, indeed, going downhill. But there was a striking sign. On the road to Saint-Bertrand he had a little garden with a detached house that was ready to be sold. The beauty of that garden was made by a very old plane tree that shaded the house. There was a storm. Lightning struck the plane tree and set fire to it.

"It's quite simple. God has it in for me."

He had an uncle who was reputed to be rich and who lived in Toulouse

"When Old Bordes dies," his friends said, "you'll be rich and your run of bad luck will be ended."

Old Bordes died. Thomas Bordes rushed to Toulouse. His uncle had, indeed, been rich, but shortly before his death he had given everything to his mistress. He had only left his nephew a collection of old bottles: bottles of large dimensions that had caused their dazzling colors to shine in the window of his pharmacy in the Rue Saint-Rome.

At first Thomas was tempted not to accept that heritage.

"Always my bad luck! Those bottles will cost me money to have them transported."

However, he reflected, and had them come. He installed them in his own shop window. But his shop was in a poorly-lit side street. It is at night when pharmaceutical bottles exert their mysterious attraction, by means of the evocation of mineral mixtures and the magic of mingled substances. No one passed along the street and no one saw the bottles.

One evening—it was the time of the gold fever—Pierre Montanagol came to see Thomas Bordes, whose father he had known. He stood there thoughtfully, considering the bottles.

"One never sees that in America. If you went to a city like New Orleans and installed yourself as a pharmacist, with your bottles well exposed, you'd make a fortune in three years."

Pierre Montanagol's word carried a great weight, because he had been to America and he had come back rich. Thomas Bordes, gripped by the general madness, had thought of having himself inscribed in Alcide Pécouret's society. Then he had recoiled. The intoxication of fortune-seeking that was blowing through the land was manifest in him under the sign of multicolored bottles. New Orleans was a vast and rich city where bottles had never been seen. It was necessary to install himself there.

It was not without difficulty that the bottles were packed up in sturdy crates made to measure, but they were, and Thomas Bordes departed for Bordeaux, and then for New Orleans. A consoling idea was born within him. The ill luck was a force attached to the continent and it would not follow him to America. Perhaps his hair would grow again.

The vessel that transported him had already been afloat on the Ocean for three days. He was rather surprised to fall down fifteen steps to small, overly steep stairway that led from the deck to the dining room. He had quit the European continent, but bad luck pays no heed to the arbitrary divisions of geography.

Small woes and petty misfortunes recommenced falling upon him. A bad tooth started aching again. An old family watch, considered as a masterpiece of horology ceased to work for the first time. A ham that he had brought, intending to eat it when he woke up at night, turned out to be mysteriously full of little white worms.

"You see," he said, explaining his case to a young man who was going to New Orleans on behalf of his father's rum business.

He was a young man of delicate health, always anxious and naturally superstitious. He listened to Thomas Bordes with an extreme attention. He examined the ham that the latter had shown him on the deck, before throwing it in the sea. He had Thomas Bordes recount all the incidents of his life that testified to the presence of bad luck.

"I'm from a Neapolitan family," he said, "the Orsini family, and one of my uncles, it appears...."

He stopped and hesitated before continuing.

"It's better not to pronounce the words. One of my uncles was marked. I often heard mention of his case. Bad luck has a close relationship with...with the evil eye. I've said it. Too bad. A man who has bad luck also has the evil eye, and it's a terrible thing. It's communicable. If one frequents one of those marked beings too much, one eventually becomes like him—and sometimes quite rapidly."

From that day on, the proprietor of Orsini rums carefully avoided encountering Thomas Bordes on the deck where they had the habit of strolling together. The threat of the evil eye was very painful to Thomas Bordes.

"I'd never thought of that!"

And he felt a responsibility. However, there was no shipwreck. The ship was not becalmed by the absence of wind, and after twenty-two days of navigation, it arrived in New Orleans.

It was the beginning of the afternoon. The customs formalities were prolonged until nightfall. Thomas Bordes had become friendly with a man of advanced age, who said: "I'm a former Frenchman. When one is young, it's necessary to be French, in order to make war and have prestige over women. But when one advances in age and has a taste for large properties, with palm trees and sugar cane, it's necessary to become American. My name is Landry. Nowadays I call myself Harrison."

He offered to guide Thomas Bordes through the streets of New Orleans. As it was late, they would come back to have their evening meal and sleep on the ship.

When they had passed over the dark quays they emerged into a street full of shops. It was the hour when they were closing. Thomas saw one of them at a distance, from which a bright light was escaping. He asked what it was, and Harrison said: "It's a pharmacist who installed himself here last year, at the time of my last voyage. He possesses extraordinary bottles, so his shop is never empty. You'll see."

Thomas Bordes saw. Certainly, the bottles of the pharmacist of New Orleans were not as beautiful as his, but it was his idea. He had been anticipated because of his bad luck. And that bad luck was a terrible genius, which had a prophetic vision, for a year earlier, when he had not yet formed any project, it had organized his pharmacy with cunning and a diabolical foresight.

Thomas Bordes had no other thought than to run to the ship to stop the disembarkation of his crates. He would go no matter where, until he had found a city in which the bottles with a thousand colors were unknown.

He told Harrison his story. That man full of experience shook his head. He invited Thomas Bordes to dinner in a big New Orleans restaurant, because of the joy one experiences in giving advice. Perhaps a perfidious thought had been born in him. Perhaps he belonged to the category of men who have a hypocritical and profound determination to drive others toward misfortune by lavishing falsely wise advice on them.

"The *Neptune*, which brought us, is stopping over in Galveston. I advise you not to try to make your fortune in that city. The marvels of civilization, in the pharmaceutical domain, must have reached there, as they have New Orleans. Don't stop at Campeche either. That city is in decay since the export of dye-wood from Yucatan has been made via Carmen. You might go to Merida, a very prosperous city where there are monuments, convents and universities, but I wouldn't advise it. There's also a school of pharmacy, and the pupils are very jealous of their privileges. After a week your shop window and your precious bottles would be lapidated. To succeed, there's only one city for you, the most distant, the most remote in high mountains, the most inaccessible, one of the most beautiful and most populous, Santa-Fé-de-Bogota, the capital of New Granada. Access to it is so difficult that it's certain that no one will have preceded you."

Thomas Bordes had never heard mention of Santa-Fé-de-Bogota.

"It will be necessary or you to take a new ship at Chagras. Disembark at Barranquillas. A propeller boat, one of those marvelous modern vessels, will take you up the Magdalena for six or eight days. You'll continue on foot or on mule-back, with your baggage. You'll re-embark for a few days on a rowing boat with black oarsmen, the Bogas, and go as far as Honda. There, you've arrived. You'll only be separated from Bogota by five days on mule-back."

It sometimes happens that the implausible and dangerous character of an adventure urges you to attempt it. Sometimes a project suddenly plants itself in the soul as if it had roots, and it is impossible to tear it out. Perhaps, too, one is driven by the mystery of one's destiny.

Among the various things that he might have attempted, Thomas Bordes chose the most redoubtable.

"Avoid Agua-de-Dios, the city of lepers, "Harrison said, on quitting him, without apparent irony. "And when you camp under the stars—for one can't sleep on the Bogas' boats because of the odor—beware of the monochrome tiger that is confounded with the vegetation of the shore and prowls around camp-sites."

Thomas Bordes had thought hard about returning to Saint-Gaudens. He preferred to depart for Santa-Fé-de-Bogota.

He was young and robust. Fatigue was nothing. But he lived in a perpetual anxiety that he bottles might be broken in their crates. And he dragged after him an even heavier burden, that of the bad luck that never quit him. It continued to manifest itself. He missed connections with boats. He always stayed in the most uncomfortable hotels for which one paid most dearly. He was obliged to wait for a fortnight in Barranquilla because the rainy season was coming to an end and the waters of the Magdalena could not be navigated upstream even by propeller boats. There was an accident of navigation that immobilized his boat for three days on a sandbank. And it was only after the rapids that he knew the true misery of that journey.

The crates, the precious crates, might be stolen. He learned that from his traveling companions who were also going to Bogota: a professor of law and theology, and a pious old lady, Señora Iturri, who was traveling with her four grandsons and returning after fulfilling a vow to pray to a certain saint, whose statue, and hence her personal power, resided in a church in Cartagena.

It was necessary to watch over the crates, and all the baggage in general, for the Bogas were terrible men. They formed a corporation that imposed the number of hours of labor and the wages, for going up the Magdalena by rowing boat demanded an exceptional strength that was only found in that aristocracy of strength formed by the Bogas. They did not travel on certain days because there were festivals of Boga gods. The travelers waited on the bank of the Magdalena while their boatmen plunged into the forest, singing and dancing. Without anyone knowing why, any necklace or jewel green in color, such as jade or emerald, exerted a temptation on the Bogas so powerful that they could not do otherwise than take possession of it.

The large boats that transported the travelers had, over two-thirds of their extent, a roof of palm leaves, but at night one could not take advantage of that shelter to sleep. The passengers only occupied half the boat, the Bogas the other half. The indelicate boatmen paid no heed to the presence of those they were transporting. Their odor was sufficient to make everyone who was not a member of the Bogs race flee. When the boat stopped it was necessary to build a fire on the bank, prepare a meal and above all, watch out that the boat, with the baggage aboard, did not slip away under cover of darkness. One such disappearance was registered every year, and neither the government of New Granada nor that of Venezuela could do anything, for the Bogas were indispensable.

Thomas Bordes did not possess a green jewel, but one of the bottles, the one in crate number three, reflected admirable emerald shades. If the Bogas had known! But the packaging done with care in Saint-Gaudens protected the bottle admirably. Would that packaging resist so many crossings? That was what Thomas Bordes asked himself incessantly, with anxiety.

The shores of the Magdalena were redoubtable. The forest frequently plunged into the tumultuous waters and there was often only a thin strip of ground where one could camp. The passengers and their servants had organized shifts on watch.

Thomas Bordes asked one of the Iturri grandsons, experienced men, why three fires were necessary. "It's because of the monochrome tiger," he replied. And he learned that among those animals there were some individuals, more audacious than the others, which were not frightened by the fire. There were cases in which they had seized sleepers from alongside the flames.

The Iturris were not in accord on that point

"At any rate, it only happens shortly before dawn."

Thomas Bordes acquired the habit of awaking up before daybreak.

There were also crocodiles, which had sometimes seized travelers sleeping to close to the water by the foot.

Thomas thought: *It's my bad luck that has sent me into a region so full of dangers.* And when he awoke he observed that, for the same reason, the cloud of mosquitoes swirling around him was always sensibly denser than the ones surrounding his companions.

The journey up the Magdalena, for those who are lucky as well as those who are not, lasts for a little longer than a month.

That's because destiny cannot do otherwise, Thomas thought.

The travelers were in Honda, and could consider themselves as almost having arrived. There was only another six days by mule. Thomas Bordes allowed his satisfaction to show.

"This is the most dangerous part of the journey," the four Iturris told him. "We'll be going alongside vertiginous precipices on paths that are sometimes carried away in the rainy season. It's now October. We're the first to go through after the big storms. We risk finding ourselves on the edge of an abyss, on a road so narrow that the mules can't go backwards, with a void in front of us because there's no more road. It might also be that the valleys we have to traverse have become deep lakes and that it's necessary for us to wait for a week or two in the mud.

"We might be victims of pestilence that emerge from the waters, and which are the cause of the goiters that one sees on so many of the inhabitants of the region. It will be incessantly necessary for us to fear paramos, which are unusual tempests particular to the high solitudes of the Andes. A mule can be carried away like a feather, even if its load consists of heavy bottles. It's necessary to know that the great condors of the summits attack humans, and that in the hollows of valleys, the mud of the river-beds contains crocodiles that the heat of fires that people light might wake up."

"But those dangers are only child's play compared to the most real, which is that of an attack by brigands. We'll march with rifles in hand, although it's true that the Iturris are known throughout the region, and our presence is the best guarantee of success."

One person's bad luck is doubtless counterbalanced by another's good fortune. The journey passed without incident. The nights were only troubled by Señora Iturri's cries.

"What do you expect? She's a Beata," said her grandsons "When the paths rise, she senses that she's approaching the heavens. She thinks she's closer that she really is, and she's calling to the angels.

Everyone was woken up by those cries, but it was necessary to be indulgent to the appeals of a Beata.

The seven days passed and they saw with amazement, after the precipices, the waterfalls and the grim peaks, an immense city displayed, full of steeples, towers and majestic monuments.

But Thomas Bordes was at the limit of his strength. He could no longer support the somersaults of his mule. He was incapable of walking. Scarcely five or six miles separated the caravan from Bogota. At that distance, the security was absolute. Night was about to fall. He saw a house a short distance from the road. José Iturri offered to sustain him that far. For a piaster he would certainly receive hospitality. His baggage was not at risk. He would find it the following day when he arrived, rested, at the Hôtel de Madrid. In any case, José Iturri promised to come back and fetch him with a fresh horse from the stables.

Thomas Bordes could do no more. He managed to reach the house. It was to be feared that it was inhabited by Muysca Indians, taciturn men who only spoke the Muysca language. To the appeal shouted by José, with the offer of a piaster, an indifferent voice replied in bad Spanish. Hospitality for the night was granted.

"They're half-breeds," said Iturri, and hastened to return to the caravan.

Thomas Bordes opened the door of the house. At first he could not see anything. He was struck by a sickening odor, tempered by the perfume of courimari, which is an odorous bark burned throughout the state of Cundinamarca to drive away mosquitoes.

He became accustomed to the gloom of the room and saw that there were two hammocks suspended from the ceiling. From one of them emerged the head of an old man who was nonchalantly smoking a long and deformed cigar.

"Lie down on the ground," said the host, curtly. "I'm smoking." He was, indeed, a half-breed who expressed himself partly in an Indian dialect and partly in Spanish.

Thomas, who was exhausted, was only too glad to lie down. He dozed. Much later, he saw a shadow moving around him. It was the old man. He ground something in a bowl and the held it out. It was a wheat broth, the evening meal. Thomas had seen the bowl on arrival filed with a yellow paste that his host had thrown outside. The odor of the broth was so nauseating that he refused it.

The old man absorbed it avidly and resumed his place in the hammock, smoking a new cigar. Thomas saw its glow above him for a long time. He was installed in the only empty space there was, beneath the second hammock. He had felt the sticky soil, but what could he do? He ended up going to sleep. His fatigue was so great that he slept until morning.

He was woken up by the daylight, and also by the sensation that thick droplets were falling at intervals on to his forehead. He thought at first that it was raining outside and he wiped it away with his hand. But he saw that the sunlight was coming in through the doorway. His host was sitting beside him. He contemplated him with horror, for he perceived by the horrible deformation of the features and the stump that was holding the cigar that he was dealing with a leper. He leapt to his feet and put the piastre on the ground, being in the greatest haste to flee.

But as a further drop had just fallen with a soft sound and he saw that it had dripped from the second hammock, under which he had been sleeping, he wondered what was in that hammock. He saw a rounded form, as if a human being endowed with a formidable immobility were lying there.

"It's my wife," said the half-breed. "She died of the disease a month ago. I'm keeping her. It's the custom."

Thomas Bordes did not ask any more. He started running along the path that brought him back to the road. He was in despair. He would never see Saint-Gaudens again, that blessed town where there were no precipices, no crocodiles and no

270

lepers. His bad luck had reached its limit. Could one imagine a horror greater than receiving on one's forehead the decomposed essence of a leper dead for a month?

The limit of the bad luck had not yet been attained.

Thomas Bordes found his baggage at the Hôtel de Madrid. But the funds he had brought with him, which represented the realization of all he possessed, were in rapid decline, and were even running out. It was necessary to hurry, to rent a shop, expose his bottles and arrange the lighting. The Iturris, to whom he had recounted his story and explained his projects, without showing any excessive enthusiasm for their success, had assured him that the bottles of whose dazzling quality he had boasted had never been seen in Bogota. He was reaching his goal.

A few days passed in formalities and requests for authorization. He finally found an admirably-situated shop in one of the busiest quarters, not far from the school of medicine. He rented it immediately, paying out the last of his money. He no longer had any, except for the small sum indispensable for procuring the pharmacological ingredients that he had not brought with him. He intended to sleep on a camp bed in a minuscule room behind the shop. He had his crates transported immediately, and, his heart hammering, he set about opening them. The packing had been particularly careful, but does one ever know? The bottles might be in pieces.

But they were intact. His joy was immense. He glimpsed a glimmer of light. Perhaps the bad luck had departed. He went out in order to take the morning meal at the hotel.

His shop was almost adjacent to an immense and very old building that was a Franciscan convent. That morning it was very hot; a monk with a thick face and bulging eyes was hanging out of a window. Thomas observed his stupid physiognomy. Scarcely had he made that observation than the monk cased a long jet of saliva to emerge from his mouth and that jet hit Thomas on the left cheek. The monk disappeared immediately, but it seemed to Thomas hat his face had reflected a

271

base malignity that proved the intentional nature of the jet of saliva.

He was respectful of ecclesiastics. He continued on his way. He ate, and then went back to his shop. He went past the convent again, and saw the same fat monk at his window.

Perhaps he'll take the opportunity to apologize, thought Thomas. *He gives the impression of being veritably stupid.*

Scarcely had that thought been formulated than a new jet of saliva departed with rapidity and, with an foreseeable accuracy that denoted long practice, immediately hit Thos on the right cheek. The monk disappeared immediately, with an audible snigger that excluded the hypothesis of distraction or that of an unfortunate hazard.

It was too much. Thomas called to the monk vehemently, and as he obtained no response he headed for the portal of the convent, determined to lodge a complaint with the superior, surely a venerable and just man.

He rang, but there was no response. He heard laughter and insulting words. A judas hole opened in the door and he glimpsed faces very similar to that of the monk with the bulging eyes, which reflected the same scorn and the same hatred. He went home, irritated, and strove not to think about the incident any more.

But later, when he went out, no longer thinking about it, in fact, and absorbed with his money worries. He felt something wet strike his temple. It was another jet of saliva. He raised his head. The window was empty. Was it the same monk, or were they taking turns? Perhaps there were several who had that extraordinary habit.

Anger seized him. With his fist and his foot he hammered on the door. Passers-by stopped, and he explained to them what had happened. He did so in his bad Spanish. But that bad Spanish, instead of exciting laughter, gave birth to hostility. Women made the sign of the cross. He was deemed to be sacrilegious. He was obliged to draw away precipitately.

He told his story to the Iturris at the hotel and to the French consul, with whom he lodged a complaint. All the faces took on the same expression of gravity as they listened to him. Everyone gave him the same advice. He had been very imprudent to insult in a loud voice the very respectable order of Franciscans. It was necessary to hope that it would not give rise to serious consequences. As for complaining to the authorities, that was a hypothesis that would lead to the worse difficulties for him.

But the jet of saliva was inexhaustible. At every hour of the day, at the same window, Thomas saw the silhouette of the monk sprawling, meditating the insulting jet. It was in vain that he brushed the opposite wall or passed by at a run, simulating haste. He heard an immense burst of laughter fill the convent then. And if he wanted to avoid passing the accursed window, the disposition of the streets was such that it was necessary to make an immense detour.

Thomas recalled the drops falling from a hammock containing a dead leper. The manifestations of his bad luck since his arrival in Bogota had a bizarre relationship between them, a horrible resemblance. What would happen next?

He installed his pharmacy. He disposed the bottles in the best possible fashion, but he did it without courage and without hope, impelled solely by the tenacity that is a characteristic of the men of his homeland.

A storm burst at dusk on the very day that Thomas Bordes had chosen for the inauguration of his pharmacy. It was a storm of unusual proportions. Thomas Bordes sat down and waited.

I've seen others, he said to himself. It's one day lost. I'll put it off until tomorrow.

But a total obscurity covered the city of Bogota. A subterranean rumble resounded, and as Thomas was heading for his door in order to open it, he was thrown to the floor amid an avalanche of stones and an avalanche of broken glass.

Confusedly, he heard cries in the street: "An earthquake!"

That cry was followed by desperate clamors, the sounds of people running and confused collapses. It was, in fact, one of the most terrible earthquakes that Santa-Fé-de-Bogota, a city built on unstable foundations, had ever experienced.

Thomas groped, chilled by horror, touching fragments of matter that he thought he recognized. He remembered the corner in which he had put the candles. He found them. He had his briquette. He lit one. He looked around. All the bottles had been reduced to shards, and lay on the floor amid the dispersed pharmaceutical substances.

He sat on the floor near the candle and at first he had a desire to laugh at such a completion of misfortune. So, he had been led step by step to this disaster! An evil will had conducted him.

His bitter hilarity was of short duration. He pictured himself, devoid of support, far from his homeland, becoming a wretched beggar. Through the chimerical spaces of the dream he saw the town of Saint-Gaudens dancing, surrounded by joyous vines and blooming roses, like a lost paradise—lost forever. He took his head in his hands and he wept.

Then he felt a slight cold impact on his forehead. It was at the place where he had received the decomposed drip emanating from the leprous corpse. Then there was another on his cheek, where the saliva of the evil Franciscan had fallen. But what did it matter to him now?

However, the impacts multiplied; he perceived their hardness. He wanted to have a broken head, but it was like a particulate stream, a regular shower of little objects by which he was covered. He had put the candle down behind him, mechanically. He picked it up and looked.

He was entirely covered by gold coins. The coins were flowing like a stream from a hole formed in the ceiling, the joists of which had been dislocated by the shock of the earthquake. He swept them up with his hand. He made a pile of them, over which he threw his cloak. A treasure hidden in the course of wars, doubtless in the times of Bolivar, had been sheltered in the ceiling of the shop and its possessor had died without being able to recover it.

At that moment someone knocked on the shutter of the shop. It was the youngest of the Iturris, who had come to enquire as to his fate.

"I'm alive, but all my bottles are in pieces. I'm ruined."

"If you're alive, that's the essential thing," said the young man, and he left.

Thomas Bordes had before him several hundred thousand francs in Spanish doubloons. It was then that he showed a genius of which he would not have thought himself capable.

He understood that if he wanted to keep that treasure, it was necessary to get it out of Bogota, where he would undoubtedly be dispossessed of it, and in order to do that, to escape thieves, precipices and Bogas. He found within himself the necessary cunning.

In the homes of the Iturris, the French consul and the owner of the Hôtel de Madrid, he went in quest of the piastres necessary to reach the shore, in the manner of a beggar, where he would find a ship capable of taking him back to France. He succeeded, after research, in finding an emaciated, lame mule of pitiful aspect, but still having the strength to cry him and his gold coins. On the eve of his departure he ripped his garments and made up his hands and face to give himself fake swellings and the stigmata of leprosy. He even hung a bronze bell around the neck of his mule, which he intended to keep as far as Honda.

It was thus that he set forth, protecting himself by the appearance of the utmost poverty. An ardent force animated him: the sentiment that the bad luck no longer existed. He even wondered whether it had ever existed. Who knows? Perhaps the long sequence of his misfortunes had been necessary to his present signal good luck.

He triumphed over all the perils. He arrived in Cartagena, where he found, thanks to the consul, a French bank in which he could deposit his gold.

A few days later, having transformed the leprous beggar into a rich traveler, he embarked for Saint-Nazaire.

Ten years later, Dr. Fazeuille, who was installed in Villefranche-de-Lauragais and had become a notable individual in his small town, went to see Thomas Bordes in Saint-Gaudens in order to question him about his one-time voyage. Dr. Fazeuille was researching the former adventurers of 1850, making a study of the success of the men in life and the returns of that success, either by virtue of the will to succeed or by chance.

Thomas Bordes had obtained a pharmacy in the center of Saint-Gaudens and had several assistants under his orders, but his commerce was not prospering and everyone was in accord in attributing that to the great sadness that radiated from his person.

"No," he said, in response to a question from the doctor, "there's no relationship between luck and happiness. I was much happier when I was unlucky, or when I thought I was, than after the intervention in my life of the events that brought me a fortune. My opinion is that the desire for luck is the greatest factor in happiness. But in fact, there is no good luck and bad luck. What one thinks is good engenders invisible causes of evil. I've bought a large property that causes me nothing but worries. The little patch of land that I once had, with a single plane tree, even burned by the storm, gave me more satisfactions. And then, success gives birth to ingratitude. When my wife was alive she was always saying to me: 'You want to crush me with your money.' Now, isn't it my son who's claiming that my business is going downhill because I'm naturally sad, and I'm therefore harming his future prospects? It's better to be unlucky."

XI. The Forests of Goazalcoalco

What initially truck the sight of the men of Comminges leaning avidly over the bow of the *Avenir* when the ship tacked toward the mouth of the Goazalcoalco was the wreck of a ship of large tonnage on a sandbank.

The Pyreneans transported by the *Avenir* were men who had not allowed themselves to be caught by promises of the gold of placers, of virgin gold. They were laborious men hardened by toil. What they had come to seek was land with streams and trees—land that cost nothing! That land would be given to them. And that was not extraordinary, they had been told. The government of Mexico had, after all, an interest in drawing to its still-wild country men like them, accustomed to hard work. Here, the land was too abundant and also too fertile, but men were lacking. Those men were desired, and would be welcomed with open arms.

But what a surprise it was to see that great ship, half-dislocated by the waves, with its masts broken and its hatchways open. They believed confusedly that once a certain size was attained, ships no longer had to fear being wrecked. And their surprise gave way to anxiety when one of them, who had a telescope, read the name of the ship, which was still visible: the *Belle Étoile*.

They had heard mention of the *Belle Étoile* in France. It was the ship that had transported a convoy of emigrants from the region of Lyon two years before. Those emigrants, they had been told, had disembarked, built houses, cleared land and planted. They could count on their example, profit from their experience.

But it seemed that the experience in question had begun with a shipwreck.

Night was about to fall. It was necessary not to think of disembarking. They would disembark tomorrow at sunrise. The wind had eased. The stars were bright. It would be fine tomorrow. It was very fortunate that the travelers had arrived in such weather, the captain of the *Avenir* assured them. The travelers on the *Belle Étoile* had not been so lucky. From group to group people repeated that they were very fortunate. Yes, assuredly, very fortunate.

At the first ray of sunlight, all the emigrants were on the deck, gazing avidly at the land where they were to live henceforth. Their baggage, their implements and their provisions were around them. What they were searching for on the shore was the silhouette of the houses that were ready to receive them. One can live in the open air, either on the sea shore or in the forest, but half of the joy of life is the product of the walls of the room in which one dines as a family in the evenings and where one sleeps in security.

They did not see any houses. How in any case, could there have been any houses there? There was nothing but trees, as far as the eye could see. And what trees! The Pyreneans had never seen any so tall. And they were so densely packed that there was something menacing about them. The estuary of the Goazalcoalco seemed to have had difficulty opening a path to reach the sea. Its borders were guarded by high rows of trees. To the right the forest rose up and one could distinguish sandy stretches in places and marshes that interrupted the vegetation. The waters of lagoons had green-tinged reflections, and they resembled wounds in the soil, the result of some terrestrial malady.

"You're decidedly lucky," said the captain. "We'll pass the bar easily."

The majority did not know what "the bar" was. A few pirogues manned by Indians with impassive faces were drifting in the bay. The beach was deserted.

"The houses must be further away, hidden by the trees," said the emigrants to one another. "It's still early. The representative of the society will arrive and take us there."

The horror of their situation only appeared a few hours later. The captain of the *Avenir* had demanded that everything be disembarked immediately, and that nothing should any longer remain aboard his ship. The mother of young Raucat, who was dying, was transported. A carpenter by trade, he installed her on the sand, after having hastily put up a wooden frame to protect her mattress from the damp. The captain's mission was limited to transporting the passengers from France to that point in Mexico. He had fulfilled it. He was in great haste to depart again. Perhaps he suspected that if he had waited for a single day, all of those who had arrived full of hope would have demanded to be taken back to their homeland.

A single day was all that was necessary to show the cutters of wood and the clearers of land that they had been duped by a cleverly organized lie. At first they waited for the representative of the society who ought to be present at the arrival of the ship to take them to the houses destined for them. An ardent sun had now risen. Fearful Indians who seemed to inhabit a few miserable huts that could be glimpsed here and there came to examine them. The stout Ouvrard questioned them in Spanish, with the utmost joviality. Did they know a certain Monsieur Leprat, the representative of a large French society?

Indifferent to that question, which they doubtless did not understand, the Indians contented themselves with staring at them mutely. Malègre climbed into a pirogue and went upriver a short way. Young Duportal took a path into the forest. Both came back equally discouraged. There was no trace of houses anywhere, nothing but swarms of mosquitoes, stagnant pools and snakes slithering through the grass. Duportal had, however, seen a few wooden huts in ruins.

Toward the end of the afternoon, two men of the white race were perceived on the shore. They were only clad in a shirt, trousers and a big straw hat. They advanced slowly, chatting. Everyone ran toward them.

One was the customs officer, whose post was a little further away on a hill. The other, an old man, was the pilot charged with guiding ships through the sandbanks heaped up by the Goazalcoalco. They listened to the complaints and shook their heads gravely.

There were no houses, and no representative of the society. Two years before, other Frenchmen had disembarked from the ship that was wrecked out there. They had arrived in the same conditions. They had attempted to clear land. They had been put in touch with timber-merchants in Orizaba and Vera Cruz. They had not succeeded. But others might succeed.

The customs officer was a worthy man, sensible to offers of tobacco. He gave advice. The most urgent matter was the construction of shelters in palm-branches similar to the Indian huts, for there might be a storm. Then they could build real hoses with tree trunks. Were there hunters and fishermen? There were some. Then, it was necessary to think about mosquitoes. Who could tell? Men accustomed to cutting wood might perhaps get them out of trouble, with a great deal of courage.

The customs officer retraced his steps as he drew away. It was necessary to light fires because of tigers. Those animals pullulated, and were incredibly audacious. Even fires were not always sufficient, and there were cases...

Night fell. They only had time to accumulate wood. The emigrants huddled together. As soon as the first evening they split into two groups. Madame Alca, a rather singular old lady who was accompanied by her son, had called the emigrants Children of the Lord and had exhorted them to prayer. She was endowed with a resounding voice and had recited evening prayers, demanding with authority that everyone repeat them. That went on for rather a long time, and the incredulous murmured. Two camps immediately formed: the partisans of the pious Madame Alca and the rest, among whom Malègre and his family stood out.

The following day, the hard labor and the difficulties began.

Everyone set to work courageously. They commenced clearing, cutting down trees, attempting to plant. Some had brought seeds, others had not. Some possessed good tools, others had counted on those that the society had promised to furnish, and that a certain Leprat was to have distributed to them. Some had a rifle, a pistol or a saber, others had no weapon at their disposal. Immediately, there was another division than the religious one, between the poor and the rich. A quarrel between a Toulousan and an Alsatian was a further cause of separation. The southerners formed a large majority. Those who belonged to northern France built their cabins apart and only joined the others in the morning and evening when Madame Alca shouted: "Children of the Lord!"

Madame Alca demanded that everyone pray kneeing down, in order to oppose impiety, for as soon as her call to prayer was heard Malègre responded to it with a loud whistle. Fatality dictated that on the second day, Madame Raucat went into her death-throes just as the morning prayers finished. Furthermore, the tide came up higher than usual and a wave enveloped the wooden frame on which her mattress had been placed. During her final moments she was surrounded by the waters, and a wave covered her, which hastened her end. Her son, who had thought that he could leave her in order to join those who were praying, ran back too late, and only succeeded in preventing her from being carried away.

"See, prayer brings misfortune," the impious Malègre never ceased repeating.

Another misfortune followed. An eight-year-old child was devoured by a tiger. He had ventured into the forest with his brother, but only a short distance from the beach. The older of the two children saw a mass pounce and heard a scream. That was all.

All those who had weapons in their possession came running, but too late. They had not believed in that danger, which had not been manifest by anything visible. For the presence of tigers entailed an act of faith. Nothing revealed their presence. The idea necessarily formed that they were prowling around, ferocious and silent. And in the evening they huddled around the fires, pointing at fireflies, which were mistaken for their terrible eyes in the process of choosing a victim.

The emigrants learned that a few hours to the north, there as a small town called Mina-Titlan. They were supposed to go there to make a declaration of their arrival to the alcalde, who was the representative of the authority. Those who went discovered vast meadows, fertile expanses furrowed by streams, and woods of cheerful aspect that rendered them hope. The pilot's house was a real house, surrounded by plantations of sugar cane, maize and bananas. Here and there they saw a small deer, or a heron in flight. The country had the richness that had been praised to them. But the part reserved for them was still in its primitive state. Would the duration of a human life suffice to render it habitable?

The alcalde came to the French camp himself. He had put on a velvet costume and an almost new sombrero, in order to give the foreigners an elevated idea of his authority. He was a taciturn man, embarrassed by the sight of that whole society. He would like nothing better than to come to their aid, but there was nothing he could do. Perhaps the superior authority would intervene in favor of the colonists. Perhaps the governments had an arrangement between them, but he did not believe it. It was necessary to wait and not to hope for too much. They could always come to consult him if they needed advice.

The hunters exploring the region were intrigued to encounter crosses quite frequently. Indians who spoke Spanish and with whom they exchanged a few words mentioned a saint who lived in the forest. The saint was a Frenchman, they said, who had been in the party of colonists who had come two years earlier. He had withdrawn into the forest. No one knew how he lived. In any case, he was respected by the tigers.

People set out in search of him. Men deprived of everything superfluous considered the presence of a saint as an important supplement. Madame Alca stimulated the searches. Many crosses were found, but they did not succeed in encountering the man who had set them up.

One evening, they heard a canticle sung in French, and all hearts were filled with emotion. They attempted in vain to locate the singer. They heard his voice fade away in the wildest part of the forest. Only a saint could confront the nocturnal dangers like that.

It was only a few days later that they saw a half-naked savage arriving, of an alarming aspect, with a large machete in his belt, who was carrying a large wooden cross over his shoulder. He went past the huts without paying any heed to anyone. When he reached the shore he set about digging and planting his cross in the sand.

All those who were present came running. "It's the saint," they said. People called to one another. They surrounded him, and Madame Alca, who had the usage of sanctity, asked him questions. Some of them began to kneel down and ask the unknown man for his blessing. But he stared at the audience with wild eyes, and asked: "Where are Julie and Dominique?" Then he pronounced his name. "I'm Leprat."

It was perceived that the constructor of crosses was a madman. They tried to talk to him about the emigration society associated with his name, and which he was supposed to represent, but it was futile. He responded by pronouncing the names of Julie and Dominique, and resumed the route to the forest.

That was a cruel blow for Madame Alca, who had said that the protection of heaven was manifest by virtue of the presence of that saint.

Hatreds were only increased in consequence of the difficulties of life. Malègre called a meeting of all those who could warrant the title of workers. He made a speech to declare that the exploitation exercised over them by a few fallen aristocrats could not go on. They had to oblige the two Bramevaque brothers to work or expel them from the community.

In fact, both of them had shown themselves to be incapable of any work whatsoever. Their minds could not settle on anything. Adhémar spent his time drawing figures in the sand, saying that he could distinguish the future thus. As for Antoine, not finding any cats, he set out in search of little tigers. Malègre took advantage of that to say he was posing a danger to everyone, by stimulating the wrath of those animals. He shouted at the two brothers violently, reproaching them for their uselessness.

That upset those simple souls. Antoine was seen with his head in his hands, weeping. The next day, they had disappeared. People searched for them in vain. Indians reported that they had seen two men going along the shore at sunrise, heading in a northerly direction. They had departed without weapons, a change of clothes or provisions.

"It's thanks to me that we're rid of those parasites," Malègre repeated. And from that day on, his tyranny never ceased to be exerted. He fixed tariffs for all manual work accomplished. What was called mutual aid was exploitation. Although he received gratuitously a share of the game distributed by the hunters, he wound not consent to lift a piece of wood without payment.

A few discouraged colonists abandoned the game and went to Vera Cruz, either to re-embark or to exercise their métier there. Maria, who had come with a former café waiter named Dubourg, initially departed for Mina-Titlan, thinking that it was a town analogous to Saint-Gaudens. She and Dubourg thought that they could establish a tavern there. They tried, but their failure was complete. Much later, it was learned that they had ended up managing a hotel in Mexico City. That was an exceptional success.

Young Raucat thought he had made a fortune. While digging his plot of ground with his friend Colomiès he discovered a marvelously sculpted stone what appeared to be very ancient. It was in the form of a cup of large dimension, with bas-reliefs representing various sorts of individuals. He had heard it said that such things could have an enormous value. Napoléon, it appeared, had brought back some from Egypt at great expense, for the Louvre. They decided to go and sell the stone in Vera Cruz. But Raucat specified that the value would revert entirely to him, since it had been found on his land. His friend Colomiès was only an employee who was paid on a daily basis.

They both set forth, and, having traversed a thousand difficulties and many dangers, carrying the stone on a sort of stretcher that they had constructed, they arrived in Vera Cruz through the Orizapa gate.

As they were walking between the first houses they heard a cry: "It's a xicalli!"

A man of tall stature, full of great importance, who emerged from a sumptuous dilapidated dwelling, ordered them to stop. Having examined the stone he summoned other people, who emerged from the same dwelling.

"An authentic xicalli! The sacrifice cup of the god Teoyamici. There isn't one like it in Mexico!"

The man asked Raucat where he had found the stone. The latter told his story, but it appeared singular to the man, who gave curt orders to his servants to take the stone into his house."

"It will go to the museum in Mexico City."

The two Frenchmen protested vehemently.

"Go fetch the carabiniers. It's necessary to clarify the matter. First of all, don't you know that any ancient monument or fragment of an ancient monument is the property of the Mexican state, and that individuals have no right to them?"

Raucat and his companion were completely unaware of that. They would be held in prison until their statements could be verified. When they were released they would each be given five piastres, by virtue of the benevolence of the lover of xicallis, a man learned in Mexican antiquities, whom bad luck had placed in their path.

They were separated, for Colomiès, in his quality of employee, demanded his friend's five piastres as back pay. As well as the xicalli, they lost their friendship.

It was shortly before the dispersal of colonists of the Goazalcoalco that the Jean Bourdin incident occurred. Jean Bourdin was a former sub-officer in the artillery who had emigrated in 1820. He had enabled a small plantation near Orizaba to prosper, and had had a daughter by an Indian woman, whom he adored. That daughter, named Asunta, died after falling from a horse. Jean Bourdin, in despair, quit the place where he had lived and started wandering at random. He had stopped not far from the mouth of the Goazalcoalco and had built a cabin in a part of the forest known as Mal-Paso, which was reputed to be full of tigers. He thought would die rapidly there, but people who want to die do not. Fifteen years had gone by and he had acquired great renown as a tiger-killer. People came to find him from far and wide when a place was unduly ravaged by those animals. He was now very old and his white beard gave him the appearance of a patriarch.

All had had left of his daughter was a coral necklace she had worn. He had set up a sort of altar in his cabin and the necklace reposed there in a box that he had sculpted and painted amorously. That was his only religion.

Now, Malègre, roaming in Mal-Paso, came across the cabin one day while Bourdin was out hunting. He went in, and saw the altar and the casket. It had a lock, which he forced. He took possession of the necklace, supposing it to be very valuable. According to him, a member of the working class ought to remain ignorant of the quality of those adornments reserved for the rich. But that evening, his more competent brother made fun of him on seeing the coral necklace. They threw it negligently into a corner of the hut in which they lived together.

Meanwhile, Jean Bourdin returned from hunting and perceived the theft, which was for him an inconceivable sacrilege. He knew that no Indian would have dared to touch anything belonging to him. He went to the colonists' camp, running and gesticulating. Everyone was preparing their meals, but they came out on hearing his cries.

"I want my necklace. Woe betide the man who has taken it."

People grouped around him to hear his explanations. Malègre declared that such a suspicion was an insult to everyone, and his gaze met the old man's.

"I'll visit all your houses!" he cried. And he threw himself into Malègre's, which was the nearest. He saw the necklace lying on the ground.

Malègre, resenting the audacity, made the gesture of throwing Jean Bourdin out of his home. The latter came out, seized his carbine, which was over his shoulder, and shot Malègre at point-blank range. Then he picked up the necklace, considered it amorously, and strode way.

Late in the night, the alcalde of Mina-Titlan was woken up by a loud noise outside his door.

"I'm Jean Bourdin. I've killed a thief and I've come to surrender to the law."

The alcalde was very embarrassed. The prison was a wooden hut that had no lock. Jean Bourdin was a man honored by everyone. Then again, he had no guard. Who would pay for the expense?

He deliberated for so long that Jean Bourdin became impatient.

"But who will kill the tigers if you're imprisoned?"

Jean Bourdin returned to Mal-Paso and continued to live for no one knows how long in the worship of his daughter Asunta, symbolized by the coral necklace.

An America ship, the *Alabama*, came cruising outside the mouth of the Goazalcolalco, and the rumor ran around that all the land on the banks of the river had been sold by Santa Anna to America for the construction of a railway that would link the two oceans. No indemnity was set aside, it was said, for recent owners of the land. As for the Indians, they fell into a great and sudden despair. Those naïve men thought that they were about to become slaves again and be condemned to work in the mines, as in the times of the execrable Spanish domination.

A wind of anxiety passed through the colonists. They abandoned their labor. What was the point of going to any trouble, since they were about to be dispossessed. The alcalde, when questioned, did not know what to reply. He would refer the matter to the governor, he said—but in the thirty years that

287

he had been the alcalde, he had never produced a case to which he had received a reply.

In vain Madame Alca appealed to divine authority. American surveyors were measuring distances and digging in the vicinity. Discouragement took hold of everyone. The colonists dispersed gradually. An epidemic killed many of them. A few were fortunate enough to be repatriated.

Madame Alca became the administrator of a nunnery in Orizaba. In the morning she continued to shout: "Children of the Lord!" but it was in Spanish.

Someone recognized Malègre's brother among the convicts who were working on the roads near Vera Cruz, with a cannonball attached to his foot.

PART THREE: THE SAVAGE LIFE

Prelude

There is a force that drives humans to go further on. There are some who pursue gold in the sand of rivers and the stone of deserted mountains. There are some who seek God in the cloisters that the forest forms, in the sanctuaries of the solitudes. There are some who are not seeking anything and who keep marching forward with the certainty that they are heading for oblivion. Many do not know why they set out. Many do not want ever to come back. A very large number do not come back.

Out there, in the land where the Indians have blue eyes, in the ancient kingdom of Cibola, where the five mysterious cities stack their adobe houses on steps raised up like ramparts, in the middle of the desert where the Zuni mountains cast a shadow in the South and which is limited to the North by the Red River, stands the rock of El Moro.[18]

---

[18] Cibola was the name attributed to the legendary "seven cities of gold," rumor of which began circulating among Spanish conquistadors in the sixteenth century. The most celebrated of those who set out to find it was Francisco Vasquez de Coronado, who reached its supposed location—in what is now the Zuni Reservation in New Mexico—in 1540 and found nothing there but ordinary towns. There he was told another story about an equally fabulous city of gold called Quivira, of which he immediately set out in search, with a similar result. Naturally, the legend refused to die and continues to thrive in fanciful popular fiction in all media. Madame Blavatsky cites the story in *The Secret Doctrine*.

It is a silhouette of a Moor that emerges from the sand, made with the eternal stone of the body of the Earth. For nature, by virtue of a strange playfulness, took pleasure in creating at the beginning of the world, when matter was still plastic and malleable at the whim of the divine force, the contours of individuals and the designs of monuments that would not be imagined until many millennia thereafter. In the times when there were not yet any seas, forests or monsters, she amused herself placing, here a cavalier, further on a cathedral, and further on a sailing ship. And in the desert of the Indians with blue eyes, she established a Moor with his burnoose, made with the granite that is the substance of mountains.

It became a reference point for travelers who came to sleep in its shadow. And at sunrise, with their spear or sword, they proudly engraved their name there, impelled by the eternal desire that men have to make it known to future men that they were alive on a certain day, in a certain place, which they have notified in stone, and then passed on.

Is this the sign of Quetzalcoatl or that of Huitzilopochtli? But were those gods worshiped in these deserts? Was this cross engraved by the Madoc, the elder son of a King of Wales, who traveled over the sea in the twelfth century and reached the kingdom of Cibola with men and women who all had golden hair?[19] Who was this Joseph de Bazenzalles whose name is there on the stone? And who was this Jean Gonzales, and that Antonio de Cochea, who was known to be Bishop of Durango and given to magical practices before disappearing

---

[19] The legend of the Welsh Prince Madoc, who supposedly sailed to America in 1170, became popular in the Elizabethan Era, when it was offered as a kind of entitlement for English pirates to attack Spanish possessions in America and ships bringing back treasure therefrom. Later scholarly fantasists popularized the myth of "Welsh Indians" belonging to various tribes—including the Zunis, who were nominated as such by several writers in the 1850s, including Abbé Emmanuel Domerich.

mysteriously? What became of all these men? Did they find the gold for which they were searching? Where do their bones repose

Not long ago, on the threshold of a grotto lost in the Sierra Madre, the skeleton of a dead man was found. The birds and beasts of the region had eaten his flesh. The Zuni Indians must have surprised him in his sleep. They had killed him and abandoned him, in order that he would sleep for centuries. His breastplate was nearby and his sword was in its sheath. But between his jawbones there was a gold nugget. "Eat that gold for which you have come so far, for which you and your kin kill, and for which you all die," those Zunis must have said then.

They did not know how truly they spoke. All those who sleep in the sands, near torrents sparkling with flecks of gold, or in sterile mountains, chew with their teeth of death the accursed substance of the earth, which they have been unable to possess while alive, and which they believe they finally hold in their immobilized phantom jaws.

I. The Document
(Dr. Fazeuille's Journal)

Nothing is as disagreeable as discovering in oneself elements of naivety, even of stupidity. I would have liked to have been a great psychologist, knowing characters in a second by means of the facial features. I am almost always mistaken. These errors are very serious in certain cases.

Thus, I have judged Bernard falsely. I thought him fundamentally good, beneath a cold exterior. He is nothing of the sort. He is the opposite of his uncle, the opposite of his brother Sulpice. How can completely different personalities be born like that in families?

We have had a conversation in the garden of the hotel in Vera Cruz. Only rather banal words were pronounced, and yet the tone and the silences that followed them, and certain...hmm...gazes have enabled me to see Bernard's soul clearly. I'm frightened. I dare not believe what I have seen, in an invisible mirror.

"What a pity Sulpice isn't with us," I said, with sincerity, without any hidden agenda.

"It's a great pity," he said, with a certain intonation, darting a rapid sideways glance at me, to see whether there was any hint of irony in my exclamation, and whether I knew that he had arranged everything in order that we would all depart and Sulpice would remain in France. I had often thought of the skill of that machination, but I had said to myself: he loves Malvina; he fears his brother. He wants to travel with her without him. I had excused his lies because of that amour, since there is a general convention that is willing to excuse everything when amour is at stake.

"You know Sulpice's ideas," he added. "Nothing could have made him depart."

"Except perhaps Malvina," I said, with the greatest possible ingenuousness.

His face suddenly expressed a frightful hatred. I understood that he had always hated his brother. He started laughing.

"There are no two people on earth who are as unsuited to one another. Sulpice is in the genre of my brother Hugues. He was made for preaching."

"Opposites often attract."

That idea of opposites attracting had the gift of irritating him.

"Malvina, you see, only likes rogues. There's a whole category of women in whom honesty inspires a profound horror—a horror that they don't admit and of which they might even be unaware. Thus you, I prefer to tell you, have no chance with Malvina."

Me? But..."

I started to stammer, always being embarrassed when someone talks about my intimate sentiments.

"For you're somewhat in love with Malvina—admit it."

I knew that he considered me not to be a dangerous rival, much too timid, and that he was scornful of me from the viewpoint of matters of amour. I knew that, but I was shocked by the expression of triumph and baseness in his features. And I said to myself at the same time: *He takes me for an imbecile, and perhaps he's right.* And I felt a profound humiliation.

"You'd be capable of telling a woman like Malvina that you love her?"

"If it were true, why not?"

He laughed again. "What folly! To be loved by her it's necessary to treat her as an inferior, to degrade her, even to beat her—how do I know? Two or three years ago an adventurer, a bandit with the physique of a dandy came to Saint-Gaudens. I now that he pleased her because he was a bandit. And here, she only had to see that murderer, that wretched Ezéquiel, once, to become infatuated with him."

"Murderer! You're exaggerating. He was a smuggler."

"No matter—you've seen the kind of man."

At that moment he stopped, and I sensed the rise of a physical rage within him. He stamped his foot on the stones of the pathway. Then a sincere sadness overtook him.

"I can't explain why I don't please her. Oh, I don't say that because of my physique. That's never the reason that causes one to please. Even you, if you weren't a simpleton, could have successes. What I can't explain is that she doesn't find in me what she loves in the other. What attracts her is a man of whom one can say: 'He's capable of anything.' Well, I feel that I'm capable of doing more than the petty adventurers to whom she's given herself, more or less. In any case, I can arrange things so as not to end up being garroted."

He remained silent for some time, and I saw that he was imagining the execution of the Alaman son with a profound satisfaction.

That's true, I thought, *I'm a simpleton. Malvina, in sum, who knows...*

It is three days since Ezéquiel Alaman was executed, and we're still at the hotel in Vera Cruz. What is going to happen? In what situation have I put myself? In what situation have we all put ourselves?

If I look back, I can see that we have all been seized by a sort of vertigo, carried away by the collective folly that passed through Comminges. We've been victims of gold folly, mingled with the prestige of a passionate young woman of captivating beauty.

I shall recapitulate. Mademoiselle de Noussoulens has received from her father a document in which there are indications for finding a place, or a treasure of an undefined nature. Monsieur de Noussoulens got that document from a Portuguese who wanted to borrow money from him and who disappeared. That constitutes an extremely vague basis, inasmuch as, although the document gives an itinerary, it doesn't specify the exact nature of the wealth to be found. Any sane person— and I am one—would immediately think that it was a story invented by an adventurer in order to borrow money. Monsieur de Noussoulens has, it appears, affirmed to his daughter that it was a matter of something very serious. *It's your heritage*, he told her.

It seems to me, now I think about it, that it's too late to go back. Now, Malvina hasn't doubted for an instant the veracity of the indications given. Bernard Borromée, to whom she has shown the document, is enthused, and has had no difficulty persuading the excellent Martin Bruno, as well as me, to depart with him to go in search of an assured fortune. Perhaps Bernard, a shrewd and reflective mind, had seen it above all as an opportunity to make the conquest of Malvina by traveling with her and becoming her mentor in matters of treasure and adventures. But he believes in the document; we all believe in it.

That comes from our race, as men of the Midi, who have a profound love of chimeras and unreal things. I am one of the sanest among those southerners and one of the most scientific, but it was sufficient for someone to mention a treasure to me, the discovery of which was enveloped in a certain mystery, for me to accept immediately to depart, without asking for any proof, prey to an interior enthusiasm that is utterly unjustified.

And now I'm wondering where all this is going to lead us. The question of money hangs over our actions. We each have only limited sums. It's Malvina, the owner of the document—and, in consequence, the treasure—who is assuming the material expenses of the expedition, but apart from that, there are the petty daily expenses. Martin Bruno and I have agreed that we will hold on to the price of a return passage to France. But can we hold on to it? Might we not be overtaken by a wave of unforeseen expenses?

I made those reflections in my room, shortly after waking up, at the time when thoughts are clear and events and events are not subject to the transformations of the imagination. I quit my bed in order to have even clearer idea, for I was under a mosquito net and that light veil inclines toward dreams.

Someone came to tell me that Anastasio Alaman wanted to talk to me.

I was very surprised. I had thought that I understood, without being affected by it, that in the group we form around Malvina, he considered me to be a secondary character.

"Have him come up," I said to the mulatto, who had pronounced his name with a profound respect, for the father of a man sentenced to death for brigandage is not attained, as he would be in France, by the slightest discredit. On the contrary, I believe that his moral surface is magnified.

I had been told that Anastasio Alaman was devastated by the death of his son. He appeared to me to be singularly alert, and with the animation that an appetite for life gives. He was wearing his white felt hat, which he took off with a grand gesture and with which he imprudently covered the ink-well. His moustache was carefully waxed and had been subjected to a special treatment in order to have straight points. He sat astride a chair, which is a sign of authority and self-satisfaction.

"I've come to see you because you're the most reasonable."

I sensed that for him, that was not praise. It was for me.

"And in, in truth, you're a doctor. That's a great deal."

"Oh!"

"Yes, yes, you're a man of science. And at the same time, you believe in magic. Don't say no. In Vera Cruz, everything is known."

I had retained a bad memory of the visit I had made with Garisse, and also a great perplexity. I contented myself with nodding my head. I any case, when people have formed an opinion of your nature, and have enunciated it, it's not what one replies to them that can change it.

"Well, I've come to talk to you about your expedition, with which Mademoiselle de Noussoulens wants to associate me. With you, I can examine things from a higher viewpoint, which I can't do with your companions. You're in progress toward an immense realization, which involves more than riches, something much more admirable, which I can't, how-ever, specify. Don't forget that it's a matter of a cathedral."

"A cathedral?"

"Yes. The document that Mademoiselle de Noussoulens possesses mentions a cathedral."

"That document, in truth, appears to me to be very ob-scure. And the more I think about it..."

"It isn't obscure. It's even quite clear, at least in large part. Very clear, from the moment one knows the name of the man who wrote it or the regions that it indicates. Paso-del-Norte is the town from which caravans set off that go between Texas and Arizona toward Santa Fe. The rock of El Moro is a rock that looms up in the middle of the desert, and is thus named because its silhouette, in the evening, bears some re-semblance to that of a Moor. I know that rock. I've slept in its shadow and I've seen engraved in the stone the name of Anto-nio de Cochea.

"That's another story. That the name is contained in the document is the dark point of our affair. Antonio de Cochea was a magician bishop of the sixteenth century. He lived in that region and left bloody memories there. He was atrocious-ly cruel and extraordinarily powerful. He is reputed to have been the master of a school of magic, certain secrets of which have been retained and transmitted. But once again, that's another story.

"The land where the Indians have blue eyes is the land of Cibola, in the region of Acoma, where blue eyes are indeed a characteristic of certain families. Acoma is a small fortified village, which is not mentioned on any map because it is in a terrible desert of stone, and no one knows it except for a few audacious adventurers who have seen the ruins of its towers from a distance and have not dared to risk climbing the three hundred steps by which one reaches it.

"I am one of the small number of white men who have climbed those three hundred steps and who have lived in Acoma. I have had the surprise of seeing that that solitary rock is inhabited by a few families of Indians, particularly gentle

297

and good—men, perhaps, such as exist nowhere else. Up to that point, you see, everything is quite simple. Where the enigma commences is with the matter of the cathedral. And yet, is it an enigma?

"A legend runs around that region on the subject of that cathedral. Somewhere in the inaccessible rocks of the Zuni mountains or the first foothills of the Sierra Madre stands an immense cathedral, which time has respected. A religious monument—note that—which is not the work of the Spaniards, but might have been built several centuries earlier by the mysterious Prince Madoc, who came to America from the land of Wales and subjugated the Zuni Indians. The mixture of the Welsh and the Zunis would be the cause of the blue eyes that one finds in the inhabitants of Acoma, whose children intermarry.

"Thus, the existence of the cathedral has at least a legendary basis. It also rests on certain facts. A few years ago, a man—an adventurer—claimed to have seen it and to have removed a solid gold object therefrom: a chalice, which he showed, and which appeared to be of great value. 'Why didn't you remove more?' people asked him, when he affirmed that the cathedral was full of unusual riches. Then, it appears, he was troubled, seemed embarrassed, and ended up saying that there was great danger in touching anything whatsoever. 'I escaped by a miracle,' he said. He was mistaken, He had not escaped. He was found dead a short distance from Santa Fe, dead and horribly disfigured. The chalice, of course, had disappeared.

"All the old Indians of the region, if one questions them on the subject of the cathedral, are unanimous in making the same response. Somewhere in the mountains there is a very ancient cathedral. But it is bewitched. One is sometimes able to see it from afar, but no man can reach it. Unless...

"There is a concordance on that conclusion. On can reach it under certain condition—but no one can explain what they are. What are those conditions? Do they correspond to the phrase in the document: *find a saint for the mass*? You know as well as I do how rare saints are. They are also, difficult to displace. One can only make conjectures. I've made many. The story of the cathedral once intrigued me greatly. I wanted to discover it. I knew Esquiros, who was a bandit. But I renounced my project as too dangerous.

"I had a certain intuition. I sensed, at that moment, that death was linked to whoever touched that cathedral. I ought to tell you that I was young, sought-after by women—in sum, that I had others things to do. And then there was—and there still is—the capital point, which is that of a certain Socrates."

"Who is this Socrates? The document, so far as I remember, mentions a certain Socrates, to whom it is necessary not to offer money. That is, in fact, rather peculiar. Why is that the capital point?"

"I don't know, exactly—and, in sum, I don't know who Socrates is. I haven't seen his face. No one has ever seen it."

"Why is that?"

"He wears a mask. One can only see his eyes, and even then, only one. What is the reason for that mask? It's said that half of his face was ripped off in a combat with a bear. It's said that he's so frightfully ugly that women would have nervous cries if they saw him. It's said that he's either a famous man or a great criminal who doesn't want to be recognized. But what don't people say? My intuition, in which I trust, tells me to fear him. I know that he's in communication with Indian sorcerers.

"What struck me most, once, was that Esquiros himself was afraid of him. Now, Esquiros was a redoubtable individual, who feared very few men. He died as a consequence of a crocodile bite. There's an indication in that. But he can only have been struck by someone who had gone far enough in the study of magic. Crocodiles, certain snakes and scorpions are animals susceptible of receiving the will of sorcerers and acting when ordered. But again, that's another story. Anyway, that's a pure hypothesis I'm making.

"What surprises me, and it's primarily for this reason that I've come to see you, is that the document says: *make contact with a certain Socrates.* Now, the person who wrote that, Maximo Avila, had received the confidences of Esquiros, he had gone to Santa Fe himself, had traveled the region, and had the best reasons for fearing Socrates. The document ought to have said: *at all costs, avoid a certain Socrates.* I'm afraid that it might be a trap. That remains to be seen. I wanted to warn you. And it's necessary that I warn you about something else. An expedition like yours, like ours, since we're associates, forms a whole—in a way, sort of moral personality..."

He stopped, and seemed to be questioning me with his eyes. He was wondering whether I understood. I am let down by my physique and above all by the lack of vivacity in my gaze, and I sometimes have a certain expression of stupidity that I have glimpsed with sorrow in mirrors. It is all the more unfortunate when I have that expression although I understand very well. I hastened to repeat back, in another form, what my interlocutor had just said, in order to prove to him that I was following his argument.

He went on: "That personality can be more or less powerful, can have more or less chance of living, and above all, be more or less good, more or less creative of evil. When one asks of a seer or a sorcerer whether something will succeed, in order to respond, he has only to scrutinize the personality of the affair in question. It is only more or less conscious than him. Well, I've studied the soul of our affair. It's impressive. It has terrible aspects. It seems that it has stimulated misfortune and will continue to do so. Misfortune is always like a chain. One link leads fatally to another. Without being able to explain why, I sense that this cathedral has a fatal character. Note that it isn't necessary for it to exist for that. The faith that one has in it gives it a sort of existence that can be sufficient to create great evils."

I must have betrayed myself again by the expression on my face, for Anastasio Alaman stopped and I saw by expression of ironic superiority on his features that he estimated that I was no longer following the subtlety of his conceptions.

"But let's leave that domain and return to practical matters. There is a caravan once a month that goes across Mexico to Paso-del-Norte and from there to Santa Fe. It's there that you'll wait for me."

"You're not departing with us?"

"No, that's better. I'll join you out there. Perhaps I'll even have preceded you. In spite of the distance, everything is known. With you, my presence would be known. Traveling alone, no one can know that I'm returning to the land of Cibola. I've made an arrangement with your companion Bernard Borromée for the expenses of the expedition, of which I shall take charge. I'll also take care of everything you need for a journey that will last about three months."

"Three months!"

"Perhaps a little more. Texas isn't very safe. The Texians don't support the American yoke very well. You'll have an interest in proclaiming loudly that you're a Frenchman, even though the Texians don't know what a Frenchman is. It will mean that you're not a Yankee. It's at Santa Fe that our real mission will commence. Between now and then, remember: beware of a certain Socrates."

II. General Houston's Slap
(Dr. Fazeuille's Journal)

Sometimes, through the faults that I am obliged to recognize in myself, I see the glimmer of a quality, like an earth-
worm in a dark forest. Am I courageous? It is necessary for
me to examine the events that I have just traversed to be able
to answer that question. If I recognize that I have courage, I
sense that I will be able to obtain great advantage in the life
that I am called upon to lead, for no virtue is effective without
the consideration given by the consciousness that one possesses it.

I am not cut out for camping in the desert. Not that I do
not support it marvelously, having received the gift of splendid health, but I prefer sleeping with my head on a pillow rather than on a saddle, and good wine is more agreeable to me
in the course of a meal than the water of a stagnant marsh. A
regret presents itself every evening at the same time, when I
roll myself up in a blanket and prepare to go to sleep. How
much better I would be in my father's little house!

Now, on evening in question, I was at that moment of regret, and also that of going to sleep. The turns that we had
organized to mount guard permitted me to spend a tranquil
night. Everyone had been in a bad mood. There are evenings
when all souls are naturally morose, as if they had communicated wordlessly an inexpressible item of bad news. In such
cases, coincidence dictates that the meal will be abnormally
bad. It had been. Strips of beef dried in the sun, which were
revived by boiling water impregnated with herbs, had been so
tough as to be almost inedible. There had been too many aro-
matic herbs, and one had the sensation that the beef had been
steeped in the liqueur made by the Carthusian monks. That
liqueur is exquisite, but ought to be drunk separately and in its
time.

The wood collected for the fire was damp, for the fire was giving off an almost insupportable smoke.

"We can't stay here!" I had cried.

"Señor, I've collected damp wood deliberately," one of the arrieros told me. "This way we'll be free from mosquitoes."

The mosquitoes were buzzing more loudly than ever, and Bernard said: "No, there's no smoke," for a slight wind was pushing it in my direction. He added, with a certain irony: "You can always move away a little."

The howling of wolves could be heard, at a distance that did not seem very great. An arriero with a hideous face had recounted while we were eating perfumed beef around the fire how he had acquired that hideousness due to an almost total obliteration of his right cheek. Sleeping with a numerous company next to a fire like ours, he had neglected because of the heat to put his sarape over his head.

"The fire was smoking like this," he said. "That must have prevented a particularly savage wolf—for there are some that surpass their fellows in cruelty—from being frightened by the flames. The wolf of which I speak emerged from a bush and leapt on me. I was woken up by an atrocious pain. With a single snap of its jaw—just one, you understand—it ripped away my right cheek."

In telling that story he took a certain pleasure in emphasizing the unique character of that snap of the jaws, for which he could not help feeling a certain admiration. Such an exploit, when it is exceptional, always retains its prestige.

The sight of those two rows of teeth laid bare had enabled me to tolerate the smoke. All the noises of the camp had died away one after another. The four or five fires around which all the travelers were extended were launching high flames into the air that communicated a sense of security. The vehicles were not sufficiently numerous to form a complete barrier round us, but disposed in a semi-circle they defended us on the north side. The east and the south were protected by large trees with low branches, to which the horses and mules were attached.

Only the westerly direction was defenseless, but an arriero with whom I had chatted during the day had taken charge of watching it, and I heard his regular footfalls coming and going. I could even follow the glow of his pipe in the darkness. His name was Tiburce, and he was an excellent man, full of experience.

"For twenty years I've been accompanying caravans from Mexico City to the Ocean, or from the banks of the Mississippi to Santa Fe. All the Indian tribes know me and I've even lived with Houston—the famous Houston, the great patriot of Texas—in a Cherokee tribe.[20] Well, I can tell you that there's no danger in the prairies except for the man looks for it. Nothing ever happens to a prudent man."

And he talked to me on the road, and for a long time, about a certain Houston, a admirable man according to him and universally known, to whom the fate of Texas was linked. That country, which only seemed to be to be composed of frightful deserts and savage mountains, had been ceded to America by Mexico a few years before. Some of its inhabitants—there must have been some, although we hardly encoun-

---

[20] Sam Houston (1793-1863) lived with a Cherokee tribe for some time in his youth, and married into it. He was the leader of what Americans call "the Texas Revolution" of 1835-36, when American colonists rebelled against the Mexican government and expelled the troops stationed there easily; Santa Anna, then President, vowed to take it back personally, but failed, was captured and ordered the Mexican army to withdraw in exchange for his life. The annexation of Texas as the forty-eighth state in 1845 precipitated the Mexican-American War. By the early 1850s Houston was a Senator and a career politician in the USA, according to the record of our history, but the text of the present story gives a markedly different account of his affiliation and that of the "Texians" he commands.

tered any villages there—had protested against that cession and were fighting for their independence. At least, that was what I understood.

So I was about to go to sleep, hypnotized by the drop of light made by Tiburce's pipe. It gave the impression of igniting and fading away, and the sound of his footsteps drew away.

He doesn't fear the wolves, was my final thought.

I was woken up by something that seemed to me to be a cannon-shot.

Our caravan did not possess a cannon. How could one find oneself, in the middle of the desert, in the presence of a troop firing a cannon? Such was my first thought.

I saw Bernard and Martin Bruno a few paces away, on their feet, and Malvina, who was hurriedly wrapping a kerchief around her face. I remembered that advice that she had been given in Mexico: if you find yourself in the presence of brigands, they're thinking primarily in terms of money and merchandise; it's rare for them to take women, but it's necessary not to tempt them by the presence of beauty; hide your face as much as possible. That was what she was in the process of doing.

An absurd precaution, I thought, as I got to my feet.

To my great amazement I was almost knocked over by a horseman in big hat, who had a rifle in his hand ready to fire. There were others around me. All sorts of cries of fright resounded. Men were running hither and yon shouting incomprehensible things. I saw a tall merchant with long hair and the head of a prophet, who was hastening to load his rifle. He was plunging the rod into the barrel feverishly when one of our arrieros snatched it from his hand brutally.

"It's too late. You'll get us all massacred."

The horses were whining and puling at their tethers. The disorder was complete. I heard: "They're Texians." And also: "So what? They won't eat you."

Some of the horsemen who had invaded our camp so suddenly had dismounted, and were bringing out all the families who had spent the beginning of the night in their wagons.

I had drawn closer to Malvina. Bernard and Martin Bruno had done the same. The latter was very calm.

"Why aren't we defending ourselves?" he said, in a loud voice.

"You can see that it's impossible," said Ambrosio, the leader of the caravan, who had heard him. "You always have the right to get yourself killed."

In fact, the foreign horsemen formed a menacing circle. The majority had their rifles aimed at us. There might have been thirty.

Malvina clicked her teeth. Bernard looked to the right and then to the left with an abnormal nervousness. I was dominated by the thought that I would not show sufficient courage, and that dread paralyzed me.

"It's shameful," said Martin. "They're less numerous than us."

"Shut up!" said Bernard, sharply—and I noticed that he had difficulty articulating those syllables, and that he was short of breath.

He's afraid, I thought. *Fear cuts off the breath like that. Perhaps I wouldn't be able to speak myself.* I felt the dread of losing my breath making my respiration difficult. I drew nearer to my companions and slowly articulated some phrase or other in order to prove to myself that I had conserved my facility of elocution.

The barrels of the rifles were turned toward us in a disquieting fashion and the horsemen advanced, deliberately pushing us into the middle of the camp.

I noticed a young man with a big nose, dressed in a garish fashion, who seemed to be the leader of the band. He gave an impression of an annoyance and seemed to be irritated by the cries. I heard him murmur: "If those children could shut up!"

Then, in a loud voice, he said: "Are they all here? None of them have escaped?"

"Except for the sentinel they're all here," said a voice emerging from the darkness.

"My God—what's going to happen?" said Malvina in a low voice to a woman beside whom she had been traveling all day, and who was holding her arm.

The one that I judged to be the leader took a step forward on his horse, stood up in his stirrups and shouted in a strident voice: "Which one among you is the doctor?"

Those words were followed by a great silence. Even the children, who did not understand, had suddenly fallen silent. My heart started hammering in my breast. So it was me they wanted! The shock prevented me from replying right away.

"I ask the doctor to make himself known."

There were whispers. To my great surprise, the eyes of the horseman who had spoken, which were wandering back and forth, settled on me. So he had recognized me by my doctor's physique!

Without making any effort for that, I was invaded by a great calm. I raised my right arm and I replied: "It's me."

With an extreme politeness, the horseman removed his hat and made me a great salute.

"Señor Doctor, I'm charmed to have been able to meet you; we've come rather a long way expressly for that and we're obliged to depart in the greatest haste. I hope that you won't hold it against me if I ask you to accompany us without any delay."

The hypothesis of refusal did not even present itself to my mind. I understood by the way that the horsemen were looking at me that I was the objective of their expedition.

"Should I bring my medical kit?"

"What?"

I repeated my question. He smiled and made a vague gesture. He must not have known what a medical kit was."

I went through the crowd and headed for the place where I had unloaded my baggage. As luck would have it I found it almost immediately. The young man with the big nose never took his eyes off me.

"Bring the best horse for the doctor!" he shouted.

"Will I be absent long?" I asked him, for I envisaged with horror the idea of losing my companions and wandering alone in the frightful wilderness.

"The future is God's, Señor Doctor," he replied, with a hint of irony that I found alarming. "But according to all anticipations your companions will be following the route to Santa Fe for several days. You can't fail to catch up with them." To the horsemen surrounding him he said: "Let's go!"

One of them was holding a horse by the bridle. "Are you a good horseman?"

"My God! I can ride...but I don't have any prowess."

"I have orders. We'll have to travel at top speed."

I did not have time to agree anything with my friends. Martin threw me a blanket, shouting that it would be cold in the morning.

"Especially in the forest," added the officer. "Good precaution. Go on ahead of me."

My horse was drawn away by the others. But a short distance away they stopped.

"It's Tiburce that has been killed," said a voice.

"It's his fault—he fired at us," said another.

I saw the unfortunate Tiburce lying on the ground, his arms outstretched, and I recalled his words: *Nothing ever happens to a prudent man.*

I wanted to dismount, but my companion seized my arm. "He's certainly dead. I know him. He was a Texian."

"But perhaps..."

"I have orders. We need to hurry. I have a chief who doesn't joke."

"Can I ask who that chief is?"

We had set off again.

"It's Houston himself—the great Houston."

And I sensed that he was trying to distinguish in the darkness the effect that name had on me.

I tried to put him off the track. "I confess, Captain,"—I gave him that title at hazard—"that the name is scarcely known to me."

He started to laugh, like someone sharing a joke. Our horses had begun to gallop and it was impossible to talk.

The moon was above our heads. I was primarily occupied with my horse, but I was able to examine the riders who were accompanying me. With the exception of their leader they were all redoubtable in appearance.

I'm in the hands of a gang of bandits, I thought, and I praised myself internally for having been able to vanquish my idleness since my departure from France and having exerted myself to perfect the little Spanish that I knew. I now spoke it fluently, albeit with a slight accent.

Sometimes the horses slowed to a walk, at other times they galloped for an interval that I found interminable. I dared not complain, but I was exhausted. We finally stopped and everyone dismounted.

"We're going to rest for a while," the officer told me, "before we go through the forest. Afterwards, we'll have an hour on the mountain."

I suppressed a fearful exclamation.

"My name is Antonio Perez," he went on, with the tone of a man of the world introducing himself. And he added, emphatically: "Of the Perez family."

He strove to reassure me. He liked the French, Paris, French women and their elegance. He dropped the names of Lamartine and Victor Hugo.

"The men you can see are very primitive, to be sure, but they're not bandits, as a foreigner might think. They're Texian soldiers who are fighting for the independence of their homeland. It's true that we've acted brutally with you, but my men have carried out their mission, and haven't pillaged the caravan."

We were sitting in the grass. Beside us were two mules laden with thick bales. I recognized them as mules belonging to the silk merchant who had departed with us. One bale had been slashed by a knife, doubtless to allow its contents to be identified, and brightly-colored kerchiefs were emerging from the rip.

Perhaps Antonio Perez saw the direction of my gaze.

"That's nothing. It's necessary that these poor fellows have some recompense for their trouble. What do you expect? I count on choosing a few kerchiefs for myself, if it's worth the trouble. But if Houston knew that!"

"Am I being indiscreet, Captain, in asking you for what reason you came to look for me, and what kind of service you expect of me?"

Antonio Perez remained silent.

"Houston is very susceptible. I prefer not to reply to you. Perhaps he'd rather tell you himself. And note that he might also insult me because I haven't told you."

We set forth again. I ought to have been anxious, even anguished. *By the grace of God*, an interior voice said to me. And immediately, I thought: *But that's a form of courage! No, it's insouciance. Let's call it strength of mind. That's it: I'm showing strength of mind in an unexpected and dangerous situation.* And I straightened up on my horse, in spite of my fatigue.

An hour on the mountain! But what a mountain! The moon was about to disappear and the first glimmers of daylight were beginning to pale. I was surrounded by blocs of lava that were reminiscent of desperate giants, prey to convulsions for thousands of years and suddenly struck with immobility.

As we were following a steep path, Antonio Perez drew nearer to me.

"We'll soon be arriving. Will you permit me to give you some friendly advice?"

"Certainly."

"Do you have strength of mind?"

I was astounded.

"I was just…yes, I believe I have some mastery of myself."

"You're going to need it. I advise you to summon up all the mastery of which you're capable. This must remain between us. It's certain that you're going to see Houston. He's a great man. But as such, he has his weaknesses. Among others, he drinks. I can tell you that, because everyone knows it. He's known as the greatest drunkard in Texas. When he's drunk he lets himself go, saying no matter what. Again, that's nothing. But he lets himself do things. It's of no importance, for there isn't a Texian who doesn't consider him as his father. Then again, to be slapped by one's father..."

"Slapped!" I exclaimed.

"Yes, it's a slight annoyance. Either in jest, or seriously, no one knows which, he can't see someone new without slapping him."

"What! I could never support that!"

"Only at table—when one has a meal with him. What do you expect? It's a habit, a mania, call it what you will. It's sufficient to get used to it, to tell oneself that he's the father of the Texians..."

"I'm French, and I swear to you that if..."

"Don't swear anything! There are exceptions to every rule. In any case, you might not have a meal with him... No, it's not certain that you'll have a meal in his company. If you're lucky, we'll learn on arrival that he's gone out tonight to set an ambush for the Americans. He comes and goes, he's indefatigable. But in sum, if the episode of the slap occurs, believe me, have strength of mind. It's a matter of a great man, the Napoléon of Texas. Consider yourself as a Texian and tell yourself that he's your father."

I felt an extreme fatigue, but that didn't prevent anger from making my blood boil at the idea of what might happen. However, I succeeded in getting a grip on myself, thanks to the decision I had made to be master of myself.

To tolerate receiving a slap, I told myself, *is an impossible thing. Receiving one from this Houston and returning it would be equivalent to certain death. Now, life is precious and all human actions tend, in sum, to perpetuate it. It would be*

311

insane to accomplish an action that would put that life in great danger. Hold on! Isn't that the advice of my natural cowardice pushing me to submit to anything rather than run a risk? True courage consists of defending one's dignity and neglecting any other consideration. But do I have courage?

I was at that point in my reasoning when the road turned; we began to go downhill. We had almost arrived. I had before my eyes a narrow valley full of trees, with meadows that were slightly dry, but meadows nevertheless. I saw enclosures with livestock and people who were going to work. At the extremity of the valley there was an agglomeration of tents and huts constructed of branches, which surrounded a large stone building that looked very ancient. A little church tower rose up beside it. How could a hacienda exist in the middle of those savage mountains, far from any town, in a territory only inhabited by savage peoples?

"Houston's army is sometimes here, sometimes there," Antonio Perez told me, "It comprises fifty men, sometimes a thousand. But the general headquarters is here. It goes without saying that you will never remember what you have seen or the itinerary you have followed."

Finally, we dismounted, after having passed under centenarian trees into a courtyard of vast proportions. I noticed a well surmounted by a faience dome with a cross at the summit. It was covered and one could descend into it by means of a narrow stairway closed by a metal door. An Indian clad in rags was guarding that door. I only noticed that because we stopped right alongside it. I handed the bridle of my horse to someone who had run forward. I was so molded to the saddle that I asked whether I could stretch my legs a little.

Day was breaking. An angelus rang. Immediately, like a house of cards, I saw all the men around me collapse. They gave the impression of having been scythed down by the invisible force of the bell. There were all on their knees, their hands clasped. The horsemen still in the saddle had leapt down. In the distance, an entire file of men carrying sacks had instantly set down their burdens in order to prostrate themselves. Criminal or joyful faces had suddenly become grave.

As I gazed at that spectacle curiously I felt someone strike my shoulder forcefully—too forcefully.

"On your knees, Señor."

It was the guardian of the well. He said that to me with a furious expression on his face, as if he were addressing a sacrilege. I saw Antonio Perez making signs to me at the same time as he said something to the guardian that I didn't understand, and in which I heard the word *gringo*. I remembered that it had been recommended to me urgently aboard the *Reine Marie* to comply with the custom of prostrating myself when the angelus sounded, wherever I might be. Anyone who refused risked being maltreated, or even killed, by the witnesses, under the pretext of heresy, by virtue of a right of violence acquired by tradition.

I did not have time to deliberate and to ask myself what the attitude of a truly courageous man would be who had long refused himself the external formalities of a religion to which he did not adhere. An obscure wisdom made me fall to my knees before reflection as to the propriety of the gesture. Already, faces of hatred were turning toward me.

What would my father, an admirer of Voltaire, say, I thought, *if he saw me kneeling like his in the midst of these fanatics?*

The hacienda was constructed on the model of all the old dwellings of the region, half-farms and half-fortresses. It had only one upper floor, with a monumental stairway, cut by a wall garnished with loopholes in anticipation of a siege. The ground floor was reminiscent of a barracks and I even perceived a large white horse before a bale of hay.

Antonio Perez drew me away rapidly. "You can rest afterwards. A room must have been prepared for you, on your own. But I ought to take you to the patient first. Don't be astonished if she talks about the stars. The stars have played an important role in her life."

It was the first time that he had made an allusion to the objective of my journey.

The first floor of the hacienda was strangely silent. The doors of the rooms were closed. Several motionless people were standing in a broad corridor. They seemed to be waiting. Perhaps it was the arrival of the doctor for which they were waiting, because there was a murmur when we appeared. I was surprised to see Indians, women clad in black with long shawls, and an enormous red-faced priest. But I could not make them out precisely, for curtains were drawn over the windows. Fatigue caused me to conceive everything as if in a dream.

"My God!" said one of the women in black, falling to her knees in front of me.

"No follies, Speranza!" exclaimed another, severely, opened the door of the room into which she gave me a sign to enter.

At first I couldn't see anything. Then my eyes adapted to a vague clarity that came from sunlight filtering through the curtains of a window and a candelabrum in which the flames of candles were flickering. The room I had before my eyes was muggy, stifling and filled with furniture, paintings and statues. There were so many that I thought: *The fruit of some pillage has been accumulated here.* Gold was gleaming, mirrors sparkling. But my attention was immediately seized by an immense crimson silk bedcover deployed over the bed. It blinded me with its sumptuousness, streaming with light between the four sculpted columns of a bed with an awning. And from that dazzling crimson a small white head emerged, the smiling face, beneath the tresses, every hair of which seemed to have received particular care, of an exceedingly old, very wrinkled, very gentle and utterly exhausted woman, who looked at me with mauve eyes full of benevolence.

She moved her head up and down, and I heard a kind of whisper. "Thank you, thank you. They were wrong to make you come. I'm well, I'm very well, I told them. But they don't believe me. I'm very well."

And after a silence, she added: "Have all the stars disappeared from the sky?"

"In the name of heaven, Señora, don't talk," said the woman in the black shawl who had introduced me, in an imperative voice. "And above all, don't occupy yourself with the stars."

The invalid had closed her eyes and I immediately took account of the fact that she was living the final hours of her existence.

I asked questions, for form's sake, and I listened to an interminable account of the highs and lows of Señora Houston, the mother of the Texian hero, a few of whose eccentricities of character Antonio Perez had revealed to me. All her life she had had heart trouble. It was a miracle that she had lasted so long. A creature of God! It was necessary to say that, because it was the pure truth—and the lady in the shawl approached my ear in order to whisper that only the remedies furnished by the Indian sorcerers had been able to do any good, and had saved her beloved mistress ten times over."

"So?" I said.

"The same remedies have done her harm. It's inexplicable." Then too, "the great light of the Cherokees" had ceased to exist. Someone had gone to Arkansas to consult him, but he was dead. Oh, he would have saved her! She had fallen unconscious twice. What was it necessary to do.

"What age is the patient?"

"No one knows. In the old days, in Texas, people scarcely counted the years. Perhaps a hundred."

There was a slight movement under the crimson bedcover. The Señora had heard. I drew nearer to her. In a whisper she told me that she had a reference-point. When she had been told about the great French Revolution she had been thirty. She was, therefore, ninety years old.[21]

---

[21] In our history, Sam Houston's mother, Elizabeth Paxton, had married in the early 1780s—Sam was the youngest of her five children—but it is unlikely, given that she was of Scot-

Ninety! The heart! Two bouts of unconsciousness. I thought about the inutility of my journey.

"What is it necessary to do, doctor?"

I nearly said that there was nothing to be done.

I ordered a small dose of coffee. Several women in shawls surrounded me. As soon as I had said those words one of them fell to her knees with a strangled sob and I felt her kiss my hand. I thought that it was the one who had prostrated herself in the corridor.

"Speranza! Stop your follies," said the one who seemed to be the most important, and who had a bony and rather terrible face.

She looked me full in the face and held back an ironic snigger. "Coffee? Is that all?"

"There's nothing to do except give her as much strength as possible."

"Nothing else to do. I wonder what the general will say when he hears that there's nothing else to do."

The fat priest moved the women aside and pushed them with his belly. He put his face with its bulging eyes close to mine, and with an air of stupid complicity, he said: "I gave her the Sacraments yesterday evening. It was seven o'clock." Then, turning to the women, he added, majestically: "Do what the French scholar says. Go fetch the coffee."

A slight whisper summoned me back to the bedside.

"Go and rest," said the Señora. "I'm as well as possible, given that soon...I don't know why they're tormenting themselves. One can't live forever, can one?"

---

tish-Irish descent and brought up in the Shenandoah Valley in Virginia, that she would have not have kept an exact count of the years. The figure of ninety cited here implies that it is now 1849, but that is incompatible with other datable references in Dr. Fazeuille's narrative—except that we now seem to be deeply entrenched in an alternative history.

I had asked to be woken up after two hours. Antonio Perez knocked on my door.

"The general wants to talk to you." He fixed me with his gaze. "He's in a very good mood. That's understandable...he adores his mother and she's doing much better." Doubtless he thought that he read an afterthought in my gaze, for he added: "His good humor won't be a reason...on the contrary...but it's only during meals that...who will ever be able to understand why?"

"Much better!" I exclaimed, pretending to have forgotten the general's habits. "But she's going to die."

"Don't say that. That would be terrible. But you've rendered her life."

I followed Antonio Perez, but we had not taken three steps along the corridor when a resounding voice shouted: "Antonio!"

I saw a giant come toward us, a giant in uniform, with little gleaming eyes and an extraordinary belt that covered a third of his body, and from which two revolvers were suspended.

"General Houston," Antonio Perez old me, in a low voice.

"You've worked a miracle, Doctor." He held out his hands toward me. "Oh, I knew that the scholars of Paris knew more than the Indian sorcerers. So I'm very grateful to you for your visit."

I thought I noticed that he blushed. He must once have been a timid individual, I thought, who slaps people in order not to be intimidated by them.

"Has Antonio talked to you about your honoraria?"

"Not yet, General," said Antonio.

"I'm so grateful to you! You can dispose of General Houston, who, if God aids him, will chase the Americans out of Texas."

"Let me tell you, General..."

But he did not let me speak. I saw that he was part of the numerous species of men who follow their own train of

317

thought without taking any account of what their interlocutors say.

"It's necessary that you know that my mother is a woman of genius. You haven't seen her on her feet. She's as tall as this." With his hand he indicated the stature of a child. He started to laugh loudly. "Well, she has a son of the height that you can see and she has a brain that embraces everything that one can know. She knows everything, absolutely everything. Isn't that so, Antonio?"

"She knows everything," Antonio Perez agreed.

"The stars, for example. She knows the names of the stars. Isn't that unusual? She calls all the stars by their names, and with that, no taller than…oh, Doctor, how I thank you! I've been very afraid. But between us, I believe that my mother has a special vitality—in sum, that she'll never die."

"General, I'd like to tell you…it's absolutely necessary that I tell you…"

But he was no longer listening to me.

"I'm expecting you for lunch."

I had resolved firmly not to leave the invalid's room again. She passed from the greatest lucidity to periods of semi-slumber during which I heard her repeating: "The Great Bear, Vega, Sirius, Venus, Jupiter…"

The names of those stars made the woman that they had addressed as Speranza shiver with wonder.

"You hear, Doctor. She loves them, her stars."

I had tried in vain to procure a little rest for the señora by having the bedroom evacuated. There were more and more women in black standing there, with their eyes fixed either on the bed or on me, murmuring: "She's saved! The Frenchman has saved her!"

I even heard one of them say to another: "I saw it with my own eyes. He added a powder of his composition to the coffee."

I had had a few minutes to reflect. The camp, even after the harassing days—the camp where my companions were—

appeared to me as a paradise. Would I ever see them again? Was I up to the circumstances? The essential thing was to remain calm, self-controlled.

Antonio Perez slipped to my side. I had to go with him, he told me in a low voice. General Houston was telling me to come to lunch with his general staff.

"Impossible! I can't leave the patient."

He insisted, but I refused to go with him.

He came back after a few moments. It seemed to me that his cheek was red. He was strangely nervous.

"It's a formal order. The general says that his mother is completely cured. He wants you at his table. Since you've seen him, he's been drinking. In such cases, there's nothing to do but obey. He's already furious that you didn't come immediately. Follow me. I don't know what he's capable of doing."

I leaned over the patient. I saw her mauve eyes fixed on mine. There was no fear in them and no benevolence, no human sentiment. She seemed to be contemplating an astonishing spectacle, invisible for me. "Venus, the Great Bear, Vega…," she murmured.

I followed Antonio. Once we were in the corridor he reproached me for having made him come back twice.

"That will spoil everything. He's another man. You're going to see another man."

Because of the heat and the flies, the room on the ground floor in which the meal was served was plunged in semi-darkness. There must have been forty people there.

I'm in the middle of a band of brigands, I thought, as I considered the general staff. There were men magnificently dressed, with an extraordinary luxury of weapons overflowing from their belts. Others were in rags. I noticed one who was naked to the waist. I thought I could distinguish two or three women sitting at the back of the room, at the extreme end of the table, one of whom was wearing a red mantilla that fell over her shoulders. It seemed to me that the silhouette in question was not unknown to me, but I did not have the leisure to meditate on that matter. General Houston, whose stature surpassed that of all the guests, showed me an empty place opposite him. He did not say a word to me, and his gaze even avoided mine.

All sorts of strange foodstuffs were among the numerous dishes on which the guests drew, some with silver or golden forks but the majority with their fingers. Some had precious vessels in front of them, other simple earthenware bowls. A large bowl that must contain mescal circulated from hand to hand. In the midst of laughter and imprecations I heard the name of the American General Norris pronounced several times. I calculated, regretfully, that the table was quite narrow—certainly narrower than the arm of a tall man.

One attracts unfortunate events by thinking about them, I said to myself. *The important thing is to be calm and spread calm around oneself by means of one's own calmness.*

Soon, joy infected everyone. I did not understand everyone, for some expressed themselves in a Texian dialect that was unknown to me. I observed Houston covertly. Sometimes he guffawed at a crude joke while leaning back in his chair or falling with his head on the table, sometimes he had a furious expression, for some unknown reason. I calculated the moment when the meal could decently be terminated for me and when I could slip away toward the door without being noticed, but Houston never lost sight of me.

An interior sense told me that I was antipathetic to him and that he was meditating something against me, but I also told myself that it was fear that was engendering that illusion of my interior sensibility, that it was Antonio Perez' stories that had frightened me, and that if I was calm, all would be well.

What followed then happened with bewildering rapidity.

An individual with a swollen face and a very thick neck, whom I had heard called "Commandant," stared at me for a moment. Suddenly, his mouth broadened, like the mouth of someone about to say something very droll. He extended his arm toward me and said, very loudly: "The Frenchman looks like General Norris! Perhaps it is General Norris!"

He turned very red, and, excited by his own words, he started shouting: "Norris! Norris!"

He was beside Houston. The later raised himself up in his chair, cried: "Idiot!" And with a loud burst of laughter, he slapped him.

That only made an impression on a single member of the audience: me.

The commandant did not even rub his cheek. He started laughing, but an atrocious laugh, so false was it, so much did it disguise baseness of soul.

It was that laughter that distressed me. The expression "My blood ran cold," was exact for me at that moment.

"General Houston," I cried, in a resounding voice, "I prefer, personally, to slap you first."

And I leaned over the table, launching my hand at full tilt in the direction of the general.

I don't know what receptacle fell. The general had leaned backwards and my hand only struck empty air.

"No, I won't wait to be slapped. It's me who will give the first slap."

I got up and launched myself forward in order to run around the table and reach the general.

I never got there. Someone—I don't know who—seized me round the body. An immense tumult went up. Everyone was shouting. I heard: "He's mad! He's mad! Kill him!"

I had enough presence of mind to register an immense amazement on the general's face. That amazement caused an expression of stupidity to appear at the same time.

"Let him return to his place!" howled the general. "I like you, doctor. Clink glasses with me. I want to have the man who slapped me facing me."

I don't know how I found myself sitting down again, facing the general.

"For he slapped me! Hey, Commandant, did you see how he slapped me?"

I was certain that I had only struck empty space. But he rubbed his cheek in a comical fashion, making a semblance of having been hurt and obstinately taking the commandant as a witness.

Reason returned to me. *How will this end?* I wondered.

Providence must have been watching—or had foreseen everything.

A young man in a uniform came in, almost running. He was covered in dust and letting his saber trail. He explained something to the general in a low voice. The young man must have been known to everyone, for silence had fallen. Suddenly, the general stood up.

"My friends, it's necessary to depart. The Americans have arrived at the hacienda of Huesca and they've been laying siege to it since yesterday.

He darted a fiery gaze around him and I sensed that I was completely outside his preoccupations. There was no longer any trace of drunkenness in his attitude.

But at that moment a prolonged, heart-rending cry rang out, a plaint such that I thought at first that it had come from some animal, perhaps a tiger-cat murdered in a neighboring room.

"Eusebio! Eusebio!"

The door opened. A black form sprang forth. I recognized the woman who had prostrated herself before me and who seemed to have the habit of extravagant manifestations. The extremities of her shawl were hanging down behind her like black wings. She traversed the crowd of the officers, who had risen to their feet, and were buckling their belts or downing a last glass of mescal. She reached the general, seized him by the neck, wrapped herself around him and cried in an increasingly heart-rending voice, the tone of which tore the nerves like a violin scraped by an inexpert hand.

"Eusebio! Weep on my heart! Let's weep together! God has taken back her soul!"

At the same time, other individuals filled the room. There was a great disorder. I saw the woman with the bony face, who paraded a gaze of hatred over all of us, and said:

"She's dead!" in the same tone that she might have used to say: "She's been murdered."

The fat priest approached the commandant, and, as an item of information destined for him personally, putting his face close to his, he murmured: I gave her the Sacraments yesterday evening. It was seven o'clock."

"Mama! Mama!" howled the general, tearing himself from Speranza's grip.

And the man I had previously seen with the face of a drunkard, and then with the face of a soldier, went past me with the face of a child, over which large tears were flowing, and the enormity of which rendered it all the more touching.

I ran out behind him. At the bottom of the stairs Antonio Perez caught up with me. "If you value your life, don't go up. As sure as I'm here, he'll kill you."

"Me! Why?"

"People will say that you've made the señora die."

Assuredly, I should have gone past and climbed stairs. Yes, I believe I should have acted thus, even though I understood that Antonio was telling the truth.

The young woman in the red mantilla suddenly loomed up before us. "Follow me," she said, in an imperative tone.

We followed her into the courtyard.

"Lieutenant," she said to Antonio Perez. "Give the doctor the horse that I ride here. It's a very fast white horse. Call Benito the half-caste, who knows the country like his pocket. It's necessary that they're gone within five minutes."

And as Antonio scratched his head and appeared perplexed by the responsibility he was taking, she said: "I'll take it all on me. Don't worry. I'll sort it out tomorrow. You know how quickly the general changes."

I had before me Carlotta, the daughter of Anastasio Alaman. I had judged that she had a strong head. I was not mistaken. She was in the process of saving my life.

I thanked her. She stopped me. "Oh, I love your friend so much," she said, "but he doesn't live in the real world. He's a poet. How quickly everything goes. Me, I need reality. Tell him, if you see him again..."

She hesitated, and then started laughing.

"No, don't tell him anything."

Hazard—or, rather, Providence—dictated that Antonio found Benito in a few minutes and the latter brought the horses.

I had a scruple, or, rather, made the semblance of having a scruple. "I ought, all the same, to have..."

"Life is precious," said Antonio.

Carlotta gave instructions to Benito.

"Don't stop until nightfall. Join the road to Santa Fe at the well of palms. If anyone pursues you, they'll never believe that you've got that far."

"I'll doubtless be charged with the pursuit," said Antonio.

I climbed into the saddle.

"You've witnessed a Corneillian scene, eh?" And as I did not reply, he insisted, desirous of showing me that he knew Corneille: "It was truly Corneillian!"

Carlotta saved my life a second time. She caught up with me as we were setting off, leapt up and placed Antonio's sombrero, which she had stolen on the wing, on my head. I was bare-headed and the sun was leaden.

"If you think of it, give it back to Benito," said Antonio.

It was, in fact, a splendid sombrero. I thought of the kerchiefs stolen from the caravan, of which he had reserved a few.

Scarcely had we galloped past the last cabins than I said to myself: *Flight is, in any case, not the courageous thing to do. A sick woman was confided to me. I ought to have been beside her, even dead. On the other hand, I haven't shown any self-mastery. True courage would have consisted of receiving the slap. Yes, true courage—but I have, all the same, given evidence of courage of a secondary order. It's necessary not to be too severe with oneself. In sum, it's Providence that di-*

rected everything. It visibly intended that I should live. Why? It has reasons that are impenetrable.

I was, therefore, certain of escaping if Houston had me pursued. I was not pursued. And when we arrived at the well of palms and Benito told me that I was a fine horseman, I felt an immense satisfaction.

Next to the well there was a cabin. I sat down on the ground, dazed, for, in spite of my qualities as a horsemen, that ride had exhausted me. I was vaguely conscious of Benito burning herbs inside the cabin. I also saw him deposit a canvas bag on the ground.

"There's dried meat in there for three days, and a flask of coffee. I've tethered your horse to that tree trunk, leaving him a few meters of rein. According to the tracks left on the trail, your caravan passed through during the day. If you leave early tomorrow morning in a northerly direction, you'll catch up with it very quickly, for your horse is a fine one. The essential thing is that you catch up before the confluence of the river Pecos with the river Penasco—oh, not because of the rivers but because of the black ogress that guards it."

I was so fatigued that I did not reply, and did not inform myself as to what the black ogress was. His words were to come back to me later. In any case, he was in a hurry to leave and did not seem to have any desire to tell the story of the ogress.

I took five piastres from my belt and gave them to him, asking myself, as I always do in such cases: *Is that sufficient? Am I miserly or generous?* He did not let anything appear on his impassive features.

As he mounted his horse, I had a hesitation. I had Antonio Perez's sombrero in my hand. I ought to send it back to that amicable man. But what would I do tomorrow without a hat?

Give it to Benito if you think about it, Antonio Perez had said. I was tired enough not to have thought of it. I kept the sombrero.

III. The Black Ogress
(Dr. Fazeuille's Journal)

Never forget to enable your soul to progress. Such was the phrase that I repeated to myself frequently. It was, in a more pretentious form, a translation of what my father had said to me on quitting me, with a hint of melancholy: "You'll acquire experience by traveling."

I also prescribed to myself to recapitulate the actions of the day and to pronounce a judgment on the manner I which I had conducted myself, the good and the evil that I had done— for there is an austere sage within me who only appears in the evening. He formulates arguments, advises and makes resolutions. But how can that sage appear when one is obliged to worry about whether a little snake or a scorpion might come to sting you during the night?

For I could suppose that one or other of them, having sheltered in the roof, might fall on my face during my sleep.

By the grace of God! I thought, putting my head on my elbow and lying down. *I should have given ten piastres to Benito. I have, in sum, inherited a superb horse. But in this country horses are of no value. I've committed a sin, lack of gratitude, in not returning Antonio's sombrero. No, I've done a thousand times better, for the sombrero, lying over my face, will preserve me from the fall of any scorpion.* It's unfortunate not to have more elevated thoughts in the evening.

And I went to sleep.

It was only the next day, when I woke up, that I had a sentiment of solitude. So much fatigue is a precious auxiliary. It was a demi-solitude, in truth, for I saw on the threshold of the cabin, which had no door of any sort, the head of my horse, which was staring at me. And immediately, I recalled Benito's words. It was necessary to catch up with the caravan before a certain confluence of rivers, because of a black ogress.

Benito had spoken without laughing. He was a taciturn person, sparing with his words—and the few he had spoken had been to exhort me to beware of an ogress. The matter merited consideration.

I departed at a trot along the trail where recent tracks of horses and mules were very visible. That reassured me a little, for I judged my situation rather disquieting. I was alone, without weapons, and I knew well enough that in this country, people kill a man for less than his horse, its saddle and bridle. I must not go astray under any pretext, for I only had dried meat, almost inedible, and a flask that I had filled with brackish water at the well of palms.

When the sun became too intense my anxiety was aggravated. I thought of the exiguity of the flask of water, and then, as happens to me in difficult situations, I made an appeal to Providence.

There is in its manner of responding an utterly disconcerting whimsy. It has an astonishing faculty of not hearing, and sometimes hearing even what has barely been formulated. My appeal had not yet taken the confused form of a thought when I saw a moving dot on the horizon. That dot became the silhouette of a rider.

In my situation an encounter might have been a great danger. I had not prepared any speech in case I found myself in the presence of a bandit. Fundamentally, my best recommendation was the title of physician to General Houston, who ought to be universally known. But there was the commencement of my appeal to Providence. It would not respond to me by putting me in the hands of a bandit. I therefore advanced with a demi-tranquility, for one cannot have absolute confidence in an entity as vast as Providence.

I uttered a cry of joy and waved Antonio Perez's hat in the air. I had just recognized Martin Bruno.

It really was him, and I had a great amicable satisfaction on seeing on his face the mark of the sincere pleasure he felt in having found me—for a man taken away by an armed troop is never sure of returning.

The leader of the caravan and the Texians who were part of it had speculated as to the event. They had recognized Houston's men and one of them, who knew the approximate location of the old hacienda where he sometimes established his general quarters, after having calculated the distances, had indicated the well of palms as the most probable point to which I would be returned, if I were to be returned. The majority of Texians had opined that if Houston needed a doctor he would probably keep him throughout his campaign, which might last several years.

I shivered when Martin Bruno reported the opinion of the Texians, who were experienced men. In spite of that, the leader of the caravan had not opposed waiting for me at the well of palms, at least for a day. All our friends had pressed him to do so; but there was the confluence of the rivers. Everyone spoke about the confluence of the rivers as a dangerous place, which it was necessary to pass as soon as possible.

Martin Bruno, Malvina and Bernard had initially allowed themselves to be swayed by the general opinion and had followed the caravan, but in the morning, when they raised camp. Martin had taken the fastest horse and had come back in the hope of finding me at the well of palms.

I still shiver in thinking how easily I might have lost them forever. Our destiny is thus suspended by a thread!

All of that was related to me by Martin in a broken fashion, and I gave him a rapid account of my adventure. But he did not attach the importance to it that I would have expected. He was preoccupied with the confluence of the rivers.

"There's a ferry," he told me. And a little later: "It's absolutely necessary to get there before nightfall."

"Doesn't the confluence have some connection with an ogress?"

"Indeed. There was mention of an ogress."

"A black ogress?"

"Yes."

"But what is this ogress?"

"I don't know. I thought at first that it was a joke. We had other things to think about. Then I understood that it was a matter of a real danger. At the moment when I left a Texian came to me and said: 'You've heard mention of the ogress? Well believe me, pay but don't accept to wrestle, even if you're very strong.' And another added: 'And what's equally dangerous is the husband's rifle shot.'"

Then I remembered one of the stories told to me by the poor guide Tiburce, who estimated that nothing ever happened in that redoubtable country to a prudent man—except death, perhaps. Tiburce had mentioned an enormous, fabulous black woman who had never been defeated at wrestling by anyone. She had a ferry in a place lost in the deserts of Texas, and she challenged men to single combat, half-serious and half-laughing, demanding a ransom from the vanquished that was always considerable. Caravans, of course, had nothing to fear from her, but preferred nevertheless not to camp near her house, so much had her evil reputation grown.

Martin Bruno and I only stopped long enough to let the horses rest and to eat the dried meat. On turning round I saw behind me a great accumulation of clouds that augmented rapidly. It was a storm in preparation, and those preparations did not last very long in that region.

Night was about to fall and the storm was racing when we finally saw before us and to our right two long lines of vegetation that indicated the presence of rivers. They gave the impression of coming toward us from the depths of the horizon, having arranged a rendezvous with the storm and with us at a given point. That point was the one at which the trail reached the river Pinasco.

The trail plunged into the sand and ended at a little beach. The river was flowing tumultuously and menacingly. On the other side, a long and low stone house was visible, the aspect of which was sinister, without it being obvious why. Further away there were a few half-demolished cabins of palm leaves and an enclosure for horses.

I experienced a disappointment, for I had hoped to see the caravan camped on the other side of the river.

We shouted in order to signal our presence, but the sound of the water drowned out our voices.

"It's necessary to hurry," I said. "Night will fall in five minutes."

Martin Bruno drew his revolver and fired a shot. He waited, and fired a second.

"Fire another," I said,

He preferred to be patient.

Suddenly we saw the door of the house open and distinguished the silhouette of a very small man.

"What do you want?"

"To cross the river," shouted Martin, in a resounding voice.

"Are you Yankees?"

"No, Frenchmen."

"What?"

"Frenchmen."

We heard him shout to someone inside the house: "They're Yankee dogs."

Then he replied to a question: "There are two of them."

There was a laugh. Night had fallen.

"They don't know what Frenchmen are," said Martin. "You talk—your Spanish is better than mine."

On the other side of the river we saw a human form of unusual dimensions advancing. A voice broken by alcohol shouted: "Look behind you."

"We can't see anything," I shouted.

"Behind you there's a storm. You've brought the storm."

"So?"

"So it's ten dollars each."

That was exorbitant. The most elevated price never exceeded a dollar.

"Let's get over first. We'll argue later," Martin said to me in a low voice.

I shouted: "It's theft, but we'll pay. Come."

Darkness had fallen. A wind damp with rain was blowing. In spite of the noise of the waters we heard a metallic grinding. The boat stopped a few feet from the bank.

"Throw the dollars in a handkerchief," said a voice that emerged from the form at the rear.

"Do you have them?" Martin asked me.

I threw them, and my companion was already holding the horses, ready to wade into the water. But the boat touched the bank and we hastened to take our places in it. There was still enough light for us to be able to make out the woman who was guiding it. She hastened to stuff the dollars into a cotton belt that supported a man's leather trousers, like those of the cowboys. She was a woman who justified by her enormous size the reputation she had acquired. Like the majority of negroes she did laugh, showing her teeth, but we saw when she spoke that the majority of her teeth were missing. Only one very long, emerged on the right side of her mouth, like a fang. Her face was cut by several scars and a section of her hair was missing, as if she had been partially scalped by someone inexperienced. The fashion in which she handled the gaffe gave us an idea of her strength.

"Oh, the Yankees! The weather is bad," she said, in a fashion that she strove to make engaging.

"Ten dollars each," Martin Bruno said to me in French, "is a scandalous theft. But on seeing the thickness of her arms and the enormity of her body, I wonder if it's not wiser to renounce our money."

Was it avarice? I suffered from the loss of that sum.

"There are two of us," I said, "and it seems to me to be reasonable to oblige her to return half that sum. Even so, we'll have paid ten dollars for our passage."

"And then, it's a woman..."

We approached the other bank.

"I believe it would be better to put on mourning for the ten dollars and go in search of shelter in one of those huts we perceived over there."

I did not reply, but deep down I thought Martin Bruno very timorous. I had known for a long time that he never made use of his strength. But in the presence of such a manifest theft, it seemed to me that abstention resembled cowardice."

"Oh, the Yankees!" cried the woman, when we had disembarked.

"You speak Spanish better than me," said Martin. "Ask her which hut we can go to."

She was tying up her boat, and we had taken a few steps over he and. She caught up with us with an incredible velocity. She stood in front of us, but Martin kept going, intending to indicate that the affair only concerned me for linguistic reasons, and that it was up to me to find a solution.

"She's only a woman," he murmured, to diminish the importance of the debate.

"Since you're Yankees, you ought to know the habits of your own country."

Anger took hold of me.

"I do know them, in fact. One never pays more than a dollar to cross a river."

The black woman burst out laughing, which pushed her tooth forward. I felt a formidable hand seize me by the neck and shake me from right to left.

"You're too thin and you can't stand up straight. But the other Yankee is strong," she said, releasing me, after looking me up and down scornfully.

Martin Bruno had retraced his steps.

"What's the matter?" he said, without enthusiasm.

"One can't come to blows, all the same," I said. "Let's renounce our ten dollars."

"I was speaking in French, but the woman understood that I had mentioned ten dollars.

"It's not a matter of ten dollars but fifty. You can earn them. But it's necessary to wrestle with me. The winner will get fifty dollars."

"Go on, Mother," said Martin, increasingly conciliatory. "We aren't people looking for stories. Keep our ten dollars.

We want to catch up tonight with the caravan that passed through during the day."

A flood of frightful insults responded to those words. Had there been some argument with Ambrosio, the leader of our caravan? I heard his name coupled with all kinds of filthy animals. The black woman had planted herself in front of Martin and she was howling in his face.

I had known for a long time that Martin Bruno, a man of great strength, was reluctant to make use of that strength, but I did not imagine that it was to the point of appearing pusillanimous. He stammered, recoiled, released the bridle of his horse and came back toward me. He seemed to be prey to fear.

I thought about the enormity of the woman, of her reputation, of the dead men she had behind her, and I thought that perhaps Martin judged himself incapable of wrestling with that phenomenon of nature.

"You, who speak Spanish well," he said to me in a voice that I did not recognize, "explain to her that if she wants another five dollars…"

I was tempted to reply that I would accept the challenge myself and engage in combat immediately. I was distressed by the grotesque character of the situation.

"You're not even a Yankee, you're a Texian. As cowardly as them."

She uttered a laugh that lifted up her belly and she waved her arms. "Anyway, I know you. I know your sister, who hooks the miners at…"

The idea that Martin's sister, a gentle young woman of fifteen who lived not far from Saint-Gaudens was known to that monstrous woman was merely comical.

"What?" said Martin.

He received a blow full in the face. The woman had doubtless given it to him by way of a warning, for she had not put all her strength into it and had delivered it with the palm of her hand.

I remembered Anastasio Alaman's advice: Always strike the first blow.

333

Nevertheless, Martin tottered under the shock.

"I beg you, tell her that I won't fight with a woman," he cried.

I rolled on the ground. At the moment when I drew nearer to attempt that explanation, she had struck me with a negligent blow of her left hand. When I got up again, they were at grips.

I saw immediately that Martin, who was holding his strength in check, as experiencing an extreme astonishment, that of someone who, thinking to strike a human being, is hitting an elephant. He recoiled, his nose bleeding. His hat had fallen off and he had rid himself of his equipment with an abrupt gesture.

Lightning was striping the sky. The scene was ridiculous and horrible. A silhouette was outlined in the doorway of the house, vaguely illuminated.

I recalled having heard various exploits narrated in Comminges relative to Martin's physical strength. At eighteen, in the Pyrenees, he had excited the admiration of all the woodcutters of Saint-Béat by lifting enormous tree trunks and hurling them down the steep slopes Yes, but would that permit him to triumph over a monster, a singularity of creation?

The black woman had obliged Martin to turn in such a way that he had his back to the house. She raised herself up, singularly supple and light in spite of her mass, like one of those elephants that one thinks riveted to the ground by their weight, but which suddenly set off, exactly as if they were provided with wings. She caused Martin to recoil, and I saw that he was ashamed of recoiling. With every blow she delivered she uttered a sort of hoarse grunt, doubtless to frighten her adversary. The silhouette in the doorway of the house was accompanied by the silhouette of a rifle.

"Look out!" I shouted.

But the combatants had seized one another around the body and were rolling on the ground. With anguish, I heard the hammering of blows. And suddenly the hoarse grunt changed into a long, piercing screech that gave the impression of being produced by a false trumpet. I saw that Martin had his knee on the chest of the woman, whose shoulders he was maintaining on the ground with his right hand. At the same time, shot rang out.

I thought my companion had been hit and I launched myself toward him. I was witness to an extraordinary exploit. Seizing the woman by the neck he had lifted her up and he was pushing her in front of him toward the house, where the barrel of a rifle was agitating. He supposed that the man who had fired had a two-shot gun. The cry of the trumpet was still resounding, but broken, expressing defeat, fear and death.

There was no second shot. The woman was thrown forward. She almost fell, got up, hesitated and then, with a cry that resembled the trumpeting of an elephant, ran into the darkness. The form of the short man who had appeared on the threshold hesitated, uttered a cry of the same nature, but much more feeble, and ran after her.

"What an adventure!" said Martin, simply, wiping his face. "The horses! Look out for the horses!"

Fortunately, they were not far away. At that exact moment, a great squall of rain fell on us.

Martin picked up the bags that we had thrown down in order to wrestle and we ran to the covered hangar that was adjacent to the house. We attached the horses there. The hangar communicated with the house by means of a door.

"They might come back," I said. "It would be wise to lock the doors."

"I'd be very astonished if the woman came back," Martin replied, with a hint of modesty.

There were large bolts everywhere. We pulled them. A single smoky lantern illuminated the room, which was extraordinarily untidy and dirty.

"The best thing is to sleep here, with our backs to the door."

Our emotions were not finished. We heard a voice calling, without being able to distinguish where it came from. It was a desperate cry coming from everywhere at once, but which was low and muffled, giving the impression of coming from the earth. I saw Martin's eyes allow more of the white to show than usual.

"If one were superstitious, one might think that the souls of men murdered here…"

I had an idea. I moved a heavy wooden table and I perceived a trap-door closed by a sliding plank.

"There's someone imprisoned there," I said to Martin.

I slid the plank away and immediately, a black-clad individual surged forth with the agility of a monkey, entirely gray under the dust that covered him.

"You took your time hearing me," he said, looking at us with glittering eyes. "Are the doors locked? Do you have anything to eat?"

We gave him dried meat, which he stated to eat avidly.

"They were going to let me die of hunger," he said, looking at us with severity. "Watch the doors while I eat."

For a moment, nothing was heard but the sound of his jaws. He had long flat hair and must ordinarily have been clean-shaven, but a graying beard of several days covered his cheeks.

He was almost sated when he interrupted himself abruptly and fell to his knees, his hands clasped. He seemed to be praying.

"I'm thanking God," he told us. "I'm a pastor. You ought to be praying at the same time as me."

He approached a shelf where there were numerous bottles and took one of whisky. He poured himself a large glass.

"And to think that there are no police before Santa Fe."

Turning toward us he gave us various orders, notably that of searching for a bag of which he had been dispossessed. If he was not dead, he explained, it was because just at the moment when the woman had seized him her husband had shouted that a caravan was arriving. He had been brutally thrown into a kind of cellar where he suspected that there must be corpses because of the nauseating odor that reigned there. He spoke to us as one speaks to servants.

"You're Texians, aren't you?"

"No, Frenchmen," I hastened to reply.

He shrugged his shoulders. As he wanted to go to sleep, he assigned us places and ordered Martin to hand him his revolver, which as the only firearm we possessed.

Marin contented himself with turning his back on him. Then we heard him murmur that perhaps he had fallen between Scylla and Charybdis.

There was no further incident. Martin woke us up before daybreak. It was necessary to depart in obscurity, he thought, because of a rifle shot that might be fired from somewhere.

The pastor gave us an order imperiously to search the cellar to make sure that there were no cadavers there. We refused.

"I'm obliged to make a complete report to the police in Santa Fe."

"I'll lift the trap-door and you go down," I said. But he shot me a terrible glance, as if I had the intention of sequestering him again.

All the same, he mounted the rump of the horse behind me, without ceasing to give me indications as to what I ought to do.

We caught up with the caravan in the morning. Its leader, Ambrosio, only showed a mediocre astonishment at what we told him. Attempted murders were daily events in the region, which were only of mediocre interest. When I told him about the wrestling match between the black woman and my friend I saw that he was smiling, and understood that he did not believe me.

"Just think," said Ambrosio. "Dick the Canadian himself, the strongest man of the prairies, found death in wrestling."

A little later I overheard a few fragments of the story that the pastor was telling. There was mention of "two pusillanimous Texian peasants who had not even dared to descend into the cellar where he had been imprisoned."

IV. The Adventures of Noël Alga

Noël Alga had quit his traveling companions in New Orleans. He had only taken his guitar and a few indispensable objects. He never gave any details of the life he led with Carlotta Alaman or the duration of the time he spent with her.

"No, I don't know General Houston," he replied when questioned, "Although I was in New Orleans at the same time as him. He made me a proposition to become one of his lieutenants, but I refused. He pulled a face when someone told him that I played the guitar and he added: 'It's necessary to choose between war and music.' It was Carlotta who reported that. The next day she asked me: 'Have you chosen?' I said: 'Yes, I've chosen.' She replied: 'Me too.' Generals have a great deal of prestige among women. But the world is full of women."

Finding himself alone, he perceived that he had no more money and that it was necessary to think of a means of existence. The sight of bearded individuals clad in animal hides who were called trappers or woodsmen, and the marvelous stories they told of their life gave him a romantic desire to plunge into the bosom of nature and to live there on the produce of hunting. He had read Chateaubriand, and also Fenimore Cooper. He knew from them that there were pure and good redskins who smoked the peace pipe in the evenings and worshiped the Great Spirit. Some men of the white race had lived among them, had shared their free life and had married women with ocher skin of an ideal beauty. At least, they said so.

Noël Alga had that chivalric worship of women that one habitually has at the beginning of life. He was shocked, evidently, to learn that wretched squaws were condemned to carry burdens, to do heavy work and played the role of vulgar livestock. One custom above all was contrary to his ideas. A woman who considered herself poorly married and had been

338

tempted to flee was condemned to the following torture: her husband, with the skill in the custom of scalping given to his ancestrally, removed the skin from the sole of her right foot with his knife. That was to prevent her from running away but not from the carrying out the duties of the hearth. A romantic idea of womanhood allied to a poetic conception of life was not compatible with such a procedure. But was there not some exaggeration on the part of those who reported such things? Noël Alga preferred to believe in the innate nobility of men who lived in the bosom of nature.

An incident contributed further to his desire for the savage life. He was then in a small hotel in a suburb of New Orleans not far from Lake Pontchartrain. He was dining alone at a table illuminated by a smoky lamp. A negro tapped him on the shoulder and made him understand that someone was asking for him at the door of the hotel. He went out. The threshold was brightly lit by a large lantern above the door. He saw a man of tall stature who appeared to be very strong advancing toward him. The man smiled benevolently and extended a hand that Noël Alga was about to take. He expressed himself in English, a language of which Noël Alga understood the common words.

"I wanted to ask you..." He interrupted himself, as if prey to a joyful surprise. "But if I'm not mistaken, that's my father's hat."

Noël Alga was wearing a bright felt hat that he had bought shortly before leaving France. The man leapt forward and snatched the hat from Noël's head. At the same time he shouted: "I've found the hat that was stolen from my father!"

Two acolytes had emerged from the shadows. "Seize him!" cried the man.

Noël Alga struggled, and felt hands rummaging in his pockets.

"Look at the mark of the hat. It comes from France; I'm French," he proclaimed, ingenuously thinking that it as an error.

"Wretch," the man said to him. "Give me five dollars and I won't lodge a complaint about the theft made from my father."

"There's nothing," said one of those who had seized him.

"Too bad, then. All the same, my father will be content."

The noise made people appear on the threshold of the hotel, and as Noël Alga called for help, the three men disappeared into the night, taking the hat.

"It's a well-known trick," the proprietor of the hotel told him, when he had recovered from the shock. "And it always succeeds, see."

But when Noël talked about lodging a complaint regarding the theft, all the witnesses were unanimous in advising him against such folly.

"You've only lost a hat. If you make a complaint and have to settle things with Big Dick, for it must be him, you'll be convicted of theft. He'll being the necessary five witnesses. And when you get out of prison you won't fail to receive a knife between your shoulder-blades. His methods are well known. He doesn't like being implicated."

Noël Alga had linked himself with a few young men who had, like him, a liking for savage nature and considered it to be possible to smoke the peace pipe one day with grave Indians with painted faces. They embarked on a steamboat that belonged to a fur company and went up the Mississippi. They were bound for Brazos Santiago in Texas. They were going somewhat haphazardly. They had heard that one could earn a lot of money by setting traps for beavers or foxes, or furry animals in general. Men full of experience had assured them of it. They even took traps with them. But their success as hunters was of secondary importance in their preoccupations. What they desired was to find themselves in the midst of savage and limitless expanses.[22]

----

[22] The geography of this fictitious America is obviously different from that of our world, where Brazos Santiago is an island off the Gulf Coast of Texas.

They were five in number but a blue-eyed Canadian quit them *en route*. They had received hospitality at a farm where recently-arrived Americans were struggling against the forest with difficulty. Those Americans had a daughter. In the wilderness, marrying daughters was not easy. The father, a simple man, came to find the Canadian as the travelers were about to leave and offered him his daughter along with a share in the concession of the woods. The Canadian accepted. He put his bag and rifle down on the ground and wished his companions good luck.

A man they called the Old Swiss was the expedition's leader. His old age was only relative to the youth of the others. He was a man of about forty-five, tall and then, with a broken nose and small eyes, His back was slightly stooped, and he had an equable humor, except in the evening. Then he took a few swigs of gin that that the carried in a gourd and set about talking untiringly about what he called "the happy times." Those times had gone by in his youth, above Lake Geneva. He had such a capacity to resuscitate the past that he sometimes wept, with his head in his hands. saying: "There you are, Charlotte! It's you, Godefroy!"—individuals from the times of his youth, whom he thought he saw appearing before him.

Lieutenant Finn had made war in Mexico in the American army, and gloried in it. "Everywhere I go," he said, "I'm popular. When the corps of volunteers that I joined was formed, officers were elected and I was proclaimed a lieutenant by unanimous acclamation." He had the coquetry of being the youngest and claimed that Noël Alga, who was indisputably younger than him, has been rejuvenated. Even in wild places he thought about elegance and always strove to make witty remarks.

The final companion of the troop only spoke one language, Spanish, which the others did not know very well. That isolated him, but he did not complain about it. Juan the Taciturn, as they named him, had no amicable exchange and did not desire any. In the evening, when they had camped under a large tree, built a fire and had a meal, he rolled himself up in his blanket without saying goodnight. But he did not sleep. He three companions saw the gleam of his gaze in his half-closed eyes. He seemed incessantly to be mulling over somber thoughts. His complexion was jaundiced and the part of his eyes that ought to have been white was the same color.

That was the time when Noël Alga played the guitar. His instrument was the most precious thing that he had brought. Lieutenant Finn and the Old Swiss never tired of listening to him. It was not the same for Juan.

"I have a horror of music," he had said several times, with a somber expression, and he always pretended to be asleep when Noël played.

"The mountains of America do not have the same appeal for me as the Pyrenees," Noël told his companions, and he explained to them that back there, on mountains covered with trees, voices came to him that incited him to take a particular path or climb a particular ridge. He no longer felt the same affinities with the animals of the Texian valleys as those that bound him to the beasts of his homeland. He was also astonished not to find the great herds that had been described to him: bison wandering freely, wild horses following the legendary white horse glimpsed and pursued by all trappers, but which no one ever attained.

"Patience," said the Old Swiss. "A moment will come when the mountains will call to you and the white horse will follow you meekly." Whereas Finn mocked Noël's discourse, he had enough experience to know that everyone has his mania and that it is necessary not to contradict it.

The finally reached the savage regions so dearly desired.

The last colonist they encountered lived with his two sons in a small for enclosed by palisades. He only opened up to them after long negotiations.

"Go back—the region is of full of thieving Indians. You'll be killed within three days."

"How many attacks have you suffered since you've been here?" the Old Swiss asked.

The colonist had settled there three years before and had never been attacked, but he claimed to owe that to his great celebrity as a redoubtable man. He was known throughout Texas, he said. He never missed his man. In spite of that, he lived in continual anxiety.

The Old Swiss did not believe in the Indian attacks.

"It's sufficient to carry a carbine very evidently," he said. "The Indians have even more appetite for life than we do, and they know that men on foot have no other property than a few animal hides."

After marching for days in a westward direction through plains covered with mescals and aloes, they reached a region of lakes and tall trees. Snakes were abundant there and the Old Swiss, who viewed all things with optimism, only made an exception for snakes, of which he was particularly fearful. Noël Alga wanted to succeed in taming them, and had made several vain attempts, either by modulating certain whistles of which he claimed to know the secret or by drawing sounds from is guitar. Most of all, he excited the laughter of his companions, but a time came when his desires were more than fulfilled.

He had quit the camp alone in the morning on the pretext of going hunting. He followed the course of a stream that would prevent him from getting lost. On the way, he noticed how much the stream resembled the streams of his homeland. It was bordered by the same reeds, from which he had once carved flutes, and it received the shade of large trees that bore an astonishing resemblance to the poplars of Comminges.

The stream plunged abruptly between rocks that he had some difficulty scaling and coming down again, and it penetrated into a narrow valley that broadened out and gave the impression of being separated from the rest of the world by steep slopes carpeted with mesquites. Nature had an unexpected richness there, a virginity that made him think of a corner of the commencement of the world, where a creator filled with poetic good intentions had wanted to realize the maximum of his possibilities.

The stream flowed placidly at the level of green meadows strewn with all sorts of flowers, but those flowers had a variety and a richness that Noël Alga had never seen. On the water there were blue nympheas and nelumbos that gave the impression of having fallen from the wings of the flamingos that were drawing away above the trees. Blooming agaves were girdled by wild roses and orchids of a thousand colors. White daturas spread droplets to which the sunlight gave hues of dazzling pink. Sometimes, three or four centenarian oaks seemed to be placed expressly to provide shade and repose. Multicolored parrots called to one another in a little wood of magnolias. Noël glimpsed a couple of peacocks that were fraying a path through flowery bushes and among bamboos that had the color and form of minarets. Enormous insects with emerald wings striped the waters, playing with flies, like little blue lamps.

A swarm of enormous butterflies with white stripes on black wings suddenly enveloped Noël. They were so numerous that when he raised his hands he touched the silky fabric of their wings and retained a golden and greasy dust like pollen. The breeze was warm. There was a music of insects that filled the air. Noël savored the voluptuousness of a joy that is unexpected but whose beauty one had imagined confusedly in ancient dreams.

The air, the water, the meadows and the trees formed a harmony so complete that he felt the need to lie down, simply in order to be nearer to the earth, to be in a more intimate contact with nature. He let himself fall at the foot of an old trunk for formed a circle with other trees adjacent to a large rock.

Suddenly, a pestilential breath reached him, a charnel-house odor so nauseating that he leapt to his feet. Had the wind changed? Where could that odor be coming from? For a second, he saw himself as a child in Saint-Bertrand, in front of the shop of a man known as a knacker, who was reputed to buy dead animals, from which he then removed the skin.

He looked around. He was, indeed, in a charnel-house. The poetic shelter formed by the rock and he trees was filed with bones and pieces of skin, on which bloody hairs still remained. It was the lair of a beast of prey of large dimensions, to judge by the size of the broken bones scattered on the ground.

The course of Noël Alga's thoughts changed abruptly to pass from impulsive lyricism to the fear of feeing the jaws of a wild beast clamp upon his shoulders or his neck. He remembered everything that he had been told about the mores of wild animals. The enormous head of a bison was staring at him with the dead holes of its empty eye-sockets. Wild birds and small carnivores had cleaned it entirely. It still had its horns. Something new and shiny in the polish of the cranium attested that it had been transported to this retreat quite recently. But to transport a bison requires an animal of powerful strength. Only a grizzly bear or a tiger was capable of that exploit. Noël knew that grizzly bears, lovers of mountains, were rare in that hot region. It was, therefore, a tiger: a tiger with red eyes that can see in the dark, only hunts by night and returns to its lair at sunrise. The sun had risen some hours before, the lair was there, and Noël Alga was there, respiring an odor of putrefied flesh that was making him feel faint.

He had to struggle against his surprise. There was, therefore, no conscience in nature. She prepared with care a place of election, a place into which she put all the beauties of her butterflies and her flowers, and she permitted a beast of prey to wallow there and to display the debris of decomposing flesh there.

But he did not linger over those general reflections. The tiger was merely late. It had modified its habits in consequence of events relative to the life of tigers. It might surge forth at any moment. Who could tell? Perhaps it was watching the intruder that had invaded its dwelling from the little wood of magnolias some distance away, for animals meditate for a long time before acting; only humans do not make use of reflection.

Noël thought about his weapons. He had a knife in his belt and his carbine. It was only loaded with lead pellets. He remembered the advice of the Old Swiss for such an eventuality: You let the tiger come within two or three paces and you fire the lead pellets into its eyes; that way, you're sure of blinding it, after which there is nothing more to fear.

The Old Swiss, who saw everything as easy, only presenting few dangers, had then informed him of another method. It consisted of killing with the knife. It is sufficient for you to have a well-furnished sheepskin; for want of that you take off your coat, or even your jacket, and you wrap it carefully round our left arm. You let the tiger reach you; then you put your left arm into its maw, as deeply as possible. It will try to bite you, but if your arm has gone far enough it will not be able to do so. You take your time and with our knife you traverse its heart, striking at the weak point in the shoulder with a certain inclination of the weapon.

Those methods, which had excited his admiration when they were explained to him, now appeared profoundly derisory to Noël Alga. But he did not calculate their chances of success. Impelled by a sure instinct, he launched himself forward at a run, traversed the valley, scaled the rocks that isolated it from the rest of the world and did not stop running until he was out of breath. Then he was slightly ashamed. He replaced the lead shot in his rifle with a bullet and told himself that, all the same, it would have been good to possess the skin of a tiger he had killed. He did not, however, think of going back.

The four companions' lucky star determined that, due to the play of the wind and the disposition of a river, they did not fall victim to a prairie fire, and only saw the end of it.

"Harm only comes to those who have no confidence," said the Old Swiss. "The man who doesn't believe in the danger isn't running any risk."

He had had confidence the previous evening, on seeing great plumes of smoke on the horizon, after studying the direction of the wind, and he had advised his companions to sleep peacefully.

In the morning, however, the little troop was woken up by a noise analogous to that of thunder, or an army on the march.

"The wind has freshened and turned," said the Old Swiss. "We're lucky to have slept."

They were under a large tree with low branches. Suddenly, they saw a large she-bear emerge from nearby bushes, followed by two cubs. Their first impulse was to climb the tree. The Old Swiss made a sign to them that there was no need. The bears passed by without paying any heed to them. They sensed that they were fleeing an urgent danger. The mother bear, having a great experience of life and knowing the bizarre properties of fire, did not turn side on seeing the embers of the fire, which were still consuming a few brands.

"It's a stampede," said the Old Swiss. "The best thing to do is to go in the same direction as the animals."

As they were rolling up their blankets they were enveloped by a herd of antelopes. The ground seemed to be animated. Snakes were slithering under their feet, as well as rats that were holding their feathery tails upright.

A confused bellowing resounded to their left. The atmosphere was heavy. All kinds of animals passed alongside them, tightly grouped, in a kind of fraternity that fear gives even to animals. Fallow deer and elands bounded while wolves ran head down, skimming the ground with their muzzles. Bison uttered desperate bellows. Wild horses were prey to such tremors that they sometimes stopped and let themselves fall, with whinnies in which there was something like a desperate supplication. A squirrel had fallen from a tree on to the back of a buffalo. It remained there, looking fearfully to the right and the left.

The men had started running, infected by the terror of the animals. Fortunately, the Old Swiss had experience of stampedes. Often, the animals, intoxicated by their own terror, continue to run long after the danger has passed. That was the case. The Old Swiss calculated, by the state of extreme exhaustion of the animals going past, that they must already have be running for a day, perhaps two. They were at the limit of their strength and were dying abruptly. Snakes stopped dead. A bison's knees buckled; it lowered its head to touch the ground with its horns and remained immobile, like a bison of stone. Birds that had participated in the animal madness were flying low, in a miserable flutter. Sometimes, one of them, renouncing the struggle, fell dead, as if struck in the heart by an invisible hunter.

But in the end, the Old Swiss gave his companions a signal to stop. The smoke was visibly drawing away behind them and they found a large and profound gorge in front of them. They descended into it, not without difficulty. Water was flowing in the bottom of the gorge and that made a kind of cutting, a neat separation from the desiccated expanse from which they were emerging. The nature of the terrain changed completely. After a region of aloes and horny bushes they saw before them green trees, prairies, and glistening reflections of pools of water. An extraordinary spectacle struck their eyes.

The animals had sensed that they had reached another world, where the scourge of the fire could not reach them. Thousands of creatures were lying on the ground, trying to recover their life, which was close to escaping. Some were licking their wounds or, in accordance with an ancient law of hygiene, removing the dust of the journey from their bodies. Others were moaning softly, with their heads slightly raised, as if they were invoking the god of animals. Some, while remaining extended, were attempting to browse the clover on which they were lying. Their extreme distress had given birth to a temporary fraternity. Innocent antelopes were gazing tenderly at a grim panther that was lying in the middle of their herd. The panther sometimes uttered a dull growl, but there was no threat in the tone of the growl. Its eyes were half-closed and it was evident that it was making a great effort to hold its head up.

The wolves had not been the most resistant. Perhaps they had traveled the greatest distance. Many lay dead. One of them was leaning its head on the tail of a horse that had made no attempt to draw away. Another had all its fur completely singed, and no longer represented anything but a strange bald being belonging to no known species.

Noël Alga was torn between a sentiment of joy give to him by the proximity of so many animals, which fear deprived of dread, and pity for such extreme misery.

A large deer attracted him particularly. It was on its knees and its eyes, full of benevolence, were fixed on him. There was a choice in those eyes, the comprehension that it was in the presence of someone that might come to its aid. Since the loss of his hat Noël Alga had been wearing a bonnet susceptible of covering his ears on cold nights. He ran to a large sheet of water that was nearby, where all the animals capable of standing up were drinking. Some furry animals had even dived in and were only letting the tips of their muzzles protrude, with round eyes widened by pleasure.

Noël filled his bonnet and carried it to the deer. At first the latter only dipped in a tongue like a piece of wood, very gently, but then began to drink with increasing rapidity, only pausing to gaze at Noël with grateful eyes.

But he heard a snigger beside him. It was Juan the Taciturn. His face had an expression of hatred.

"It would be better to kill the deer and roast it for supper."

Noël made a semblance of not having heard, and, cutting a handful of grass with his knife he handed it to the deer, which was already beginning to clamber to its feet and parade a circular gaze around it, doubtless to search for the members of its dispersed family.

Lieutenant Finn was moved by the antelopes. He took them in his arms and carried them to the water. He stumbled over a large python that was as motionless s a tree branch. It was to lost or abandoned bear cubs to which the Old Swiss rendered his cares.

An old emaciated jaguar made an exception to the great fraternity of fear. Perhaps it had already had a similar experience and fear was absent from its aged soul. It approached a splendid fallow deer, crawling, and had a gleam of death in the embers of its red eyes. Noël Alga chased it away without difficulty, with the butt of his rifle.

However, the day was coming to an end. The Old Swiss killed a bear cub for supper.

"I do it with regret," he said, "for there's a truce."

Because of that truce they decided not to kill the furry animals of whose pelts they were in quest. Juan was the only one to think that decision stupid.

The deer had followed Noël Alga step by step. In the evening it came to lick salt from the palm of his hand, and it lay down not far from the camp.

The Old Swiss lit a big fire because, he said, savagery might resume its rights during the night. That was, in fact, what happened. The nearby grasslands and woods filled with roars and plaintive cries. He deer got up and fled. When the sun rose, nothing any longer remained but the cadavers of dead animals.

The four men had decided to rest for a day or two in that place, where there was a lake surrounded by trees and which was protected by the depression overhanging the gully.

Noël regretted the disappearance of his deer. He was looking round in the hope of finding it again when he suppressed a cry of joy. He had just seen it appear timidly and stop some distance away, between the trees. It advanced, stopping at almost every step. Noël bent down to take salt from his bag. A detonation resounded behind him. The deer reared up on its hind feet and fell back. It had been hit in the heart. It was the Spaniard who had fired. Noël ran forward to make sure that the animal was dead, and came back pale with anger.

A violent argument ensued.

"By what right did you kill that deer? Couldn't you see that I'd tamed it and that it belonged to me?"

Juan burst out laughing. Were they not hunters? The previous evening, he had been prevented from taking advantage of the marvelous opportunity that was offered. That could not go on. He would kill whatever it pleased him to kill. Finn and the Old Swiss put him in the wrong, however. Then he abandoned himself to an irrational fury. He drew his knife. He had lost control.

"If one of you three has anything to say about what I do, let him do as I do, let him draw his knife. I'm ready for him." And as his amazed companions did not move, he dead: "Of course, you're all too cowardly!"

He was possessed by a hatred that he must have repressed, and which had finally burst forth. He relieved himself by means of coarse insults and then, throwing his rifle over his shoulder, he marched away.

Communal life had linked the three men with a solid amity. They deliberated as to what to do. They could not think of separating in those solitudes, where humans could only live by means of the mutual aid of a group. It was agreed that the Old Swiss would talk to Juan when he returned and would strive to discover whether there was a secret motive for his rancor.

"Everything will sort itself out," he said, with his habitual optimism. "Juan doesn't sleep at night. He has insomnia. In the wilderness, insomnia disturbs the mind."

Al three of them admitted to one another the anxiety to which their companion's attitude had given rise for some time. They had all glimpsed his expressions full of malevolence and were in accord in thinking that he nourished the most hostile sentiments against them.

"He has a secret," said the Old Swiss. "Perhaps there's a crime that is weighing upon him. When does go to sleep he wakes up abruptly, crying: "Inès!" and remains sitting up for a long time, his eyes haggard."

The afternoon came to an end and Lieutenant Finn was returning to the camp when there was a detonation behind him and it seemed to him that a bullet passed not far from him, breaking a branch. The shot had been fired from a considerable distance, and Finn was not absolutely sure that it was in his direction. When he reached the camp he interrogated his two friends as to whether one of them had fired the shot. They had been there for more than an hour, digging a hole in the ground and lighting a fire above it in order to cook a joint of bison in the Indian manner. They were in agreement that the author of the rifle shot could not be anyone but Juan. But had he wanted to hit Finn?

A little later, Juan came back. He did not say a word. He had not been hunting. He seemed exhausted.

The Old Swiss offered him a few mouthfuls of gin, which he had conserved preciously in the bottom of his gourd. It was his final reserve. Juan contented himself with shaking his head.

"I'll drink it, then," said the Old Swiss.

Those few swigs were sufficient to take him back to the happy times. While eating the roast bison he talked for the hundredth time about sunlit mornings when he went down toward Lake Geneva to find the beautiful Charlotte near Chillon, who was waiting for him leaning on a wooden balustrade.

Finn and Noël Alga chatted for a long time in low voices. The Old Swiss had gone to sleep and Juan was pretending to sleep. Much later, Noël saw the latter get up quietly and go to pick up a piece of wood, with which he came back and of which he made use to do something that the firelight did not permit him to distinguish. Then a shot rang out. In a second, they were all on their feet, except for Juan, who was dead. He had put the barrel of his rifle in his mouth and had used his foot to activate the piece of wood attached to the trigger.

The Old Swiss searched him, and found nothing but the portrait of a little girl, wrapped in soiled paper, on which was written: *Inès, aged four*. The three companions were never to know anything about the drama that had acted upon the man's conscience.

They buried him in the morning. The cadavers of the dead animals had attracted thousands of birds, and in addition to the charnel-house odor that was rising, the Old Swiss claimed that when birds of prey are very numerous, they become conscious of their strength and do not hesitate to attack humans.

They asked one another a thousand questions on the subject of Juan the Taciturn.

"Was he truly a bad man?" asked Noël Alga.

"Ah, how can one know?" concluded the Old Swiss. "One never knows." When one encounters a jaguar, perhaps it's a good jaguar what would go away if one let it alone. But one always assumes that it's evil and fires at it, which sometimes results in the hunter being devoured. Life would be simpler if one knew who is good and who is evil."

Confidence protects you until the day when it kills you.

They had arrived in a region where there were traces of Indians everywhere.

"There's nothing to fear," said the Old Swiss. However, he was careful only to light fires between rocks, in such a way that they could not be seen from distance. But as he had acquired the habit of going hunting alone, early in the morning, he did not consent to change it.

"Perhaps the opportunity to smoke the peace pipe will come," he said, laughing.

One morning, he left and did not come back. He never came back.

Noël Alga and Finn waited for a fortnight in the same place. They searched the surrounding area for a considerable distance. One day, torrential rain had washed away all the tracks. Had the Old Swiss fallen victim to a panther or a bear? Had he been killed by Indians? No clue revealed the truth.

In the end, Noël and Finn resumed marching westwards, but they could not detach their minds from the memory of their friend, who, they sensed in the depths of their hearts, had gone forever to find Charlotte, Godefroy Lake Geneva and the eternal times of youth.

V. The Friendship of the Pelican

In the deserts, in the cities and on the oceans, Noël Alga had a great many adventures. "I didn't seek them," he said. "They came to me naturally, like pigeons that, on seeing a dovecot, come to perch in it."

He spent an entire year with Finn setting traps. But he did not do it without remorse.

"I shall no longer be the friend of animals if I kill them to take their skins."

They returned to the banks of the Mississippi, where Finn embarked on a steamboat that went downriver. He transported more than three thousand dollars' worth of furs that he was to sell in New Orleans. It was agreed that he would deposit Noël's share in a bank. The latter preferred to depart again with a troop of adventurers who possessed a secret. Somewhere on the border of Arkansas and Texas there was a valley full of precious stones.

Noël Alga searched for that valley for a long time with his new companions. But he lost them and plunged on his own into a region situated between the tributaries of the Red River and the Sabine, which was known as the region of dead ponds. There were long extents of marshes, forests half-covered by the waters, and quicksands.

It was there that he killed a cawana, a hideous and terrible monster unknown to natural history, which is a belated representative of a vanished antediluvian fauna. The cawana is half-turtle and half-alligator. It has scales as impenetrable as steel, whose extremities are curved into fangs. It can grow to twenty feet in length and lives in the sand of deep lagoons. The one that Noël killed belonged to the largest species.[23]

---

[23] This description of the cawana is taken, in its entirety, from *The Travels and Adventures of Monsieur Violet* (1843; Fr. tr. 1846) by the English novelist Captain Marryat, which pretends

But Noël then perceived that he had no more powder or bullets. Surrounded by water, he spent days in the lower branches of an enormous tree. Rain had caused the waters to rise and he had been obliged to spend the greater part of his time contending against snakes and fishing with a net that he had improvised, and which he ate raw because he had lost his briquette.

He was saved by an officer of the United States army and two surveyors sent by the Federal Government to delimit the frontier. They were traveling in a large flat boat and had only strayed from their route because large flocks of birds converging on the same point had notified them of the existence of a cadaver. It was that of the cawana, the body of which the birds had succeeded in opening in spite of the thickness of its carapace. They found Noël on his tree and took him away with them. They told him that he had accomplished a rare exploit in killing a cawana of the large species, that animal being greatly feared in the region because it seized horses in passing and dragged them, with their rides, into the depths of the wet sands.

In the habitations where they stopped during a long voyage through the ponds Noël was called "the man who killed the cawana." He was also "the man who has tamed a pelican," for he brought back a young pelican of the species of spectacled pelicans. But the later had the peculiarity of being entirely white around the eyes. Noël had found it alone in the hollow of a tree; its parent must have fallen prey to some snake. He had nourished it on little fish, and thanks to him, the young pelican had always carried an abundant reserve of nourishment in the membranous pouch that it had, like a goiter, beneath its beak.

---

to be a factual account of travels in America by a young Frenchman in 1830. Various other details are borrowed from the same text. The tern "cawana" appears in other texts as a variant of caiman.

Noël arrived in New Orleans with his pelican, which grew and became increasingly attached to him. He baptized it with the name Vénasque, in memory of the Pyrenean pass above Luchon called by that name. A merchant of curiosities offered him a hundred dollars for it, which he refused. He was glad to find the share that reverted to him from the sale of the furs made by Finn, who had deposited it faithfully in his name as the two friends had agreed.

Vénasque had witnessed his master's refusal to sell him, Noël saw—or at least he affirmed it—the natural malignity of its gaze change to gratitude. The bird's attachment increased. It sometimes flew over Lake Pontchartrain in order to catch small fish there, filling the pocket that it carried under its beak and served as a larder. It did not remain absent for long. But from the day when Noël had refused to sell him—from that day exactly—it adopted the habit of disgorging all the fish that it had just caught on the window-sill of the room where Noël lived and was waiting for him. It had a debt of amity, and repaid it.

Noël explained the matter thus to incredulous comrades: "He obviously did not understand the value of the hundred dollars that I refused, but he perceived the impulse of affection that passed through me at the idea of losing him."

Noël was, moreover, to receive a greater mark of affection on the part of his pelican.

"Why have you come to live in this ill-famed quarter?" a French maker of musical instruments asked of Noël.

"A quarter where there are palm trees," he replied, "is always favored."

He had taken lodgings in a narrow avenue bordered by old palm trees, which must have dated back to the foundation of New Orleans and ended at Lake Pontchartrain. He had chosen the place because of the facility that his pelican had in going to fish in the lake. It could also stand in a broad stream of water that ran alongside the small houses of the avenue.

Those houses were, in fact, inhabited by an entire population of former slaves, the dregs of the city, with whom the police did not occupy themselves At the extremity of the avenue near the lake there were even a few ajoupas constructed with mud and palm leaves, in which the most wretched lived. In one of those ajoupas lived a white-haired negro known by the name of Noah the Albino. Some said that he was a saint, others that he was a madman. On some evenings he harangued he negroes of the neighborhood, exhorting them to virtue and the love of their African God. At other times he danced savage dances, drank rum and delivered knife-thrusts.

"I have the strength of God," he said, for he was extraordinarily strong.

He was immediately exasperated by the sight of Noël Alga, less because of his person than the guitar that he played outside his door.

Noël's first concern, as soon as he arrived in New Orleans, had been to buy a new guitar, for his own, the one that his mother had given him, had remained in the waters of the land of dead ponds. But the new instrument did not have, in his opinion, the interior genius that had inhabited the wood of the old one. He did not hear it sighing during the night. It was a guitar that did not yet have a soul. *It's necessary to give it one*, Noël Alga thought, *by playing it often and exposing it to the light of the stars, which has a direct action on guitars.*

In an adjacent street, which Noël often took in returning home, there was a house with a low balcony in sculpted wood, were a young woman was almost always sitting, whose gaze met Noël's when he passed by. She was a mulatta with hair parted at the front, who spent her time laughing in company with another mulatta with hair similarly parted at the front, but not as pretty. The second mulatta remained in a room inside and must have said things that were extremely funny, for the one of the balcony replied to them with incessant bursts of laughter. Noël Alga heard that laughter from a distance and thought that the adolescent soul of his guitar would benefit from it in its formation.

But at length, the master of the guitar perceived that he was more impressed by that hilarity than the instrument was, and one evening, moved by an irresistible impulse, as the delightful face of the mulatta was leaning forward in the midst of the large red flowers that surrounded the balcony, he pushed a little wooden gate, traversed the garden and went to the house.

He had no hidden agenda. The features of the young woman had such a purity that Noël would have considered it a sacrilege even to kiss her fingertips. He climbed a little spiral staircase and found himself in a room on the first floor of which a bed enveloped by a mosquito net occupied almost the whole extent.

The ingenuous mulatta showed no embarrassment or reserve. She expressed herself in bad Spanish and the slightly hoarse sound of her voice contrasted with the angelic purity of her face. She had made a sign to Noël to sit down in a chair with one place, and sat down beside him without playing any heed to the exiguity of the chair, seemingly to tell him that her name was Eva.

"Miama!" she exclaimed, with the imperative tone of a child, "part the mosquito net and leave us."

Noël almost asked why.

Before she disappeared, Miama's smile expressed the humblest servility.

I no longer have the habit of talking to women and understanding them, Noël thought.

With a rapid gesture, the young woman removed from her neck the several coils of a heavy necklace of carved wood. But at the same moment her gaze turned toward the garden and the expression of her face changed, expressing the most vivid terror. Noël looked in the same direction and saw Noah, the insane preacher, who was rushing toward the house, while a scream uttered by Miama resounded.

"Run away," said Eva. "He'll kill you."

The purity of his intentions blinded Noël and took away the sentiment of danger. But an immediate danger of death was revealed to him by the flame of dementia that shone in the negro's gaze when he loomed up before him.

Noël tried to speak. He received a blow in the chest that caused him to fall on to the balcony. He got up and heard a hoarse, savage cry uttered by his adversary, in which there was the intoxication of murder. At the same time, he had drawn a long knife from his belt.

Eva had fallen on to the bed in a sitting position, as if overwhelmed by a fatality about which she could do nothing. She seemed resigned with an inconceivable facility to a form of misfortune that was familiar to her.

A second went by during which the negro savored the certainty of killing. Noël took advantage of it to seize a stool and hold it in front of him like a shield. But his adversary, celebrated for his strength, seized the stool with his free hand and snatched it away.

At that moment, there was a shadow obscuring the balcony and a great flutter of wings, and a howl from the negro, who dropped his knife and covered his face with his hands.

"Help! I can't see any more!" he cried. The pelican's beak had only plucked out one eye, but the bird was thinking about the other, and with a great knowledge of the weak points of a body, it was striking the face.

Noël had retreated along the balcony. He had the presence of mind to whistle Vénasque with the tone that he employed when he demanded an immediate obedience, and climbing over the balustrade, he leapt down into the garden.

How had the bird known the danger that its master was running? Perhaps, perched in a palm tree, it had seen him enter the house from a distance. Or did it have a prescience of certain events, as certain species of birds have the prescience of catastrophes, and emigrate before they occur?

Noël perceived outside his door that, in order to fight better, the pelican had rendered all its reserves of little fish.

Ordinarily, the individual who renders a benefit is linked by that benefit as much as the one who receives it. That is true for humans but is perhaps not true for birds, Noël decided to

leave New Orleans, where he had had nothing but disappoint-
ments and where he would always be followed by the unique
eye of an insensate negro. The acquaintance of Monsieur Harvard gave him the opportunity. He embarked for Merida in
Yucatan.

Sitting on the deck of the three-master that was carrying
him away, he had his guitar to his right and his pelican to his
left. The bird manifested no anxiety or regret. When Noël
looked to see how it was supporting the descent of the Mississippi, he saw its eye, filled with malice, settle upon him as if
to say: *Don't worry; I'm here*. Then it lost itself again in the
endless reverie of animal creatures untroubled either by
thought or ennui. But there came a time when the horizon
broadened, when the shores became distant and disappeared,
and when the sea breeze blew. Abruptly, without the slightest
visible sign allowing the decision to be anticipated, the pelican
opened its wings and took off. It rose very high without hesitation, and flew in a straight line toward the land it had just quit.

VI. Yellow Fever

When Noël Alga recounted the vision he had had of that city he said: "It was Cartagena!" But then he stopped, reflected for a few moments, and went on: "Was it really Cartagena? It's just that I've seen so many cities!" Then he picked up the thread of his memories again.

"It was Cartagena. I had been taken on as secretary by a Belgian, Monsieur Harvard, a very rich man who was a passionate about the zoology of the past. He was in America to search for the last specimens of a race of extinct birds, the queczalms,[24] whose tails had several meters of resplendent plumage. Those birds only live close to volcanoes and the Aztec kings attributed to them the power of giving joy to those who possessed them. They sent expeditions in each of them all the way to Central America near the volcano Tajvancelco.[25]

"Apart from his obsession, Monsieur Harvard was a charming man who was extraordinarily generous. In fact, was he generous? 'I'll give you a thousand piastres for the expenses of this voyage,' he said. At the moment of departure he gave me three hundred piastres. 'But...' He patted me on the shoulder, laughing. 'One can do a lot of things, at the present time with three hundred piastres.' And when I pointed out to him that he was mistaken and there were only two hundred

---

[24] Author's note: "A few of them exist at present in the zoological gardens in Chicago." The birds in Chicago zoo were undoubtedly quetzals, which do not bear much resemblance to the fanciful description of the species cited here, for which I have retained the author's spelling, although he is surely working from an exaggerated description of the resplendent quetzal, *Pharomachrus mocinno.*, and exercising his customary liberality with known data of natural history.

[25] Presumably Tajumulco, not far from the city of Quetzaltenango [i.e. the place of the quetzal bird].

and eighty piastres he cried: 'Two hundred and eighty piastres! But that's enormous! Give me back thirty piastres, you'll have more than you need with two hundred and fifty.'"

"You'll join me in Cartagena," Monsieur Harvard had said to Noël Alga. "The hotel is a very old dwelling, with paintings, facing the cathedral. In the disposition of the walls, according to Lord Kingsborough, we can find Jewish traces."[26]

Monsieur Harvard did not only have the specialism of queczalms. He believed, like Lord Kingsborough, that the first civilized peoples of America had been Jewish tribes that had passed over the Behring Strait. He was looking for their traces.

"The Jews passed this way," he said, when he left Noël Alga ill in the care of a French family in Porto-Bello. "It's only a short step to take to rejoin me in Cartagena."

That short step was a mariner's step, which comprised a crossing of a few hundred miles in the most agitated part of the Sea of the Antilles. As soon as he was cured, Noël took a berth on a schooner of low tonnage whose captain was a black man who only spoke Portuguese, a language unknown to Noël. All the same, he was able to reach an understanding with him regarding the price of the passage, which seemed to him to be exorbitant. There was a reason for that excessive price, which was explained to him at length, but Noël, who still had a residue of the fever, did not understand it.

At the moment when he embarked, four or five passengers who arrived with their luggage argued with the captain and went away again. Noël even remarked that they did so with a certain haste, but he had been in bed for a week, he was in a state of agreeable languor, he was installed on the deck and the earth and sky seemed strangely beautiful to him. Then

---

[26] Edward King, Viscount Kingsborough (1795-1837) was an Irish antiquary fascinated by the notion that the indigenous people of America were descended from a Lost Tribe of Israel; he found supposed evidence of that thesis in Mexico, especially among the relics of the Mayan civilization.

too, he had bought a striped poncho and experienced a puerile joy in wearing that garment.

The crossing was fortunate and devoid of incident. Two days later, in the evening, when they were in sight of Cartagena, Noël was surprised to see the black captain having whisky and rum brought on to the deck and insisting that he drink, and drinking a great deal himself. Noël having limited himself to one glass of whisky, the captain explained to him that there was nothing to pay for the drinks, which were a generous offering on his part, and refilled his glass. The captain also pointed out that the crew, composed of five men, had received a double ration of rum and that they were taking copious advantage of it. There was an uncustomary liberality in that.

The afternoon was about to reach its end and Noël saw before him a great mass of stone, surmounted by towers, domes and steeples, which loomed up and drew nearer, and remained strangely silent and inanimate. He knew that between the Fort of Galeras and that of Saint Julian the Spaniards had striven to render the channel impracticable during their war with England the previous century, but he had not been able to imagine a port so abandoned, so dismal and so deserted. Two or three brigs were aground in the mud. There was a file of thin pirogues. All of them seemed dilapidated. There was no silhouette on the forts, no customs officers, no fishermen mending nets.

He looked at the captain, whose complexion seemed to him to be gray with apprehension. To that interrogative gaze he responded, while raising his arms to the havens: "*El vomito!*"

Noël was only aware of epidemics in the form that they presented themselves in Europe, and did not think that yellow fever was susceptible of changing the exterior aspect of a city.

"*El vomito!*" said the negroes of the crew, opening their eyes enormously wide. The schooner had passed through the channel of Boca Chica and stopped on the waters of the harbor, similar to those of a pond. The shore was covered with parasitic plants, debris and wreckage. The ancient stone fortifications raised up their high fissured walls a little further away. There were blocked loopholes and the vestiges of crenellations. Plants had grown between the blocks of stone, and even a tree with twisted branches. Two crows flew away from it. But there was no trace of any living being.

Noël was obliged to borrow the schooner's dinghy in order to disembark. He left his valise aboard. "I'll send someone to fetch it this evening," he said. The captain responded by raising his arms to the heavens and explaining confused things in which the name of God recurred. He was due to depart the next day and he exhorted him to leave with him. And he made the gesture of washing his hands.

As he set foot on the sinister quay Noël heard a chant in the distance that resembled a canticle sung by many voices. At the same time a bell rang, and Noël perceived something like a dance tune played on a guitar. The city was not absolutely deprived of human life, but an atmosphere of evil sorcery and lugubrious enchantment hung over it.

Noël saw a staircase of worn steps. He climbed it and found himself on broad ramparts covered in walkways on which empty platforms could be seen and the emplacements of vanished cannons, where weeds were growing. He went down another staircase, the guard-rail of which had fallen off, and which led to a street.

Finally, a street! It was deserted. What was the cause of that silence and solitude? Perhaps a ceremony of an exceptional order had caused the entire population to flow to a particular point. The essential thing was to know in what direction to head. The street was straight, with large protruding balconies, in the Spanish fashion, and perforated windows that sometimes dominated the silhouettes of miradors. On a stone bench Noël perceived a man sitting in the attitude of someone holding his midriff in order to master a burst of laughter. He waited a few seconds for him to straighten up in order to question him. As the man did not budge, Noël called out: "Hey, Señor!"

He touched him on the shoulder. It was as if he had touched a mannequin deprived of a center of gravity. The man fell at his feet. He was dead. His black face had retained the open mouth of his last plaint. Several large flies flew away. Noël leapt backwards.

He started to run. He did not understand very well. Why had that dead man been left on a bench? He saw that the portal of an ancient dwelling of fine appearance had been left ajar. Someone there would be able to inform him. He rapped with a bronze knocker representing the head of a Spanish king, gazing with the solemnity of absence that the empty eyes of sculptures confer. No one replied.

He pushed the door gently and took two or three steps. He was in an interior courtyard surrounded by marble colonnades. There was a fountain in the center where a minuscule jet of water was dancing, like a soul on the point of extinction. And around the fountain, struck by a terrible immobility, on seats disposed in a circular fashion, sat several individuals, all of one family, some sitting up straight—too straight—others frightfully contorted: an entire family of corpses.

Noël could not make out whether they were of the black race, or whether the malady had given them that somber tint. An old lady, her head completely enveloped by a veil of white lace, seemed to be smiling softly at the death that had struck her in the midst of her family. A man with large side-whiskers and a long soiled black frock-coat had clung on to a column on dying, but he turned toward Noël Alga a face that appeared disproportionately broad, with enormous teeth.

Noël remember having heard stories in which such people had been abruptly struck together and had died all the more rapidly because their reciprocal terror had acted as a stimulant. He recoiled before that familial assembly of dead mulattos. And as he was about to cross the threshold a horrible mortuary odor swept over him like a breath. He darted a glance to the right and glimpsed the zaguan, the reception room of old families, dimly illuminated by the light filtering through the closed blinds.

The antique Spanish furniture was in disorder. A great red velvet curtain had been torn down, doubtless by someone struggling in the spasms of dolor. And Noël perceived, half-hidden by the curtain, a young woman sitting on the mosaics. Her face was decomposed. Her neck, once pure, was deformed by swollen glands. Her mantilla was hanging over one shoulder and she was biting one of her undone tresses.

Outside, the heavy air of the approaching dusk seemed redoubtable to Noël. He launched himself in the direction from which the singing was coming, accompanied by an incomprehensible music. He nearly bumped into a man who was emerging from a side-street: a living man. In his disturbance, he questioned him in French, and was pleasantly surprised to receive a response in the same language.

"Yellow fever! Do as I am doing and leave as soon as possible for the mountains. They've paraded the saints of the cathedral in order to drive away he malady, and it appears that the bishop has advised combating the disease with the joy of living. It's the best solution. General San Miguel's widow has had his entire cellar of Spanish wine distributed to the poor. But they won't have time to drink it. It's better in France than here."

And the man departed at a run.

Noël emerged into an immense square dominated by a basilica. The bell was still ringing at full tilt and a procession, emerging from a street to the left, headed toward the church. It was a strange procession, and Noël remained motionless. He heard someone call to him from a low balcony protruding from a house of beautiful appearance beside him. Lifting up a sheet of crimson silk that was veiling the balcony, a fat woman in a lace dress covered with frills had raised herself up in the armchair in which she was sprawled. A part of her face was hidden behind her fan with determined coquetry, Noël saw a large black kiss-curl, exaggerated greasepaint ineffectively covering profound wrinkles, a lasciviously engaging smile, a gaze heavy with desire beneath eyelids charged with make-up. Was that the joy of living counseled by the bishop?

The procession traversed the square diagonally. A few Indians were carrying candles. Terror caused them to tremble and they were darting hectic glances to the right and left. A little old man clad in black mounted on a donkey, was telling rosary beads, and two equally old ladies, veiled by mantillas and enveloped in shawls, were holding the reins of the donkey and muttering prayers. All alone, naked but for a loincloth, an Indian of ascetic thinness was playing a barrel organ, his face contorted by a musical ecstasy.

Four children sustained a painted awning of which one section was coming away, and the bishop marching beneath it was wearing a miter of extravagant dimensions, with his arms crossed over his chest. Sometimes he stopped, turned round and put his knee on the ground before the statues that were being carried behind him.

Each of those statues, life-sized with wooden pedestals, was being carried by two men. There was Saint Joseph, Saint Anthony of Padua, Saint John and Saint Peter. Their naïve author had painted them in bright colors and had sculpted their heads as large as their torsos. Doubtless to express sanctity, the eyes had the same disproportion as the heads and the mouths were stretched in a hilarious expression. The key that Saint Peter held was as large as him, and a dove was sitting on Saint John's shoulder. They preceded a crucified Christ, four Roman soldiers and a hideous being representing Judas, the extremity of whose tresses formed the heads of serpents and whose breastplate imitated the scales of a crocodile skin. Behind them marched four individuals who were recognizable by their gravity as notable men of the city.

The procession was about to reach the cathedral. Suddenly, it stopped. The ringing bell stopped dead and a muffled and distant sound came from the belfry, as if a body were falling down a staircase. Everyone much have thought that the bell-ringer, afflicted in a devastating fashion by the disease, had let himself fall down the stairway of the tower.

"Jesus Maria!" cried the shrill voice of a woman.

The procession seemed to be shaken by a spasm. The bearer of the crucified Christ made a false step, tottered, and let his burden fall. It collapsed on to the paving stones of the square with a sound of splintering wood. Fear passed through the audience, whose members rushed in disorder toward the threshold of the church. There were cries of despair. The candles went out. The statues rolled and swayed on the steps giving access to the portal. The bishop was carried away in their midst toward the darkness of the protective cathedral.

Night fell like a wave, which the setting sun tinted red. The square was empty in a matter of seconds.

The fat woman with the kiss-curl said: "Psst!" and leaned over the balcony, trying to reach Noël Alga's shoulder with her hand.

But he fled. Fear emerged from all the houses. He looked behind him several times with the vague sentiment that he was being pursued by the old woman with the kiss-curl and the saints with hilarious faces.

He emerged into an intersection where three musicians were playing under a lantern. Young men in Sunday dress, whose sleeves had ruffles, and señoritas in short blue or violet skirts, with silk rebozos covering their foreheads and shoulders, formed an admiring circle around a couple of dancers. They were dancing the balbuco, an old Indian dance. The man was a monk with the thin face of an ascetic and a black beard. His tonsure, larger than ordinary tonsures, covered almost all of his cranium. He was moving his jaw as if he were chewing and he had the fixed stare of someone who knowing that he is being watched. He had lifted up his robe as far as his belt, and his fleshless legs were visible, like bones. He was striking his heel rhythmically around a young woman with lowered eyelids, who moved her body slowly, possessed by an interior music, until the moment when the monk took her in his arms, at which point they began to spin recklessly. Then, as if it were a signal, all the watchers imitated them, twirling and striking their heels around the musicians, who started to agitate themselves and accompany the balbuco with their feet.

Noël was seized by the vertigo of the dance. He spotted a young woman beside a little old woman, who seemed to be looking at the ground in a bizarre attitude. He was about to approach her when she looked up, uttering a frightful scream, and Noël saw that her face was decomposed by agony. She let herself fall to the ground, howling, while the little old woman threw herself upon her, invoking God. But the whirl of the dancers enveloped them and their cries were drowned out by the sound of heels striking stone.

A little later, the freshness of the stagnant water of the port, the stones of the ramparts and the shadow of the mast of the schooner, close enough to the quay to be hailed, were for Noël the rediscovered paradise, after the inferno of yellow fever.

VII. The Adventures of a Star Dancer in the Land of the Seminoles

It was through the intermediary of Monsieur Harvard and at the moment when the latter went to Europe that Noël Alga met Monsieur Poussielgue and was engaged in his expedition. Monsieur Poussielgue had been at the French legation in Washington for two years and had only come to America to study nature there in its state of virginity. He thought that here were certain secrets that might be revealed in absolutely savage lands, secrets that were only discovered via the intermediary of animals and plants.

"He knows the language of birds," Monsieur Harvard said to him, indicating Noël Alga to him.

And Monsieur Poussielgue took that formation literally, to such an extent that when an owl uttered a cry with an unusual modulation on evening, he asked Noël Alga: "What does it mean?"

And Noël replied without hesitation, translating the owl's state of mind.

Monsieur Poussielgue, as he recounted himself, had equipped a small schooner, the *Découverte*, and with three servants and three sailors he wanted to travel along the coasts of Florida and explore the maze of its rivers, its lakes and its inundated forests. It was in that voyage that Noël Alga accompanied him, having the function of copying the daily notes and classifying the plants in herbaria.

Monsieur Poussielgue intended to go up the Saint John River. The *Découverte* steered toward its mouth and went past the Hazard Lighthouse, built on an islet two leagues from the coast to indicate the entrance to the passage, and to prevent ships from getting stuck in the midst of the moving sands.

Someone came to tell him that a human form had been made out at the top of the lighthouse making signals with a white cloth and that the signals seemed to be a request for help. He had the anchor dropped, put the dinghy to sea and headed for the lighthouse, accompanied by Noël Alga.

The lighthouse was a broad tower about sixty-five feet high, whose base was almost bathed by the waves of the sea, and entirely covered with wrack and seaweed. At first glance it seemed inaccessible.

Noël and Monsieur Poussielgue saw a miserable rope ladder swaying along the tower, which was the sole means of communication. The ascent seemed perilous. Nevertheless, they scaled it, one after another, all the way to the platform bordered by an iron balustrade. Alongside the glass dome that formed the summit of the lighthouse they saw the opening of a spiral staircase, by which they descended, astonished not to find anyone to greet them.

They called out. No response. They found themselves in front of a hermetically sealed iron door on which there was the number 18. Monsieur Poussielgue knocked on it forcefully. But they waited in vain for a few more minutes, continuing to shout fruitlessly. In the end they were getting ready to depart, believing it to be an inexplicable mystery, when the door suddenly turned on its hinges and a smiling young woman appeared, with rouge on her lips, carefully coiffed, with long curls, wearing a white dress with cerise knots and an ample crinoline. She seemed ready for a ball.

"It took a little time for me to make myself decent in order to receive you," she said.

It required a few seconds for Noël Alga to recognize Margarita de Querigut, whose choreographical debut he had witnessed in Saint-Gaudens. Dancing, adventures and misfortunes had contributed to embellishing her. She had put on weight and her face had lost its former resemblance to a death's-head.

Noël had the spontaneous surge of pleasure that one experiences when one finds a compatriot far from one's homeland. "Mademoiselle de Querigut!" he said.

But Mademoiselle de Querigut, in spite of adverse fortune, had not forgotten that she belonged to a noble family,

371

and had as a principle that a woman who wants to be respected must keep her distances. She knew Noël, having encountered him a thousand times throughout her childhood. *Petty people*, she had heard someone say, and she had not exchanged salutations with him. She maintained the same reserve and contented herself with nodding her head, addressing herself to Monsieur Poussielgue, whom she had sensed to be the more important of the two men.

"I've been a prisoner of this lighthouse and its guardian for ten months, and I'm counting on you to save me."

At that moment a lamentable groan filled he spiral stairway. It was the plaint of a man suffering cruelly.

"I'll explain it to you," said Margarita de Querigut. "Come in. It's necessary that you know my story."

She showed the two men into a cell that was her bedroom. They sat down and she summarized everything that had happened to her since her departure from Saint-Gaudens. Sometimes the story was interrupted by a long plaint rising from below. The listeners could not suppress a movement of anxiety. Margarita reassured them with a gesture, saying: "A little more, a little less!"

"I ought to tell you that I'm a star dancer. I made my debut three years ago before the entire aristocracy of the Midi."

She turned toward Noël, giving the impression of searching for his name. "Monsieur...Monsieur Fagan...no, Faga..."

"Noël Alga," Noël corrected.

"Monsieur Alga was perhaps there, and can testify to the success I had before people of my class. But since! Since then, I have had the greatest success, but more popular. For that has been the misfortune of my life. An evil destiny has dictated that I can only produce myself before an inferior audience, ignorant of great art and true beauty. Yes, I, who departed with the hope of conquering the suffrage of America elites, have only danced before cattle drovers, who came with their prods, and redskins, who came with feathers on their head, and have even arrived at dancing in a cell similar to this one before a sea-dog become a lighthouse-keeper and a somewhat idiotic negro. What a destiny!

"The impresario who engaged me in France had promised mountains and marvels. I left for America in order to become the star dancer in a company that was first to perform in New York and then in all the great cities of the New World. I embarked at Saint-Nazaire. There were other stars with me. Firstly, a trapeze-artist, remarkable for extraordinarily curly hair, which he spent his time caring for when he was not in the process of doing gymnastic exercises in the rigging. Secondly, a dwarf, the dwarf Mignapouf, who was to compete, it appears, with the celebrated General Tom Thumb, recently launched by the American impresario Barnum.[27] He was known as Maréchal Mignapouf. Then there was a fat matron who was an opera singer, the daughter of a gendarme whom advertisements presented as an houri escaped from the harem of the Sultan of Constantinople. It was agreed that, in order to give plausibility to that title, the houri would remain veiled. In addition, that masked a large wart that disfigured her.

"That was the company in which I departed. That's the theatrical life, I said to myself. But the administrator who accompanied us, a certain Peyrade, did not inspire confidence in me. He was a poor devil, a former bit-part player who, every time the sea was rough, could not help remembering the time when he had played a sea-wave himself in a fairy play, agitating his back under a blue-painted canvas. I was obliged to put him in his place, for he claimed to know something about dancing and he said to me almost every day: 'With your physique'—he addressed me as *tu*, as everyone does to everyone in the theater—'to succeed, you ought to make yourself up as a skeleton and represent Death.'

---

[27] "General Tom Thumb" (Charles Stratton, 1838-1883) had actually been touring with Barnum—his adoptive father— since the age of five, and had made a triumphant appearance at the Vaudeville in Paris in 1845. He grew a little taller thereafter, but not a great deal.

"He said that to me under the pretext that I was slightly thin, and he wanted to paint ribs on me, saying that he had been a painter and was a master in the art of make-up! 'To succeed in the theater,' he added, sententiously, 'it's necessary to make use of one's physique.'

"I passed through all the difficulties that a young and beautiful artiste can support who finds herself on a ship full of unoccupied passengers. Can you imagine that I was obliged to resist the attempts at seduction of the dwarf, who, taking advantage of his small size, had hidden under one of my dresses in my cabin one evening! Can you imagine that the former bit-part player, who had been a sea-wave at the Ambigu-Comique, wanted at any price to marry me! 'On the ship, American style,' he said. 'It will be good publicity for us.' It appears that the captains of ships have the right to make marriages. Oh, I've seen things in all colors! When one is a young noblewoman, it's very hard. And yet, the period of the crossing was still the time of hope for me!

"My misfortunes commenced on my arrival in New Orleans. They are linked to a certain Forbes, the director of the troupe to which I belonged. 'I've bought you, like slaves,' he said to us, in the manner of a joke, the first time he saw us. That Forbes, a veritable brute, was a former French seminarian—a former seminarian! How can such a being ever have been able to think about God at any time in his life? I believe that he boasted about it in order to give an appearance of morality that he contradicted by singing obscene songs all day long. 'I have an iron hand,' he said. 'It's necessary to obey me militarily.'

"He began by giving us roles to learn. Apart from the exercise of our art we were to form an acting troupe, performing plays in verse and prose. We protested our ignorance in vain. 'Well, you'll improvise. It will be sufficient for you to know the subject.'

"I had to learn Shakespeare, Racine and Molière. I must say that I didn't come out of it badly. But there was a hilarious scene when the trapeze artist was charged with doubling the role of Othello. They wanted him to rehearse it in case the American actor who was playing Othello fell ill. He came to the rehearsal in a leotard—note that he was extremely hairy, a veritable ape-man—and said: 'Ask me what you like, to walk on my hands, to carry weights, but not to perform plays. If you insist, I swear to you that I'll come on stage like this to play that Arab role.' And he made a tour of the stage on his hands.

"Oh, that was a singular thing! Before a public that only knew English or Spanish, we performed in French, and a few artistes played opposite to us in English. Between two acts, under the name of Stella the Light Breeze, I did a dance number, and I can assure you that then, even before the uncouth fishermen of Florida, I had an unimaginable success. People cried *encore* every time, and I had to do it again.

"See the jealousy of artistes: when I recommenced my number, Peyrade, the former bit-part player tried to stop me going back in stage, saying: 'What's got into you? No one's calling for an encore.' I said: 'Yes, they are,' He called as witnesses the other artistes. 'Did anyone call *encore*?' he asked. Well, see the jealousy of artistes: they put on the most ingenuous expressions and replied in a unanimous fashion: 'We didn't hear anything…'

"I recommenced anyway. Oh, one sees hard things. And that bit-part player, pursued by his obsession, never failed to add: 'You won't have any real success until you let yourself be made up as a skeleton for a dance of death.' He was obsessed with the idea of painting me.

"It appears that Florida is the land where one can make a fortune. Forbes took us to Florida. Nothing but marshes. Once, a woodsman jumped on to the stage in order to kill Lady Macbeth. 'She's gone too far!' he shouted. We never knew whether he was mad, or whether he believed that the drama had really happened.

"Then Forbes perceived that he was mistaken. Florida didn't bring in the receipts. I told him that it was to New York that it was necessary to take us. And one day, he abandoned us in a remote village, taking the stage-manager with him. The

Americans in the troupe would have got out of trouble eventually, but we French would have died of hunger if God hadn't sent us a benefactor. I say God...I had something to do with it, for the benefactor was in love with me. He was a tobacco planter who had just lost his father and inherited a large fortune. A charming young man, with spectacles, who had studied in England, spoke French and was a poet. Harry Brown! Oh, what memories. He was in poor health and was inflicted with a precocious paunch. But he was so charming! 'I'll take you all to my château!' he told us.

"That was providential, but I only accepted with the most honorable intentions of course. The dwarf, the trapeze-artist, the opera singer and I left for a château on the shore of Lake Dunns, Palm House. I'd imagined a château like those in France, but it was something else entirely. It was a matter of an enormous stone building, almost devoid of furniture, fortified and built on piles. It was surrounded by two sets of palisades, with loopholes for rifles, and the perron went down to a pond of rather lugubrious appearance. The fortifications had been constructed thirty years earlier to protect it from Creek and Seminole Indians. Those Indians had made peace with the white men, but fatality dictated that at the moment when we arrived, they recommenced hostilities. The only amenity the château had was a large circular veranda on which one could drink punch in the evenings while gazing at the stars and the horizon of marshes alternating with tobacco plantations.

"The opera singer started to sing, but it happened that her voice was drowned out by the cries uttered by the crocodiles. People think that those monstrous animals are silent. Nothing of the sort. They utter cries that resemble those of young calves. And as there are millions in those stagnant waters, you can imagine our soirées. When one is a star dancer and one has dreamed of theatrical glory, imagine living with a dwarf and a trapeze-artist in the midst of crocodiles!

"And yet the time passed. The castellan was such a pleasant fellow. It was there that I lost the slimness of my body slightly. Perhaps we ate too well. The trapeze-artist complained about it. 'I'm becoming less supple,' he said. He had installed his trapeze in the mud and did exercises all day long. As for the dwarf, he claimed that he was growing. The singer was anxious because she thought she had noticed that her wart was becoming larger under the influence of the climate.

"But all that didn't last. Harry Brown asked me to marry him, for I was beside him with honorable intentions. And then he died. He had a weak chest. I was his fiancée. I should have had rights, shouldn't I? I wasn't able to assert them. Emerging from who knows where, alerted I don't know how, came a sort of savage clad in crocodile skin, Harry Brown's uncle—or so he said—a tobacco-planter like him, who filled the château with his howls. I couldn't even talk to him. 'Throw out all this vermin!' he shouted. If the steward, who was a worthy man, hadn't intervened, he would have delivered us to the crocodiles and the Creek Indians. He even wanted to stop the trapeze-artist from recovering his trapeze.

"In the end, we were able to leave and reach a town called Picolata. How surprised we were to find the impresario Forbes there with a few artistes. He was there looking for us. He'd bought the apparatus of a magnificent traveling theater for the price of a loaf of bread, with its scenery and such beautiful costumes that it was sure of success. A fortune-teller had told him that he would make a fortune in Florida. 'But I need a few attractions of the Barnum genre.'

He had found a woman whose skin was covered in scales, and by means of an ingenious arrangement he made a siren of her. He flew into a fury because I had put on weight. The stage-manager had ended up giving him an idea—he had talked about painting me too, but he changed his mind. 'We're about to fight our great battle in Saint Augustine, the largest city in Florida. You can play Desdemona in *Othello* and dance after the play.' He had no suspicion of the kind of battle he was about to fight.

"It was no great distance from Picolata, where we were, to Saint Augustine, but the road went through a particularly savage region of great forests. Forbes hired carriages and an immense wagon pulled by six oxen, in which all the dazzling costumes were put. As the carriages weren't very numerous, part of the troupe including me, took our places in the wagon.

"At the moment of departure the rumor ran around that the Seminole Indians—or rather, what was left of them, for they had been dispersed and massacred twenty years before— were attacking and pillaging solitary houses. We received that news without attaching any importance to it. We set out.

"We traveled at the pace of oxen. At first we walked, singing as we went, to distract ourselves. Then there was a downpour and we got back into the wagon. The time appeared very long to us. What should we do? We were very intrigued by the splendor of the costumes that we were going to wear, which we hadn't yet seen. A wicker basket covered with canvas carried the inscription: *Othello and Desdemona*; it was the costumes for the two leading roles. 'Shall we try them on?' said the actor who was to play Othello.

"My dress was in violet velvet with a crimson bolero and a blonde wig falling almost to my feet. Othello was a young man with a splendid physique, an Irishman gone astray like me in that third-rate troupe. His name was O'Connell. We dressed up, as he had proposed. To my great surprise, he uttered a loud burst of laughter as he looked at me when I was ready. I was about to ask him why, but I was never to know.

"A fusillade burst forth around us, and savage cries resounded at the same time. The wagon stopped; the driver had fallen, his arms outspread, on to one of the animals he was guiding. It was the Seminoles who were attacking us. The wretched Forbes, who was in a carriage at the head with three musicians, gave his driver the order to whip the horses and he escaped. Note that he had two revolvers and would have been able to defend us.

"I saw a band of half-naked men with painted faces throw themselves on the second carriage and murder those it contained, who contented themselves with joining their hands. The stage-manager was there, the trapeze-artist and a charming young woman who couldn't have been older than sixteen. In such events, things happen so rapidly that one doesn't have time to become emotional. I was struck by amazement, and it was without emotion that I saw horrible savages bounding toward the wagon, who had emerged from the undergrowth of the forest. I ought to say that the forest formed a vault above our heads, and that everything was happening in a twilight that gave it a dream-like atmosphere.

"O'Connell had rushed to the rear of the wagon and with an admirable presence of mind he had pulled out a packet of theatrical weapons, some of them made of wood—but in the middle of them there was a huge two-handed sword, which was a real sword and very old. We had looked at it in Picolata, astonished by its weight, and had wondered how it had gone astray in the midst of those fake swords.

"Casting off his white cloak, in a theater leotard, O'Connell pushed us aside, leapt outside and split the head of the first Seminole who advanced toward the wagon. A pusillanimous clown, instead of helping him, shouted out beside me: 'It's better to surrender and let ourselves be taken prisoner!' A spear came into the wagon and went clean through him. The man who had thrown the spear was almost cut in two by O'Connell's sword. In his starry turban, like a hero of the Middle Ages, such as one sees in engravings, he fought in a magnificent fashion. What a handsome man! I was palpitating, watching him strike to the right and left. Then he put his hand to his breast and collapsed. One of the Indians pounced on him like a tiger, tore off his turban and started to strut around, showing his teeth and uttering cries of satisfaction.[28]

"I thought that I was doomed, but I was calm. The idea of being killed in that wagon seemed frightful to me. I don't know what force impelled me forwards. The wagon was high

---

[28] Author's note: "For several years, the presence was glimpsed during attacks by rebel Seminoles in Florida of a chief wearing a large theatrical turban." In fact, a kind of turban was a standard item of Seminole headgear.

on its wheels and it was necessary to jump to reach the ground. I hesitated momentarily and I saw something extraordinary. The Indians, who were forming a circle, and were about to rush forward, recoiled at the sight of me. I saw an expression of amazement and admiration on their faces. The extraordinary color of my dress and my wig covered in sparkling gold dust made them believe that it was an apparition, the advent of some goddess.

"It did not last. They questioned one another. There are always a few intelligent individuals among the stupid. The one who had Othello's turban on his head, and who must have been the chief, howled words at his companions that I didn't understand and which must have been an exhortation to massacre. I had delayed that for a few seconds, perhaps a minute, but that was sufficient to permit Providence to intervene.

"I heard the rumble of running horses. All the Indians dropped to the ground and threw themselves into the long grass bordering the road as if diving into water. The garrison from Fort Frazier arrived on horseback. It appears that every time there was an attack, the commandant of the fort was warned by an Indian in exchange for a bottle of alcohol, but he was always alerted late enough for the attack to have happened. It is necessary to specify that the alcohol would only have been handed over if the warning had arrived sooner.

"The dead men were put on the wagon along with us and the oxen set off again. 'I'm the daughter of a gendarme, me, and I wasn't frightened,' said the opera singer, clicking her teeth. 'A gendarme's daughter is never afraid.'

"The news of the disaster had preceded us to Saint Augustine. The bishop and an immense crowd were waiting at the threshold of the city, singing the canticle for the dead. A troop of armed volunteers shouted that we would be avenged. They were prancing and firing rifle-shots into the air. You can imagine the sensation that I caused when I appeared at the opening of the wagon costumed as Desdemona, with a wig full of sparkling gold.

"I was installed at the City Hotel, the former palace of the corregidors, transformed into a hotel. I had a room six meters high with a solid oak four-poster bed, Venetian furniture and wall painted in emerald lacquer. It was, in truth, the perfect frame for the wife of the Moor of Venice. I hadn't been able to put on my bloodstained dress again, nor buy a new one, because it was Sunday. I stayed in my crimson bolero, my violet dress and my wig for two days and the entire city came to see me.

"I stationed myself in the patio of the hotel and I had to tell the story of the Seminole attack incessantly. All the ladies of the city wanted to offer me a dress and I had a hundred at my disposal. There was even a collection in favor of the survivors of the troupe, but it was Forbes who collected it, I don't know whether the other artistes got anything. They all embarked on the steamboat that served the coast. If only I'd gone with them! I was retained by my celebrity.

"I ceded to the instances of Captain Brandt—ceded is a manner of speaking; I consented to see him, and I went out with him. He was a superb man. That was ten months ago. I don't understand how the human form can deteriorate with such great rapidity. There are people who retain the same physique for forty years, and others who change completely in a matter of months. What a power of transformation humans have!

"Captain Brandt fell in love with me immediately. With the most honorable intentions, I can assure you. He was a man of austere mores, a former mariner who had entered in the service of the arsenals. He was the image of strength and authority. One could not resist him when he commanded and looked you in the face. He gave me an order to stay in Saint Augustine and I stayed. But what drove him mad him was a dance performance that I gave at the City Hotel. He confessed to me afterwards that he had never seen dancing in his life, except for a savage tribe in Oceania. He was a mariner, wasn't he?

"'You have to come and dance in my tower,' he said.

"'What tower?'

"He didn't reply. I assumed that it was a matter of some old family château.

"In brief, he abducted me. My situation in Saint Augustine was becoming difficult in any case, because of the rivalries of certain men. One evening we were walking near the landing-stage with one of his friends, who was in command of the cuter charged with coastal surveillance. They put me, almost by force, into a launch and then the cutter.

"'You'll see how you can enjoy yourself in my tower. And what a view! It's sixty-five feet tall'

"I didn't really know what feet were and I was still thinking of the tower of a château. It was a terrible night. The sea was rough. The cutter danced. I was frightened.

"'What a wedding night!' said the commander of the cutter. I didn't understand. They were both looking for the tower in the middle of the darkness of the sea.

"Finally, a tall silhouette appeared. I thought the land was behind it. I was carried to the launch. There was a cargo of crates to unload. That time there was an iron staircase that went up in a spiral to the summit of the tower. I climbed it without understanding, and it was only in the morning, when the sun rose, that a realized that I was in a lighthouse. Yes, Captain Brandt was the guardian of the Hazard lighthouse and he had chosen me to share his solitude.

"I wept and cried out, in vain. The cutter had disappeared. I was the prisoner of Captain Brandt, with a somewhat idiotic negro as a servant. And I've been here, Messieurs, for ten months.

"Captain Brandt destroyed the iron staircase that permitted descent to the base of the tower. One could only reach the sea by means of the vertiginous rope ladder that you climbed. There was a dinghy, which was hoisted forty feet into the air by means of a pulley, which permitted the receipt of provisions once a month and went to take letters to the steamboat that goes along the Florida coast, but when the steamboat passed, Captain Brandt locked me in. In any case, it stopped a long way from the lighthouse because of the sands. We have tinned food, medicines, wine, and, above all, gin, for several months.

"Human nature is a mystery. There were two men in Captain Brandt. One was gentle, even artistic, and had no other aspiration than seeing me dance for him all alone, in a minuscule room, to the sound of a flute—which, moreover, he played very badly. He lay down on a mattress and gazed at me ecstatically. He told me then that I was the most beautiful woman in the world and he thanked God, putting himself on his knees, for having permitted him to savor such happiness. And he was sincere. He shed tears of joy and gratitude, and sometimes got up shouting: 'Tom! Tom! I don't have the right to be alone in seeing this spectacle!' And he made the negro slave, who is a mindless creature, come to watch me.

"But there was another Captain Brandt, who was a gin-drinker and was inconceivably coarse. I noticed that it was generally at the time of the full moon that that vulgar Captain Brandt appeared. He once pursued me in the interior stairway of the lighthouse threatening me with an iron rod, and another time he labored me with blows. Afterwards, he wept and begged my pardon.

"You can imagine what my life was like. One day I took advantage of his sleep to read a letter he had received, which had an official heading. It contained the felicitations of his superior hierarchy. Lighthouse-keepers don't stay in those terrible posts for longer than a year, after which they return to land. Now, he had just written that he found himself so comfortable that he had agreed to stay at the Hazard Lighthouse in perpetuity.

"I nearly went mad with horror. Tom was to go to land with the dinghy. I confided letters to him in which I explained my situation to two or three people in Saint Augustine. One of them, a chivalrous young man who was smitten with me, would not have failed to come to my aid. But what can have passed through Tom's obscure mind? He never came back. He took advantage of it to become a runaway slave, and doubtless went to join one of the bands of pillagers of houses who are said to be rife in Florida.

"Our solitude became terrible. The steamboat stopped in vain at sea. We no longer had a dinghy in which to reach it. But Captain Brandt took that very lightly. 'I have you, that's the essential thing,' he replied, when I represented to him that we were going to die of hunger.

"I noticed that he was changing with great rapidity. He could no longer climb the stairs except with extreme difficulty. He complained of pains. 'It's my rheumatism,' he said. But his condition got worse. His joints swelled. He had an intense fever. He treated himself by alternating gin and quinine. But his primary remedy was gin. I don't know if it's very good for rheumatism, but the quinine ran out two weeks ago.

"For a week he's only emerged from successive bouts of unconsciousness to cry out. You heard him, in any case. I thought I was going mad, and it was a veritable miracle to have perceived your ship on the horizon, a miracle that you've come."

Monsieur Poussielgue reflected momentarily as to the best thing to do. "We could transport Captain Brandt to the schooner and deposit him in Saint Augustine along with Mademoiselle Querigut."

The latter uttered a piercing scream. "That's impossible! That man has been a torturer, but the slightest movement would cause him intolerable suffering. I refuse to augment it voluntarily. Just think! He obtained so much pleasure from seeing me dance!"

Monsieur Poussielgue reflected that they could not get an immobilized man down a vacillating rope ladder whose use he feared for himself.

"Well, I'll send my domestic Tobie up here with provisions and all the quinine I have. You can come with us and we'll notify the marine authorities whose responsibility it is to do what is necessary in such cases, although this case seems to me to be prodigiously exceptional and difficult to resolve. In the meantime, let's go see the invalid. Perhaps our coming…"

Mademoiselle de Querigut extended her arms in front of the door to the staircase. "No! The sight of strangers here would be too cruel a blow for him."

"Come with us, then, and my domestic Tobie will replace you."

Mademoiselle de Querigut wrung her hands.

"I was his companion, with the most honorable intentions, but I see now that it's impossible for me to abandon him. I've already left him alone for too long."

Before such contradictions Monsieur Poussielgue remained perplexed. But night was about to fall and it was necessary to go back to the schooner. Monsieur Poussielgue decided to send Tobie with the quinine and the provisions. As they drew away in the dinghy, Noël Alga and he noticed how the silhouette of the lighthouse resembled, in the twilight, an individual in a black robe, with a huge malevolent and menacing head.

Pablo, where there was a post office, was only a few leagues from the mouth of the Saint John River. Monsieur Poussielgue arrived there the same evening and sent an urgent message requesting help for the Hazard Lighthouse.

A few days later he was rejoined in Jacksonville by his domestic, Tobie. Captain Brandt's rheumatism had reached his heart and he had died two days after Monsieur Poussielgue's passage, shortly before the arrival of the steamboat sent to assist him. Tobie had witnessed desperate adieux and a strange scene of Mademoiselle de Querigut dancing—a dance that the dying man had solicited, but which he had not ceased punctuating with terrible cries of agony. The Captain's body had been thrown into the sea, and during the ceremony, they had been obliged to hold on to Mademoiselle de Querigut because they feared that she might throw herself in with him.

Moved, Monsieur Poussielgue made plans to stop in Saint Augustine to search for the young woman and, if possible, do something for her. Tobie added that such anxiety was needless. He had waited for the boat for a few days in Saint Augustine. Mademoiselle de Querigut had immediately found her former admirers and scandalized the city with her liking for nocturnal suppers, to the point that the bishop had forbidden her entry to the parish church of the Calvary. She had departed on the yacht of a rich sawmill owner.

"Doubtless with the most honorable of intentions," concluded Monsieur Poussielgue.

VII. The Apparition
(Dr. Fazeuille's Journal)

Man is tossed between two currents. When he is in the country of his birth, he only think about the beauty of other parts of the world, about adventures, and the fortune he might make far away. When he finds himself far away, in countries that are not his own, among men who do not speak his language, have a different skin color and dress bizarrely, he regrets the folly that caused him to quit familiar places.

When I was in Lauragais, the diligence that took me to Toulouse appeared to me to be the road to life. When I was a student in Toulouse I aspired ardently to go to Paris. Then I was seized by a vertigo, and here I am in a city called Santa Fe, with which I have no interior rapport. The Indians are incomprehensible for me and deprived of the power of expression. The Mexicans seem to me to be limited and cruel. The Americans are uniquely occupied with horses and dollars. Good faith does not reign anywhere. Will it be given to me one day to hear the wind in the poplars that border the Hers, to see again the vines and the maize of Lauragais, those landscapes without great beauty but which I love, and where I know that my father is walking slowly, smoking his pipe?

Santa Fe! What have I come to do in Santa Fe? It is a city with flat roofs, with old Spanish dwellings, ruined churches and gardens full of centenarian trees and deformed plants full of redoubtable thorns.

I have come in search of chimerical riches, but I perceive that I have found something else. If I look into my soul I no longer have the same severity for it. Many of my faults have been attenuated. Certain virtues have been acquired. I believe that I'm courageous. I'm not entirely sure about that, but I am convinced that, if I were thrown into the midst of dramatic events, I would conduct myself courageously. I have observed within myself a certain cupidity, the sordid self interest that I find despicable in others, but it seems to me that I am disinterested. I no longer have any desire to see the enterprise in which I have foolishly engaged myself succeed. If it were only dependent on me, we would not find anything and would depart again poorer than before.

And there is a more important transformation in my soul: I am no longer an atheist. My conception of the world has changed. How and why, I don't know. Is it the grandeur of the landscapes contemplated, the dangers run, or the sentiment that my life is very little and that I might lose it at any moment?

I sometime surprise myself making an appeal to a power that is above me and which directs human beings. That power exists, but I am not sure that it omnipotent. It has created an immense order and it is obliged to respect the laws that it has created. And in that order there are passionate and insensate men who suffer and die, and to which it can only bring help in a certain measure.

I believe in that power. I remember that in the times when I did not believe I talked about God one day with a man of the countryside. They are the only men with whom a conversation on that subject is possible.

"What is it that makes you believe n God?" I asked him, from the height of my superiority.

He smiled, because he was certain of the strength of his argument. "It's quite simple. It's impossible that God doesn't exist."

At present, I think like that countryman. And in sum, merely for having sensed the value of that argument, it was worth the trouble of having come to Santa Fe.

We are staying at the Hotel España, which is remarkable for a garden filled with giant cacti, where tame parrots swarm that chatter all day long. Señor Alvarez, the proprietor, resembles the idea one has of a Spanish grandee. He has a large white moustache and he hands you the key to a room as the Grandmaster of Calatrava must have handed over a sword sanctified by the Archbishop of Toledo. He has one obsession, that of redskins, and considers himself to be permanently in danger of being scalped.

Perhaps that danger exists, but not for at last three days' journey into the heart of the desert. The region of Santa Fe and Albuquerque is full of ranches, livestock and houses, and the question of scalps does not arise.

"Be wary, young man," he said to me on the first day. "Try to keep your hair if you stay in our country. It's a miracle that I still have mine. I've been a trapper and I know the redskins. And they know me! Every time I killed one I made a cross on the butt of my carbine. In the end I ran out of space, so I made lines, and then dots.[29] I'll show you that weapon. But believe me, don't go too far from Santa Fe. One never knows."

Bernard's room is next door to the one that I occupy with Martin Bruno. This morning I went to see him in his rom. The door was unlocked and I went in. He was in the process of writing a letter. As the room is very small I immediately found myself against the table and involuntarily, with no intention on my part, I saw the first sentence that he was writing.

I believe that I can count among the qualities I possess that I have a horror of listening at doors, reading letters that are not addressed to me and surprising secrets that have not been confided to me. I would have liked not to have looked at the sheet of paper that was on the table. But I had looked at it. In any case, with a rapid movement, Bernard turned it over, making a semblance of drying it on a sheet of blotting paper.

---

[29] Author's note: "When he returned from America, it appears that the novelist Gustave Aimard showed his friends his own carbine, with marks that had the same significance." "Gustave Aimard" (Olivier Gloux, 1818-1883) was a prolific writer of popular fiction who produced numerous adventure stories featuring American Indians, which routinely—but implausibly— claimed to have some basis in his own experiences.

Now, I had read this amazing phrase, which was the beginning of a letter to his brother: *My dear brother, Malvina has just died...*

Bernard did not suppose that I had been able to read that beginning. In spite of her parsimony, nature has endowed me with a particularly remarkable sight. He started pacing back and forth, saying to me that he was sending news of us all to his brother.

"The postal service is a prodigious thing," I said, to disguise my confusion at having read that phrase and the astonishment that it had caused me. We were lost in the midst of deserts and mountains and we could nevertheless communicate with France!

"In abut thirty-five days my letter will be there," said Bernard. "Naturally, I'm telling Sulpice that we're all very well." And he repeated to me for the tenth time: "What a pity he didn't come with us."

I could not get over such hypocrisy, and I remained silent. I remained so for too long, for I sensed that Bernard was wondering whether I might have read the beginning of his letter.

"Those parrots are make a deafening noise," I said, in order to say something.

The parrots touched a sore spot in Bernard. He hated those birds. Since his arrival in Santa Fe he had been woken up before sunrise by their piercing cries. Malvina was as importuned as he was.

"Martin Bruno and you aren't sensitive beings; you sleep like logs and certainly don't hear them. But the best thing to do would be to leave his hotel and rent a house where there are no parrots. Anyway, we'll be in Santa Fe long enough, and a house is necessary. Perhaps a moment will come, if we succeed, when we'll be required to hide certain things, and pack them up in order to transport them."

I saw with surprise the certainty of success becoming ever greater in Bernard as it declined in me.

He went on: "We'll then have great difficulties to overcome. In the meantime, it's necessary to find a house that isn't too dilapidated, and set out in quest of a certain Socrates."

"The one to whom it's necessary not to offer money."

Bernard started to laugh. "What a joke! As if there were a single man who can't be bought!"

"It appears that it's necessary to employ a great deal of caution for that."

"Get away! There are only two methods of dealing with people: either to buy them or to use force. This Socrates must be like any other man."

Certainly, it then depended on me to reflect, to wonder why Bernard was telling his brother that Malvina was dead when she was very much alive. I could have, and ought to have, written to him to reestablish the truth. But I was embarrassed by the thought of confessing that I had read by surprise the beginning of Bernard's letter. I put off searching for the motive that might have impelled him. I have remarked that focusing one's thoughts for a long time on a problem initially judged enigmatic, after a certain time, the solution presents itself of its own accord. I did not use that psychological method, or, rather, I put off doing so.

Then again, one has no desire to write long letters when their fate is so uncertain. The Santa Fe post had no special functionary. It was necessary to wait for the passage of a caravan heading northwards. Letters were confided to the leader of a caravan and traveled toward Kansas City, where they found a railway line.

Whatever the reason, I waited. Such is the enchainment of things. That postponement was to be the cause of my friend Sulpice's misfortune.

I shall retrace in their order the events that followed. Not, certainly, to do the work of a storyteller, of which I am quite incapable, but in order to be able to examine them and see, with the aid of hindsight, the measure in which I might have been able to modify them, if I had been more intelligent or wiser, and change evil into good. If one proceeds thus one might be able to see in many situations a benevolent *deus ex machina*, on condition of foreseeing it. But how difficult foresight is!

Bernard had departed with Martin Bruno.

"We're going to explore the region," they had said, as they drew away on horseback.

"I have to talk to you," Malvina said to me.

The day was not too hot, and we started walking along the near-unique street of Santa Fe, which is dominated by an ancient cathedral with a double steeple.

I had never been able to be alone with Malvina without being invaded by a certain disturbance and inhibited by a certain timidity.

"It's curious," I said. "The church of Villefranche-de-Lauragais had two steeples exactly like the one in Santa Fe, which it resembles in a striking fashion."

"It's curious," repeated Malvina, who had not heard me and was only thinking about what she had to say to me.

In a conversation, each person only things of succeeding in taking their own thought where it needs to go.

"I'm addressing myself to the physician today. In sum, André, it's a consultation that I'm asking of you."

She never called me by my first name. As soon as she pronounced the syllables I sensed the extent to which I was acquired by her, and said to myself at the same time: *What a simple procedure! How little is sufficient for women to capture you!*

"Yes, I'd like you to be the judge of my case—for I am a case. I'm an invalid, a poor nervous creature who does not know either what she wants or where she is going."

She fixed her splendid eyes upon me. Around her head and shoulders she had a rebozo with red stripes, which gave her a Mexican appearance. She had stopped and had put her hand on my arm. It seemed to me that her lips were trembling. I did not know where she was trying to get to. Everything is always possible with women. My heart started to beat faster, as it does when an event important for me is in the process of being determined.

"You see, I like you. Those are the words to employ, because I know that no thought of amour can intervene between us. Desire is always what kills amity. You're a friend, and that is better than anything."

I was tempted to ask her whence came the certainty that no thought of amour could intervene between us. I almost did so, stammering: "You think...but in sum..."

She laughed lightly, as curtly as a trenchant blade. That laughter was provoked by the evocation of something confused, but risible because of its extreme improbability.

"I'm going to talk to you as a friend, as well as a physician. First, it's necessary that I ask you..." She searched for a few seconds for how to express herself. "Do you believe that the dead return?"

I had not expected that question.

"Personally, I have never been witness to any case of the return of a dead person—I mean a convincing case. The power of illusion is very great. Those who believe firmly that it's possible for a dead person to appear might be susceptible of seeing one."

"But how can one distinguish what is true from what one imagines? I would like so much to think that everything is my imagination. Oh, I haven't see the dead appear. But certain phenomena are produced for me. What I'm going to tell you, I wouldn't tell anyone else; it's a secret that must remain between us. In any case, what I have might be no more than an illness that can be treated."

We had emerged from Santa Fe by the southern road and we had passed a few Indians with mules laden with forage and wood. We had taken a trail that led to a large abandoned building and were now coming back toward the road by a path bordered with cacti.

"Two years ago I was deeply impressed by the death of someone, someone who might have loved me, and whom I saw lying dead beside me."

Malvina's features had stiffened and her gaze had become fixed at the evocation of that memory. We had reached the road again and we were heading back toward Santa Fe. The morning sun was high in the sky. Crows, inhabitants of the abandoned building, which had not ceased to accompany us with their cries, had fallen silent, and here was an oppressive silence. The luminous landscape was contrary to any evocation of phantoms.

"It's always when there's an absolute silence," Malvina went on, "that the phenomenon is produced of which I am the victim."

We were walking slowly because Malvina stopped frequently.

"I told you that the person whose death struck me forcefully might perhaps have loved me. Yes, perhaps, because one never knows, does one? Amour, in this case, has a great deal of importance because if the dead have some kind of life after their death, they remain attached to the beings they loved while alive. Well, what is produced for me is the sentiment that the dead man of whom I speak is behind me, that he follows me, that I can hear his footsteps..."

"But think about it...that sound might only be a creation of your mind. If a dead man were walking behind you, his body, devoid of weight, wouldn't make any sound and you wouldn't hear him."

Malvina had seized my arm. "Listen! Can't you hear anything?"

I cocked an ear. "Absolutely nothing."

"However, I can hear footfalls, a very light tread, like the one I sometimes hear in the evening."

"That's it," I sad. "You hear it in the evening. It has to be in the evening, because darkness is favorable to illusions, even auditory illusions."

Malvina was still motionless. Behind us there was a bend in the road that we had just passed.

"It's easy to take account of the fact that there's absolutely no one there."

No sooner had I said that than I had the sentiment that someone was walking on the road. It was a light, slightly muffled tread.

"It's a coincidence," I said, "but someone's coming."

And internally, I was astonished by that disposition of nature to create curious correspondences between things, as if a deliberate whimsy presided over that creation.

"My God! It's always the same sound of footsteps," said Malvina, in a low voice. She squeezed my arm very strongly and stiffly, and half-turned around, she gazed at the place where the road turned. I looked in the same direction.

"You'll see...," I began

Indeed, a man as advancing toward us. I only looked at him for a second, and I distinguished a well-dressed man with a symmetrical and pale face, framed by short side-whiskers under a large hat.

A cry of horror resounded beside me. It was Malvina who had uttered it. Her arms extended, she seemed to be protecting herself against a terrible vision.

"My God!" she cried. "It's Maximo! Maximo Avila!"

I saw her totter and I thought she was feeling ill. I took her in my arms in order to prevent her from falling. But losing consciousness is not a possibility given to everyone. I had often perceived that it was a means of providing a solution to a difficult situation.

Malvina, her eyes widened by fear and sustained by me, contented herself with recoiling. A few seconds sufficed to reveal to her the living reality of the man who was before us.

"I'm not Maximo, I'm Henriquez Avila."

The stranger had taken off his felt hat and, as if to take me as a witness and excuse himself for that bad impression, he turned to me and said: "You understand that the señorita must have mistaken me for my brother Maximo, who is dead." And he continued forcefully, as if there were some glory in it: "I'm Henriquez, the younger. It's a mistake that I understand very well. Suddenly to see someone that one believed to be dead! Maximo and I resembled one another so closely."

There was an unctuousness and a displeasing excess of politeness in the man. Meanwhile, Malvina recovered gradually.

"Maximo's brother! Is it possible?"

The man went on: "In spite of everything, I am very glad to encounter here someone who has met my brother. After such a voyage! I've come from very far away—from Portugal! In any case, here come my companions. I preceded them on foot as soon as I perceived the steeple of Santa Fe. Traveling by mule is exhausting. But what luck to encounter compatriots on the very threshold of the city toward which I've been traveling for three months."

We were speaking in Spanish. I hastened to say that I was French.

"I divined that," he said. "I call compatriots all those who are not the savage inhabitants of this region."

A little caravan composed of a few arrieros and a few mules laden with baggage had just stopped beside us. In the middle was a strange old man with long graying hair falling over meager shoulders. A goatee of the same color hung over his breast. He was wearing dark glasses, and gave the impression of a Don Quixote who was also an aged Bohemian painter.

"This is Master Ascanio, who wanted to accompany me all the way here. If you knew my brother he must have mentioned him to you."

Malvina made a vague gesture. She was still leaning on my arm and she made me understand that she wanted to go back to the hotel as quickly as possible.

The Master, doubtless lost in a profound meditation, had not perceived our presence. We started walking toward Santa Fe.

On the way, Henriquez Avila explained to us that it was a great pleasure for him to have been able to being a great man like Ascanio. "His presence," he added, "will doubtless ensure the success of my voyage."

I led the newcomers to the Hotel España. It was hardly possible to stay anywhere else. I hastened to take Malvina to her room. She was still too upset to give me any explanations. But when I said to her that I could not understand how the presence of a great painter could ensure the success of an expedition to New Mexico, she smiled weakly, and told me that Master Ascanio was not a painter but a magnetizer, who was a master of what are known as the occult sciences.

This is only a memento of events in which I was involved. In reporting them I am neglecting the dramatic interest, and with the sole care of the order in which they occurred. I am noting as reference points a few details and certain words that have no other importance except that of having struck me at the time.

"You didn't tell me that you were a friend of the Avilas," Señor Alvarez said to me, with a hint of respect that he had not previously had. "I knew his brother well. What a handsome man! More handsome than this one."

I was obliged to correct his misapprehension and explain to him that I had met Henriquez Avila that same morning.

He was not listening to me. "Above all, let him be careful!" He made a circle round his head.

Night is about to fall and I meet Henriquez Avila as he is going out. He is very preoccupied because he has changed clothes and has not been able to have his frock-coat ironed.

"Is it necessary to make a declaration to the police on arrival?" he asks me.

I explain to him that although the Americans replaced the Mexicans five years ago, there is no organization of police and that order is assured by the officers at the fort.

"We're in a very primitive country as regards its government," I tell him. "Thus, at Leguna, it appears, it's an old trapper who cannot write who has the functions of notary, and the cross that serves as his signature has official value."

397

"At any rate, I'll explore. When I arrive in a city, it is first necessary to have my clothes ironed and then for me to see what the place looks like."

He retraces his steps to ask me whether he creases in his frock-coat are very visible. I assure him that they are not. But he is very preoccupied about that matter of grooming.

Scarcely an hour has gone by. We are having the evening meal in a large room, poorly illuminated, which looks out on to the street. Malvina is thinking about something else and Bernard is in a very bad mood. The door opens and I hear an authoritarian voice that says: "Take him through head first."

A bearded man of short stature comes in and takes us as witnesses. "These Indians never understand anything. I said head first!"

Two Indians come in carrying a man whom I judge to be dead from the way his head is hanging down.

The man conducting them cries: "Alvarez! He certainly lives here. Alvarez will recognize him. He's a man who has just been murdered."

I recognize him immediately: it is Henriquez Avila.

It seems that in Mexico death appears to be a more usual phenomenon than in France. Even death by violence does not cause an enormous emotion.

"I would have bet on it!" exclaims Alvarez. "But I wouldn't have thought that it would happen so soon."

One is not the master of certain thoughts that invade your mind without reason. Henriquez Avila had fallen in the mud and during the examination of the wound, the transportation of the body into a room at the bottom of the garden and the formalities that followed, I could not help thinking, as if it were a obsession: *What would the poor fellow say if he could see the state of his frock-coat?*

I did not find myself alone in my room again until midnight.

What events! I thought. And before anything else I took up my pen to record in this notebook the following remark, which appears to me to be the result of my experience:

When one is on a little-frequented road in no matter what country, if a carriage goes by, one can be sure that one or two more will pass by immediately afterwards, as if there were an understanding between carriages to travel a short distance apart. In the same way, on the road of life on which a man is marching, few events occur, but when there is one, it is always followed by others. Events happen in series.

I had scarcely had the time to write that, and I was putting my pen down on the table, when someone knocked on my door. After midnight! I started. Was it another event?

It was.

The hotel doorman had come on behalf of the proprietor to ask me to come down with my medical kit for an urgent case.

In spite of the annoyance of being disturbed I was not sorry to have a confirmation of the theory of series.

At the foot of the stairs Alvarez was talking to a man entirely enveloped in a hood that surmounted a long Mexican poncho. The man was as motionless as a statue and rather impressive by virtue of the absence of a face, for the hood prevented his features from being distinguished. He was listening without making a gesture to Alvarez, who was in the process of praising my medical prowess to the skies and speaking of me as a master of medicine. Alvarez was one of those men who believe that they are magnifying themselves by delivering pompous eulogies about the people they know.

Perhaps for the same reason he introduced the man in the hood to me as the most important person, not only in Santa Fe, but in all of New Mexico.

"Yes, yes," he said, in response to a gesture of protest. "The Americans must reckon with him. He's the idol of the Indians. There isn't a trapper, a cowboy or a ranchero who doesn't talk about him round the fire in the evening. You, a stranger, will thank me for having introduced him to you. It's a matter of accompanying him not very far from here and see-ing someone who is very ill."

"Even, I'm very much afraid, on the point of dying," said the man, in a somber voice.

"But does one ever know?" said Alvarez.

And as we went out, he murmured to me in a low voice: "In my opinion, you have nothing to fear." Which is never reassuring when one is following, in the middle of the night, in an unfamiliar city in which someone has just been murdered, a man whose face one has not seen.

In the street, by the light of the hotel lantern, I saw a gleaming eye—only one—fixed on me from beneath the hood.

"Let's be quick," said the man. "It's a matter of an old man who has been poisoned."

I was intrigued by the enigma of the form walking beside me.

"Excuse me," I said, "but Alvarez speaks so rapidly and so much. I didn't hear your name."

"My name is Socrates," said the man.

IX. A Certain Socrates
(Dr. Fazeuille's Journal)

If I were giving titles to these notes, as if they were chapters in a novel, I would entitle the one that follows: *The Discovery of a Personal Charm Exercised over Certain Persons*. I am enumerating events in order to know how my qualities and facts were manifest therein and in order that I can identify them to myself.

As soon as we began walking silently through the darkness of the streets of Santa Fe I was aware that a current of sympathy was circulating between the man known as "a certain Socrates" and me. Yes, the sympathy that links two men is caused by a faculty of seduction, a sort of opening to amity that they exert upon one another. That sympathy increased incessantly because of the views on death and on life that we exchanged in the course of the night. Nothing unites men like a community of ideas regarding death. It is to that unexpected sympathy that I owe having been enlightened as to the goal of my voyage and the motives causing the people around me to act.

It seemed to me that we traversed a garden and that we found ourselves in front of a large building that seemed to me, in the darkness, to be enormous. A form crouching on the threshold stood up and spoke a few words in a low voice.

By the light of a smoky Quinquet lamp we climbed a worm-eaten wooden stairway, several steps of which had given way. We went through rooms that I judged to be empty in order to arrive at a room where three candles were burning, one near the door and the other two to the right and left of a bed formed by blankets piled on top of one another, of which the rich colors, patterns and stripes were immediately visible.

On the bed was an old man who was supporting his head with one arm and who appeared astonishingly calm, filled with the serenity that the approach of death only gives when it is welcomed with a tranquil conscience. By the ruddy bronze of his face and the form of his temples I recognized that he was an Indian. Beside him, almost invisible, was someone who came toward Socrates. He was also an Indian. I heard him say something in an unknown dialect and designate me with a gesture signifying that my presence was futile.

In Socrates' response, which I did not understand exactly, the word "American" figured twice, and I thought that he was saying that the presence of a doctor was necessary because of the American authorities. Then, with a rapid gesture, he took off his cloak and at down beside the motionless old man. His presence appeared to wake him up, for the latter raised himself up gradually; his eyes opened, he looked at Socrates with an infinite tenderness, and he extended a hand, which the other took.

An inappreciable time went by. No one moved. Sometimes, an air current inclined the flames of the candles. My mind was dominated by the regret of not having brought a coat. I was embarrassed by my inutility. And while I was struggling with the vanity of my thoughts, the old man died.

Everyone suddenly knew that, without it being possible to know how. Abruptly, he had appeared to wake up, and I heard him murmur: "Kionata!" His gaze had followed some sign or form in the air; he had an expression of very pure joy on his face, and simultaneously, a sort of timidity.

Socrates got up slowly and I saw then that half of his face and one of his eyes were hidden by a headband. He picked up a candle and gestured to me to follow him. On the threshold of the room we encountered three or four Indians with grave faces, dressed as well-to-do Mexicans and only different from them in the tresses of hair that fell over their shoulders.

Socrates took me with him into a room that had a door, the walls of which were entirely covered by Indian blankets that seemed to me to be of considerable value. The question of money is so closely linked to our wretched conception of all things that in the presence of no matter what, one cannot help translating its monetary value. I was surprised to see Socrates light a large number of candles that were in old Spanish candelabra.

"It's necessary that light be made," he said.

He invited me to sit down, adding that it was appropriate that I be enlightened as to the events of the evening, in view of the fact that I would undoubtedly be required to give testimony.

"The man who has just died is Toscalor, the great Toscalor, the last descendant of the Zuni kings. He had only one weakness, for which he paid dearly—that of living in the manner of white men. That was because of his daughter Kionata. He came to live in Santa Fe a few years ago, and he bought the most beautiful house there, the old palace that we're in. I don't know what destiny he dreamed of for the young queen of the Zunis. Nor do I know why the white men exerted such prestige on him. He could pretend to anything among them because, for your race, nothing counts except wealth, and only those who possess it can have a place in the sun. The king of the Zunis was able to dispose of incalculable riches. You know that when Cortés asked Montezuma from which region he obtained the masses of gold that were visible in Mexico, the Aztec sovereign contented himself with pointing to the north. He was designating the land of Cibola and the region west of Albuquerque."

I did not know that but I nodded my head as if I did. I was, in any case, glad to know it.

"Kionata was only an ingenuous child and Toscalor, a old man, did not know what an abyss separates the Indians from the white race. Fatality determined that he was only in communication with men of the lowest order. One of them was called Esquiros and was an exile from his own land; I do not know for what reason. The other called himself Maximo Avila and passed himself off as the descendant of a great Portuguese family. That impressed the naïve Toscalor—who was, however, filled with wisdom, since there was not a Zuni Indian who dared to make a decision without consulting him. But the more elevated wisdom is, the more easily it falls victim to human baseness.

"That Maximo Avila seduced Kionata. When she was on the point of having a child by him, he must have feared the shame of becoming the husband of an Indian woman and he fled. Kionata went mad and died while giving birth to a stillborn child.

"Toscalor remained in Santa Fe. His daughter had been his entire reason for living. I was his friend and I saw him almost every day. He considered the extinction of the family of the Zuni kings, with the death of its last descendant, as the last link of a chain of fatalities that had to lead his people to total extinction; for since his youth he had seen the number of Zunis diminish with a rapidity that increased with the years.

And it is not only life that diminishes but the facility of action. It is as if the Zunis have been afflicted with immobility. If you go into the pueblos of the region that extend between the Pecos River and the Rio Grande you will see the inhabitants of those villages sitting outside their doors, immobile, as if they were meditating. They are not meditating. They are just there. They leave the fields fallow. They neglect hunting and fishing.

"And Toscalor too, from the moment that he acquired this house in Santa Fe, no longer budged. He sat in the garden and he waited. For what? Doubtless the continuation of his misfortunes. It required the desire for vengeance—or, rather, for punishment—to make him get up. Every day he went to the road by which the caravans from Mexico arrive. He was sure that Maximo would come back. He was sure of it because he had confided certain secrets to him relative to gold, and he knew that, for the possession of gold, men of the white race are ready for any sacrifice, even that of their life.

"I often accompanied him there when I found myself in Santa Fe, I accompanied him there yesterday. In recent times he had aged greatly. He had difficulty walking, leaning on a stick. He was very old. I did not believe him to be any longer capable of a punishment about which, in any case, he had ceased to talk. I knew, however, that he still carried beneath his deerskin jacket the long, straight knife that all the Zunis carry.

"Yesterday, we went past you. You did not notice us. I saw Toscalor's piercing gaze pose successively on all the faces. But he did not allow the slightest sign of emotion to appear. For myself, I had seen immediately that the man accompanying you was not Maximo Avila but someone much younger, smaller and more insignificant. The similarity was only a family resemblance. I assumed that Toscalor had made the distinction, like me, or that he had not noticed any similarity.

"I did not worry about it any longer. He must have lain in wait and struck him as soon as he came out of the hotel. He had always told me that when he had avenged his daughter he would go to join her in the place where the Great Spirit had put her."

Socrates leaned toward a large fireplace where faggots were piled up. He lit them with his briquette and the room filled with a delightful odor of incense and resin that Mexican wood emits.

I warmed myself with satisfaction, because it was cold, and I supposed after that gesture that my host did not want to see me depart immediately.

"No, I don't regret not having foreseen what was about to happen," he said, as if he were replying to something I had said. "The man would have died a little later, as all those die who come to extract from the ground the cause of inequality, hatred and the misery of the world. If it were to be recommenced, I would let Toscalor act as he acted. He has not known his scorn and he has died satisfied, having accomplished what he had to do, or believing that he had accomplished it, which is the same thing. The essential thing, for happiness after death, is to die with a tranquil conscience."

I found myself, with regard to my interlocutor, in a state of inferiority, since I was one of those who had come to extract from the ground the cause of all misfortunes. But was I one of them, in fact? Something rose up in me to protest. Before that fireplace, by the light of the wood full of sparks and little explosions, a sort of interior revolution took place. I was a disinterested man. Driven by a collective movement, carried away, I had accompanied a group of friends who had departed for the conquest of a chimerical wealth. To be sure, wealth was of scant importance to me. I affirmed that to myself. And it was with an absolute sincerity that I set about blackening the avid adventurers who were precipitating from all parts of the world toward Mexico and California.

Socrates' piercing eye posed upon me. He did not add anything. He continued to follow in his thoughts the destiny of Toscalor after death.

"Dreams are realized, wishes are granted—but only for the good. I know that in principle, a doctor, for having studied life as a simple phenomenon, is tempted to believe that everything terminates with death."

I protested that there was nothing certain about that for some doctors. Death was perhaps a door opening to the veritable life. And to my great surprise, I explained with sufficient facility and eloquence ideas that were presenting themselves to my mind for the first time and to which I adhered as they presented themselves. Those ideas, strangers in one sense, were nevertheless mine, since I was the one who exposed them. Doubtless they reposed in my mind and were only waiting to manifest themselves for that nocturnal encounter with an almost faceless man next to a fire of perfumed wood. Thus, expression permits the soul to create itself, as it renews itself in accordance with the rhythm of events.

We talked for a long time beside the fire. I was astonished by the idealistic personality that surged forth within me, of which I admired the new aspects, and no less astonished by the personality of the man who was before me. He appeared to me to be cultivated and very different from all the men that it had been given to me to frequent since my arrival in the New World.

But as our conversation went on, I sensed that Socrates, while speaking and listening to me, was asking himself questions about me. Sometimes he interrupted me, not so much to have the response to what he asked, as to be able to make a general judgment of me. He was, in sum, subjecting me to a sort of psychological examination. And I sensed that the examination was favorable. I felt a certain pride in being able to be in sympathetic rapport with that redoubtable man. But I did not know at the time that in that conversation I might have determined my existence and that of my companions.

It was very late when Socrates accompanied me back to the hotel. He did not say anything more. When we came out of the garden, where I distinguished a great silhouette of a dead tree, he raised his head toward the sky and said in a low voice: "I loved Toscalor. He was a pure soul. There will soon be no more pure souls on the earth."

At the moment of quitting me, he added: "We shall see one another again." He was already drawing away into the darkness, but he retraced his steps. "Between now and then, if an Indian guide, of which there are many in Santa Fe, proposes to lead you through the desert of San Juan, don't accept."

X. The Land of Acoma

One has a great deal of difficulty attributing intelligence and extensive knowledge to a man who only has one eye and a part of whose face hid hidden by a bandage. I only accustomed myself gradually to the idea that Socrates was a remarkable individual.

Having encountered him the next day, he asked me to accompany him to his home. He lived in the part of the city where the steps that it forms reach the Rio Chiquito. I was surprised by the modesty of his house, which was made of adobe, with a flat roof, and only comprised a single room in the middle of a garden. There was nothing in the garden but reeds and bizarre cacti in the form of candelabra with three branches. A narrow path led down to the river.

The room did not contain any furniture. In one corner there was a machete, a bow, an old rifle and a blanket on which he must sleep. An earthenware pot was full of maize porridge.

"I have a similar house in Acoma," he told me, "Although a little smaller, here I live for almost all the year."

I understood that he was letting me know that he was a resident of Acoma and that he was only participating accidentally in the destructive civilization of Santa Fe.

"What a different there is between certain men," he added, "even though they live in proximity."

We strolled for a while in the garden.

"I'm called Socrates because I've often given medical advice. For the Mexicans of this region, Socrates was a famous Egyptian, or perhaps Greek, physician who lived a long time ago. I'm half-French. My father was expelled from Haiti at the time of the revolution and came to settle in America. It was him who gave me the ideas regarding the destructive influence of wealth that I still have. He had freed his slaves and shared his property between them, and that earned him the hatred of everyone. He took refuge in America, where I was born, and, disgusted with humankind, he wanted to live in the middle of a desert, far from contact with men. That is very difficult. The earth is full of deserts, but there are savage men everywhere around them who will kill you in order to rob you.

"Contrary to the theories of Rousseau, with which the New World is filled at present, he taught me that humans are fundamentally evil, evil in the roots of their instincts. He came to install himself on the banks of the Rio Grande in a log cabin that the two of us built, and his ideas about human nature were abruptly transformed. He made the discovery of good and simple men with an unalterable purity of heart. Yes, there was such a marvel in the land to the south of Santa Fe and Albuquerque."

"Is that possible?" I exclaimed. I did not believe that Socrates was speaking seriously.

"There are marvels in the world, and there are greater ones that exist without anyone being able to recognize them. If you happen to encounter the people of Acoma, although they rarely descend from their village, you will find nothing special about them. They have the same impassivity as all Indians, the same haughty reserve that one finds in the Apaches beyond the Rio Grande and the Navajos of the west. Their costume, their habits and their mores are the same. However, there is something that distinguishes them, a particular characteristic—with exceptions, naturally, such as nature always produces. The Indians of the pueblos of Laguna and Acoma all have blue eyes.

Blue eyes. I immediately recalled the brief indications of the document that Malvina possessed, and what Alaman had told me about the land of Cibola and a Welsh prince called Madoc who had subjugated it three centuries before the advent of the Spaniards.

"I've heard mention of that," I said. "Isn't there a story of a cathedral attached to it?"

Socrates shot me a glittering glance. "You know that a cathedral exists in the land of Cibola? That's a story that it's better not to know."

"Why is that?"

"Because misfortune befalls those who search for it."

That day, he did not tell me any more.

In the New World—at least, in the part of the New World adjacent to the desert—the death of a man is a matter of scant importance. There was no investigation on the subject of the death of Henriquez Avila, and when I had declared to an American officer of the garrison that I had witnessed the death of the murderer, everything was concluded.

Nevertheless, that death was to have an unexpected consequence. Anastasio Alaman arrived the day after the event, and even though he did not know Henriquez Avila, he was impressed to an unimaginable extent. In the evening he came to see me in my room.

"You're the most reasonable," he said to me, again, "and when you're reflected, you'll follow the path of reason. I say when you've reflected, because it's hardly sensate to have left France, made a journey of several months, braved dangers, fallen into Houston's hands and to have arrived in Santa Fe and then to go away without having attempted to find what one is searching for. I remain convinced that the true source of gold isn't California, to which all the world's adventurers are flooding, but the region enclosed by the ruins of the seven ancient cities of Cibola. It's from there that the gold of the Aztecs originated.

"The legend of the cathedral that some say is made of solid gold is only a symbol. It probably exists. Perhaps it contains riches. Perhaps it's a ruin. But its location must be an inestimable indication. Only you can see how things happen. Esquiros, and then Maximo Avila, once fled. There are reasons for that. They wanted to come back, but doubtless with a numerous troop. I've participated in your project because I thought that times might have changed something here. I'll continue to contribute materially, as has been agreed. But you can see how things are. As soon as he arrived, Maximo's brother has been killed. You're younger than me, and aren't known to anyone. I'm going to let you continue your search without me and leave as soon as possible. You'll tell me that that's lacking courage."

"I don't say..."

"I don't lack it before real dangers, but I confess to not having any for those that prowl around us like phantoms."

I thought that we were could talk about that the next day, with him and my companions, but the next day we learned that at daybreak, a small caravan of merchants had gone south, and that Anastasio Alaman and Master Ascanio, and the arrieros he had brought, had gone with them, in order to travel with more security. We remained alone in Santa Fe.

"Do you attach a price to human life?" Socrates asked me, one day when we left Santa Fe on horseback, heading westwards."

"It depends..."

"God doesn't care about it. He causes death from day to day. He sends wars and epidemics. Why should we be more scrupulous than him?"

"We're human..."

"And he strikes the good and the evil indifferently. I don't say that we ought to strike in the same fashion, but isn't it our duty to act in accordance with the will of God, as he indicates it to us? It's not a matter of recompensing the virtue that we call virtue, of punishing the vice that we call vice, for we might be mistaken. It's a matter of acting in the same way as God, when one has glimpsed that way by means of an indisputable sign."

"That way is very difficult to discover."

"That depends. I'll take an example, that of this country. Visibly, the divine will, what one might call the order of things, wanted this country to remain as it is, with its peace, its uncultivated terrain, its villages of good people, its solitude and its silence. It ought not to be disturbed by the dregs of society driven by the desire for gold. Look at what has happened in California and parts of Arizona. There were doubtless villages out there where Indians lived with patriarchal mores, whose only commerce was a little barter, not even thinking about extracting a little alcohol from maguey. What have they become now? For it's a curious particularity of the red race: those who are nomadic and live in tents are exceptionally cruel, whereas those who are sedentary, like those of Acoma, have conserved a soul such as humans had in the days of primal innocence.

"The cause of the evil is the folly of metals that Europeans possess. It isn't only gold, it's also copper, silver and tin that they want to extract from the ground. And for that they turn everything upside down, destroying landscapes, diverting rivers and corrupting souls. The greatest human crimes happen around mines. Well, isn't it the duty of those who are conscious of that evil to prevent it in the measure of their means, or at least to slow it down? The man who acts thus is acting in accord with God, so why respect human life any more than he respects it himself? If one is his instrument, if one is acting on his behalf in a disinterested fashion, it's legitimate to make use of the same methods."

I listened with surprise to the man clad in hides and primitive in appearance, who seemed to be claiming to be carrying out the work of God. Perhaps he read a little of my surprise in my expression.

"Plants, animals and simple men act in harmony with God. It's only from the moment when desires develop in them that they act contrary to his will. There's no doubt about it; God wanted the face of this land to remain as he had created it. He gives indications on that subject; I've distinguished one of them.

"Recently, as the cemetery of Acoma was full, it was thought that one could dig in the location of old tombs dating back several centuries, in order to place new corpses herein. It was perceived that the substance of the soil in question had intrinsic powers of conservation. The body of a Spanish lord from the times of the conquest was exposed, who had been buried with his weapons. Only his eyes had disappeared, but his parchment face had retained the expression of faithful gravity that it had had while alive. He could no longer see, but he still lay there, such as he had been put there.

"Thus things ought to remain, similar to what they were. If, on a mountain of stone such as the isolated rock of Acoma, a few families live in peace, almost entirely ignorant, practicing human virtues—disinterest, fidelity to faith, reciprocal love—it is because God has so far taken the trouble to protect them. Perhaps it's a matter of an experiment of a divine order, the range of which escapes us. It's the task of those who have understood to perpetuate it by all means. And that's why I think that one ought not to take any account of human life when one is collaborating with God."

I was disconcerted by such a conception on the part of such a man.

"It's necessary to be very sure of that collaboration," I said.

"I am. Many years ago, following a great chagrin, after having wandered all over America, I returned to Acoma, to which I had been brought by my father when I was a very young man. The presence of genuinely good people is, I believe, a sovereign remedy for all ills. I have sworn to defend those inoffensive and pure people, whose race is dying out.

"I imparted my sentiments to Toscalor. Since then, the adventurers that have come to this region have almost all been subject to the same illusion. They have encountered an Indian who, in consequence of various circumstances, has come into possession of a secret. Either it is a river easy to deflect from its course, or a part of the mountain that encloses nuggets in a rocky matrix.

"That Indian would have difficulty deceiving those men on any other subject; they are usually men whom the battle of life has rendered suspicious. Well, they believe; they believe without proof; they always believe. They believe in a cathedral of gold, the treasure of Montezuma.

"You see those mountains in front of us. Behind those mountains is the San Juan desert. They venture into it haphazardly, with a guide who disappears when they have gone too far to turn back. In any case, they do not think of turning back. Gold is at the end of the journey—far away, because they never come back. I have the weight upon me of a certain number of lives; they do not weigh heavily. Thus far, I have been able to protect this country from death, and I believe that I have acted in accordance with the law that has been traced for me."

"However," I said, with a certain timidity, while we were returning in the direction of Santa Fe, "among those adventurers who have remained in the desert of San Juan, there must have been worthy men, as there are in any human company."

"No just action is accomplished in the world that does not entail in its realization a measure of injustice. Have you been to Tucson, which is not very far from the land of the Zunis? Have you seen the inferno of the mines, the unleashing of crimes, the devastation that alcohol brings to souls? If I can spare this country a similar fate, or even slow it down, I consider that the sacrifice of a few human lives is very little."

"Everything depends on the height at which one places oneself in order to judge. I'm an average man who would not dare to elevate himself to any other point of view than that of average men."

"Men are only valuable by virtue of their capacity to elevate themselves above the level at which they are placed."

We completed the return journey in silence. I thought that he was right and I had the disagreeable sentiment of a mediocrity that bound me to the human point of view, and of which, in spite of everything, I did not want to rid myself.

No, I said to myself, that old conception is firmly attached to me. One ought not to kill one's fellows, even for a very elevated goal.

And Socrates also said to me: "Remember that, under the pretext of I know not what riches to be found, or for archaeo-

414

logical discoveries, men who install themselves in Acoma never fail to dig up its ancient cemetery. Now, it's there that my father lies. And I can't think without trembling that he might appear in the sunlight with his face intact, to be deprived of the peace and darkness to which he has an inalienable right."

I do not recall with pleasure the time that I spent in Santa Fe, although that time was part of what I call the heroic time of youth, and everything connected with youth is clad in a powerful attraction. No mode of life is agreeable in an atmosphere of bad feeling I did not note at the time the petty daily occurrences because they had a depressing effect to me. I am only summarizing that comes back to memory.

The event that was one of the principal causes of trouble was our change of residence. We left the hotel and went to live in the large dwelling, once aristocratic, to which I had accompanied Socrates and where I had witnessed the death of Toscalor. An old Indian woman prepared our meals there; another, equally old, did the housework.

"You can install yourselves there," Socrates said, as he handed me the keys. "Toscalor was the owner of the house. His heirs are in Acoma. No power in the world would make them penetrate the place where their king and is daughter died in succession. Consider that you're in my home."

Even now, I cannot see the motive that caused him to do that. I can only find an explanation in the personal sympathy that I inspired in him. But that was precisely what caused my relationship with Bernard to deteriorate. Naturally, I had announced on the first day that I had made the acquaintance of Socrates. Perhaps I had done so with too much satisfaction. It excited Bernard's jealousy to an extraordinary degree.

"You've made the acquaintance of a bandit, that's all," he said. "I've asked for information about him. He is, as we know, a very dangerous man."

Bernard's anger only increased the next day when I was obliged, the following day, to put off until later the moment when I would introduce him. Socrates had declared to me in the most formal fashion that he never spoke to strangers. Bernard, whose curiosity was sharply stimulated, had difficulty disguising his chagrin.

"Above all," he said, when I mentioned the house, "make the arrangement—but I don't want to encounter that sinister individual."

In reality, he was bearing a grudge against me because that encounter had not taken place. If he consented to be his guest it was because he was only preoccupied with one question, the only important one in his eyes. That was Malvina. The journey had been, for him, a period of waiting. He had hardly any opportunity to be alone with her and she avoided any such opportunity carefully. He sensed the determination she had to avoid it, and that aggravated his exasperation. He thought that in a vast solitary dwelling, there would be more opportunities for drawing closer than in the hotel, where our rooms were adjacent and only separated by thin walls.

It is not for me to map out the episodes of the drama of resistance and disappointment that was played out alongside me. Malvina was a creature submissive to her desire, and as ardently delivered to sympathy as to antipathy. "She knows what she wants," is commonly said of such natures. Perhaps the sentiments that she had always had for Sulpice had something to do with the distancing she experienced for his brother. Now, nothing renders greater bitterness than being rejected by the woman one desires.

Martin Bruno and I sensed the tension increasing in the relationship between our two companions, so we were not surprised when we heard cries coming from Malvina's room in the night. Bernard had arranged to have his own close by and I had thought that disposition did not augur well. It was on the second day of our installation. Marin Bruno and I hastened to arrive and we saw that Bernard had tried to put into practice is theories regarding the prestige of brutality and insult. But he had failed.

Malvina, her hair falling over her shoulders and the top of her dress torn, had seized an old sculpted poker that must have dated from the sixteenth century and had threatened to strike him with it if he came any closer. He had not gone any closer—not because of the poker, which it would have been easy for him to avoid, but because of the expression of fury on Malvina's face. There was also disgust in it, for women susceptible of giving themselves spontaneously and joyfully have equally violent sentiments of repulsion.

When we arrived, Bernard was motionless and was looking at Malvina with an amazement mingled with rage and despair. One might have thought that he had only then had the revelation of the sentiments that he inspired in her. Perhaps he was also surprised by Malvina's tragic and slightly theatrical beauty, which harmonized with the black velvet curtains, the heavy cedar beams of the ceiling and the high walls covered with Indian blankets.

I sensed by the expression on his face that he would never pardon us for having witnessed his humiliation. He attempted a burst of disdainful laughter, shrugged his shoulders, as if it would be wrong to attribute any importance to an incident that had none, and he left. We heard the entrance door of the house slam.

I do not know where he went during the three days that followed. He had told me that he had found a place where Americans gathered in the evenings.

"There are extraordinary characters," he had told me, "but they're not your sort of people."

The place was called Teddy's. Teddy was a half-caste who sold a little of everything, but mostly powder and alcohol. At night, there was gambling there.

In the course of one of our conversations, Socrates had said to me: "Not one of the horse-thieves who frequent Teddy's will return to his homeland alive."

So, when Bernard came back to tell me that he was going to accompany a Canadian who knew the country admirably and had decided to cross the San Juan desert, I protested, and gave him once again an exact account of my conversations with Socrates. I had already done so.

He did not take any account of what I said to him. According to him, I was the dupe of an impostor who might have some information about the gold that could be found beyond the San Juan desert and who invented fanciful tales in order to put off those who might be able to supplant him. I was one of the naïve individuals who fell into the trap.

"We'll have Zuni Indians with us," he told me. "Since you believe blindly in what a man you don't know told you a week ago, I won't ask you to join us. In any case, neither you nor Martin Bruno could understand the mentality of a man like the Canadian O'Ready." He burst into laughter that he tried to render joyful. "I would have liked to see Malvina and O'Ready come to grips."

He returned a part of the funds of the expedition, which he held. I only found out later that he had kept the lion's share.

"In that regard, you realize don't you, that if Anastasio Alaman gave us the money, it was uniquely for Malvina's beautiful eyes."

I replied that I had no idea on that subject.

"We've all been the famous dupes of that..." And he added several injurious terms.

I thought how very different the effects are that voyages on people. Since our arrival in America, certain ideas had come to me about God and human duties that I had not had before. Bernard, on the contrary, had developed the bad side of his nature. He manifested an increasing liking for inferior men, by virtue of the law of souls that determines that similar ones attract one another.

As I tried once again to deflect him from his project he called me a coward and quit me, manifesting the greatest scorn for men who had water instead of blood in their veins.

XI. The Legend of the Invisible Cathedral

Hugues Borromée could not forget the words of the man who had been his teacher and master at the seminary, Père André.

"There are signs," he had told him. "You will never be abandoned. If you find yourself in the midst of the greatest dangers, remember that the signs are around you, to tell you what you ought to do."

But he had added: "Except that the signs aren't always comprehensible. The language of God is sometimes clear, but sometimes it's an enigma that it's necessary to decipher."

Why? Hugues did not understand why the response was not always explicit, why it was contained in a sort of divine rebus. And that question, which he could not resolve, weighed heavily upon his soul in crises of doubt.

For the doubt never quit him. On certain days, he was afflicted by it without any reason. On those days, he woke up in the morning with a dolorous desiccation of the soul. It was as if a bitter wind had blown over his thoughts during the time that they had escaped his control in sleep. He could no longer rely on the certainty of the previous day. Everything was called into question again. Former reading returned to his mind in which his faith had been destroyed by the arguments of science. Then he took refuge in prayer, but he only prayed with his lips, and behind the words he sensed the negation of the prayer.

Gradually, involuntarily, that doubt had become personified in a form. It had taken on the outline of an individual represented in an illustration in a romantic book. It was a tall, thin man dressed in black, with a large black cravat, to whom the artist had given the arched eyebrows and pointed goatee that is ordinarily given to the classic face of Mephisto. And the gaze was both persuasive and seductive. Hugues could not remember the book in which he had found that illustration, nor what hero it incarnated. But that hero, so far as he recalled, was represented in the book as a man of superior intelligence. By virtue of an incomprehensible whim of his memory, doubt was associated in his mind with intelligence.

The novelty of travel did not distance the black-clad companion from Hugues, as he had hoped. It even caused him to come more frequently—intermittently and fugitively, but faithfully.

Doubt seemed to exasperate the faith that was within him. There were days when it seemed that he would never have the time to realize the good that he sensed within him. How many creatures there were to save, how many retarded souls that were in need of enlightenment! And how few men there were, in sum, who devoted themselves to that task! When he thought about the number of creatures who lived in ignorance of the word of Jesus, he wondered why there were not more Christians passionate to go and teach them that it is necessary to love one another—for there were very few, especially in America. Once-prosperous missions were now in decay. The twelve Franciscan missions of California that had claimed a host of proselytes among the Indians had been expelled forty years ago at the time of the Mexican revolution. The Christian Indians has been dispersed in the forests and the mountains. Where were they now? What did they believe? Were they happier?

But that question was terrible for Hugues. Abruptly, the character from the romantic book loomed up before him and raised his bony and excessively white hand. Yes, he said, they were happier. Christianity brings garments to those who were naked. It gives scruples of conscience to those who had none, it obliges them to the discipline of labor. It is a cause of pain for those who were living in insouciance. It diminishes the sum of the happiness that God has distributed over the earth so parsimoniously.

And Hugues wondered then if he was really following the path of verity.

Having disembarked in Santa Cruz he had first to reach a small Franciscan mission recently created at Queretaro. He did so by means of Mexican stagecoaches, and caught a fever traversing the marshy regions beyond Santa Cruz. He was obliged to spend a few days in the Queretaro mission directed by Père Amédée, the missionary who knew America best, having traveled it in all directions for a long time.

Père Amédée was a man of great authority, who only spoke to criticize the disorders of the Spanish clergy in the places where that clergy was left to its own devices. His first words to Hugues were to advise him to avoid the priests who lived in a scandalous manner, living with women and having children, as much as possible. Pope Pius IX had tried to remedy that state of affairs. He had created an apostolic vicariate at Santa Fe. Monseigneur Lamy had recently arrived and he was about to undertake the task of reforming the clergy. Would he succeed?[30]

But for Père Amédée there was an influence that surpassed human range. Mexico was the land on earth where evil had the greatest action. Men were more cruel than elsewhere. He had witnessed the majority of the revolutions. At twenty he had been enclosed voluntarily in the besieged city of Cuautla in order to obtain from Morelos that his troops would respect women and children. He had gone to make the same request of the Spanish general Calleja. He had been witness to all sorts of atrocities and claimed that those who committed them were prey to a demonic possession whose like had never been seen before.

"You see," he said, "when the soil of this country is left to its own devices, it only yields cacti bristling with spines, a

---

[30] Author's note: "Monseigneur Lamy had been sent to New Mexico in 1850 with the title of Bishop of Agathonica, having come from missions in Ohio and Kentucky." Jean-Baptiste Lamy (1814-1888) is now most famous as the central character of Willa Cather's novel *Death Comes for the Archbishop* (1927)—he was promoted to Archbishop of Santa Fe in 1875.

vegetation that gives the impression of being made to lacerate and cause suffering."

Thus, he prescribed to the half dozen missionaries who were with him in Queretaro not to leave the enclosure of the mission. It was a former monastery of the time of the Spanish conquest, partly ruined, only one wing of which had been restored. In a cell overlooking a vast cloister invaded by weeds, Hugues was cared for by Brother Antoine, an old Spanish monk come from no one knew where, whom the missionaries had collected. He did the cooking and went to the market, thus sparing the missionaries the contacts with the population of the town that Père Amédée judged dangerous.

Brother Antoine was short, fat, red-faced and absolutely bald. He was a curious mixture of joviality and mysticism. He had a very extensive knowledge of all things, which he continued to augment. Heaped up in boxes he had found a large quantity of books that must have constituted the library of the former possessors of the monastery, and he spent a large part of his time plunged in their study. At other times, in the cell next to the one that Hugues occupied, he plunged himself into prayers that, on some nights, extended until the time when he went to sound the Angelus in the chapel tower. But that did not prevent him from doing the cooking lovingly; nor did it prevent him, very rarely, from drinking an excess of the coarse cane alcohol known as aguardiente.

Perhaps because of his youth and perhaps because he considered him as a child whose reproaches he did not fear, he had made Hugues his confidant. One evening, when the convalescent young missionary had said that he felt weak, Brother Antoine had brought him aguardiente in great secrecy, which gave him strength.

"The roads that lead to God are various," he said, and everyone must find his own. "Now there is in these alcoholic spirits that come directly from the earth a means to reach very high. It's necessary not to say that to Père Amédée. In any case, it's necessary to know how to make use of aguardiente, which, like an explosive, can't be handled without danger. Aguardiente has two aspects, which it's necessary to know."

Brother Antoine said the gravest things while laughing, with the result that when he was joking no one knew whether or not he was serious.

He took Hugues into a cell that served as a storage room for gardening implements. He showed him bottles lined up behind a broken wheelbarrow and an old watering-can. They were uncorked.

"You don't know why I've taken the stoppers out of those bottles, at the risk of letting the liquor deteriorate in contact with the air, or permitting some fly to fall in. I could say simply that it's with an objective of purification, but the real reason is more serious. The quintessence of juices of the earth that the sugar cane had condensed exerts a powerful attraction on the souls in torment that prowl around the places where they have lived and seek the effluvia of those they have loved. Those souls in torment, which are blind and unconscious, enclose themselves by virtue of their desire in the bottles of aguardiente. They are inferior souls, those of prostitutes or drunkards. Thus, I put a term to their captivity and I pray with their intention, in order for them to be elevated."

Having said that, he laughed—but the tone of his voice contradicted his laughter.

"You've devoted your life to saving souls, and I've always thought that that was the greatest duty of a man who has faith. I've always planned myself to go and evangelize savage peoples. I've even learned the barbaric Indian idioms of the Apaches and Navahos, and attempted to study the language of the Chippeways, for I dreamed of going north. I dreamed of reaching a land where there would be no aguardiente, and, above all, no women. I never went, for I'm a great sinner, aging and repentant now, whom God has permitted to be, at the end of his life, a servant of true holy men and has granted him books. in order to permit him to redeem himself."

Hugues gradually confided in the old monk. One day, he talked to him about his crises of doubt.

"Yes, doubt is a terrible enemy," Brother Antoine relied, "but how can you explain that the man who believes and never doubts acts no better than the one who doubts? It's not certainty that is the most necessary thing, but the will to rid ourselves of the desires that are beyond our flesh. Lust is the greatest enemy of humankind. I'm an old man who believes, and even knows, for God, after appeals that last several days, has been kind enough to favor me with certain visions.

"Well, lust is still in me, dormant but alive. And there are images that have the power to resuscitate it. I've talked to you about the souls that are subject to the attraction of agardiente. Well, it's happened to me on certain nights, when walking in the cloister, after having drunk perhaps a little more than is appropriate, to be followed by phantoms of poor fallen creatures that I had known in the past. Fallen, but beautiful, for one isn't exclusive of the other—and that beauty brought me forcibly down to earth, oh, far from God! And it was at that moment that I had a desire to leave the monastery and start running to a back-street in Queretaro where I know that, in a low house, a lamp is burning...

"Then again, the one who doubts has a refuge in prayer," he concluded.

"But if one doesn't have faith within oneself, one only prays with the lips."

"If one has a sincere desire to have faith, a moment always comes when God appears, or, if he doesn't appear, he gives a striking proof. Look at the example of Eusèbe-François Kino."

But Hugues did not know who Eusèbe-François Kino was.

"The story of Father Kino is linked to the legend of the invisible cathedral. Has anyone told you that legend?

Hugues did not know the legend of the invisible cathedral either.

"In the convent of Dolorès, at Zacatecas, a town in Mexico not far from Queretaro, there was an old Jesuit father named Eusèbe-François Kino. He was reputed to be a very holy man who was tormented by crises of doubt. He resolved to accomplish some great work to the glory of God in order to obtain, as a recompense, the absolute faith that he desired. He was going to depart on his own to go and evangelize the savage populations of the north, solely with the strength of the cross. Your case is, in sum, the same as his.

"In the meantime, he heard it recounted that in the distant land of Cibola, which the Spaniards hadn't yet reached, near a city called Grand Quivira, built by the predecessors of the Aztecs, stood a stone cathedral surmounted by the Christian cross. It had been constructed, it was said, four centuries earlier, by a Welsh prince who had conquered the land. The prince had been massacred along with his companions, but the women they had brought with them had been spared and a blue-eyed race resulted from the interbreeding of the Welsh and the Zuni Indians.

"Father Kino made a vow then. Barefoot, he would march in the direction of the land of Cibola, in spite of the snakes and the spines of a vegetation hostile to humans, until he had found the cathedral of the Welsh prince. He had no doubt that he would then receive the faith, as a gift of grace, for he was desperate to find a supernatural aid within him. It's necessary to know the nature of the terrain, to have seen with one's own eyes the deserts to the north of Mexico, to know what a martyrdom a march of several months over that accursed soil represents."

"And did Father Kino find the faith?"

"He set off, only accompanied by a negro named Esteva. For a long time, nothing was known of his fate, but after two years of absence he came back, and he was a different man, possessed by divine illumination. Not only had he found faith but he seemed to be carrying God perpetually within him. He had, incessantly, the delight that we simple mortals only attain at rare moments of exaltation. He had reached the land of Cibola and had said mass in the cathedral, of which he made a description. It was thanks to the information that he gave of that unknown region that the Spaniards were able to conquer it a little later.

"He set off again, with several other Jesuit fathers, and he founded a mission, which is now abandoned, in the Sierra Madre. But all the evidence is not concordant. Some documents say that Father Kino had lost his reason by virtue of having contemplated things that were too admirable in the old cathedral."

Hugues had listened to that story with a passionate interest.

"The story of the cathedral doesn't end there. The great revolt of 1680 expelled the Spaniards from all their northern possessions. They took them back gradually. The cities had been destroyed. Grand Quivira was no longer anything but ruins. But of the cathedral, which was somewhere in the vicinity of Grand Quivira, no one could ever find any trace. And there's another legend.

"A bishop who was reputed to have devoted himself to magic and to have made a pact with the Devil, Antonio de Cochea, famous for the cruelties he inflicted and the sumptuousness of his life, supposedly extracted large quantities of gold from the mountains in which the cathedral was built. Fearing that it might serve as a reference point for those who wanted to search for gold in the same sources as him, he was said to have rendered it invisible to human eyes by means of a diabolical process analogous to the charms the Oriental magnetizers are said to know. It can be seen, it's said, but it can't be reached. It's confounded with the mirages that are born of the illusions created by deserts and the sun.

"That enchantment cast by the bishop magician not only rendered the cathedral invisible, but also keeps away from the region men capable of restoring it to its former splendor. That influence will be perpetuated beyond death. The land of the seven cities of gold—seven cities now in ruins—will be rebellious to Christian influence and condemned to immobility and solitude. To be sure, it's only a legend, but it's curious, all the same, that the once-prosperous region in question, that region full of riches, remains savage to the extent that no one knows the exact location where the vestiges of Grand Quivira can be found, and no one is searching for gold in Cibola, when crowd are flooding into California and Arizona. There's a mystery there..."

Hugues' decision was immediately made. The next day, in the chapel of the convent, he made a solemn vow to reach the cathedral, barefoot, as Father Kino had done. He had no doubt that faith would be given to him in exchange for his effort.

Everything was, in any case, arranged to permit him the realization of that vow. It was in Texas that the most savage Indians were found. A few tribes were still anthropophagous. Père Amédée moreover, was counting on him to carry a letter to Monseigneur Lamy in Santa Fe. The region of Cibola was on the route leading from Queretaro to Santa Fe. If the cathedral existed and he ought to reach it, God would guide him to it.

He wanted to depart like Father Kino and try to follow his itinerary. Brother Antoine found that itinerary, approximately, in the archives of which he had custody. He drew a map that would permit him to navigate.

"Father Kino left with a negro and a mule. A mule is indispensable to carry provisions, water and also the consecrated stone, the sheets, the crucifix, the chalice and the priestly vestments that are all necessary for saying the mass. But a man is necessary to lead the mule, because human strength is limited. It's necessary in the evenings to cut wood, build a fire, construct a shelter and prepare a meal. I'll make you an inestimable gift in giving you Codrillo, a Christian Indian who, although he isn't very intelligent, at least possesses purity of heart. When the goal is very elevated, it's necessary for the means to be pure. It's reported that in all the villages through which Father Kino passed, the negro Esteva pursued the Indian women and seduced them with promises of money. He was, moreover, killed by a jealous husband on the return journey. Thus, the saintly Father Kino, in pursuit of a high ideal, was accompanied by an atmosphere of lust. For lust soils everything. Do not let it penetrate your soul, or your surroundings."

Brother Antoine added to Hugues' baggage an ointment for the wounds that would not fail to lacerate his feet, and a provision of huaco, the snake-herb, which is reputed to counter the mortal effects of their venom.[31] He accompanied him for some way along the route. Hugues had set forth before sunrise in order to take advantage of the matinal freshness. Daylight had not yet appeared when they separated.

"I'd like to go further," said Bother Antoine, "but I'm fat, alas, and soon out of breath."

Hugues was going on alone with Codrillo, who was holding the bridle of the mule, when he heard running footsteps behind him. It was Brother Antoine.

"You'll succeed, as sure as I'm a poor sinner condemned to die obscurely without having done anything. I was watching you draw away and I saw that you weren't going alone. There was a luminous form walking behind you."

There are petty prophecies, sketches of visions, that one is not supposed to believe, but which are nevertheless a powerful aid. In the course of his journey Hugues was to remember those words of the old monk, and to draw great comfort from them.

---

[31] Huaco, or guaco, also known as snake-herb—plants of the genus *Mikania*—had the reputation of permitting its users to handle dangerous snakes, not so much by providing an antidote to their venom but by giving rise to a repellent sweat that deterred them from biting.

XII. The Marvelous Journey

Hugues' vow entailed traveling in the same conditions as Father Kino. There were no inns in those regions; Hugues was therefore obliged to sleep on the ground rolled in his blanket. When it rained, a barn or the crown of a tree served as shelter. That fashion of traveling did not provoke any astonishment from the taciturn Codrillo, for he had never known any other.

And I believed that I was accomplishing an extraordinary exploit! Hugues thought, on seeing him lie down on the ground beside him and go to sleep in a matter of seconds.

The first part of the journey passed without encumbrance. The travelers were walking on roads and Codrillo knew the states of Zacatecas and Durango, which they had to traverse, perfectly.

"Here, old Mexico!" he said, sometimes, with a tone of respect in his voice.

They had nothing to fear but thieves, very numerous on Mexican roads, but what would they have be able to steal from the missionary's meager equipment?

Hugues did not stop in the towns. He even tried to go around them in order not to see them. He avoided Durango and Cullacan and headed toward Sonora.

A moment came when the aspect of things changed. The villages became increasingly spaced out. Steeples became less numerous. There were great forests to traverse. The people they met had a different appearance. In the same way that when one draws close to the sea one sees a different race, the approaches to deserts and savage regions engender a new humanity. Hugues passed gold-prospectors carrying the barreta over the shoulder that they used to strike rocks in order to extract gold; vaqueros, or herdsmen, bringing immense herds nourished on the desert vegetation back to the towns; hunters laden with the hides of wild animals; and also men recognizable by their weapons and appearance as highway bandits, and who did not seek to hide the fact.

"Here, dangerous land," said Codrillo, when they arrived in Arispe, the last town, after which there was an infinite extent of ancient forests, great stony expanses and sandy deserts, where there were no longer any habitations, nor any trace of human life, excepts for ranches separated from one another by long distances, or an occasional pueblo of taciturn Indians in a hollow in the mountains, composed of a few wretched cabins.

And when they had arrived in La Puerta del Cajon, at the place where the Rio San Miguel hollows out a profound bed in the earth, enclosed by walls of steep rock, where nature put on a redoubtable face, as if to announce that another world commenced there, Codrillo said: "Now, accursed land."

But there could not be any accursed land for Hugues if the land in question was the road that led to the peace of the soul.

There would be signs, Père André had once said. Hugues searched for the signs in everything he saw on the earth and in the sky. In the evening, when he had meditated over the maps made for his use by Brother Antoine and had assured himself of being on the same path as Father Kino, he listened to the silence of the night and tried to translate the sounds that became audible. Were there not warnings in the manner in which the light of the stars filtered through the branches? When an owl uttered its cry nearby, was it not bringing a message? And could not the howling of the wolves themselves be interpreted?

He always went to sleep with the sentiment that he had not been able to understand, and sometimes with the sentiment, a thousand times more bitter, that there was nothing to understand, that the earth was silent and dead for the desire of the soul.

It happened that Christian Indians begged him to come to a distant pueblo lost in the mountains in order to carry out baptisms and marriages. The nearest parish priest was a week's journey away, and also demanded too much money for them to get him to come.

At points where trails crossed and where there was a stream or a spring, he suddenly found himself in the presence of a few wooden huts where alcohol was sold, where there was a corral for horses and where cowboys spent their nights gambling. Such places of pleasure sometimes had two or three women, who were usually fallen Indian women. A priest was always welcome, but he caused a general embarrassment. Hugues suffered in such milieux, and passed through whenever he could without stopping.

He got lost in the foothills of the Sierra Madre while searching there for the remains of Father Kino's mission. He finally discovered, in the middle of a valley, large stone buildings—storehouses, granaries and workshops—grouped around a church. But all the buildings were devoid of roofs and the church had lost its belfry. Hugues explored all the rooms, went through all the doorways of those phantoms of houses, searching for some souvenir of the past. Numerous pillages must have stripped them; nothing remained. Vegetation had invaded everything. A fir tree had split the floor of the church, parting the paving stones and, with its arboreal strength, had separated the vaults, extending the circle of its branches over the walls, with the consequence that it gave the impression of protecting the roots of the pillars and the arches of the chapels.

Hugues spent two days in that place filled with the melancholy of destruction and death. He waited; but there too, no sign came.

After months, he reached the little village of San Diego. The fatigue caused by poor nourishment and lack of sleep was beginning to make itself felt. His feet were lacerated and without Brother Antoine's ointment he would never have got that far. He still had great distances to travel across New Mexico. He thought of resting for a while with the parish priest of San Diego. Night had fallen when he went along a long street where there was nothing but abandoned Spanish houses. The

431

Indians preferred to live in adobe houses that they had built with their own hands.

The air was full of music. Light shone in the cracks of doors. Having interrogated a man who was passing, Codrillo learned that it was the festival of Saint Guadalupe. Hugues recalled that Bother Antoine had told him her story. She was a poor half-caste who had entered a convent of Franciscan nuns as a servant two centuries before, in the time of San Diego's prosperity. She had died of dolor at twenty because she could not do enough good for those whom she saw suffering.

There was a particular animation in the square in front of the church. People were dancing and singing. Cowboys, who had doubtless just arrived and were still in the saddle, were drinking from glasses that a fat woman brought them. She was running from group to group, laughing, bumping into the horses in the midst of pleasantries and bursts of laughter. One horsemen, in the midst of dancers, was beating time for the fandango by clapping his hands.

"Who is that man?" asked Hugues.

He pointed at a jovial individual with a red face who was dancing with a soutane lifted half way up his body and was wearing a blood red belt. While dancing he was calling out to people. He seemed to be the animator of the feast.

"What, you don't know him? But that's the parish priest of San Diego."

Hugues continued on his route.

As he was passing the last houses, an old man called to him: "Señor Priest, you'd do better to remain in San Diego. The famous bandit José Archilidon is in the vicinity. You know what they say about him. He tortures women and kills men for nothing, for pleasure—especially priests. It appears that he's no longer in his right mind. If you encounter him on the road, you're a dead man."

But Hugues did not take any account of those words. He slept in the open and set forth again in the morning. He reached the crest of a ridge from which a large valley was exposed. The ribbon of the winding trail could be seen extending

432

far into the distance. As he started moving again he saw five horsemen coming toward him. Soon he was able to make out the glint on the sunlight on their weapons and the contours of large hats and ponchos. Was it the brigand about whom he had been warned, with some of his companions? Hugues sensed that his guide was tempted to mount the mule that he was holding by the bridle and flee.

"I prayed his morning to Saint Guadalupe to protect us," said Hugues.

He pronounced those words with such a complete assurance that Codrillo rediscovered his courage. But deep within himself, Hugues did not believe in the intervention of saints in human affairs. What could Saint Guadalupe do? he thought. The causes are already engendered in the invisible and what must happen will infallibly occur.

The five men had reached a bend in the trail where a cabin could be seen near a little cedar wood. They stopped abruptly. A silhouette had emerged from the trees, an arm was raised.

"It seems to me that that's a young woman with an orange rebozo," said Hugues.

The silhouette was partly hidden by the trees. Codrillo could not make it out. He thought, however, that it was more probably a young man in a yellow hood.

That only lasted for a few seconds. The horsemen turned around and departed in the opposite direction. What could have caused that unexpected change? Hugues continued to advance, promising himself to interrogate the author of the intervention whose result had been so immediate. But when he arrived at the little cedar wood he could not see anyone. He approached the hut, which was only a shelter of mud and branches, such as there often were beside roads. The hut was empty. He called out, but in vain. Only a few minutes had gone by, however, since the scene he had seen. He continued on his way.

An hour later, however, when he had traversed the valley, there was a sound of horses behind him. There were about ten riders. This time there was nothing to fear. Codrillo had recognized a troop of Vigilantes—which is to say, militia of the kind that all the American towns in the frontier regions had formed against brigandage. These asked Hugues whether he had seen five horsemen heading toward San Diego. They were in pursuit of José Archilidon, who had just pillaged and burned a hacienda, and they knew that he was due to return to San Diego in the morning with four members of his gang. Hugues explained the encounter that he had almost had and the sudden apparition of someone he believed to be a young woman.

"They have accomplices everywhere," said the man who seemed to be the leader of the Vigilantes. "They must have known—I don't know how—that we were coming, and someone lay in wait in the road to warn them. But that's a puzzle, because no one could have known that we would pass through San Diego this morning."

The Vigilantes continued their route. Codrillo affirmed thereafter that he really had seen a young man. Hugues did not insist. He was sure of his own testimony and remained attached to it. It was Saint Guadalupe, who had heard his prayer and had come to save him. Saints are linked to the places of their birth, like simple mortals. They stay there after death. There, they hear more clearly those who pray to them and they grant the wishes when they have heard the prayer, in the measure in which it is only a matter of creating an image or producing an illusion. Hugues wanted to believe that. He attached himself to that hope of protection. A great joy accompanied him that day.

That joy was further maintained by another event. He found himself before a river in flood, which was carrying uprooted trees and the bodies of dead animals. After a bend, the trail ended at a place where there ought to be a ford. The detour in the trail seemed to give an assurance of it. That was Codrillo's opinion. The mule, however, was resistant. The travelers were about to attempt the crossing in spite of the strength of the current when they saw a horseman on the other bank who was making signs and shouting to them, in spite of the din of the water, that the ford was a little further on. He seemed to be heading in that direction himself.

Hugues and his companion went downstream and did, indeed, find a place where the water was calm and the crossing did not present any danger. But it was in vain that the young missionary wanted to thank the providential horseman. There was no one there, and he searched the trees and vegetation of the other bank in vain.

To his great surprise, Codrillo did not find the circumstance extraordinary.

"He must have gone in the other direction."

But Hugues sensed the idea of an invisible protection extended over him becoming firmer.

Unfortunately, the pain of the body wears away the certainty of the soul, instead of consolidating it. Redoubtable days were commencing for him. The cuts in his feet became infected. His strength weakened. It was the beginning of the rainy season, and it was necessary to endure great downpours that left him shivering. He always had a slight fever, and the provision of quinine that Brother Antoine had confided to him when he left Queretaro was running out.

Along with the weakness of the body, his anxiety was increasing. He wondered whether the goal he was pursuing might be insane. He was, after all, going toward a cathedral that no one had ever seen. What was known about Father Kino and his travels was in part legendary—everything that pertained to the mystery of the cathedral, at least.

Assuredly, to begin with, Father Kino had explored the land of Cibola. Assuredly, he had founded a mission with other Jesuits. Texts of the epoch reported that. Hugues had had those texts before his eyes. He had recently seen the ruins of the mission in the place indicated. But everything relative to the cathedral was nothing more than stories transmitted orally by credulous monks fond of marvels.

Perhaps Father Kino had begin by doubting divine truth and, after a long journey, his doubts had dissipated, but what proof was there that there was a particular place in which he had received a revelation? What proof was there that the place in question was the illusory cathedral? And even if he admitted the truth of the legend, did he not have reasons just as good for doubt and dread?

A bishop occupied with magic had intervened. Antonio de Cochea! The religious history of the Spain of the Occidental Indies slid over his story, dissimulating the role that he had played. Why? In principle, Hugues refused to believe in the power of magic. But who can tell? Why should a diabolical power not be exercised around that cathedral? For unknown reasons, God sometimes permitted demonic endeavors to be realized. It was a question of enchantment, of rendering the cathedral invisible. Why, then, would he see it? Only men of great faith were powerful enough to vanquish occult traps, to overturn diabolical barriers. He sensed that he had courage enough to give his life, to offer God all his blood, but how would he give the subtle blood of faith, knowing that he was deprived of it?

As they were traversing a desert, a tempest blew up.

After that desert, Codrillo thought, they ought to reach the sources of the River Zuni, in the very heart of the mountains of Zuni territory, where Brother Antoine had placed on the map the red cross denoting the cathedral. After the entrance to a canyon, which resembled a portal to Hell, he had said. And after passing through that canyon, it would be necessary to reach a ring of symmetrically-superimposed layers of lava so singular that only God could have disposed them, playfully, at the origin of the world, when the earth was plastic and modeled in accordance with the divine dream.

The wind blew with such force that tall columns of sand rose up and began racing from one edge of the horizon to the other. It was dark. A red moon was in the sky and it gave the impression of running in the midst of sandy turbulence. Behind a rock that sheltered them, with their blankets over their heads, the travelers struggled in order not to be buried.

It was necessary to set off again the next day, to walk without any trace of a path, to endure the torture of thirst. Toward the end of the day, the mule collapsed, and did not get up again, for animals do not have the hope that sustains humans.

Only Codrillo's intuition guided them. He sensed the water of the river ahead of him. First there was the apparition of trees in the mist of sand. Then they climbed depressions in the terrain, and saw rocks and ridges looming up that had masked the tempest from them. The wind ceased to blow at nightfall. Running to their right they saw a steep mountain chain that joined another in the distance. According to the Indian's memory, two rivers ought to intersect at the foot of those chains, and several Indian pueblos were suspended over their course.

In the shadows they made out white cubes formed by adobe houses. There was no baying of dogs, no bellowing of captive livestock woken by the fear of wolves. An impressive silence hung over the village. No one responded to their appeal. The doors were ajar. The pueblo was abandoned.

But that must have happened very recently, perhaps that very day, for in the house into which they penetrated the ashes of the fire were still warm; there was maize porridge ready to be cooked and water in the pitchers.

They were exhausted. They went to sleep without wondering about the cause of that abandonment.

They only found out in the morning. They explored the houses neighboring the one in which they had slept. In one of them they found two cadavers. They were young men whose death was recent. The redness of their faces and the pustules that covered them showed that they had died of smallpox. Hugues leaned over them to ascertain the nature of their disease, recoiled and uttered an exclamation. He had just seen that they had blue eyes.

Smallpox struck the Indian race like lightning, and the disease, which very often left people of the white race alive, killed all the men of the red race afflicted by it inexorably. The Indians had found no other means of escape than flight. When the first case appeared in a village, the inhabitants went up into the heights. It was said that they went in search of the sacred fire, the symbol of their ancient gods, which had not ceased to burn in some grotto on the mountain, and was secretly worshiped even by the most Christian among them, and which they brought back to the village in order for it to destroy the disease.

The two travelers were so weary that they resolved to stay in the village for two days, until the tempest ceased and good weather permitted them to resume their march. When that time had elapsed, however, it was Codrillo who could not set forth again. An intense fever had gripped him and Hugues realized that he had been struck by the epidemic.

Everything happened for the young missionary as if in a dream. He was sustained by the ardent will that unexpected possibilities give the body. In that deserted village, having nothing around him but cadavers, only eating the food that they had left behind in dying, he did his best to care for his traveling companion. But the latter sensed death with the same intuition that had enabled him to sense the direction of the river in the heart of the sandstorm.

During the third night he strove to tell his master everything that he could about the direction to follow in order to reach Santa Fe, the rallying point when all hope of finding the cathedral had been lost. Shortly before daybreak, he died.

In the lugubrious hut, where the vestige of oil that had previously given a little light had just run out, next to the terrible corpse, of which he could confusedly distinguish the terrible appearance, Hugues felt the human horror of absolute solitude. He was surrounded by the images that fever brings, and it was those images, by virtue of their strangeness, that deflected despair.

Brother Antoine stood by his side.

"I made you a precious gift," he said, pointing at the supine Cordillo, "but remember the man Esteva, who accompanied Father Kino. It's necessary to beware of lust. It dooms all men."

Having said that, he disposed bottles of aguardiente around the room and uncorked them one after another. A white vapor emerged from each one, which became a woman.

They were women of the lowest order, of whom Brother Antoine had spoken—those who spent their nights drinking aguardiente with him—for he recognized them and showed them to Hugues, calling them by their names. They circled around him in procession—and that lasted until the first ray of sunlight.

Then he went out. He closed the door and barricaded it solidly with branches. The hut would be a tomb in which Codrillo's body would be sheltered from the wolves. He loaded on to his back all that his wavering strength permitted him to carry, in addition to the objects necessary for the celebration of the mass, and he set forth again along a path that led northwards.

He could not evaluate the length of time for which he walked, but a moment came when his strength abandoned him and he let himself fall to the ground. He was surrounded by cacti of menacing forms. Some were out of all proportion and had swellings and pustules, as if they had been afflicted by a vegetal smallpox. Agaves rose up to an unusual height and enabled excessively beautiful flowers to burst forth, like the blossoming of that race of plants bristling with spikes. One cactus, however, by virtue of a bizarrerie of nature, launched regular arms to the right and the left in the form of a cross.

Woe betide the man who wants to assume too heavy a task, Hugues thought. *There is no supernatural protection. There is only a series of coincidences that are sometimes ingenious enough to make us believe that an omnipotent will accompanies us and defends us. Men are abandoned to themselves in the midst of the pitiless intersection of the laws of life.*

He had the sentiment of touching a certain truth, so simple and so obvious that it had no need of demonstration.

He raised his head, and saw, in the distance, a horseman advancing in his direction.

XIII. The Liberating Mass

Socrates and Hugues were now walking side by side. They went very slowly because Hugues was almost fainting at every step. Faithful to his vow, however, he had to attain—barefoot, as Father Kino had done—the cathedral toward which he had been marching for months.

For he was about to reach it. At least, his companion had told him so. Why had he confessed to him in full? There was nothing in his face, half-covered by a headband, that encouraged confidence. But Hugues sensed that he was at the end of his effort. The mountain landscape that surrounded him was that of a hallucination. The man who had leaned over him and given him something to drink had appeared to him to be a divine messenger.

"The cathedral exists, and I'll take you there," Socrates had said, simply. And he had added: "Not everyone knows the end of its story. There are some who say that a saint will come, barefoot, from far away, and, by saying mass in the cathedral, will liberate it from the malediction that covers it."

"Alas, I'm not a saint, but a sinner."

"Sinners become saints by means of the actions they accomplish."

Socrates had wanted Hugues to spend the night in the place where he had found him. He had lit a fire, prepared a meal with the dried meat that is the nourishment of all travelers in the desert, and had watched over his slumber. In the morning, they had set off again.

"We'll arrive during the day," Socrates said.

Hugues' soul was divided between hope and uncertainty. Yes, he was a sinner. Was there a greater sin than doubt? And suppose the legend was true—that the cathedral was invisible to the eyes of those who did not believe?

They walked over stony plateaux where trees no longer grew. A dazzling sunlight made the stones resplendent. Eagles were flying high above. Walls of granite barred the route to travelers. The world gave the impression of finishing there.

They plunged into one of the profound corridors known as canyons, where the sun seemed infinitely distant, and then climbed upwards by means of a vertiginous path hollowed out in the stone. Sometimes, between two rocks, a cactus had grown.

Am I not dreaming? Hugues asked himself. *All these cacti are in the form of a cross.*

The cacti gave the impression of being milestones place on the route.

They emerged from the shadow of the canyon and discovered another universe. It was barred on one side by a gigantic wall, like a giant's fortress, and at its foot unfolded curving cliffs, granitic funnels, around a grandiose circular space where series of mat stone steps were superimposed, separated by gulfs of erosion whose sheer walls shone.

There were circular precipices with slopes of petrified mud, dead lava. Plateaux were stacked between the vertical walls, and crevasses plunged down, rendering series of superimposed geological strata visible. The life of vanished millennia emerged from eternity and revealed the mysteries of successive condensations of stone. Here there had been, at the origin of the world, a special labor, an experiment in which the subterranean fire, combined with that of the sun, had tormented matter in a cosmic inferno, to give it that aspect of bleak petrifaction, that special color of a frozen planet, a desperate and silent moon.

"The cathedral," said Socrates, showing his companion, with his hand, the center of the immense circus.

Hugues leaned over, his heart hammering. Was he about to see?

And he saw, not one cathedral, but a host of cathedrals. They were of all forms, some with two massive spires like the village churches of the French Midi, others with a single tower and a steeple that cleaved the sky. Fantastic architectures opened immense portals in all directions. Some had seven naves and others three. There was one that resembled Notre-Dame with its ring of apsidal chapels and its parvis with three portals, and another that resembled the basilica of Saint Sernin in Toulouse with its two crucial red brick arms and the stages of its forceful tower.

But the belfries were too high or too low. There were strange disproportions in the contours of the naves. Some must have caused the columns supporting them to buckle and others leaned to the right or the left, as if the crypts where the ossuaries reposed had collapsed.

Those cathedrals were incomplete. They were only the stone cladding of a place of prayer that did not exist. They were not animated by the supplication or the grief of human beings. They were only masses of silent and inanimate stone, in which the bronze chorus of bells had never sung its hymn of life, where there was neither altar nor sanctuary. It was a unique play of nature that had built those incomplete monuments, within the seething of some vanished crater. Perhaps the creator spirit, when the earth was born, had amused itself sketching with plastic lava the dreams that it had formed, which humans would only realize after millennia had gone by.

But among those dead cathedrals, Hugues recognized one that was alive. In the harmony of its proportions, the fall of its lines, the rise of its octagonal tower, he sensed a perfection that was not found in the essays in stone formed by the hazards of fire and matter in fusion that a creative thought had directed confusedly. Among the hasty projects of the divine dream there was a human realization. In spite of the destructions wrought by time, it was recognizable by virtue of the regularity of forms and a winged mystery that escaped therefrom because human prayer had vivified the stone.

"I see it," Hugues said.

He did not think of being astonished by the immense work that such a construction represented, with the labor of pilasters, buttresses and beams, in the solitude that nature had struck with sterility.

"Let's go," said Socrates. "It's me who will serve in the mass."

And they went down the winding path.

"Before night falls…," Socrates had said.

Hugues tried to imagine Father Kino marching over the slopes of the circus, which they were descending slowly, between those immutable walls, three hundred years before. How was he? What forms of doubt did he bear in his soul? Did he sense those great waves of emptiness coming from the utmost depths of his interior being and swallowing all his thoughts of God, of the future life and his own eternity? And why would faith have been rendered to him here, in this inferno of stone, in this demonic place where the fantasy of an exalted Christian had wanted to erect a basilica? But that final doubt only appeared in a furtive manner, and he also remembered the words once heard in the mouth of his uncle, Nestor Borromée.

"Miracles come by unknown paths, at an appointed time and in a place prepared by a superior order."

The masses of stone that the travelers went around had an almost formless appearance. The true cathedral stood in a location that was almost in the center of the circus, and it must have been the void that had once been there that had given the Welsh prince, the conqueror of the land of Cibola, the paradoxical idea of building a basilica to the glory of God in the midst of a thousand caricatures of basilicas.

Nothing any longer remained of the glasswork, if there had ever been any, and the wind passed through the casements, whistling softly. The thickset columns had resisted the centuries and bore with fidelity the riches of vaults with beautiful lines. In the highest shadowed corners, bats had established their roosts, and echoes awakened by human footsteps gave birth to quivers in the clusters formed by their wings.

Successive pillages by savage Indians had despoiled the church of all the riches it must have contained. It no longer had anything but the skeleton of a vanished splendor. But the empty plinths and pedestals, the empty niches, and the stone frames of the armchairs where members of an ancient chapter must have sat, attested that the church had been, in times long past, animated by statues, lamps and ornaments, clad in the magnificence of flamboyant candelabra and accumulated ex-votos.

Hugues had placed the sacred stone and the cloths of the altar. He had set up the crucifix, lit the two candles and prepared beneath his veil the chalice with its hosts, as well as the sacrificial wine. Assisted by Socrates, he put on the amict, the alb, the stole and the chasuble, and, pale but no longer unsteady, possessed by the special illumination of the priest who is conscious of being the intermediary between God and humans, he climbed he steps of the altar.

Behind him, Socrates knelt down.

As soon as he had made the sign of the cross and commenced the mass, Hugues sensed that he was engaged in a mysterious combat with unknown powers that were present around him, and which became increasingly numerous. The sign of the cross had been akin to a summons. The pure serenity that he hoped to have conquered definitively was put in question again. He accomplished the ritual gestures but his soul was not in harmony with his gestures. Doubt reasserted its rights. He was the victim of a kind of duplication.

A priest before the altar had just said: "*Miseratur tui omnipotens deus…*," but another sensed profoundly the vanity of those words.

Lord, please forgive us our sins…

What sins had he committed? Did he not see behind him a life of privations, prayers and sterile hopes? His sufferings, hours spent on his knees, his appeals remaining without response—were those his sins? Was he to be punished for his own misery and his own love of that misery?

And as he kissed the altar and his gaze embraced the profundity of the church, he had the sentiment of no longer being alone.

444

Sitting on a mosaic near the altar, he saw an individual, with his legs folded, gazing at him, smiling. He recognized him immediately. It was the man of the old romantic engraving that had troubled his youth. As in the book of old, he had the same black garments, the same arched eyebrows, and he was clutching his goatee. He seemed to be saying:

I've reflected for a long time on the sacred mysteries of all religions, I have been impassioned by what I believed to be their truths, and now I laugh at them, as you ought to laugh.

"Per omnia saecula saeculorum..."

Through centuries of centuries humans had believed in the power of God, but ought modern humans—those who had meditated by the light of their intelligence—to be believe as naively? And what if negation appeared to them as the final word of intelligence?

But then Hugues perceived that the man clad in black was not the only witness to the mass that he believed he had said on his own.

Had they emerged from the portal that opened on to a horizon of stone or through the low doors of the chapels? A host of witnesses were present. And Hugues recognized them. There were all his relatives, all the members of his family, the long line of Borromées who had been ecclesiastics or monks. He saw the one who had been a cardinal, such as he was represented by his portrait, with his long sad face and his hands of wax; Michel-Auguste Borromée, prior of the Franciscans of Toulouse, with his head of a Roman Emperor and his great ascetic body; Philibert, the missionary, who had been martyred in Canada and whose corpse, it was said, had been fed to the wolves; and others more obscure, perhaps more modest, who had gone unmentioned but had played the role that their destiny had marked out for them, and who had all been animated by the faith and had spread around them the benefits of that faith. All the Borromées had known that faith is the essential element of the soul and they had come to witness the combat that would decide the fate of the youngest among them, with their arms folded and their eyes fixed. Hugues' circular glance had permitted him to distinguish his large nose, the family nose, and the light mist that moistened his eyes.

"Remember, Lord, thy servants..."

The servants of both sexes were similarly present at that mass, the benediction of which they had been waiting in their tombs of centuries. The depths of the church were filled, for Hugues, by the crowd of those who had come in the past to witness the masses that his unknown predecessors had celebrated. There were the ingenuous newly-baptized, the Indian builders of the church, those who had given their sweat and their toil to move the blocks of granite, to drag from the nearest forests the tree trunks that had become the unshakable beams. There were the first conquerors and those who had conquered again, the Spaniards of Cortés, Niza and Coronado; Hugues saw their armor gleaming and mat gold over somber damask velvets.

In the stalls, suddenly replaced on their stone foundations, the members of the ancient chapter came to sit, ecclesiastics in black robes; old men with sashes around the neck, holding their square bonnets in their hands; and a tall Indian chief clad in his ceremonial robe of beaver-pelts, holding the stick with seven knots, the symbol of his authority over the seven tribes of Cibola.

Per omnia saecula saeculorum...

In the middle of the transept, the tombstone that indicated the opening of a crypt rose up of its own accord and, emerging from an invisible subterranean stairway a radiant young woman appeared, who must have reposed for several centuries in the silent shadow of that tomb reserved for the illustrious dead. Was she a saint, the daughter of Prince Madoc himself, the builder of the basilica, whose remains has been transported so far? Beneath her light crown of roses and in the linen of her veil she was standing upright, in the heart of the church, at the ideal point that was the middle of the transversal nave forming the arms of the cross. Her hands joined, she seemed, with her serene beauty and her blue-eyed gaze, the spirit of the monument, resuscitated and attentive.

446

Hugues' ideas succeeded one another rapidly in his head. But he saw his ideas, he judged them, and the expectation of the revelation rendered that revelation impossible.

What must I render the Lord for all the benefits he has given me?

And immediately, an evil voice whispered in his ears: *What benefits? Is that the lacerating doubt from which you have suffered since your youth?*

The cathedral was illuminated. All the lamps of old were flamboyant in all the solid gold chandeliers. And on the empty pedestals, the statues took their places again. Saint Paul raised his hand; Saint Denis carried his head in his hands; Saint Martin extended his cloak. A painted mural brightened in which the Magi advanced with their curly beards and their miters covered in silver strips. Black slaves were swinging cassolettes in front of them, and Hugues thought that he could smell the perfume of myrrh and the incense that came to swirl around him; he thought he could hear the chant that the caravan guide walking in front of the Magi was intoning, as he indicated the guiding star. The relics had taken their places in the stone niches. To the right and the left of the altar stood Jesus Christ and the Virgin. Hugues was officiating in the midst of the reawakened dead, sacred figures and holy flames.

I'm the victim of a prodigious illusion engendered by fever, he said to himself. *Images are unfurling around me to which my mind has given birth, and when they have disappeared, faith will not have returned to me and I shall be the victim of the same desperate desiccation.*

And he remembered what Père André had said: "Visions are deceptive. Only the interior word that springs from the depths of the soul is true."

And that word did not come.

He uncovered the chalice and took communion.

Enable us, Lord, to keep a pure heart...

But his heart was not pure. He sensed doubt, the accursed force of reasoning, within him. Everything was finished now. He was defeated. The symbol of the presence of God in his body had not given him the anticipated faith.

He had the sensation that from all directions, the witnesses were leaning toward him was reproachful faces. The Borromées were whispering to one another. The members of the chapter had risen to their feet. The young woman with blue eyes had extended her rms. And he had a desire to cry out, to strike his breast, to beg pardon from them all for the malediction that was extended over him forever.

Ite, missa est.

And then the cathedral, with all its dazzling lights, its host of attentive people, its divine statues, collapsed before him. And he found himself alone in the silence of cosmic spaces devoid of images, devoid of light, devoid of symbols of any sort, and he knew that he was in the presence of God.

No majestic face appeared to him; no voice called to him: "My son!"—but in the depths of his being he sensed the ineffable delight that no words can reproduce, and whose marvelous beauty is no longer effaced.

A few weeks later, Hugues Borromée, convalescent, was sitting beside Socrates at sunset, on the high wall of the village of Acoma. It was on his back that Socrates had carried the missionary in order to enable him to climb the three hundred steps of the vertiginous stairway leading to the solitary pueblo.

Hugues never wearied of hearing from his companion's mouth the story of the hours that had preceded their first encounter. He made him repeat once again that if he had been on the route that evening, it was without a reason, because an imperious intuition had forced him to set out. He saw in that, without any doubt, an intervention of Providence. Nor did he weary of having recounted yet again the story of Father Kino and that of the cathedral, such as it was reported by the last Zuni Indians of the land of Cibola.

It was autumn. It had been raining. The sun had, however, pierced the clouds and was parading a bloody radiance over the bleak landscape of stones that extended from the foot of Acoma. Now the two men were reflecting.

"There is always a hidden truth beneath legends," Hugues said, "and sometimes it can be interpreted variously. Now, it was said that when a barefoot priest came and celebrated mass in the abandoned cathedral, there would be a sort of enchantment that ended. This immobile land closed for centuries would be opened to men of all races come from far away; it would be evangelized again, but it would have the fate of other adjacent lands; it would be prey to all the adventurers of the world, whose presence would hasten the end of the Zunis with blue eyes, whom you love with so much reason. You have confided to me what the goal of your life was. Would it not have been wiser to let me die on the route, where I had fallen?"

Socrates lowered his head.

"That's true. But the beauty of great actions," he said, slowly, "has a power that one cannot resist. And then again—and this is the most incomprehensible thing in the world—evil is born of good and good emerges from evil without one ever being able to discern either the secret reason, or the point of contact at which the transformation takes place."

PART FOUR: THE SHADOW OF THE PYRENEES

Prelude

How beautiful the mountains are when one has been born in their shadow and one sees them again after having quit them years before! There is in the waterfalls of the Pyrenees a music that other waterfalls do not have. There is in the triangular thrust of the fire trees a sad sweetness that other trees do not have; and the gentian and the artemisia at the edge of torrents, mingling their perfume with that of the damp earth, have the odor of youth.

Behold the plane trees of the road, the diligence at the entrance to the village, the houses beneath their slate roofs, the old men beneath the arches of doorways and the chestnut trees climbing the slopes, as powerful as the stones into which they plunge their roots! Behold the beneficent bridge that never wearies of hearing the water of mountain streams passing beneath its vault and recounting stories of glaciers and snowy peaks. One can hear the sound of sawmills in the valley and the song of the cuckoo on apple trees in flower. There is nothing more beautiful than spring in the Pyrenees. How insensate men are to quit their native land when it teaches them the lesson of such beauty!

There are different beauties in every country. Nature has spread herself over the earth with an incomparable variety. But the beauty that suits each human being, the one that gives the heart perfect plenitude and joy, is the beauty of the land of his birth.

We have seen suns decrease over oceans, we have seen continents surge from the mist and those masses of trees above isles that give the impression of verdant bouquets cast to the middle of the waves. We have seen phosphorescences in which flying fish dance, bays in which ships run aground and beaches where unknown people laugh. We have walked in the tumult of ports, heard the sirens of steamships about to depart, contemplated the extent of deserts, the passage of great rivers, bizarre monuments, the craters of volcanoes, forests charged with shadows, and heights where the luminosity is inexplicable.

Nothing is worth as much as the color of the Garonne, the song of the cricket next to the poplar, and the beautiful garden surrounded by a wall that is beside every village and where the graves of our parents are.

We are coming back poorer than before. Great voyages are the cause of suffering. We have been hungry, we have been thirsty. We have seen bad men and we have learned that evil is, above all, in the souls of those who disown the land where they were born and wander here and there over the vast earth.

We have known the extent of the world, the lack of welcome, the hardness of hearts and the desperate fear of solitude in the host of a foreign race. But what does it matter, since the apple trees are in flower, the cricket is singing beside the poplar and there is a little house where cherished beings are waiting for you?

I. The Return of Noël Alga

"Have you any news?" Madame Alga asked Madame Bruno almost every day, when she encountered her at the market in Loures, and sometimes she made the ten-minute walk that separated her from the Bruno house, in order to know whether a letter might perhaps have arrived.

Oh, how rare the letters were! The two mothers had each received one dated from New Orleans.

"More than a month to get there! Think of it!"

From New Orleans, Noël had written again to say that all was well, that he had a thousand plans. Accessorily, as a matter of minor importance, he had announced that he had separated from his companions. And then time had passed.

"Oh, I'm sure that he hasn't forgotten me," said Madame Alga. "But he's in terrible lands. And so far away!"

"Have you had any news, Madame Alga?"

That question, which Madame Alga no longer asked, became an obsession.

"Eh! News! There must be people out there who steal letters."

Another time, she said: "He must be among savages. Then again, you understand, there's no post, among those people who don't know how to write."

After two years had gone by she received another letter, again dated from New Orleans.

"Oh, that city! He must like it, since he's gone back there. It appears that it's on the edge of the sea, with lots of steamboats."

Madame Alga had suffered too much from telling everyone that there was no news. From that moment on, every time someone mentioned her son to her, she had a satisfied expression. He was well. He was content. Fortune would come one of these days.

Then came a time when she said: "He's in Florida now."

And once she ran to make several visits in order to announce: "He's now in a country that's absolutely unknown to anyone. I've written it on a bit of paper—look."

And they read: *Venezuela*.

"Indeed, it's absolutely unknown."

And she felt a certain pride, as if her son had discovered Venezuela.

"Oh, what he'll have to tell when he comes back!"

But the years passed. Many people who had departed in the epoch of the great folly had come back. Martin Bruno was one of them. The expedition organized by Mademoiselle de Noussoulens and Bernard Borromée had not succeeded. Bernard Borromée had gone into the desert with men whom everyone agreed in considering to be scarcely recommendable, and there were all sorts of reasons for believing that he was dead. Mademoiselle de Noussoulens had stayed in Vera Cruz. Why? He did not know. Would she come back? He did not know that either.

In any case, everyone who came back told the same story. They had endured great suffering because of the climate, the harshness of mores and men, and regret for their native land. In those distant lands—Mexico, California, or America—there was a force hostile to newcomers. Simple and honest men could not accustom themselves to the bitterness of the struggle, to the law of the strongest that regulated human relationships inexorably. No one had made a fortune. They came back as poor as before.

But since Noël had not come back, Madame Alga said to herself, he could not have suffered all those misfortunes. Where others had failed, he had succeeded. In any case, he must be content.

For a long time she lived on that argument. An intelligent young man like her son could go anywhere. He would get himself out of trouble where others had not been able to do so.

But gradually, time did its work. There is a pitiless logic that comes from the sentiment of time passed, and which insinuates itself into souls. All the arguments lost their value; all

454

the illusions vanished, and gave way to the bleak despair of not seeing her son, not knowing where he was and the fear of dying without having seen him again—for even those who never think about death, by virtue of insouciance or simplicity, sense at a given moment that there is a term to hope and that the limit is fixed by a power of which one cannot know anything.

Madame Alga went to market with her eyes lowered, went rapidly past neighbors with whom she had loved entering into conversation, and became self-enclosed. And time, which brings good and evil, brought her the habit of dolor. In the same way that the face wrinkles a little every day with old age, the soul hardens. Madame Alga became less adept at suffering with the passage of the years. Then she had weaknesses and dizzy spells. It was at that point that Madame Bruno went to Dr. Tonniens herself to ask him to go and see her.

"Well?" she asked, afterwards.

Dr. Tonniens, who only subsisted thanks to infinite precautions, being of feeble temperament, placed the idea of health in debility.

"It's still the same thing. She eats too much. Everyone eats too much. I've forbidden her meat. Without that, one of these days…oh, the heart! Everyone dies of the heart."

Madame Alga's ideas were restricted. Her mind no longer embraced more than a small number of things. There was, however, one fixed light in her: the return of her son. Would he come back before the day of her death? And there came a time when, without any appreciable reason, she felt certain that he would come back. Had not all those who had left—Martin Bruno, who was a woodcutter now and worked in the mountains, and all those who lived in Saint-Gaudens, the officers, the pharmacist, Malbosque and Mademoiselle de Querigut—come back? There had certainly been those who had died, but at least their deaths had been announced. Children did not die before their mothers, or it is very rare. Noël would return, one day or another.

At what hour? She could not know that. Perhaps he would take a diligence in Toulouse that only went as far as Saint-Gaudens. Or he would take the one that went to Luchon and get off at Loures. But that diligence arrived late, long after nightfall. There were bad days and dark nights. What if Noël were unable to find the little path and got lost in the darkness?

Madame Alga remembered that Noël sometimes used to come back very late, with his guitar on his back, after an excursion into the mountains. It was agreed then that she would light a little lamp, the flame of which was visible from a distance through the panes of the window facing the direction of Loures. Well, she would light the same lamp to guide him. Who could tell whether that lamp might not be a sort of ex-voto, a mysterious appeal that would contribute to making him come back. Strange things happen.

She did that, and every evening the lamp was lit. That coincided with an increase in her weaknesses and dizzy spells. But as nature has, in certain cases, a kind of foresight, that was accompanied by a sight detachment, a certain insouciance, a little optimism.

"Yes, yes, Madame Bruno, thank you, I have everything I need and I'm much better now that I'm convinced that Noël will come back one of these days, or perhaps one of these nights."

Noël Alga had had many adventures, like all those whose soul is full of various and ill-defined desires.

After having spent a year in Florida, he had rejoined Monsieur Harvard and had participated with him in further expeditions, the goal of which was chimerical.

With him he had searched for the traces of Mayas in Yucatan. Monsieur Harvard had studied the civilization of those conquering people and had deduced from what he knew that the conquerors had only subjugated other people is order to have the liberty to build convents in inviolate solitudes to which their elites had retired. There were warriors that had made war in order to permit those sages to meditate in all tranquility. Monsieur Harvard had the proof of it in fining and exploring the ruins of Ek-Balam and Tuloom.[32] In the midst of the virgin forest he had encountered the vestiges, still standing, of those convents, with their cells appended to great stone halls that were—at least, so he supposed—the meeting-places of the Mayan sages.

Noël Alga participated in those studies. He returned with Monsieur Harvard to Mexico, and accompanied him on his explorations of volcanic craters. Monsieur Harvard was convinced that various secrets relating to the constitution of the earth and the origin of life might be revealed to someone who descended far enough into the interior of the globe. Noël Alga recounted later having sailed with him on a lake of unusual beauty, the waters of which were slightly luminous, at a great depth within the earth. But he sometimes exaggerated.

Perhaps Monsieur Harvard neglected the advice of his Indian guides. According to them, one should only descend into craters masked, and after having sacrificed two white birds. They did not give an explanation. It had to do with the god Quetzalcoatl. In the course of a descent, Monsieur Harvard broke a leg. It was necessary to take him back to Mexico City, where he renounced all adventurous enterprises.

In Mexico City, Noël encountered a young man named Alphonse, known as the Pelé because he was afflicted with an obstinate dermatitis, whom he had met in the deserts of Texas, and left with him and two other comrades who had nothing better to do. It was a matter of accomplishing a disinterested act of justice. A savage haciendero was keeping prisoner, in a hacienda in a remote corner of Sonora, a beautiful young

---

[32] Authors note: "In 1885 or thereabouts Monsieur Desiré Charnay explored these cities again and gave description of them in *Le Tour du monde*." The reference is to the explorer Claude-Joseph Desiré Charnay (1828-1915), one of the first to employ photography to document his discoveries. He visited Yucatan in 1886. The title is that of a journal in which he published his account of that expedition.

woman abducted by violence from her family. Details were lacking, but Alphonse the Pelé could not support the idea of that captivity.

After various researches, they discovered the hacienda, penetrated into it on horseback and fired rifle shots. An old woman with an energetic face barricaded herself on the first floor and fired at them with an old rifle. The haciendero was absent. They negotiated. There were explanations. It was the old woman who had been abducted, but by her own choice. She had been married twenty years before. She had gone to see her father the year before, and as there were quarrels over money with her husband, who was slightly crazy, he had kept her there by force. Her husband had been obliged to come to search for her and carry her away on his horse. A legend had been created.

The four horsemen departed again, full of confusion. Or rather, three of them were full of confusion. Alphonse the Pelé was not. "I'm very glad to have clarified that story," he contented himself with saying, without apologizing for having made his companions traverse all of Mexico unnecessarily. The latter were obliged to abandon him because he was talking about going to kidnap the alcalde of the town of Alamos, under the pretext that he only rendered justice in exchange for cash, in order to oblige him to better conduct.

Having returned to Mexico City, Noël met a small group of men in possession of a secret that they were enthusiastic to confide to him. With them he embarked for Venezuela, having paid for a large part of the expenses of the expedition with his savings. It was a matter of recovering the treasure of the Incas hidden between Quito and Archidona in the Italo Mountains. It was a terribly savage country. The secret had a real basis, but the expedition learned that for fifty years the Indians of the Italo Mountains had been going to Quito every year in order to make purchases with a considerable mass of gold. They probably had knowledge of the treasure and had exploited it.

The expedition departed again to harvest rubber. Noël Alga was taken prisoner by geophagous Indians. The absorption of soil had developed a monstrous development of the stomach in them. They wanted to force Noël to eat soil like them and deprived him of nourishment. Later, Noël recounted that soil, as an aliment presented in a wooden bowl by people who nourished themselves thereon, eventually exerted a kind of fascination, but the sight of the geophages' deformed stomachs had prevented him from yielding to temptation.

He was rescued, sold rubber, met a very saintly missionary who lived on the bank of the Amazon and had two huts, one for himself and the other for a family of domesticated tapirs. Noël Alga built a third alongside and lived happy days, as much because of the missionary as the tapirs.

"They are, in sum," he said, "the animals most ready to sympathize with humans."

He spent a lot of time domesticating an anthill and a boa, but the missionary died and he set forth again.

He went back to Mexico, then to California and Arizona, in search of adventure. He never quit his guitar, which served to charm his hosts of an evening, or himself when he was alone. He was a miner in the placers of Sacramento and a horse drover in the ranches of Texas. He played cards in dives in Tucson and descended along the stone walls of the canyon of Chelly; he slept under the giant trees of Calaveras; he attempted to decipher the hieroglyphs engraved in the rocks of the Tuba River; he pursued the first railroads on horseback; he fought; he had amours; he was happy; he suffered; he lived.

And after years, the desire came to him to see his homeland and embrace his mother, who was waiting for him—for he did not doubt that she was still alive. He had given addresses in the rare letters that he had sent, but he had always gone before the time that a reply would have taken to reach him. When you are a dyed-in-the-wool optimist, you do not doubt that life will conform to your desire. Noël Alga had no doubt that he would find his mother on the threshold of her little house.

I shall arrive at the beginning of spring. There will be nasturtiums and convolvulus around the door.

To his great surprise, he was able to traverse the greater part of France by railway. He was a little disappointed. But in Toulouse he had to take the coach, as before. The railway was only a project.

He had dreamed of coming back with a great deal of money and dazzling his mother with his wealth.

Bah! Money has always been irrelevant to her. The essential thing is that I've come back.

The diligence was late. It was Easter week. Passengers got on and off at every stop.

Noël Alga had ceased to tell stories, astonished not to know anyone. People looked at him with some suspicion because of his cowboy hat, his bronzed complexion and his leather jacket. He was vexed when someone said: "You talk the language with an English accident. It's obvious you're not from around here."

The diligence arrived at Loures in the middle of the night. The inn was open.

"Is Père Castillon here?" Noël asked, joyfully, on the threshold.

A stout brunette waitress burst out laughing. "Père Castillon? But that was ages ago. It's five or six years since he died. It's his son-in-law who's replaced him."

The son-in-law appeared. He was from Lannemezan. He remembered the guitar.

"For sure your mother's waiting for you. Poor woman! You've arrived just in time."

"So you're one of those who left? Oh, the poor fellows!"

There were two or three men around a table who had come to wait for the diligence. Noël was surprised not to excite any admiration, scarcely a little curiosity. But it was his leather jacket that attracted attention. One of the men got up and felt it "Does it protect well?"

Noël sat down and asked for a bottle of local wine. Travelers came in. He heard someone ask: "Isn't that the son of old Madame Alga?"

And someone added: "All the same, he might have come back sooner. When one has an old mother..."

Noël was penetrated by an infinitely painful sentiment.

The inn was about to close. He left his trunk and set out, only taking his guitar, which he thought it imprudent to abandon.

"The night isn't very bright. Will you be able to steer?"

"I haven't forgotten the way."

He recognized trees, walls, and the mass of the church. It seemed to him that he was provoking a reproach, that there were whispers saying: "He's very late!"

He hastened his steps. Was it an illusion? The plane trees along the road were also saying: "He's very late!"

Noël was penetrated by the delight of seeing is homeland again. He saluted internally the contours of Saint-Bertrand-de-Comminges, which loomed up before him, and the mountains of Barousse and the forests of which he glimpsed the indistinct shadows by the light of a few stars. But his delight was spoiled by the confused sentiment of being very late, by the bitterness of ingratitude.

And suddenly, he uttered a cry. At the extremity of the little road to the right he saw a light: a light that he knew; the light of a lamp; the light of the old oil lamp that his mother placed behind the panes of a window to guide him when he came back from the mountain.

Tears moistened his eyes. His mother was there and waiting for him. It was true, he was very late. He had only thought of himself and his egotistical pleasure of enjoying life. Well, he would beg his mother's pardon and make up for it.

He ran along the little road. Everything was the same. A wooden gate that hung badly. A yard with the well and the same gardening implements that were always forgotten on going in: a watering-can, a bucket, and a little shed to one side that never closed, and in which there as wood.

Noël's heart dilated. He had a desire to seize the watering-can, to go to the pump, to devote himself to little tasks, to resume life where he had left it.

He went to the door of the house, but he hesitated as he was about to knock. Once, ten years before, his mother had said that her heart leapt when she woke up with a start. That might have got worse, ten years later. It was very late. The night would not last long, and his mother always got up with the sun. It was better to wait and surprise her while she was making her coffee.

He even feared having made too much noise running. He circled the house on tiptoe. Who could tell whether he might not find one of his friends, the hedgehogs or the crow that knew the time and came to tap his window with its beak?

But no. There was no hedgehog, even though those animals have an active nocturnal life. Little wooden houses once constructed by Noël for the beasts had fallen into ruins. The crow must be in its nest. There were only chickens in the henhouse. One of them woke up and considered him with a round and stupid eye in which there was no amity.

And the mole? Who could tell whether...? But no, the mole must be in some subterranean corridor, gazing at the darkness with its blind eyes.

Oh, what a surprise his mother would have! Al the same, it was a great joy that he was about to cause her, him, the ingrate! He looked at the sky, which, far away, in the direction of the Ariège, was beginning to pale. He sat down on the stone bench. He would not be there for long.

Then, gradually, the world of forms became visible around him. As if a sea had withdrawn soundlessly, the trees emerged, then the gables of châteaux and the steeple of the church of Saint-Just. A file of poplars gave the impression of running toward him like messengers of the dawn. The sky was a celestial blue. The stars are more luminous at five o'clock in the morning, and seem to be illuminating the world of the angels. The summits of the Pyrenees were bathed in a fiery glow. One might have thought that the mountains were hiding from view a gigantic crucible in which all the terrestrial darkness was mutated into flames.

Noël Alga had an idea. It was the time when his mother woke up, and after getting dressed, moved round the house. He knew how to let her know that he was there, gently and gradually, without emotions. He picked up his guitar and began to play. And while playing, he lent an ear to the sound of clicking shutters and the latch of the door.

But the shutters did not click and the door did not open.

Noël thought that his mother had changed her habits. She must get up a little later than before. It was her age, wasn't it? He waited again, and then he recommenced playing.

Suddenly, the lamp behind the window emitted a slightly more vivid flame, and went out. All the oil was consumed. It had burned to the last drop, and its flame was dead.

Noël stopped playing. He stuck his face to the window and saw a little wisp of smoke that faded away in the lumber room where the lamp had been placed, and which the rising sun tinted red.

Then a fear took hold of him. He ran to the closed shutters of his mother's bedroom and knocked, gently at first, and then more forcefully, calling: "Maman! Maman!"

But he obtained no response. Never again would he obtain a response, at least for mortal lips. For it can happen that the prodigal son is greeted by the silence of death.

The inconceivable mystery of coincidences had determined that, during her sleep, his mother had quit this world of waiting and vain hope, at the very moment that the sound of her beloved son's guitar had resounded nearby, in the light of a new day.

II. Curves of Destiny
(Sequel to Dr. Fazeuille's Journal)

I am resuming this journal, which I have kept in a very intermittent fashion for ten years, because I had very little to say to myself. But I am taking it up again in order to note a few conversations and a few reflections that are related to the only problem passionate in my eyes, that of destiny, that posed by the why of things, the why of the enchainment of events. That problem, moreover, impassions everyone—except that people are unaware of it. They give the problem all sorts of names. They call it destiny, chance or hazard. They attribute merit to events and criticize God for what is annoying.

In 1850 a certain number of us from the same region, in approximately the same conditions, departed for America in search of fortune. A common cause precipitated us into adventures and led to different results. Since then, some have died, some have disappeared, others have come back sick, and poorer than before, and a very small number have found themselves more favored than before their departure.

Profiting from the summer and the liberty I grant myself every year, in having myself replaced by a young doctor from Toulouse, I resolved to go and spend a month in Saint-Bertrand-de-Comminges and to research what had happened to the men of the region what had departed in search of gold, not in order to have stories of adventures—my own are sufficient for me—but to search for the secret spring that moved human life, the part played by their will and that by what is called destiny, and above all to measure whether that superior power, destiny, is a blind and indifferent force, or whether it is sage and conscious.

My personal case is the most difficult to study. I brought nothing back from my voyage materially. The money I had obtained from my father when I left had been a heavy charge for him. It was necessary on my return for me to obtain from

464

him, once again, the sum that the brothers Garisse had lent me for my return journey and Martin Bruno's. I had infinite difficulty in completing my medical qualification in Toulouse. Two years spent on horseback on the roads of Texas causes the habit of mental labor to be lost.

It is true that I came back with a rich experience of life. But during the same time I could have acquired in France a different experience of another and more useful order. I left with many faults. I came back with a few qualities, but that was owed solely to the inexorable analysis to which I subjected my soul, and the voyage contributed nothing. I can say that I only bought back one thing from my adventures. That is the knowledge of God. To be sure, that is capital.

On the first of August, therefore, the diligence deposited me at Loures, from which I reached Saint-Bertrand-de-Comminges. It is the virtue of old towns of stone, build on the foundations of ancient fortresses, to remain immutable, similar to themselves, insensible to progress.

Monsieur Mauvezin, the proprietor of the hotel, welcomed me with great marks of satisfaction. He was still shrewd and talkative.

"There will soon be a railway, which will doubtless bring us tourists. Unfortunately, the project presently on the drawing board will not go through Saint-Bertrand itself. The people of Loures and Barbazon have conspired, and Saint-Bertrand will not be on the line."

"That's a great good fortune for your town," I said—for I have become reactionary. I think that what is called progress is a bad thing and that railways, in particular, will harm humanity. People have no interest in being transported rapidly. Slowness is an element of human happiness, and the immobility of the active man who labors in his homeland and remains there is the ideal.

Monsieur Mauvezin made no reply. He does not contradict his clients.

"I was very glad," he told me, "When I heard, at the time, that you had returned. There are so many who never

465

reappeared, whom California and all those distant lands absorbed and did not return."

It was from him, from Sulpice and the people of the area with whom I was able to converse, that I was able to learn a few series of adventures, a few curves of existence.

There was one soul that was saved. It was that of Jean-François, who nicknamed himself the Sinner because he had once embezzled money from the community from the Brothers of Saint-Jean-de-Dieu. Doubtless he had profoundly rooted in his soul the faith in his salvation, and there is no example that faith does not save.

His story is poorly known because he never recounted it, but its broad outlines are known.

He was seen for a long time in San Francisco gambling, drinking and holding forth, an object of ridicule for some and admiration for others. He appeared completely fallen, reported a young man from Toulouse, a certain Laurent Figeac, who had departed with the intention of reaching the region of the placers but retreated before the threat of the dangers.

"Personally," he said, "I thought him mad and I avoided him when I saw him. That opinion was confirmed when I saw him for the last time. He was talking to himself as he walked. with a kind of abnormal excitement. He saw me and he said: 'Finally, God has spoken to me. He has sent me one of his angels. I'm saved.'

"Six months later I was told that he had amassed a large quantity of gold in one of the most distant placers beyond the sources of the Sacramento. He had arrived there without weapons tools or provisions. The owners of claims in that area, who were all Yankees, were in distress and ready to leave in spite of the richness of the claims. The place was haunted, they said.

"A week before, they had burned a negro alive who had killed one of theirs in single combat. The combat had been entirely fair, according to the rules that were recognized, but the Yankees made use of that pretext to get rid of the negro, who was the real owner of the land and had accomplished all the formalities to assure himself of its possession. They simulated a trial and suspended the negro over a blazing fire. They had buried the remains nearby. Now, every night, the negro appeared, wandered through the camps, moaned and made threats, approaching sleepers with a hideously burned and contorted face.

"The Yankees had summoned a man who was reputed to be a sorcerer and lived on the medical advice that he gave. He came sixty miles on horseback from the place where he lived. He simply said: 'You haven't buried him deeply enough. Dig him up and dig a grave five feet deep,'

"Having given that advice and been paid, he left again. The negro was disinterred, and the five-foot grave dug. But the nocturnal presence of the negro was affirmed more frequently, with more lamentable groans and a more frightful aspect. It was certain that the weight of the soil did not inconvenience the phantom.

"When he arrived, Jean-François listened to that story and didn't give any advice. But perhaps he angel that had appeared to him had prescribed him to go and pray in that place. He knelt down and prayed.

"The claims were at the beginning of their exploitation and the place was very rich. The Yankees didn't come back. No one knows how Jean-François turned himself into an improvised miner and washer of gold, and how, six months later, he returned to San Francisco with the value of a large sum of money in nuggets and gold powder."

The end of the story was reported by a monk in the region of Pau, where there was a prosperous community of Brothers of Saint-Jean-de-Dieu. Jean-François presented himself one evening at the door of that community. He was pale, old and seemed slightly cracked. He asked for the prior and had a great deal trouble getting in. His story had been forgotten; he was believed to be dead. He brought the gold from the accursed placer as he had extracted it from the ground, the value of which was far superior to the sum that he had once misappropriated. He was allowed to stay in the convent and died shortly thereafter.

The story of the two Bramevaque cousins is more uncertain and has a slightly marvelous character. Perhaps it has been transformed by multiple retellings.

The two Bramevaque cousins, old gentlemen, ruined and somewhat feeble-minded, had been among those who found misery and death along the banks of the Goazalcoalco. They went along the shore, enduring great sufferings, and their reason was completely disturbed. They knew that by following the coast they would reach a town called Alvarado and another called Medellin, where they would have the resource of begging. Before arriving there they met a German names Görres, who was the guardian of the lepers relegated to Alvarado Island, in the middle of the lagoon of the same name.

A guardian of lepers can only be either a saint or a brute. Görres had been chosen for his functions because of the total insensibility of his soul. He put the two cousins into his boat and, in exchange for a little nourishment, he engaged them as servants. He already had three negroes with him charged with preventing the lepers from escaping. Görres was a detestable individual who experienced a horrible joy in terrorizing the two Bramevaques, employing them for the most vulgar tasks and reducing them to the condition of slaves. Antoine, the elder, died of distress, but Adhémar resisted. He became increasingly weak and was about to die in his turn when an unexpected event occurred.

The Mexican administration exercised little surveillance but all the same, there was some. One day, a Mexican officer disembarked on the island charged with making sure that order reigned among the lepers. He was accompanied by a person about whom all that is known is that he had a grandiose appearance and was full of authority. He was struck by the extreme misery of the white man who appeared to be the slave of the black slaves, and he interrogated him.

468

Görres had forbidden him to say his name, but a glimmer of light nevertheless traversed Adhémar's brain. He replied: "My name is Adhémar de Bramevaque," and he handed the stranger the ring given to him on the day of his departure by an unknown horseman who had said that the ring might perhaps save him in some great peril.

What is extraordinary is that he had been able to conserve that ring, that he had not exchanged it, and that Görres had not taken it from him. Perhaps a secret instinct had made him hide it.

It appears that the unknown man looked attentively at the rose and the cross engraved on the stone of the ring; then he considered the unfortunate Adhémar and said: "In France, there was once a great Bramevaque."[33]

He gave orders to the men accompanying him, and Adhémar was taken away. He was cared for, recovered a little of his reason, and was embarked for France, having been recommended to the captain of the ship and given a sufficient sum of money to return honorably to Toulouse. By virtue of a mysterious order, there was a family there that took him in. He did not live much longer. Those who asked him to what he attributed the beneficent power that had protected him received no response—or, rather, no intelligible response. One of his ancestors, he said, vaguely, had been a very wise and very good man, and he had heard it said that goodness was the only virtue that was never lost and which transmitted its benefit to descendants.

In truth, a host of strange things happen in the world that are never explained.

---

[33] Readers familiar with Magre's works would have recognized this observation as a reference to Michel de Bramevaque, the protagonist of *Le Trésor des Albigeois* (1938; tr. as *The Albigensian Treasure*), and, in a broader sense, to the particular version of the legend of the Rosicrucians that Magre developed in several of his works.

Those who came back were the favored ones, but they were the minority. Of Bramevaque it was said that he appeared to have a magic ring. Of a pharmacist who was reputed to be unlucky but became rich, opinion concluded that it was because he had too much, but had not known it and had thought he had none.

"Oh, Monsieur, he was the cleverest," said one of his neighbors, when I went to see Thomas Bordes in his pharmacy in Saint-Gaudens. "He managed to cheat destiny itself—for that happens. If you say, since your childhood, that you never have any but bad luck, there is a law of compensation that is set in motion and sends you one day any enormous stroke of good luck by way of compensation. And as that law, fundamentally, is God, one can say that Thomas Bordes has deceived God."

But there are all those who did not come back, all those who are lying in the sand of distant shores or under the stones of unknown mountains. There are those about whom no one speaks and who, at the moment of death, measured the poverty of a failed life, the sadness of never again seeing one's homeland and those one has loved. There are those who died of exhaustion, those who were devoured by wolves, those who were killed by thirst and hunger. There is no legend for them, who are the most numerous.

And for the small number who found out there a means of living in abundance, even for them, there will always be a regret: that of the house where one was born, the air one breathed, the trees in whose shadow one walked as a child. Men are egotists and struggle against one another for life; but there is a little fraternity that circulates in spite of quarrels and divisions between those who are born on the same soil, who speak the same language and have a similar form of skull. Within that fraternity, good fortune is better and wealth futile, and from it the appeal of the homeland comes to which it is impossible not to respond.

Sulpice Borromée, to whom I had written, had arranged to meet me in Saint-Gaudens, where we had lunch at the Hôtel de France.

Since my return I had had opportunities to see him frequently. He had come to Villefranche and I had gone several times to the vicinity of Saint-Martory where he had a small property and where he grew vines. There I had the opportunity to meet his wife, for he had married.

His marriage, which had taken place while I was in Santa Fe, and about which I had learned out there, was for me the occasion of a case of conscience that I put to myself quite often. I was, in a certain measure, responsible for that marriage. It is true that my responsibility was very indirect. The true cause of the marriage was Bernard's perfidious machination, about which I only knew on my return.

Sulpice had been naïve enough to write to his brother that his Uncle Nestor had the intention of marrying him off. It was a question of a naïve little goose, of which he naturally did not want to hear mention. Three months later, Bernard's letter reached him in which the latter announced Malvina's death, without giving any details. Bernard's calculation was not very expert and had had been made somewhat haphazardly. He had thought of encouraging his brother to marry by suppressing any hope that he might be nourishing of one day having the woman he loved. It might have succeeded or failed. It had succeeded. How Bernard counted on explaining the lie subsequently I do not know. It is noticeable that those who tell enormous lies for reasons of interest never think about the manner in which they will justify them. I believe that he was counting on Providence. In despair at Malvina's death, Sulpice had accepted the marriage as a form of suicide.

When I had received the news I had welcomed it as good news. I do not know whether I was wrong, for the silly goose turned out to be a charming young woman, and then an excellent wife. It is certain that there are individuals who seem, at the beginning of life, romantically promised to one another A supraterrestrial voice has designated them. Then the voice falls silent. They are united with another creature, for whom they do not seem to be made, and with whom they are very happy.

"Malvina was the great love of my life," Sulpice had said to me, naturally, in a melancholy fashion. But his life went by in a tranquil fashion that can warrant the name of happiness.

I told myself that I had hindered the play of destiny by the delay I had put into writing a letter; but when destiny has made a firm resolution it is not prevented in its realization by the negligence of a man.

"Do you remember Margarita de Querigut?" Sulpice asked me, while we were eating lunch.

"Of course."

"Well, look to the right, at the back of the room. She came back three years ago, married to an American from Florida. Travel had enabled for to fill out, but the local air has returned her skeletal physique."

I did indeed perceive her, very similar to what she had been before, in spite of a bizarre accoutrement. Ten years ages thin people more. But she resembled a joyful skeleton. She was joking with a very fat man with a thick face, who must have been her husband, and who was reminiscent of a benevolent and well-nourished bear.

"She lives in Toulouse but she's in the process of restoring the old Querigut house, which she's bought back." Smiling, he added: "She's given up dancing."

We went for a walk through the streets of Saint-Gaudens. In August, in the early afternoon, the streets of the villages of the Midi are as deserted and silent as those of Mexican villages. We were waiting for the time of the departure of the diligence for Saint-Martory.

Suddenly, the sound of voice came from a barn whose door was ajar.

"Touché!"

"No!"

"Decidedly, it's too hot!"

I only darted a single glance in passing. I had time to see two old men in shirt sleeves, who were throwing down two long wooden laths in the firm of sabers.

"That's the fencing arena of Colonel de Chalabre and Colonel Espondeillan. They've resumed their old habits. They came back recently, aged and full of bitterness. A change of regime in Mexico obliged them to leave.[34] When I said 'Colonel' I ought to have said 'General.' They had obtained that title. They can be seen at the Hôtel de France. They live as before but never stop talking about a certain Santa Anna."

"And the other officers?"

"The majority are dead. One of the last was buried recently—Zenon Fabregat, the one with the wooden leg. Poor Madame Compans, who considered them all as her children, has now lost her reason somewhat. Women don't resist old age as well. She had the habit of saying familiarly to Commandant Fabregat: 'Zenon Fabregat, you're an ass!' When she attended the funeral, to which she came in a costume of the Empire, she insisted on going all the way to the cemetery. Her old domestic held her by the arm; he led her to the coffin, where everyone in turn had sprinkled a little holy water. She was very emotional, but with the authoritarian voice that she had never lost she shouted: 'Zenon Fabregat, you're an ass!' And she left in tears."

Memories have an indefinite power of revival. They are only melancholy because everyone, in reviving them, cannot help reconstructing them differently, imagining another order of things that would have rendered him happier, or richer, or in possession of a more enviable situation. I know that memories were sad for Sulpice because he told himself that if he had

---

[34] Santa Anna's final term as president, which began in 1853, ended in 1855, so it cannot have been his fall that prompted the return of the colonels. He was replaced by the liberal Ignacio Comonfort, who was overthrown in 1858, when the conservative Genera Féliz Zuloaga and the liberal Benito Juarez disputed authority for some years thereafter.

been less timid in accomplishing some action or other his destiny might have been different and he might have been able to realize the great love that he had had in his youth for Malvina.

Having received Malvina's confidences I knew that Malvina had once formed the same dreams in his regard. But what good would it do to tell him that? Would it have been right to trouble his peaceful life? Then again, there is an inexorable law that marks certain individuals. At the beginning of life they see one another, they have the illusion of recognizing one another, and they sense that they are irresistibly made for one another. But that is only a game of the great power that rules us, and for which we are perhaps only the pawns in a game of chess, the rules of which are unknown to us. It is agreed that certain people who are called, who have put their hope in the fraternity of one soul, will never be united with it. And against that mysterious law humans can struggle as much as they like, but it will be in vain.

Sulpice only spoke to me about Malvina as little as possible. It was only when the diligence was on the point of leaving and he was shaking my hand that he said: "If you want to see Malvina you have only to write to her. I heard from my Uncle Borromée that she has been back in the country for a few days. You'll certainly have pleasure in evoking memories with her. But I prefer not to see her again, never to see her again. There's an art that consists of changing suffering into beauty. Time is an element in that art, which I've been doing my best to exercise for a long time. I don't want to destroy in a matter of minutes the work of effacement that has cost me so much trouble."

III. The House in Villefranche-de-Lauragais
(Dr. Fazeuille's Journal)

Malvina had replied to me immediately and had arranged to meet me in the cloister of Saint-Bertrand-de-Comminges on the morning of the day when I planned to see Monseigneur Borromée. I waited for her with a certain impatience. I had not seen her for eight years and I dreaded finding her aged. There are admirations that one has a great deal of trouble losing.

It was with regret that I had left Vera Cruz. At the moment of departing for France again I had begged her in every manner to come back with Martin and me. We had spent long months together in Santa Fe, where we made it a duty to wait for Bernard's return. In the end, we had learned of his death, which Socrates had assured me was inevitable since the first day.

We had had the extreme surprise of seeing Hugues Borromée arrive, guided by Socrates. He latter had cared for him in coma He only spent a few days with us. He had agreed with Monseigneur Lamy, the Bishop of Santa Fe, to go and evangelize the most savage tribes of Navajos on the banks of the Colorado. He would attempt while traversing the San Juan desert to find his brother's remains and give them a sepulcher. I thought that he was going to certain death, but Socrates accompanied him and I learned later that he had realized all that he had projected. I could not realize, myself, my desire to see Acoma and the pure people who, according to Socrates, lived there. He only replied to me evasively.

"What good would to do?" he said to me. "First of all, the purity of souls is not evident to everyone. Those will now disappear gradually. It's better to leave them to their solitude."

It was with much regret that I quit Socrates when he departed with Hugues, although he had let me see that there were degrees in the sympathy he gave. We no longer had any reason to stay in Santa Fe

And we joined the first large caravan traversing Texas and heading for Mexico. Hazard determined that it was Ambrosio who was leading it. He assured me that General Houston, now tracked by American troops, no longer had any but a few partisans with him and was incapable of coming to remove a physician from his troop by force.

In Vera Cruz, which we reached after a long time and various troubles, we were awaited with impatience by Anastasio Alaman. Whence came that impatience? I thought at first that, since he had ventured money in an enterprise, he was awaiting the results of that enterprise and the accounts that were due to him. There might have been a little of that, but very little. I perceived very quickly that the attraction that Malvina exerted upon him was the sole cause. It was, above all, the astonishment of seeing us return alive. Socrates inspired a frightful terror in him. When he left us in Santa Fe, he had thought that we were condemned to death.

"Sincerely, in riding rapidly along the southward trail, I told myself that I had seen you for the last time."

I permitted myself to say that, in that case, he might have insisted that we leave with him.

"It was necessary to let matters take their course and allow you to take your chance." And, without thinking about Bernard, who was dead—or perhaps thinking about exactly that—he added: "In the end, everything has worked out for the best."

He was a seductive man but very cynical. He combined an extreme generosity with a bizarre avarice. He did not take any account of the money that the expedition had cost him. "We gambled, any we lost," he said. But when I talked to him about a loan to pay the expenses of our embarkation he demurred. He asked for guarantees.

"Martin Bruno is a peasant, and you're from a mediocre family—from the viewpoint of fortune, that is."

I nearly replied: "At least there's no one in our family who's been sentenced to death." But I kept silent.

That was one of the most disagreeable moments of my life. I would rather have been dealing with General Houston himself. It was not a matter at that moment, of course, of Malvina's voyage. She had told me that she was hesitant, that she was reflecting, that she regretted Mexico. But Anastasio Alaman was already quite certain that she would not leave.

Bewitchment is the word that immediately springs to mind when I think about the relationship between Anastasio Alaman and Malvina during that period. It was not a matter of course, of a wax figurine and material sorcery...and yet, when I think about it, was that so certain? Malvina was subject to a sort of bewitchment. Perhaps she was gripped by the memory of Ezéquiel, who had inspired a sentiment of desire in her all the more violent because she had scarcely known him. Did she think that she could rediscover the son in the father? Or had Anastasio been able to make marvelous promises shine in her eyes? Did Malvina see a solution to her life, at a moment when a return to the Château de Noussoulens must have frightened her? Perhaps all those motives were in play at the same time.

She decided to stay in Vera Cruz. The Garisse brothers had spontaneously offered to lend me the sum that Martin Bruno and I needed. The ship was leaving the next day. We had said rapid farewells to Malvina. Like all women in such cases, she disguised the embarrassment she was feeling under an extreme coldness. I only found out later that she was living in Mexico City and that she had married Anastasio Alaman.

No, Malvina had not aged, as I had feared.

I could almost say that she appeared to me rejuvenated when she appeared in the midst of the roses of the cloister of Saint-Bertrand-de-Comminges. In a gray hat from which a feather hung, the mass of her blue-tinted hair brought out the pallor of her gilded complexion. Her eyes were sparkling. I understood that something fortunate had given her that animation.

I must admit that my first thought was to explain that radiant delight by the pleasure that she experienced in seeing after such a long time the old friend that I was for her; but a disappointment awaits me every time I allow myself to yield to a little personal vanity. The cause of her happiness was of a more profound order. After the first amicable words that those who are meeting again pronounce, she immediately told me the motive.

"I experienced a great joy yesterday. I went to confess to Monseigneur Borromée. Oh, why didn't that thought come to me sooner? But it's a complex history, my entire history, of which I only obtained the explanation yesterday."

I note only in passing that after ten years had gone by, the joyful Malvina did not think of asking what had become of me, my situation and my own existence. Only her own occupied her. When I thought myself obliged to tell her that my father was still alive, that I was practicing medicine in Villefranche-de-Lauragais, which was the realization of a modest dream, and that I had a numerous clientele, I sensed that she was listening to me distractedly. Her gaze became vague and she waited, repeating: "I'm delighted, entirely delighted…," until I had finished, in order to talk about herself again. That was, fundamentally, what I wanted, but all the same, I would have preferred that she gave proof of a greater interest in what concerned me.

"First, do you now that I've been a widow since last year?"

I did not know that, and I saw no need to pronounce conventional words on that subject.

"We had gone to live in Mexico City. My marriage! That's another story. It was written that dramatic events would be attached to my life. Well, if I'm happy today it's because everything has just been disentangled for me, thanks to a conversation I've had with a saintly man."

Gripped by the need for confidence that the soul has when it sees a bright life free of threats extending before it, Malvina repeated for me the story of our voyage, but going back much further, beginning with the arrival of Maximo Avila in Saint-Gaudens, continuing with the drama that had occurred in her house and telling me the story of a confession she had made to Bernard Borromée, believing that she was making it to his uncle.

The sun was dazzling. Insects were humming. The stone saints gave the impression of listening to her words and consecrating their truth by means of their mute approval. An enlightenment dawned in me with regard to everything that had once happened to us.

"How could we have succeeded?" I said. "We were under the sign of the lie."

"You could even say that it was evil that was driving us. The evil was in me."

And Malvina gave the impression of looking back, through days gone by that were now detached from her, and the consequences of which she no longer had to suffer.

She went on: "The evil is in the desire," Monseigneur Borromée said to me. "I was possessed by desire: not the ordinary desire of all creatures but by a desire for insensate amour, for fabulous riches. I wanted everything to excess. I have had nothing. Was there within me an evil influence, coming from far away, from before my birth? That's possible. All those who have loved me have died tragically. One can do nothing about such things. Monseigneur Borromée says that Providence makes humans follow unknown paths whose turnings are incomprehensible."

Malvina meditated for a few seconds on her own words, and then said: "It's already a great deal to have glimpsed that there is a mystery, and that one will never understand it."

She picked three roses from one of the rose-bushes that were climbing around the pillars in the cloister.

"I'm leaving again in a few hours. I have nothing more to do here. The Château de Noussoulens is too sad. There are too many memories there. The liberating words that I heard yesterday have sufficed to dissipate all the phantoms, but I wouldn't be able to vanquish the daily ennui. I'm going to live in Bordeaux, where I have a few relations. I have the possibility of living there honorably. Life is to recommence, but I don't fear the unexpected. Perhaps we'll see one another again if you pass through Bordeaux one day."

I began to explain, perhaps at slightly too great a length, that when one is the only doctor in a small town, one quickly becomes the slave of one's patients, and one has scruples about quitting them.

I sensed that Malvina, having become distracted, was scarcely listening to me, and I stopped.

"Here," she said, simply, handing me the three roses that had flowered in the midst of stone saints. And she went away.

I had the weakness to receive that little present with emotion.

When I got back to my house in Villefranche-de-Lauragais, it was the end of the afternoon and I experienced a sentiment of delight that had no precise reason. It was primarily due to the fact that I was reprising the slightly keen air of spring in that familiar landscape, were there were no cacti and no Mexicans.

My house is modest and only comprises a ground floor with an old plane tree outside the door. It is situated on the road to Nailloux and on one side, one can see the two ancient bell-towers of the church of Villefranche, and on the other the line of poplars bordering the Hers. There are vines to the right and maize to the left. On the gate in rickety wooden fence, which has never closed very well, there is a placard sating: *Doctor.*

I can never see that placard—and I see it every time I return home—without feeling a certain pride. I have arrived, as a consequence of efforts, fraught with difficulties, in being the physician of Villefranche-de-Lauragais! There are even people who come from Castelnau, where there are other doctors, to consult me. In any case, I have no other medical pretention. I shall never be a luminary of medicine. I shall never make discoveries, or, if I do make one, it will be by chance, for I have not undertaken any special research. I am content to practice medicine in this corner of the land as conscientiously as possible. I do not spare my time or my trouble. Sometimes I have to hitch up my little carriage myself at five o'clock in the morning in winter, in spite of my horror of cold, to go and see a patient in Baziège, or even further away.

But on the subject of cold and the trouble I take, I have made a discovery of great importance. The cold and the trouble that accompany the work I accomplish are what give that work its veritable value. Work ought to be accomplished with effort; that is a general law, which applies from one end of the earth to the other. And as one discovery leads to another, I have discovered that work is the support of existence and the cause of all joy. If I did not hitch up my carriage myself to go to Baziège, or if the patient from Baziège came to find me, I would not have the profound satisfaction of duty accomplished with effort. So I continue to keep the modest place that fate has fixed for me. I shall be the doctor of Villefranche-de-Lauragais, with the joy of being nothing but that.

Let Providence by praised for having limited my horizon to these hills planted with maize, these vines that are verdant or gilded in accordance with the season, and these melancholy cypresses that are nevertheless able to make signs of amity when their human brother passes along the road in the evening.

IV. The Protective Tree

That same year Hugues Borromée had come to spend six months in France.

"How can I lodge you, my poor child?" cried his uncle Nestor when he arrived. "My house is empty of furniture. I no longer have more than one bed, one table and one chair for myself."

Hugues Borromée had laughed. He was now a vigorous man with broad shoulders and a large black beard. No furniture! That suited him marvelously. By dint of spending his nights on the hard ground beneath the stars he could not sleep enclosed in a room, in a bed with a mattress. Two nails with which to hang his hammock were sufficient for him.

Now he was leaving again. The caretaker of the church of Saint-Just had put his trunk in a wheelbarrow and was preceding him along the road. His uncle was accompanying him. He was leaning on his cane and was obliged to walk very slowly.

"So far," he said, as he went past the chapel. "You're going so far! There are Borromées lying here, under the paving-stones of that chapel. They all accomplished their task in their homeland. Is it necessary to go so far to do what one has to do?"

Hugues knew that his uncle only approached that subject with a great deal of circumspection. He was surprised to see it come up again at the moment of his departure.

"Do you remember, Uncle, the conversation we once had on this same road when I was about to leave for the first time? I was suffering. I was in doubt. I questioned you and you aid: there are aides…there are protectors…it's necessary to appeal to them. Well, I appealed to them and they responded to me. They are the ones who told me that there are, in certain regions of the world, beings deprived of all enlightenment, who have never heard about goodness, for whom the word love is devoid of meaning, corresponding to nothing. I'm not only talking about those who are called savages. Those consider cruelty as a virtue, but they have nevertheless a primitive faith in powers that are above them. It's a faith of sorts. I'm talking about the men of our race, those whom the quest for gold attracted out there and who have voluntarily renounced any idea of good. It's necessary to go urgently, Monseigneur Lamy said to me, with reason. The most urgent are those miners, the men brought together by desire, who represent everything the earth has engendered of the most evil, creatures who retrogress voluntarily, who have a love of evil. I have the certainty of not being mistaken in attempting to enlighten those terrestrial infernos of a sort, trying to save, here and there, a soul gone astray."

Often, already, Hugues had told his uncle about the results he had achieved in the region of Sacramento, which he had reached. He had described the church of logs that he had succeeded in building for the miners, the men to whom he had rendered self-awareness.

The bishop knew all that.

"You see," he said, "until the last minute, one has need to justify one's life before one's own judgment. To me too, the aides and protectors have brought their help. But one is never sure of being in the right. Who knows whether I should not have done, long ago, what you have done? Last year I made an attempt to rise toward God in absolute isolation, in the manner of the ancient ascetics. My brother Romuald had died and I was summoned to the Pyrenees on that occasion. Catherine accompanied me. I went all the way up to the cabin in which he had lived, and was tempted to remain there.

"First it was necessary to clean the cabin, and I accepted that work as a preparatory penitence. God knows the state to which a man who has returned to the primitive life can reduce a cabin! There were still the wolf-heads. Well, I perceived very rapidly that my soul was losing its strength, was going out like a lamp without oil. The reading of the gospels no longer brought me the same richness. The sound of the wind, the calls of the crows, disorganized my mind. Then I thought about Catherine, who must be weeping, and certain people who had need of me. I had had the pride of thinking that I might perhaps obtain the high destiny of a saint. It was necessary for me to be humble and to descend again among ordinary men."

"It's not necessary to live in a solitary cabin to be a saint, Uncle."

"Does one ever know? I have not been a man of action, as you are, and I have not been a man of meditation, as I would have liked to be. On the other hand, I no longer have the smallest object to give. I sold the portrait of the superior of the Franciscans a long time ago—the only one that had any value, I still don't know why—and I distributed the money from it. I no longer dispose of anything but a tiny income that just permits me to exist, thanks to Catherine's skill. I can give almost nothing materially, and I observed a long time ago how much more importance people attach to material gifts than to spiritual gifts. I see the solicitors diminishing. I'm very old. I feel increasingly useless as I advance toward death."

"You're mistaken, Uncle. Your mere presence in this region is a guarantee for the regularity of its life. What would become of people if the best among them deserted their homeland in order to pursue personal aims in solitude, even if those aims are very high? Look what happened here ten years ago. A wind of folly that blew throughout France had a deadlier result in Comminges than anywhere else. That's doubtless because the men of our race have brains more prompt to desire and illusion than others. I remember the disorganization of intelligences, the distaste for labor engendered by the possibility of immediate wealth.

"It's necessary that a certain number of sensate and just men are always present in the midst of their brothers, in order to remind them of the necessity of the order, goodness and labor that are necessary for all souls to move modestly, and without being aware of it, in the direction of perfection. That a man like you is here, and growing old here, doing the good beyond human measure that you do, has more utility and a more profound range, than there is in a cathedral with its pilgrimages, its ceremonies and its spire launched toward the sky.

"You know full well what woodcutters do when they clear the flanks of the mountains and roll the tree trunks down into the valleys. Desirous as they are of sending the tallest trees to the sawmill, they nevertheless spare the largest and most robust oaks, and leave them at intervals like guardians. They are the guardians of the earth, which extend a barrier with their roots, defending the soil against the despoilments caused by waters, protecting humans from floods and avalanches. Uncle, you are like one of those protective trees."

They had been walking slowly. The diligence had arrived. The loading of the baggage was almost complete.

"Yes, perhaps it's necessary...," said the old man. "There are two ways...to depart, to help brothers in difficulties far away, or to stay among one's own. And one doesn't choose. Everything is inscribed in a great book, the book of God."

The two men embraced. Hugues darted a final glance at the circle of the mountains, the heights of Barousse, the Cagire and the chain dominated in the background by Sauvegarde,

"That's curious," said the bishop. "It's six o'clock and there's no shadow. The Pyrenees have no shadow. Their chain follows the same direction as the sun. It's taken me all my life to notice that."

Hugues smiled. "There are men who are the same. The light is always above them."

The door of the diligence had closed.

"When you come back," the bishop murmured, "it's probable that..."

The coachman cracked his whip and Hugues made a gesture signifying that there was no separation.